the light of

falling

stars

j. robert lennon

riverhead books, new york

RIVERHEAD BOOKS
Published by The Berkley Publishing Group
A member of Penguin Putnam Inc.
200 Madison Avenue
New York, New York 10016

Copyright © 1997 by J. Robert Lennon
Book design by Judith Stagnitto Abbate
Cover design © 1997 by Marc J. Cohen
Cover photograph © Xavier Guardans/Berstein & Andriulli, Inc.

First Riverhead hardcover edition: August 1997
First Riverhead trade paperback edition: April 1998
Riverhead trade paperback ISBN: 1-57322-682-3

The Penguin Putnam Inc. World Wide Web site address is http://www.penguinputnam.com

The Library of Congress has catalogued the Riverhead hardcover edition as follows:

Lennon, J. Robert.
The light of falling stars / by J. Robert Lennon.
p.   cm.
ISBN 1-57322-066-3
I. Title
PS3562.E489L54   1997   97-10972 CIP
813'.54—dc21

Printed in the United States of America

10 9 8 7 6 5

for Rhian

The volcano trembled in another ether,
As the body trembles at the end of life.

WALLACE STEVENS,
"ESTHÉTIQUE DU MAL"

the light of

falling

stars

part *one*

1

A plane crashed. It was August, a hot, dry day. An hour before it happened, Paul was sitting on a metal folding chair at the edge of his shriveled garden, thinking about the end of his mother's life.

It was the garden that reminded him. The last three months, she hadn't moved from her bed, and except to tend to her, Paul hadn't left her side. Her demands came in a hoarse monotone that sounded like the cracking of a distant whip. There was little light in the bedroom, owing to her sudden distaste for the outdoors, and Paul could only see outside through the crack of window left exposed beneath the blind. The crack revealed, in the yard below, the back of a cushioned wrought-iron bench and the desiccated corpse of the flower garden that his mother had not had energy or concern to water since she took ill.

This was back in Tuscaloosa, Alabama, where Paul grew up. The Beveridge house stood in the Caplewood section of town, a towering plantation-style without a plantation; their money was inherited from Paul's father's grandfather, a speculator in the American frontier. Paul's mother gardened, threw parties, and drank. Paul's father gambled and drank. Paul went to college in town, feigned poverty, grew his hair long, and graduated in seven years. Then his father died of pancreatic cancer, which he had apparently concealed with superhuman stoicism for a year, until he passed out and fell down the curving stairs of their home, breaking his neck in the process. He lived two days, blanked out on painkillers in the hospital. Paul found this out nearly a week later, having been unreachable because he hadn't paid his phone bill. The black woman his mother employed to clean the house showed up at his door. "Your daddy's dead," she said, never taking her hand from the doorknob. "And your mama's in bed. She says she won't ever get out. She says to go tend to her."

"What?" Paul said, barely awake.

"When you get there you can tell her I quit."

This was the beginning of the end of Paul's life in Alabama.

As she died, his mother demanded strange things, then scoffed when he brought them. Three yards of white cotton, scissors and thread. Buttered grits. Clothespins. She ate almost nothing; he fed her until she told him to stop ("Get away from me, you shit," she frequently said when sated), then he would eat the rest. They didn't talk. For some reason Paul didn't actually believe she would die of whatever it was she had. He fully expected things to return to normal once his father's ghost had fled the premises, and for his mother to return to the garden with her kerchief and trowel and hip flask. The possibility of her death did not occur to him.

It came in late August. He went to the kitchen to make her a bowl of oatmeal, then returned to the bedroom and set it on the bedside table. She ignored it. He picked up a magazine and began to read. After a while he put the magazine down, scooped up a spoonful of food, and brought it to her lips. She didn't take it. Her mouth was slightly open, so he moved the spoon between her lips and dumped the oatmeal. She didn't chew it. He ate some of the oatmeal himself. Then he shook her and found her body cool and unresponsive, and found himself alone in the room, alone in the house, in the world. An orphan. The phone had been shut off long before, so he walked to the hospital and asked what he should do.

Later, the doctor who pronounced her dead would glare at him with untethered hatred. Her body had been riddled with deep, caustic bedsores. Hadn't he noticed? the doctor wanted to know. Did he not have an ounce of compassion? At this Paul cried, not for his parents' pain or loss, which wouldn't move him for some months, but out of fear for what he didn't know: the things he'd missed, the things yet to come.

Now he lived with his wife, Anita, in Marshall, Montana, at the edge of the Salmon National Wilderness Area, in a renovated fishing cabin once owned—and never used—by his father. The garden had been Anita's idea. She thought it would be good for him, therapeutic. Paul had agreed. He liked the idea of growing their own food. It made him feel like he was pulling his weight. They had dug it together, a long plot thirty by twenty feet, its rows separated by sunken walkways, and planted according to Paul's research: what went next to what and how far apart, which week to plant, how deep to bury the seeds and how many to drop in the hole. After that, it was Paul's responsibility.

It worked for a short time. They ate fresh salads every night, and Paul diligently pulled weeds and inspected for bugs. Then the weather turned. For the previous three years they'd lived here, summer had been wet and gloomy, the sun a pale disk of little consequence. Yet by the first of this August, there had been a full week of arid, scorching air that supported none but a few pathetic shreds of cloud. The garden sprang to life in the sun, then began to wilt. Paul watered, but the earth made short work of it, the water hissing away into the dirt like drops on a hot pan. He forgot to water one day, and once the following week; and today, at the end of August, he realized that he had lost it. The leaves were bored through and sucked dry, the tomatoes slack and rotten and drooling dark fluid. The greens were gnawed to stumps by rabbits or shriveled flat, and even the potatoes were coming up wrinkled and soft.

He'd come out here intending to give it one more shot, but it was no use. Anita would be disappointed. She'd been giving him significant looks for weeks and commenting with forced nonchalance about the heat. Now he shifted his body, and the parts of the chair that had been exposed to the sun burned his arms and legs. He picked up the bottle of beer he'd pressed into the dirt and drank from it. It was warm.

Anita had been able to take root here in a way that he hadn't. She had a job, taking loan applications at First Marshall downtown, and she'd had her way with the cabin, sanding and polishing and painting so that it finally gave up on its dank dilapidation and relaxed into a ramshackle coziness that made Paul feel, if not at home, at least welcome. It wasn't that he couldn't get jobs. He'd had plenty over the past three years, odd ones mostly. He worked at a tree service for a while, pruning, and had copyedited contracts for a real estate developer; he was a lifeguard one summer and a housepainter the next. But he was aware of an aura of impermanence that surrounded him, and he felt powerless to hang on to anything. His jobs evaporated, his employers told him they had nothing left for him to do. The people he had worked with seemed to know this about him and kept their distance.

It was only Anita who stuck with him, and only she he felt he could hang on to. They had been married four years now, and when he thought fondly of anything in his past, it was Anita: the things they'd done together years before; their holidays and weekends; their shared possessions, the artifacts of their life as a couple. They had met in Tuscaloosa, shortly after Paul's mother died. He bought a suit to wear to the funeral, and the day after to the bank, where he intended to settle his parents' estate. The woman who helped him was barely out of college. She wore a blue blazer and a crisp white blouse, and her desk was in perfect order. This was Anita. She had the cleanest forehead Paul had ever seen, a smooth, white, near-impossible expanse of clear skin. When she looked over his parents' papers, her sweet smell drifted across the desk and fell around him like confetti.

"The house is ours," she said. "After we take what they owe us, you'll get about ten thousand dollars."

Paul leaned over the desk, into the clean cloud. "I don't get it. From the house?"

"No, from everything," she said. She had light brown hair, pulled back from her face.

"That's not right. They're rich."

"Not anymore, I'm afraid."

"I don't understand."

She sighed, then reached across the desk and touched the back of his hand with her fingers. "I'm sorry, Mr. Beveridge," she said. "They ran out of money. There isn't much left, only the ten thousand. And a few hundred more." She showed him the figure on a piece of paper. "You see?"

"Sure." He scanned the rest of the paper. The ten thousand was the highest number on it. He began to calculate how much time this would give him. A year?

But there was a safety deposit box too, and this was where Paul found the deed to the land in Marshall, a place he'd never been to or heard about, and a photograph of the cabin, and a key. The deed had been signed by Paul's grandfather and father. Not long after their wedding, when Paul could barely stand Tuscaloosa anymore, it was Anita who suggested they move there.

His beer was gone when she came home, her car trailing dust. It was a Subaru, a four-wheel-drive wagon. When they'd first moved here, it was what people told them to buy, and they did. He saw her head bobbing behind the windshield and willed her to wave. She did, and he waved back. She stopped the car in the wide patch of dirt they parked in, and got out, briefcase in hand.

"Hey!" he called out.

"What are you doing out there?"

"Gardening."

She shaded her eyes with her hand. "I don't see any garden."

Paul shrugged. "C'mere."

"Wait a second," she said. "I'll be right out." She jumped onto the porch and went inside. A few minutes later she came out wearing cutoffs and a T-shirt and carrying her briefcase. She came to him across the clearing and sat cross-legged on the ground near the empty bottle. Her foot snaked out and kicked it over.

"Drinky-poo?"

"Just the one."

She unlatched the briefcase, turned it on her lap to face him, and opened it. "Happy birthday!" she said. There were three small presents there, wrapped in shiny silver paper, and a white envelope.

"You remembered."

"Duh. Open the card."

On the front of the card was a watercolor of a bouquet. A florid script read "To My Love on His Birthday." Inside, Anita had crossed out the poem printed there with a red marker, and had replaced it with the words:

YOU LOVE ME, I LOVE YOU
HAPPY FUCKING THIRTY-TWO

"How sweet," he said.

"I know." She smiled at him and slapped his calf. "Open 'em left to right."

He lifted out the first package, a flat, oblong box about five by eight inches, and shook it. Something thunked against the sides.

"Come on."

He tore off the paper and handed it to Anita, who folded it neatly while she watched him. In the box, he found a note. "Good luck on your NEW JOB," it said. Underneath it was a magnifying glass.

"Cool," he said.

"You can look for clues."

"I don't think it's that sort of thing," he said. Tomorrow he would start working for a private investigator. He didn't want to let on, but he dreaded it. What if he made a mistake? He held the magnifying glass out at arm's length and concentrated the rays on a dead plant. "I can roast bugs, though."

"Open the next one." She handed it to him.

This box was larger, but lighter. He unwrapped it and found a gently folded square of green silk. He raised his eyebrows at her and she smiled. When he lifted it out, it unfolded into a thin nightdress. He held the dress up by its straps and a breeze filled it for a moment, bringing it to life. It seemed to have no weight.

"It'll never fit me," he said.

"Here." She reached out. "Want to see me in it?" She stood up and pushed off her sneakers.

"Anita," he said. "Come on. We're outside."

"Oh, Paul. Who's going to see?" She grabbed the nightdress from his hand and walked around behind him. He heard her zipper, the jingle of a belt. "Don't look."

But Paul was looking away, at a spot over the trees, where a plane, still just a dot, was flying low. He could hear its drone from here. He had the fleeting urge to be on it.

"I'm almost ready," she said.

"Okay."

"Close your eyes."

He heard her feet in the grass, and then her voice. "Open 'em," she said.

He did. She stood before him, posing, one hand behind her head, one on her hip: a joke pose, but she was still beautiful. The wind moved the night-dress, and he could see that she wore nothing underneath.

"It's very nice," he said.

"That's it?" She sat on his lap. "Nice?"

He felt the words coming, assembling in his guts and floating up to his lips like a gas. He thought, I am such an asshole. "I thought we'd . . ."

"What?" she said, and they looked into each other's eyes. She stood up. "What?"

"No, nothing."

They were frozen for a moment, their eyes on one another, the hot air and light and the noise of the oncoming plane fixing them more soundly in place with each passing second. Finally she said, "All right then," and bent over to pick up her clothes.

"No, don't," he said.

"I'll take it back. I'll get a refund and you can have the money, how about that?"

"I'm sorry. That was stupid. I knew you didn't mean—"

"No, no, I know what you thought I meant." She tossed the clothes into the briefcase and shut it as far as it would go. The corner of a sock hung out the side. "For once I wasn't thinking about having a baby, just so you know. That was part of the gift, giving that to you. No, whatever you were thinking, I deserved it. It's my fault."

"Please, Anita. I'm just in a rotten . . . Please keep it. Don't take it back. I like it."

"Forget it. Every time you see me in it, you'll think about how manipulative I am. Forget it."

But she didn't move. She stared at the trees behind him, her shoulders rising and falling with her breath. "I was dumb to think you would ever change. I was dumb to think I could love you enough."

"Hey."

"That's what I learned today, Paul. It only goes so far."

"What?"

"Love," she said. "It'll only take you so far, and then you're stuck there."

"That's not true," he said. "I'm starting this job tomorrow. That's a change, right?" He struggled for words. "It's my birthday."

"You've started jobs before." Her eyes found him, and her expression was so pitying, so hopeless, that he wanted to run for the woods. Over her head, the airplane had grown, and its wings flashed in the light like broken glass. "It's not you, it's me. I overestimated you," she said. She slipped her thumb under a shoulder strap and rubbed it. "I'll take this back. I'm sorry I bought it." She turned to the house.

"I didn't mean to . . ."

"I know," she said over her shoulder, the plane's rumble nearly drowning her out. "That's part of the problem. You just said it without thinking."

He watched her as she walked away, and could think now about nothing else: the shape of her body beneath the silk and how her skin would warm it, how sweet it would be to slide the straps over her shoulders and let it fall in a green puddle at her feet. He missed it deeply, this gift she'd given him and now taken away, and there was nobody to blame but himself.

"Paul." She'd stopped just short of the porch and was pointing at the sky.

He looked. The plane was nearly above them now, a passenger plane. They flew over all the time. "What?"

Then a popping sound, and the plane changed direction.

Paul laughed, a defensive gesture, the same thing he did once when he'd been slapped by a woman in a bar. What other reaction could there be? He could no more undo the slap than he could reach into the air and set the plane on its proper course. Something small and dark dropped from the plane, trailing smoke. The plane screamed. He watched the dark object fall for a moment and noticed, with the easy, opportunistic logic of a dream, that it was coming toward them. Then he remembered his wife.

"Anita!"

She turned to him, astonished.

"Get behind the car!" he shouted. The words vanished in the noise. He pointed—"The car!"—and ran for it, then angled for her instead. "Down! Down!" And at the edge of his vision, the thing falling toward them. He reached her, grabbed her arm, pulled her to the car and pushed her down.

The ground shook, flinging him onto her. He heard, or maybe only felt, her grunt as the air came out of her, and off at the edge of the woods, motion, something fast and black, rumbling away like a great and awful beast. The air stank flatly. The sound of the plane receded. He rolled off her and crouched on his knees in the dirt. "Anita!"

She rolled onto her back, coughing, the nightdress covered with dust and bunched around her stomach.

Then, from the distance, an uneven rattle like an old machine gun's, and a terrible wrenching groan, and a double-bass thud like two punches to the stomach. He toppled again, and a sharp rock found his spine and gouged him there. His back arched automatically and he swept the rock out from under him. Above the trees, a cloud of smoke rose, sudden and black.

"Anita?"

"Oh my God," she said.

"Did you see? Did you see that thing?"

"No."

Paul got to his feet. The back corner of their house was crushed, sheared away as if by a giant claw, and debris dotted the grass around it like bones. Beams jutted, broken off and bent. A crater the size of a car yawned ten feet beyond the house, and past it a wide, rough track of torn-up earth led across the yard, through the wasted scraps of their toolshed to the edge of the woods. There, between two trees, sat the object, crumpled and smoking like a cigar stub, its butt end blackened. An engine, an airplane engine. The light grew dim as smoke filled the sky.

He helped her up, noting with alarm the red marks his fingers had left on her arm. Her mouth hung open. "Oh, my God, Paul."

"Are you okay?"

"Wait," she said. She stuck her arms out at her sides, the fingers splayed. Her eyes squeezed shut. She inhaled deeply, held it for a moment, then let it out. "Okay. Go call nine-one-one."

"Right."

Paul ran into the kitchen and picked up the phone. He dialed. The living room was weirdly illuminated by natural light; its corner was gone. A photo that had been hanging there was gone. Their records had fallen from the shelf and lay now on the floor, fanned like a deck of cards. The window had shattered, and pieces of it were sprayed across the couch and floor. Through the empty window frame he could see Anita stepping into her underwear and pulling on her sneakers.

"Emergency," said the phone.

"A plane just crashed," he said.

"You say a plane crashed?" It was a woman's voice. She pronounced each syllable separately, like a schoolteacher.

"In the woods near our house. Part of it hit our house." Outside, Anita knelt on the ground, tying her shoes. "It was a passenger plane, I think."

"We haven't heard anything on this yet."

"It just happened. I mean, a couple seconds ago."

He heard the click of a pen. "Okay. Where are you?"

"Way out on Valley Road. Two-one-five-four-oh Valley Road. On the left, right before the Salmon Wilderness." Anita stood up and ran toward the woods. "Oh, geez."

"Sir?"

"Get police and ambulance and fire. Fire, definitely. The woods'll burn for sure."

"You say it's a big plane?"

"Yeah, pretty big, I think."

"Can you—"

"Yeah, hey, I gotta go." Anita plunged into the trees, her sneakers flashing white in the shadows.

"Sir, I need your name."

"Paul Beveridge. B-E-V-E-R-I-D-G-E. I really have to go. I'm sorry. Please send them out here."

The briefest of pauses. "Okay."

He ran into the woods. At the edge of the clearing stood a few aspens, still a vibrant green and white despite the drought. Beyond them the conifers thickened around him like a soft, damp cloth. The smoke, acrid and coarse, had already drifted this far, and he lifted his T-shirt to his lips as a filter. Ahead he saw only haze and more trees. He called out to Anita, but his words got lost in the pine needles and murky air. Somewhere ahead there was a stream; it ran down the valley and into the river. He slowed to get his bearings and saw the stream up ahead, glistening weakly. By the time he reached it, he could see what must be the wreckage in the distance—there was an eerie glow, fire, and the shifting trunks of trees allowed him a glimpse of gray and white and the gentle, unmistakable curve of metal. The stream was low from lack of rain, and he hopped over it easily.

"Anita!" No answer.

But not far ahead, he saw her: the slim expanse of her back, motionless beneath the green silk, and the pink bottoms of her shoes. She was kneeling at the foot of a tree.

"Anita!"

She turned to him, and her face, framed by spruce trunks in the middle distance, appeared like a ghost's in the haze. Then she turned back.

He ran toward her, and came suddenly to a small clearing, where sunlight drew his attention to something in the grass: a woman's purse. It sat there, open, as if someone had simply set it down for a moment, its shoulder strap trailing along the ground like a garden snake. He stopped and peered inside: the usual jumble of stuff. He crouched over it, reached in and pulled out a checkbook.

The forest was perfectly quiet, and he felt watched. He stood up with the checkbook. Looked around. Nothing, no people, only Anita, still hunched under the tree.

The checkbook cover was black plastic and had a cartoon of Bugs Bunny embossed on it. Bugs wore a tux and munched a carrot. Inside, the checks had been printed with scenes from famous Looney Tunes: Sylvester chasing Tweety, Fudd chasing Bugs, Daffy whipping his head back and forth like a dog. The owner's name was Pamela Kinyon. She lived on Southwest Weir. Paul recognized the address, an apartment complex somewhere near Bi-Lo, where he sometimes went to buy beer. He flipped through the carbons, noting where the woman had been and what she had bought: $5.00 at Starbucks, $27.50 at Elliott Bay Book Company, $19.00 at an Italian restaurant, Santori's. A trip to Seattle. Earlier checks were made out to her landlord, to AirAmerica. He looked up again, through the woods, at the wreckage. The smoke was thicker now, the plane harder to make out, the glow of fire eerier, like the light from a jack-o'-lantern. He turned back to the checkbook and a drop of liquid fell there: sweat. It was getting hotter.

Replacing the checkbook, his hand brushed something that felt familiar, and he pulled it out. It was a film canister, and he shook it. A roll of film clattered inside.

"Oh! Paul!"

He went to her, shoving the film into his back pocket as he ran. His eyes had begun to sting. When he came up behind her, he noticed the heart-shaped sweat stain blossoming on her back and the defeated, rounded set of her shoulders, and so didn't see the boy until he had almost arrived. It stopped him short, six feet behind her.

"Jesus Christ."

The boy lay on his back at the base of a blue spruce, his left side burnt black, his hand, his foot, his face. Paul stepped closer, knelt, and rested his hand on Anita's shoulder. Her skin leaped beneath his touch. The boy's right leg was cut deeply just below the hip, and the ground around it had blackened with blood. His right hand gripped a branch, and he wore a white T-shirt, much of which was burned to his body. It read, in black letters partially obscured by burns, "Skate or die." His right eye was open and blank. He couldn't have been more than eleven or twelve years old.

"Are you all right?" Paul asked her.

"No."

"There was nothing you could have done."

"I guess," she whispered. There was a terrible smell, the turpentine stink of burning sap, and urine and the greasy stench of meat. Paul couldn't look up now, couldn't look at the crash, afraid that the woods would open up before him like a picture puzzle and reveal a grisly tableau of human debris where before there'd been nothing but trees. He closed his eyes and reached for his wife. His hands found her arms and he pulled her up. She leaned against him, her hands hanging motionless at her sides, and when she found her footing and pulled away, they turned together in the heat and started back.

At the creek, they stopped and let the water soak into their shoes and socks, and splashed it up against their legs. Anita's knees and ankles were black with blood, and as she washed she uncovered a two-inch gash across one knee. Her own blood flowed bright red from it. Blood had dried on the nightdress. She rinsed it and squeezed it out again and again.

In the distance, sirens.

In the night, after the reporters and police, Anita lay in bed, her eyes open, while Paul sat at the kitchen table, looking through the living room, through the hole in their house to the trees. Lights flashed, voices crackled through radios and walkie-talkies, ambulances hunkered in the dark like icebergs, their doors opening and shutting. On the table in front of Paul stood the film canister, unopened, and Anita's briefcase, which he had rescued from the yard. He reached out and pulled the briefcase to him, took out Anita's T-shirt and socks and shorts. Under them he found his last birthday present. He quietly unwrapped it.

It was a cardigan sweater. He set the wrapping aside, pushed back his chair and stood up. He pulled the sweater on over his T-shirt, and fastened each button, careful to align them all properly, to smooth out the wrinkles and adjust his arms in the sleeves. The air had grown cold, and the sweater felt good.

2

Lars felt sorry for unhappy people. At the moment, Toth was one of them. Toth had been dumped. They were driving to the airport to pick up Megan, Lars's girlfriend, who had spent the summer living in Seattle with her brother and working for his landscaping business. The car they drove, a red Chevette, was hers, and its farthest reaches were cluttered with her things: cassette tapes, blankets, clothes, a filthy stuffed animal that had served as an emergency rag once when they needed to check the oil on a trip. Lars himself was happy. He anticipated a nice dinner with Megan and Toth, and then afterward some time alone with Megan.

Toth had fully reclined the passenger seat, and his voice came to Lars from the back, where his head now was. "I'm trying to figure out when it started. I've got it narrowed down to two possibilities."

"You mean the coffee shop."

"Yeah, that's one," Toth said. Toth had spent about a week theorizing, Kennedy-assassination-like, on the particulars of Julie's affair. One theory was that she first encountered her lover at Banana Karenina, a University-area coffee shop and deli, where she worked long hours. "The other is the movie incident."

"Sorry?"

Toth reached for the seat adjustment and ratcheted up until he was even with Lars. "Okay, we go to the movies about a month ago, and right in the middle of the movie she suddenly gets up and goes out to the lobby to get a snack. Just gets up, right in the middle!"

"Hungry?"

He frowned. "Who gets hungry in the middle of a movie?"

"Lots of people. Me."

Toth shook his head. "So she's out there, like, for*ever.* And when she comes back, no snack! So I say to her, What took you so long? And she says, Line. So then I ask her why she didn't get anything and she says they were out of Raisinets and that was what she wanted. Then later, after the movie, we pass by the counter." He nudged Lars. "So, what?"

"What what?"

"Whaddya think is out there?"

"Raisinets?"

He slapped the dashboard. "Raisinets. Like, a hundred big yellow boxes of 'em."

"Maybe they'd just restocked for the next show."

"I thought so at the time." His voice took on a hoary, incriminating rasp. "But now I'm not so sure."

Toth was chronically unlucky in love. This owed, Lars believed, not to any lack of appeal—girls seemed to love his wan, Buddy Holly–ish looks and his nervous manner—but to the fact that Toth didn't really seem to like any of them, including Julie. Julie was pretty but didn't have much to say. Toth, on the other hand, spent much of his time talking. Why this breakup upset him so much was not clear. Lars wondered if all those conspiracy theorists actually gave a hoot about Kennedy himself. Probably not.

Lars didn't much like anyone either until he met Megan. The women he'd met in college hadn't seemed serious enough for him, and even if they had, he wasn't very good at making friends. With Megan, though, it was easy. They met in a huge lecture class. He remembered exactly what he was thinking when she sat down next to him: that it would be great if the professor, a diminutive man shouting from a stage, wore a throat mike, which would transmit via a wireless control box to tiny speakers fitted into the arms of each chair in the hall. He remembered this because of what Megan had asked him when she sat down. "What are you thinking?" she said.

"What?"

"You were gaping into space."

"Uh . . . it's kind of complicated."

"Tell me after class," she said, turning back to the stage, where the professor was writing something illegibly on a blackboard. "I don't want to miss Shorty's talk."

He thought she was cute. She had small features spaced in an Old Masters kind of way. Her hair was black and rolled into a little ball on the back of her head.

Over lunch he told her what he'd been thinking. He told her a lot of other things he'd thought about too, and to his surprise she not only understood them, but seemed genuinely interested in the entire act of thinking. She shared some of her own ideas. Tax breaks for people who grew their own food, book-buying subsidies for the poor, electric cars you could charge by hooking them up to an exercise bike. "I've changed majors about fifty times," she told him. "Right now I'm a business major, but it's getting old. All those people talk about is numbers." She leaned forward. "I wanna talk about *stuff*." Lars was smitten. He couldn't stop looking at her tiny ears. He wanted to cover them with his hands.

"Can I touch your ears?" he said.

"Go for it." They went out again that night, and again the next. That was almost a year ago.

Marshall International Airport had recently been remodeled to look like a giant hangar. A bank of revolving and automatic doors were set beneath a series of tall, thin windows, all under an enormous arc that stretched to the ground on either side. The airport expressed a certain World War II–ishness Lars found charming, and as it had been built outside the city limits on a bare expanse of prairie, it had an aura of top secrecy, like a military enclave or missile base. It was an exciting place to meet somebody.

They parked and walked to the entrance. Toth lunged into the revolving-door compartment with Lars, and tiptoed behind him as they looped the loop.

In the lobby stood an eight-foot stuffed grizzly bear encased in glass and flanked by two vending machines offering cigarettes and snacks. They walked up a flight of stairs to the gates, all four of which were down the same stretch of hallway, and found the AirAmerica desk. People milled restlessly around it. A digital clock read 5:40.

"I don't see any plane out there," Toth said.

Lars leaned over the desk and said to the attendant, "Is flight one fourteen late?"

She looked up, flustered. Her lips were chapped and the lower one bled from a crack in the skin, which she licked, wincing. "Should be in shortly. Are you here to pick someone up?" The name tag over her breast said "Jeanne."

"Yes."

She bit the lip now, nodding. "We'll be . . ." she said, then stopped. She cocked her head like a bird. For a moment, Lars thought she was listening for something in the distance; then he noticed the headset she was wearing, earphones and a tiny microphone that curled across her cheek to her mouth. Hi-tech, Lars thought, cool. "All right," she said into the mike. Her forehead creased. "Yes. Yes. . . . No, I know. Thank you." She looked down at her desk a moment, then turned back to Lars. "We'll have everything worked out shortly," she said, grinning. The cut in her lip bled freely now, and she wiped at it with a finger. "Why don't you have a seat?"

"Sure." He watched as the attendant curled the fingers of her left hand into her palm. Then she spread them out flat and stared at them as if they were the strangest things in the world.

They went downstairs to the bar and drank glasses of beer. The decor was something Lars had seen before, a style he and Megan liked to call Nouveau West. Cheap chairs with chrome frames and gray upholstered cushions were pushed under varnished knotty pine tables; mounted elk heads and fake Indian art hung on carpeted walls. Lars liked Nouveau West. It was tacky and ill-conceived, perfect for a bar. As if to complement it, a dour cowboy sat drunk at a corner table behind a small cluster of empty beer bottles. His eyes were red, and they focused on a shot glass, which he turned in his hand like a specimen jar.

Toth was talking about Julie again. "You didn't seem too keen on her when you actually had her," Lars told him.

"Yeah, well . . ." Toth swirled the beer in his glass. "It got better." He put the glass down and wiped his mouth with the back of his hand. His head hung.

"What?"

"Nothing."

Toth had lately been prone to these sudden clam-ups. Lars didn't dare ask much about them: more than once, when he had, Toth had suddenly found an excuse to get up and leave.

In the corner, the cowboy tipped back his head and poured in the drink. His Adam's apple bobbed. He blinked, held the glass one inch over the table, then dropped it. At the sound, the bartender looked up from behind a cash register. The cowboy picked up the glass and spun it like a top, and it careened into the empty bottles. One fell over.

"Check this out," Lars whispered. Toth turned.

The bartender walked to the table and said something quietly to the cowboy. The cowboy didn't look. The bartender took a dishcloth from his back pocket and pulled it taut between his hands. Lars heard the words "problem" and "somewhere else." The cowboy nodded. His arm slid from his lap, and it swung free a moment at his side before he noticed and reeled it in. The bartender watched, then returned to the bar.

"Think he's taking off or picking up?" Toth said.

"Passing out."

Toth snorted. "Falling down." They laughed, then sat in silence for a moment, staring at their glasses.

"I don't mean to bug you," Lars said, and Toth straightened himself in his chair. "You just switch off like that lately. I mean, I have to ask."

"Yeah, it's okay."

"I'll lay off. Just, you know, if you want to talk about it . . ."

"Sure." He drained his glass. "It's nothing. *Weltschmerz*. Angst. You know."

"You can talk to Megan about it too."

He raised his eyebrows. Lars was aware it had come out wrong, as if he had meant Toth could borrow Megan from him.

But Toth let it go. "Yeah, sure."

A squeal of feedback sounded over the PA system. A few people in the bar looked up, surprised. "Those waiting for AirAmerica flight one fourteen, please report to gate two," came a woman's voice. Then she said it again.

"About time," Toth said, standing. Behind him, the cowboy stood too, bracing himself against a post.

Upstairs, there was a message on the arrivals and departures board: "See Attendant." A small crowd had gathered around the desk. The attendant was talking to a family of four. She nodded solemnly at the father, a balding man wearing a black satin jacket. ". . . with you in a moment," Lars made out.

"Canceled in Seattle, I bet," Toth said.

The father stepped closer to the attendant and raised his voice. Her face flushed. "I'm sorry," she said.

A tall man appeared wearing an AirAmerica cap and pilot's jacket. He touched the balding man's shoulder and spoke some quiet words. The mother pulled her daughters closer.

"What's going on?" a woman whispered to Lars.

"I don't know." But the room felt strange, united in a way airport crowds never are. People hunkered in little groups, glancing over their shoulders at the uniformed man. The cowboy lurched into the crowd. He looked sick.

The uniformed man raised his arms into the air, like a priest. "Ladies and gentlemen," he said. His voice was deep and loud, seemingly without effort. "Let me thank you for your patience. You've waited a long time, I know." Lars looked at his watch: 6:14. It hadn't been a long time at all. He glanced out the windows and saw no planes anywhere.

"If you'll follow me," the uniformed man said, "I can explain." A murmur broke loose in the crowd, and he moved to go. At this, the attendant bent over the desk and grabbed his arm. Her lips moved silently and quickly. He whispered back, and she closed her eyes and nodded. Then she covered her mouth with one hand.

Toth bit his thumbnail. "I don't like this."

They followed the man down the hall, past the stairs and through a door into a glass-walled room full of high-backed wooden benches. The uniformed man stood at the front, beside a low pulpit, his hands behind his back. On a table at the side of the room were a freestanding crucifix and a menorah. Two potted plants and a stack of books—Bibles, Lars guessed—sat on a narrow shelf running across the back wall. Everyone sat down and nobody spoke.

The cowboy was the last to enter. There were empty seats, but he walked directly to the back and stood there, next to one of the plants. The uniformed man walked to the door, pulled it shut, and returned to the front of the room. Lars looked through the windowed wall to the desk. The attendant was gone.

"I'm afraid I have bad news," the man said. "Flight one fourteen crashed during its descent into the Marshall Valley. We have no reports from the crash site, but it appears . . . serious." He brought his hands before him and pressed them together. "You must prepare yourself for the worst. Passengers have certainly died."

Silence. Then a man burst suddenly into sobs.

At first Lars didn't make the connection. It was not the kind of thing Megan was likely to get herself into. She might be flighty, but she was safe. She always used her turn signals. Lars felt Toth's hand on his shoulder and jerked away, irritated. Words came to his lips—*Knock it off*—but he didn't say them.

The uniformed man's eyes were half-lidded, his face stoic. "I will be here until we receive further information. I will answer whatever questions I can." He swallowed audibly. "In addition, this is a chapel, if you wish to speak to your God." Two more people bent over now and began to weep. Lars heard himself whisper, "Stop it." Someone in front of him turned.

"How did this happen?" a woman asked, her voice wheeling in the air like blown paper. "Does anyone know how it happened? Was it the pilot's fault?" The uniformed man looked alarmed. He seemed to have nothing left to say.

Lars imagined Megan tightening her seat belt and strapping the oxygen mask over her face. Its white rubber strap tangled in her hair. She was sitting next to a child and helped him with his mask. Her hand touched the child, brushed hair off his face. That touch—Lars's breath rushed up into his throat and stopped there, and he doubled over, his chest on fire. When the fire receded a wave of fatigue washed over him. He wanted all this straightened out. He wanted to sleep.

"I don't know," the uniformed man told the woman. "Nobody knows yet." Quiet returned. The criers cried in silence. Lars felt Toth's hand on his arm and the arm felt hot beneath it.

"Lars."

"What." He raised his head. Toth's face was open and empty as a dog's.

"Lars, man . . ."

He was enraged. "Leave it." Behind them, off to the right, stood the cowboy. His arms were crossed over his chest and his hat lay on the shelf behind him, next to the Bibles. His hair was matted into the shape of his hat, and he hadn't bothered to fix it. His mouth was open and his eyes glittered. The sight of the cowboy made Lars tremble—it was wrong, this whole situation was all wrong—and he gripped his knees with his hands. As he did this he noticed the shorts he was wearing, a pair of cutoff chinos, and suddenly thought they looked ridiculous. He picked at the strands of thread that dangled from the edges. Toth wasn't touching him now.

"What are the chances?" a woman somewhere cried. "What are the chances they're okay?" Lars looked up. *What a stupid question.*

"I'm afraid we just don't have that information, ma'am. I should say it doesn't look too good."

The woman was sitting in the front row. Now she nodded her head in wide, sorrowful arcs.

"If anyone would like to be alone, feel free to leave the room and sit elsewhere in the airport. Listen for the loudspeaker. We will call you back if we have any news."

Lars looked at his watch. Six-thirty. He had made dinner reservations for seven. He should call. He stood, and so did several others, their faces stricken, and they all moved toward the door. Toth got up and followed.

"Where are you going?" he said in the lobby, too loudly. "You're not going anywhere—"

"I'm going to use the phone."

Toth stopped. Lars walked another twenty feet before he turned.

"What?" he said. *"What!"*

"Who are you calling?" Toth began to slouch, his arms hanging limp, like empty sleeves. "Are you calling her parents?"

"I'm calling the restaurant."

He nodded as if he understood, his face crumpling. "Lars."

"What?"

"She's my best friend, Lars." His shoulders began to shake. "What do we do? What do we do now?"

Lars marched back to where he stood and grabbed his shoulders. He had planned to shake Toth until he stopped crying, but now that he had grabbed him he didn't want to.

"Lars!" Toth cried.

Lars lowered his head to Toth's and their foreheads met. It was hot in here, everything was hot despite the air conditioning, and he thought about the three of them, himself, Toth, and Megan, getting into the car with her bags. He thought about them driving into town, talking loud over the noise of the street. He'd never felt so hopelessly held fast, so trapped in a place, as in this airport.

"What are we going to do?" Toth whispered to him.

"We're going to use the phone."

Lars remembered Megan six months before, at his apartment, a winter morning. She went into the cold bathroom to run a shower, and a few minutes later he followed: he undressed, went to the bathroom, pulled back the shower curtain and stepped in. There she stood, her back to the spray of water, her shoulders and breasts and stomach and her cupped hands before her face all covered with a pink mixture of lather and blood. Blood dripped down the wall at her side and vanished in the swirling water around her feet. Megan's eyes were wide and blank as saucers in the steam.

It was a bad nosebleed. They stuffed her nostrils with toilet paper and cleaned up the tub, and everything was fine. But this was the moment Lars gave himself over to her—the moment she first betrayed a crack in her invulnerability, standing stunned at the failure of her body to follow the rules she'd set for it. To Lars, her surprise only pointed up how astounding her faith was in the first place. He was in love.

But now the memory terrified him. Now he preferred the earlier, invincible Megan, the one who could not be intimidated.

"Lars."

"Yeah." They were back in the bar, both of them with drinks. Somebody had tipped off the bartender and the drinks were free. Neither drank them. There was a TV in the bar, but it wasn't on. Lars was glad.

"Do you think she's alive?"

"Of course she's alive."

"What if she isn't?"

"Stop it," Lars said. Toth's face was damp with tears and sweat. A whorl of blond hairs stuck to his forehead.

"Lars," he said, whispering now, "I think she's dead."

"I'd know it if she was dead," Lars said.

The call came at seven-thirty. They mounted the stairs to the gate, passing happy people from another flight. Upstairs the crowd, now subdued, gathered in the chapel, many with their arms around each other: there seemed to have been some coalescence Lars and Toth had missed, some declaration of solidarity, and a few people eyed them with suspicion when they entered. Lars recognized the woman who had asked whose fault it was. Her eyes were wrinkled with anger, but her mouth hung wetly from her face like a washcloth and he thought she might fall over. The cowboy was still there, in the same place, though his hat was back on. He had it pulled down over his eyes.

The uniformed man returned. He cleared his throat. "I'm terribly sorry," he said. "There are no survivors."

Next to Lars, Toth made a choking sound, then began to moan.

"It will take some time to identify the victims," the uniformed man said. He seemed to be losing control of his voice, and he turned away, fished a handkerchief from a back pocket, and pressed it to his face. The sounds of crying had spread through the room. Lars wanted to stand up and scream at them.

"Pardon me," the uniformed man said. "The pilot and copilot were my friends. I know they were . . . capable men. They—" And he stood there, his mouth open, looking out through the chapel wall.

A moment passed, and the uniformed man shook himself. "Pardon me," he said again. "It is important that we identify . . . We realize that you must make arrangements . . ." He cleared his throat. "Jeanne will take your names and telephone numbers. We will need access . . . We may need . . . dental records.

"I'm sorry. I'm sorry. You should all go home. I'm sorry," he said. He pressed his thumb and forefinger into his eyes. "When the victims have been identified, we . . . somebody . . . will call—"

Lars felt more than saw a quick motion at the back of the room, then turned to see one of the potted plants sliding down the shelf toward the other. It struck and the pots shattered, spilling dirt and red potsherds onto the floor. The cowboy flung his hat onto the ground. "You all shut the hell up!" he screamed. "You all shut the god damn hell up!" Everyone was watching. He bent over, panting like a beaten prizefighter. He growled. He kicked his hat across the back of the room, into the pile of dirt. Then he stumbled out, leaving the hat behind, and stomped down the stairs.

The uniformed man stood at the front of the room gaping, then with shocking speed stormed to the door. He strode stiff-legged down the hall, pushed the men's room door open with his shoulder and disappeared inside.

Lars gave his name and number, and her parents'. He patted his pocket to make sure he still had the car keys, her car keys. Toth was leaning against a window, looking out over the tarmac.

"Let's go, Toth."

"You aren't crying, man. Why aren't you crying?"

"I don't know."

"Let me come stay with you."

"I'll be okay." He marveled at how easy it was to say that. *Okay, okay, I'm okay.* Much later he would remember this moment and realize it was Toth who needed *him,* that Toth was making no pretense of being okay.

Toth rubbed his face with both hands. "Oh, Jesus."

"It's time to go."

They drove back to town with the windows open. But this is her car, Lars kept thinking. We're in her car. She's sitting right next to me, she's wearing sunglasses. But when he looked, there was Toth, leaning against the door, his head half out the window.

Toth lived on the North Side. They drove over the bridge that spanned the train tracks, through pocked and patched streets, and stopped at Toth's house. Tarpaper peeled off the sides. The porch roof sagged. One of Toth's housemates, a sullen art student, was sleeping in a cat-shredded armchair just outside the door, a beer bottle on the porch floorboards beside him. The car idled.

"Why don't you come in, man," Toth said. "I can fix you something."

"I'm not hungry."

"What am I gonna do in there? What'll I do?"

A rock band often practiced in Toth's basement, and Lars could hear them now, imprecise and loud. For a second he felt sorry for Toth and his haphazard, sloppy life, but the feeling gave way to a desperate longing for home, not his apartment but Wisconsin, his old bedroom, his mom, the dog.

"I should be home. I should wait for them to call."

Toth's breath caught and Lars watched as his chest hitched once, twice. He fell against Lars and let out one sob, ragged and awful. Lars held him with one arm. When it was over, Toth straightened up. "I'll call you," he said.

"Don't. The phone."

They sat in silence. On the next block, a child wobbled around on a yellow bike.

"Well. I'll be here if, you know, you need anything."

"Thanks." Lars was watching the child. She traced a figure eight in the street. Toth waited another moment, then got out of the car. He climbed the steps to his porch, passed the sleeping housemate, went inside.

The little girl moved to the curb when Lars passed. Their eyes met and she looked away.

I have her car, he thought. Everything's okay.

"*Hellenbeck here.*"

"Mr. Hellenbeck?"

"Yeah."

"This is Lars Cowgill." Nothing. "Megan's boyfriend."

"Yeah, sure," he said. "Howyadoin, Lars?"

"Not so hot, sir."

Another pause. Lars was sweating. His cat stood ten feet away, next to its empty food bowl, meowing.

"What's going on here?"

"I have bad news."

There was some sort of disturbance on the other end, something brushing the receiver. "Look, what is this? Where's Megan?"

"She's not here," Lars said. "Her plane crashed."

Lying on the bed was a gray sweatshirt of hers. Lars stared at it. It looked alive there, like it might suddenly fly across the room at him. He began to shake, and for a moment forgot where he was or what he was doing.

"What in God's name are you saying?" Mr. Hellenbeck was yelling.

"I was just at the airport. They said it crashed. They said nobody lived."

"You're calling me with this bullshit!"

"I'm sorry. I gave them your number." Why did everyone have to yell?

"I have to hear this from the likes of you! I don't have to take this from you, you sonofabitch! I don't have to take it!" His voice was somewhat distant now, like thunder. Lars imagined him holding the receiver at arm's length.

"Mr. Hellenbeck?"

"Fuck you!" he screamed, and the connection cut off.

He didn't want to stay here, but even more, he didn't want to go anywhere else. The phone had a long cord, so he moved it to within reach of the couch. He closed his eyes.

Everything is quiet after the crash. She unbuckles her seat belt and drops the oxygen mask. She stands. No one is speaking. She climbs out into the light through a giant hole. She is in a wide field. Crows caw. She walks and walks; it's a long way. She comes to a gas station. I'm okay, she tells the people there. She digs into her pocket for a quarter. She dials.

The phone didn't ring. It was eight o'clock, but not yet dark. He realized he knew nothing at all about the crash—where it had happened, or why. Nobody had called him about it. Except for Toth, everyone he knew was gone from town, graduated and lit out for somewhere to start new lives. I ought to turn on the radio, he thought, but he made no move toward it.

He remembered the desolate yawn of tornado sirens, and thought of his mother, living by herself. Stoughton, the town where he grew up. He thought he should call her—but why ruin her evening? And what good would it do him? She'd offer to fly out and see him, and he'd refuse.

He picked up the phone by reflex, and before he could get it to his ear he realized he was going to dial Megan's number. It was what he did when things went wrong. He set the receiver back on the cradle and lay down. His hands were cold and he thrust them between his legs.

Sometime later he fell into a kind of shallow sleep. He kept waking up, twice before the late summer dark, then again and again in the night. Once he walked across the room and fed the cat, and another time let him out. Otherwise he didn't move. At some point he'd covered himself with a blanket. When daylight came again he let the cat in and sat back down next to the phone. He examined the cord that ran from the receiver to the cradle, and the one from the cradle to the wall. He cried finally, briefly, but only for a few minutes and mostly because he made himself do it. He sat up very straight on the couch and watched the cat.

The cat's name was Hodge. He was striped orange. He was asleep on the bed, on the other side of the room. Lars looked through the papers on the floor until he found a blank piece and a pen. He spread the paper on his lap, with a magazine underneath for support, and drew a map of the apartment. There was the bedroom/living room, where he was now, the kitchenette, the bathroom. He drew a little toilet and a sink. He drew a bed and a couch, a table and stove. Then, on the drawn bed, he made a mark, corresponding to Hodge's position on the actual bed.

Ten minutes later, Hodge got up and stretched. He hopped off the bed and walked toward the kitchen. On the map, Lars traced the cat's path with the pen. When Hodge finished eating and came to Lars on the couch, Lars drew a corresponding line.

In this way he passed the morning and early afternoon. By three o'clock the paper was dense with crisscrossed paths. Many overlapped; others strayed off alone and looped erratically, often when Hodge was distracted by insects or drifting motes of dust. The paths converged on several loci: the food bowl, the corner of the bed, and Lars himself. From where Lars sat he could see into the bathroom, and he had followed carefully as Hodge drank warm water from the dripping faucet in the sink, or tightroped around the perimeter of the tub. Mostly the lines stayed near walls, then veered off toward objects.

The game ended when Hodge walked to the door and stopped. Lars got up and opened it. For a moment he thought about following the cat through the neighborhood—he would have to draw the park and the river, and his neighbors' houses, and the streets and trees and the patches of dirt where Hodge liked to roll—but he only stood at the open door and squinted in the bright sunlight. It was Saturday afternoon.

He went to the kitchen and toasted bread. He spread each slice with butter and jam and put them on a plate. He held the plate with both hands, then set it down on the counter and left it.

On his way back to the couch, the phone rang. Lars stopped, terrified by the sound, and then by the fact of the sound. It rang again, and again.

He sat on the couch first, then pulled the phone onto his lap. It rang again. He had no answering machine.

It rang again.

He knew when he picked it up. There was an antiseptic quality to the air around the earpiece, an official hiss he knew could not come from a friend. It was three-fifteen, and finally they had found her.

3

At the end of July, Trixie Bogen got a letter in the mail:

Trixie,

Well, I suppose you're surprised to hear from me. Caitlin's dead now as you probably heard and with her kids gone and me retired, I've got a little extra time on my hands. I'll get right to the point. I want to come see you there in Marshall sometime around the end of next month. I'm thinking the 25th.

If you don't want me coming, you ought to say so. But I'm going to go ahead and make the reservations, in the hope you'll say yes.

I know it's been a very long time, Trixie, but I think we would have a lot to talk about. I got your address from Bette Spraycar, who I saw in the city. She was visiting her kids. I hope you don't mind.

Write soon.

Hamish

When she first pulled it out of the mailbox, it was no shock; the handwriting was as familiar as it had been thirty-five years before and for a second it *was* thirty-five years before, and their children were still children and the letter was only something she'd seen lying around the house. But then she saw it for what it was and opened it, wondering what he could have to say after such a long silence.

Hamish was her husband; she still thought of him that way. He'd left her alone with their children and an eternity of unpaid debts, had gone off to Seattle and remarried, but still he was her husband, because nobody else was before him or after him. And for some reason he wanted to come see her again.

She wrote him back immediately, telling him no, of course he couldn't come. She stuffed the letter into the mailbox at the end of the drive and raised the red flag. But all that morning she eyed the mailbox out her kitchen window, and when she saw the mail truck coming in the distance she ran out and took the letter back. What was the harm? It was his dollar, his disappointment, whatever he thought would happen here, whatever he thought he would get. Her next letter told him to come. She made it as cold as she knew how. *If you think it's a good idea,* she wrote, *I won't stop you.* But a few days later a postcard came:

Trixie,

Your letter made me very happy. I'm coming on Air-America, flight 114. That's Aug. 25, 5:42. You can pick me up if you want but if you don't, okay, I'll get a cab.

No more now—see you in a couple weeks.

Love, Hamish

The first time she saw Hamish, he was carefully signing his name to the accounts ledger at Paris Dry Goods. A pair of blue jeans and a stiff brown work shirt lay on the counter at his side. This was in Great Falls in 1950, when she was twenty-seven and thought she would never marry. Years before, it seemed inevitable, her right, but the war was on then and it was all boys were interested in. It wasn't the war that bothered Trixie, but the boys' singleness of purpose, which to her defined men. What could she talk to them about? She got a job typing for one of the cattle companies, lived at home. And when the boys returned they were no longer boys, and she was unpracticed with them, and evenings out felt wrong, as if she had not been asked on the date but had asked to be dated. There were others for them to marry, and they did, and she gave up on them without particular bitterness. Men liked Trixie but she had managed without them, and this suited her.

But Hamish was a different story. She read his name in the ledger when she bought the thread she'd come for, and its rhythms seemed to her to match the self-possession and easy motion of his body: Hamish Bogen. She asked around. Ranched with his father outside town, no wife, no fiancée. Her friend Netta, a seamstress at the dry goods, set up their first date, blind for him: a dance at the Grange Hall at the end of summer.

He drove a truck to town to pick her up. His skin was dark, his suit pressed, his hat black and unsullied by dust; he stood in the center of their living room with the slightest of smiles on his lips.

"Your friend Netta told me you were pretty."

"Thank you," she said, feeling like a child, though she didn't know if this was a compliment or merely a statement of fact. *Netta told me.* Trixie's parents, who'd introduced themselves to Hamish when he came in, had found some reason to go up to the bedroom, where they certainly listened.

Hamish leaned toward a wall hung with photographs: recent ones of Trixie and her parents, a few old pictures of grandparents and great-grandparents from the East.

"Who's this?" he asked, pointing to a tall girl in a family portrait, whose arms encircled Trixie's neck. "Do you have a sister?"

"She died," Trixie said, ashamed to tell him this, as if it would curse her. They called the sister Schatze, and she had died of pneumonia at ten.

Hamish looked at her, weighing his words. "Was it long ago?"

"A long while."

He nodded, seeming to know that any condolence would only embarrass her, and for this she was grateful.

Nearby was hung a photograph Trixie's father had gotten at the dry goods. According to the label on the back, it had been taken in 1895 in Giant Springs. In it, a man with a white mustache stood on a railless footbridge over a shallow sluiceway of the river. He was looking down and to the right, at a man in a white suit who appeared to have fallen; the fallen man's hand was in the air and his back to the camera. Nearby, two women in long dresses held parasols. Though nobody seemed to know the identities of the two women or the fallen man, the man with the mustache was the writer Mark Twain, who had visited Montana at the turn of the century and written about it. Trixie's father loved Twain; so did Trixie. Sometimes they sat together looking at the photo, making up wisecracks for Twain. *If you want to try the water, James, just jump in. Do you want me to help you, or are you only saying howdy?*

"Who took this picture?" Hamish asked her.

Her dress itched and she tried to keep herself from scratching. "Don't know. My father got it at the dry goods."

He nodded. The way he stood—his hands behind his back, holding his hat, his legs relaxed and parted just slightly with a cowboy's easy dignity—made her itch in the chest and want to take his arm.

"That's Mark Twain," she told him.

He leaned closer. "Which one?"

"The man who's standing."

Hamish nodded. "He came here, did he?"

"Yes."

He turned around and smiled at her, and she thought, Yes, that's it, he's the one. He said, "Did you read any of his books?"

She nodded. "My father's read them all. He used to bring them home from the library."

"I read *Huck Finn* when I was in school. Then later I read the other one about the river."

"Life on the Mississippi?"

"But I never finished it. There isn't much time for reading." He turned again to look at the picture and said, "I'll bet it was the very same book, the one your father borrowed." His voice was full of wonder as he said it. "Now isn't that something? There I was, reading a book you'd read, and now here we are."

"Yes."

He spun and stuck out his hand. For a second Trixie wasn't sure what she was supposed to do with it. "Are you ready to go? I'm not much of a dancer, now."

"I'm ready," she said. "And I don't mind."

Now she sat in the old wing-back chair, looking at the photo. It was one of the few things she had from the house in Great Falls. The chair was another, and the ottoman that went with it. It was five o'clock and the sun was still high. In an hour or two the house would start to heat up and fill with evening sunlight, and just when she thought she could take it no longer the sun would set, and the air would turn cool. By then she would be sitting in the kitchen with Hamish. She'd open the good whiskey, to let him know she hadn't forgotten about his drinking, and drink it with him to show that all was forgiven. She had forgiven him; she'd done that a long time ago.

She had decided to go meet him at the airport. Driving bothered her—the sound of the tires against the pavement put her to sleep, and she sometimes found herself stranded at traffic lights, forgetful of her destination or direction—but to sit at home and wait would be agony. Though she lived alone, she was rarely lonely; only when she was forced to wait for someone else did the quiet take on weight and become a palpable enemy. She made a cup of tea to keep her awake on the drive, and drank it at the table. At quarter past five she picked up the phone and dialed the airport, to make sure the flight was on time.

"Wait a moment," a woman told her. "I'll check on that for you." Trixie heard the plasticky clacking of a computer keyboard.

"Oh, I'm afraid that one is running a little late," came the woman's voice.

"Well, how late exactly?"

"One moment." The woman said some words to someone else, and a man's voice answered. She couldn't make out either. "I'm afraid we don't yet have any information."

"I see."

"Are you picking up?"

"Yes, I am."

"Why don't you call back a little later?"

"Well, all right," Trixie said. "How much later?"

"Oh, twenty minutes. Even half an hour. You won't miss your party."

Miss my party, she thought, hanging up. Nobody's thrown me a party in fifteen years.

She decided to take a walk. Her body still worked, even if she had a few more aches than she used to, even if she did seem to be getting smaller. She stopped wearing her dresses about five years ago, when their hems started dropping, getting tangled up in her ankles, and she switched back to jeans, which she'd worn on the ranch with Hamish when they were first married. She even wore some of the same pairs she'd packed away when they came to Marshall. All they meant to her then were the old problems. Now, she liked the feel of something a little closer to the skin, something to keep the tall grass and bugs off her in the woods. And rolled up, they looked good on her: where before they were a young girl's way of kidding herself, now they were an old lady's way of slogging through the mess of life.

She followed a well-traveled trail through the woods behind her house. The house was the second she'd lived in here; the one they came to in 1958, the one they sold the ranch to buy, was downtown. She used to drive past that house sometimes on the way to the library. The grass was worn away to dust now and the door always propped open. Children played with toy guns in the yard. She didn't feel much like passing it these days, though; her own house was perfect. It was small and made of logs, and her few neighbors were kind and quiet. Though she didn't need it yet, they checked in on her from time to time. She gave them tea, the way old ladies are supposed to.

Trixie still thought of trees as a luxury. On the ranch, the only trees were in the windbreak, and they always seemed in danger of drying up and dying. She sat under them whenever there was time, which was rarely, and all the water she used to wash dishes and clean the house she tossed under one or another of her favorites, to keep them alive.

At first the ranch wasn't so hard. She took the ailing Mrs. Bogen's place as cook and nurse to a succession of part-time hands, a job she enjoyed. The men were friendly to her, and Hamish's company each evening was a delight, far better than anything she could have imagined. They lived together in a small house Hamish had built with his father in anticipation of their marriage. They planned to run the ranch together when Hamish's father retired, and eventually build a larger house where they would raise their family. Every Sunday Mr. Bogen (and sometimes Mrs. Bogen, when she felt well enough) picked up Hamish and Trixie in the truck, and they drove to town for church; afterward they always bought a newspaper from the drugstore on Central Avenue and read it over lunch in the kitchen of the big house.

Trixie had never been much of a churchgoer. Her parents weren't religious and only attended the Catholic church in Great Falls on Easter, for the spectacle. But this new routine suited her. She read along silently when the congregation said their prayers, and during sermons she imagined their new house, the children they would someday have. She made mental lists of things that needed to be done at home.

One Sunday when Mrs. Bogen was too sick to come, they didn't stop for a paper. The ride home was unusually quiet. Trixie knew little of Mr. Bogen's relationship with Hamish; the older man didn't say much in Trixie's presence that wasn't specifically about her and Hamish or their plans. But as they pulled into the long dirt road that led to the ranch, Mr. Bogen turned to Hamish and said, "I hope you prayed for her."

Hamish nodded. "I did."

"She hasn't been up all week, you know. I've had to bring her food to her."

"Figured as much," Hamish said. Trixie was sitting between them and he squeezed her hand.

Instead of driving the extra quarter-mile to the big house, Mr. Bogen stopped at the gate in front of their small one, and let the truck idle there a moment. "Well," he said.

"She ought to be in a hospital," Hamish said, staring out the windshield.

"Doc comes by, gives her a few things."

"Doc's a vet."

"He's a good man."

"She's dying. He doesn't know a thing about it."

Mr. Bogen shook his head. He and Hamish seemed to be watching the same thing, something distant that Trixie couldn't make out. "Not the kind of talk for a Sunday, Hamish."

Hamish opened the door and stepped out, held it open for Trixie. She patted Mr. Bogen's arm. "Thank you, Dad," she said. She'd never called him that before. He looked surprised but said nothing, and she got out of the truck.

Before he closed the door, Hamish leaned back in. "People are still sick on Sundays," he said. "As many people die on Sunday as any other day."

Mr. Bogen nodded. "You going to close that door?"

Hamish did.

That night, while she stood at the counter drying the dinner dishes, Hamish said to her, "I'm not going next week."

"You're not?"

"It doesn't sit right with me anymore."

They had only been married a year, and Trixie was not yet sure how to respond to such a comment. Their conversations had all been practical or speculative: what to do, what would someday be done. She said, "But your father."

"He can keep on going."

She stopped working. "I don't understand."

"He doesn't want to admit it," Hamish said. "He likes to think God will fix her or God will take her. God doesn't have a thing to do with it. It's cancer that does, not God. She's wasting away, it's obvious. And that vet knows it too."

"Maybe it's what she wants. To stay home."

"She's in too much pain to stand up. They could give her medicine."

"I'm sorry, Hamish."

He looked up at her. "You'll stick with me. Next Sunday."

"Yes," she said.

The following week his father came as usual. Trixie watched through the window as he stepped down from the truck.

"Why aren't you dressed?" he said when Hamish opened the door.

"I'm not going."

Mr. Bogen looked from Hamish to Trixie, who stood behind, by the sink, and then back to his son. It's all wrong, she thought. We should have talked to him sooner.

"What's the matter, then? You feeling all right?"

"I just don't want to go anymore."

"Anymore!" He turned to Trixie again, this time his face red with betrayal, with embarrassment. "You too?" he said to her, and she had to turn away.

All three waited, and when nothing changed Mr. Bogen said, "Well, all right then. We'll talk about this tonight, Hamish." He turned to go, his shoes scraping on the porch boards.

"I don't have much to say," Hamish said.

"I got plenty."

That night, as Trixie lay in bed in the next room, their words came to her muffled through the walls. Why was he rejecting them? Mr. Bogen wanted to know. How could he insult them like that?

I'm not rejecting *you,* Hamish said. I just don't think God is responsible for everything. I don't think God made Mom sick and I don't think praying's going to make her better.

So what is He responsible for? his father said. You think he's responsible for some things and not others? You think you know what He wants, is that what you're telling me?

I'm telling you I don't believe in Him at all.

Mr. Bogen didn't say a thing for some time, and she heard a chair scrape on the floor. What am I going to tell your mother? he whispered finally.

The truth.

She's dying.

I know that.

You owe it to her. Even if . . . you don't believe, you owe it to her.

She doesn't have to know I'm not going.

You'll go.

Dad—

When she's gone, you do what you want on Sundays. But until then, you go to church and pray for your mother.

The sound of footsteps, the door opening.

She'll be dead soon enough, Mr. Bogen said. Then you'll have your way, believe me.

Later, he crawled into bed beside her. "Trixie."

"I'm awake."

He reached for her and she moved into his arms. His body now was both familiar and strange, and she felt something illicit about the embrace, something dangerous that hadn't been there before, and she felt she must be careful. "I'm sorry," he said.

"I heard it all."

"I know."

"Will you go to church?" she said after a time.

"Yeah. You don't have to come."

"I'll come."

"Trixie, I want to start a family."

She touched his face in the dark. "I do too."

"Right away."

She held her breath, then let it out. "Now, Hamish?"

"Yes," he told her.

Soon they would have a daughter, Kat, and in time a son, Edward. Years later, when Kat was older and had gotten away from them, Trixie often wondered if she was conceived that night, if somehow Hamish's fight with his father provided the wedge that would drive her from them. But after a while she stopped wondering; that kind of thinking did nobody any good.

As she walked, Trixie noted familiar things: a tree that had fallen and blocked the path fifteen years before and the new bend she had cleared to avoid it; a pile of rocks, once the foundation of a long-abandoned cabin, that she'd seen a black bear rummaging through in search of bugs; an eagle's nest on a skeletal spruce, the eagles elsewhere. The physical integrity of these objects clarified her memories, making them more real, giving them texture, and they returned to her with greater urgency than they ever had before. She could almost feel the skin on Hamish's hands, weathered and warm, like sun-soaked boots, hear his roughened, easy voice.

But when she emerged from the woods and her house came into view, she got the sudden impression that he wasn't really coming, that he had changed his mind. There was little to explain the feeling, save the fact of her house, so real, so perfectly fitted to life without him. She let out a sigh, nobody around to hear it but herself, and went inside.

She didn't pick up the phone yet. Instead, she went to the bedroom, opened the closet door, and knelt carefully on the floor before the clutter of objects inside: a wooden box of buttons and thread, photo albums, her wedding silver, which she hadn't had cause to bring out in years. In the back, behind the broom and dustpan, she found a tattered shoebox repaired with tape, and pulled it out. She'd moved the box a dozen times, but had never bothered to open it. She knew what was inside.

She took off the lid to reveal a pile of papers and junk, yellow and rough with dust. On top was Hamish's wallet. Why hadn't he taken it with him when he left? She didn't know, probably an oversight. The desire to leave must have come upon him in a rush, and after that there was no going back. The wallet hadn't been opened since. It was worn out, shiny in the middle and cracked at the fold. She remembered that it used to lie in the same place every day—on top of the icebox, next to a bunch of dusty mason jars and the pile of change she dipped into when she sent Edward to the corner for an egg, or whatever.

She opened it up. There was no money inside—of course that was probably the first thing she took out when he left—but there were papers. Receipts, business cards. A thin piece of lined paper three inches square on which was written:

8 dress
10 blouse
7 shoe
6 skirt

Her sizes. Of course he had to have this; he used to buy her things to wear every birthday and Christmas. She remembered, suddenly, a Christmas at the ranch, playing Monopoly with Kat and Edward and wearing the new wool dress Hamish had bought her. Would he remember this, if she showed him the wallet?

She also found a brittle, yellow newspaper clipping, and recognized the type from the *Great Falls Tribune*. It was a classified ad:

WANTED. Winter sheepherder, Paradise Valley. Must be willing to work alone, no phone/mail, live small quarters. Good pay.

The ad listed a post office box in Conrad. When had Hamish considered this? she wondered. How long had he kept it with him before he left? Two weeks? Two years? Ten years? To think that this was there on top of the fridge, right under her nose if she wanted to see it.

But she did see; anyone could have.

Perhaps he started leaving her as early as the summer of 1953, when a month of rain gave way to the single hot, humid day when Mrs. Bogen finally died. There was the money for the casket and funeral, and then the rain returned, with autumn in tow. Fields flooded, the hay never dried, and they had to buy it elsewhere. Dozens of cattle fell and drowned, or got sick from floodwater; the flu took several ranch hands for a few weeks. By the middle of October it was clear they wouldn't catch up this year, probably not for several, if ever, and then one morning Hamish came back to the house at six, just as Trixie was getting up to cook.

"You're a little early for breakfast," she said, and then she saw his face:

pale and cracked open like an egg. "What," she said, as she went to him. "What happened?"

Hamish didn't move, didn't open his arms to take her. "My dad," he said.

Walking out at dawn, he had seen Mr. Bogen sitting against the base of a tree behind the stables. At first, from a distance, it looked like he had sat down to clean his shotgun and fallen asleep. But it was Wednesday morning, no time to go out looking for birds, and soon Hamish was close enough to see that the shotgun wasn't over the old man's shoulder like he thought, but jammed into his mouth.

By this time they had a daughter, Kat. They spent that Christmas with Trixie's parents in the Bogens' big house. It was their first week living there. To Trixie it still spoke of the Bogens; their bedroom remained untouched, and they'd been sleeping in Mrs. Bogen's sickroom, on a mattress Hamish had recently bought and that they could not afford, but was needed to replace the deathbed. Trixie's parents didn't know what to say to Hamish, so they played with their granddaughter and talked about Trixie's childhood. For the first time in years, Trixie missed her sister and wished they could commiserate about married life. She wished her daughter could have an aunt.

The next year the cattle companies came sniffing around, asking about the land and the stock. Hamish spoke little to these men and sent them on their way. Meanwhile he got up earlier and went to sleep later, and sometimes Trixie was barely aware of him at all save for a dark presence beside her in the bed. She stayed with the baby now during the day, and though work went well in the spring, she knew they were losing money. They were alone out there with more responsibility than they could handle and nothing else to occupy them. She could feel herself becoming hard and suspicious, and worst of all resigned—to a life without ease, without anything but the same for their children, to drudgery and endless debt.

Trixie got pregnant again. It wasn't what either of them wanted. Kat was three years old.

"We can't afford it," Hamish told her.

"We don't have any choice."

He opened his mouth to speak but shut it before any words came out. His hand found hers. "Okay, then. I think it's time to think about selling."

"The ranch?"

"That man came around yesterday. He mentioned some nice numbers, if it's numbers you're looking for."

She leaned forward to meet his eyes. "Hamish, we can get by. We'll find a way."

"Nah, it's the right thing." He shook his head. "Don't have the heart without Dad, you know that."

"You don't have the heart for anything else."

"I'll find something."

Though she let herself believe him, later she would see that it wasn't true. Hamish blamed himself, his loss of faith, for his father's death, as Trixie would certainly have done in his position, as anyone would. But away from the ranch this wound would fester and spread, and he would come to see the decision to sell as a decision he'd had to make for her, would begin to see Edward as a child only she had wanted to conceive and forced him to father. And as the rift between them grew, he would pit her children against her, and what influence she had with them would evaporate like so much water in the heat of blame. But this was all ahead of them, and saying goodbye to the ranch, painful as it was, gave them the first glimmer of hope they'd had since Kat arrived.

On their last night there, they couldn't sleep. They whispered plans to one another in the dark, Hamish expressing a tentative excitement at giving town life a try, Trixie thrilled about the extra time they would have—to spend with the kids, to go hiking and fishing, to live in a place with a good library and good schools and neighbors they'd see every day. They had decided to move west, to Marshall. A distant cousin of his, Karl Spraycar, had a job for him at a construction firm, digging foundations and laying concrete, and Hamish thought it a fitting job, helping to build a growing town, working outdoors and close to the land. They would stay with Karl, who was little more than a kind stranger to Hamish, until they found a house.

"I thought I'd be here my whole life," he told her. "Didn't think I'd ever get married either."

"No?"

"Nope."

"Did you get disappointed?"

He waited a moment before he said, "I just got surprised, is all."

"You love me, then? Or am I still just a surprise?"

He reached over and put his hand on her stomach, where she'd only just begun to show. "Still love you, after all these years."

"Four."

"A long time, for something you don't expect."

Trixie was still awake when his breathing evened out and the sky began to lighten. For four years, this was about the time they had been getting up; now, for a change, it was when Hamish finally fell asleep. They were to leave before noon, arrive in Marshall around dinnertime, and then everything would start over again. She wondered when their life would settle down, whether Hamish would learn to expect its surprises, and she hoped it would happen soon, hoped with all her heart it would happen at all.

She set the wallet aside and rooted around in the box: letters, photos, of course, but other things too: key chains, loose keys; several shot glasses; a comb, a deck of cards in a clear plastic case, a number of dice, none of which matched any others. Not exactly a memorable set of keepsakes, but the box hadn't been carefully planned. It was only the by-product of throwing out Hamish's things when he left. She'd swept through the house while the kids were at school, grabbing anything that had been his or reminded her of him and flinging it into the trash. Over the years, then, when she came across the things she'd missed that day, into the box they went. She kept it on the refrigerator, where the wallet used to go. When the children were gone and she moved away from the house on Main Street, she considered tossing it out without even looking inside. But she didn't. She left it closed, moved, and put it in the closet, where it had remained for twenty-five years, until today.

It was getting late, and she still hadn't called the airport. She didn't want to go and come back empty-handed. The thought made her ashamed: if he wasn't coming, he wasn't coming. She'd know soon enough.

Before she called she took the phone off the wall, memorized the number as she had written it on her bulletin board, and got herself comfortable across the room, in her chair. She dialed and picked burrs off her jeans while it rang.

"Marshall International, please hold." And a click.

She wondered if Hamish knew how many people lived in Marshall now. Everyone here was rude on the phone these days. They'd had a party line out on the ranch. Couldn't be rude on it, she remembered; chances were somebody'd have heard and would hold it against you.

"Marshall International can I help you?"

"I want to know if a late flight has arrived. AirAmerica one fourteen? Coming from Seattle."

"Oh . . ."

"It's still late, is it?"

"Please hold."

Another click, then more ringing. She switched the phone to the other ear and felt her legs throb and the blood well in them. The walk might have been a mistake. Already she dreaded having to get up and bend them again.

"AirAmerica." In the background, a lot of noise, people talking. It just came in, she thought.

"Is flight one fourteen in yet?"

"Ma'am, are you waiting on a friend or relative?"

"A friend, yes. Has it come in?"

"You may want to come here, to the airport, ma'am. I'm afraid something terrible has happened."

"I beg your pardon?"

"Something terrible, I'm so sorry, it's the plane, ma'am, it's crashed. It was coming into the valley and just crashed."

"Crashed!" This couldn't be right.

"I can't give you any details, but if you could come to—"

"Do you mean crash-landed? Or do you mean crashed?"

"Crashed, ma'am. It's . . . oh God."

Trixie felt a sudden need to plant her feet on the floor, and leaned forward in the chair. "Tell me what happened."

"Oh, I'm not supposed . . . This is ridiculous." It seemed the young woman was crying. Crashed? How could that be?

"Go on, please."

"They all died, ma'am, that's what they're saying. My friend Denise, she was on it, she was a flight attendant, you know. I'm so sorry, it's just awful. Ma'am? I didn't want to be the one to tell you that, I've had to tell all these people . . ."

Crashed. Hamish, dead? She stood, walked to the cradle and hung up the phone. It was strange—she'd never thought of Hamish as being alive or dead, only as being gone, disappeared. *Crashed.* It was as if the entire thing had been made up for her benefit: the letter, the flight, the weeks of wondering what it was all about, of recalling things she didn't expect ever to think about again. And the crash.

She went to her bedroom and lay down on the bed. No memories there. She wanted to rest her legs and think about all this.

But she fell asleep almost immediately. She dreamed she was watching herself sleep from across the room, and that the dreaming self left the room and walked out into the kitchen, out the door and into the woods, where everything was familiar and easy, and that the path there brought her to a clearing where she could look up and see through the trees. Stars blinked like Christmas lights, and something streaked across the heavens trailing a brilliant band of blue, a glowing ribbon that faded slowly, deepening, widening as it went, until it was indistinguishable from sky.

She woke to the creak of floorboards in the living room. It was dark. The steps traced circles, stopping every second or so. For a moment she was at the ranch. "Hamish?" she said, but the sound of her voice brought her back and she shuddered and turned on the lamp. "Hello?"

Into the living room, the kitchen: nobody. The front door was latched.

When she returned to the bedroom, her eyes fell on the cardboard box, and she suddenly remembered a photograph she had seen earlier. She picked up the box and set it on the bed, then went through the pictures until she found it. Hamish, his back to the camera, watching a pregnant cow. Hamish's hat was on straight as the horizon, and the cow's neck stretched out in agony, as if pointing to something distant and awful outside the frame. Trixie had written on the back: *Hamish, waiting for calf, 1952.*

She remembered now. She was pregnant herself then, with Kat, when she took the picture.

This more than anything else made her cry. This, and the lonely sound of steps in a house where the only steps were hers, and the unanswered questions that now would never be answered, and her dream of the vanishing light from a falling star.

4

She had to run bent over through the woods to keep the smoke away from her eyes and mouth, and once the trees had swallowed her and she could no longer turn to see their house, Anita allowed herself the luxury of thinking that none of this had actually happened, that somehow they had been mistaken about the plane and the smoke was from a distant forest fire that put nobody but herself in danger. The woods were as quiet now as they must have been half an hour ago, and aside from the smoke, as putrid and toxic as acid, little seemed out of place.

She ran blindly for a minute or so, her sockless feet sweating in her shoes, before she stopped to get her bearings. Ahead the smoke seemed thicker, and there was light—whether a patch of sunlight or fire she couldn't tell—off to the right, beyond the rise that gave way to the creek. She took off running toward it, and when she felt the ground sloping, slowed to a stop. She topped the rise and looked ahead: the creek; a clearing; and glowing between the trees, a fire, a quarter-mile away, already burning hot enough to billow the nightdress against her legs. It *was* a forest fire by now—these trees were dry enough to burst into flame spontaneously. She felt for a breeze, but there was none she could discern.

Nobody could survive in that, she thought. If the crash didn't get them, the fire . . .

She ran down the bank and jumped the creek, slowing to a jog to scan the trees for something out of place. The clearing ahead, cluttered with tall weeds; a strangely gnarled aspen that looked, for a second, like a man. A patch of moss at the base of a tall, scrawny spruce. A squirrel running across a log, to her left. Nothing.

But then some movement, to the right this time, near the patch of moss. She walked toward it, wiping the moisture from her face; the heat was so bad here that her arms were already crusted with salt from her sweat. She pulled the silk from her skin and riffled it, letting the air in.

What had looked like a patch of fungus against the tree trunk fell to the ground, and she saw then that it was a human arm, and the moss a body, lying on its back.

She ran, gulping in the bad air, and fell coughing to her knees where he lay: a boy. At first she thought he was lying half in shadow and looked up to see what dark object hung above them, but there was nothing, and when she turned back to him she saw that it was not shadow, but burn. His arm and leg, his hair, the side of his face—it was all blistered and black, and stank. His left eye was gone, evaporated or burnt over. But the right was open. It blinked.

"Hello?" he said.

Anita stood up and ran ten steps before she retched, and when she was through her stomach clenched and unclenched like a beating heart and her pulse rang in her head. She breathed as deeply as she dared, then went back to the boy's side. It was even worse than she'd noticed: his right leg was gouged as if by a butcher's knife, the cut clean. Blood ran from the wound and covered the ground. She knelt.

"What happened?" he said. His voice was folded strangely over itself, as if an old man were speaking his words with him. "I can't move."

"Just relax," she said. She had begun crying briskly, without ceremony. The boy didn't seem to notice. His eye spun untethered in its socket.

"We were almost there," he said.

"You're here now."

"I am?" He tried to lift his right arm, the good one, but it only flopped over lifelessly in the humus. "I can't move," he said.

"Don't. Don't try."

"Are you okay?" he asked her. His eye seemed to have settled, though it wobbled now when she looked at it. He blinked.

"It's fine. I'm fine."

His head moved just slightly, a twitch. "My uncle."

"What's that?" She leaned closer to his face.

"My uncle . . . I'm supposed to stay with him. He'll worry."

Anita said nothing. The boy squinted. He drew in breath and let it out. "Oh . . ." he said.

"My name's Anita."

"What?"

She moved her lips to his ear. "Anita. I'm Anita."

"I'm so tired."

"Do you want me to do anything?"

She heard her name being called then and turned. It was Paul, at the top of the rise, waving to her. He had his shirt bunched up over his mouth and his belly was thin and white.

"Ma'am?" the boy said.

She turned back. "I'm here. I'm here." Somehow, his hand had found a twig and held on to it. She stared at this delicate hand and tried not to look at his other side.

"Tell my uncle I'm here."

"What's his name?"

"Uncle Larry."

"Sure, of course I will." She wrapped her own hand around his fist. If he noticed he didn't show it.

"Will somebody bring me to his house?"

"Yes," she said. "They'll bring you wherever you want."

"Fishing," he said.

"Yes."

He was quiet a long time, and the eye went halfway shut. His hand was cold. She thought he was dead, and then he said, "I'm beat."

"I understand," she said. She thought she must be empty of tears now, but there they were, still going. The boy said something she didn't catch, and she leaned closer. His smell rose up to meet her, the chemical tang of blood and metal.

"What's that?"

"You have a nice accent," he said.

"Thank you." And after that, he said nothing else.

She didn't know how long she had been there when Paul came for her. "Anita," he said. "Jesus Christ." She felt his hand on her shoulder, and then at her elbows, lifting her to her feet. "Come on," he said. "Let's go, now."

He turned her around and took her arm, then led her back through the trees. They walked together in short, slow steps. She felt like she was in a dream or on the moon, unable to gather momentum, unconnected to the earth. She tried to turn, but he held her fast.

"Are you all right?" he said.

"No." She watched her legs move, each knee crusted with pine needles and blood.

"There was nothing you could have done."

"I guess."

She didn't want him here now, touching her, and shook his hand off her arm. But somehow he interpreted this as need and slipped his arm around her shoulders. She had no energy to speak. The arm stayed.

They came to the creek and wordlessly stepped in together. Her shoes soaked through instantly, and the coolness of the water seemed to her a great and generous gift. Paul knelt in the current and began to splash water onto her knees. She let herself feel gratitude for this, even pleasure.

"Better?"

"I'm fine," she said.

"I didn't see anyone else. I didn't want to look." He stopped splashing her and scooped up water into his hands, then rubbed it into his face.

She could still see blood on her ankles and the sight of it filled her with revulsion. She reached down and finished washing it off, and when the blood was gone she kept rubbing her legs until the feeling came back to them. There was a raw, jagged wound on her knee, deep but barely bleeding. She felt no pain from it. The silk nightdress was covered with blood. She tried to rinse it, but it wouldn't come clean.

"I can't believe this," Paul said. "Did you see the plane?"

"Yes."

"I didn't see anybody at all. Maybe there weren't many people on it."

"I don't know."

"I just can't believe this."

She looked at him crouching there, shaking his head. She took a step back.

"You don't have to be so excited about it," she said.

He stopped and looked blankly at her.

"They're all *dead*," she said.

"I'm sorry."

She stared down at the water, at the mud and moss Paul had upset flowing over and around her shoes. "That boy was alive when I found him."

"What?"

"I talked to him."

"What did he say?" He stood up.

"Nothing," she said. "I just talked to him. He was alive. He didn't know what happened, and I didn't tell him." Paul only watched her, his face slack and wary. The default face for Paul, the reason he didn't know anybody. Her feet had grown cold, and now were beginning to go numb; the air had thickened. She felt urgent, pulled with increasing strength in two directions, neither any good.

From ahead came a flurry of snapping twigs and footsteps. She looked up, startled. A black man with a thin beard, dressed in white, appeared on the rise. He was carrying an orange plastic box with a cross on it.

"Hey! Are you all right?"

"Fine," Paul said.

He ran down the incline and stopped at the edge of the creek, his breathing heavy. A surgical mask dangled at his neck. "Were you all in the crash?" he said, his eyes frantic. He looked from Anita to Paul and settled finally on Anita.

"No," she said, pointing. "We live in the house."

"Did you see . . ." the man began, then looked past them, to where the woods burned. "Sweet Jesus," he said.

Then, from over the rise came the others: people in white, masks strapped to their faces, carrying stretchers and bags and boxes. They splashed past Anita and Paul, their faces grave, their eyes locked on the scene ahead. The black man fumbled with his mask and ran, disappearing into the mass of them as thoroughly as a drop of water into the creek. When they passed,

Anita turned and watched them go, sunlight flashing on their uniforms, swift and quiet into the smoke, like angels.

Light poured through the hole in the house. Anita and Paul sat on the sofa. A record, apparently knocked free of its jacket, lay on the floor at their feet, and Anita pressed her toe to it. A wet print appeared on the vinyl, flecked with dirt. There had already been newspaper people, and now they milled in the yard. She dreaded the rest of them, who were sure to come.

"I'm sorry," Paul said.

"About?" Though it could have been anything now, as far as she was concerned, any one of his inadequate reactions to trying circumstances. But I must give him a chance to redeem himself, she thought. I always do.

"Outside, before. In the yard. This," he said, pointing to the green night-dress, now beyond repair. For the first time she felt naked, and smoothed the fabric over her thighs.

"Oh."

"I was a jerk. It all seems so stupid now. I'm sorry, I really am."

"Please stop that."

"What?"

"Apologizing." She leaned back and closed her eyes. From outside came the sounds of car doors opening and closing, of men calling things out to one another, of people asking questions and other people answering. It had already begun when they stumbled out of the woods together: ambulances and police, firemen in a red car with a flashing light. She stood up and looked out the hole. A ripped-up track led in a gentle curve to the trees, where the fallen object, clearly a jet engine, sat half-blackened in the shade. Two policemen had come and wrapped the trees around it with yellow police-line tape, and they stood just inside the tape, talking, cups of convenience store coffee in their hands. As she watched, another police car pulled up and parked halfway into their garden. Two more officers got out, a man and a woman, and marched to the police line, but when they got there, they only stood, joining in the conversation. The scene had a peculiar, festive air to it.

"We'll have to fix this," she said. "Or at least put some plastic over it."

"As soon as these people leave, I guess." Paul said.

Two more people approached the cops now, men wearing jeans and identical green golf shirts. The taller one held a clipboard. They ducked under the tape, said a few words to the police, then walked around the engine a couple times. The short one pulled out a tape measure and held lengths of it up to the engine, and the tall one scribbled on the clipboard. Soon the tall one moved away from the engine and walked along the trail of ruined earth, while his partner stayed behind and talked to the police. He used his own tape measure to record the length of each mark on the ground, and its distance from the next. In a couple of minutes he had reached the hole in the house and examined its edges.

"May I?" he said to Anita, holding out the tape measure. He wore a neat red beard and reminded her of a cigarette ad, though he wasn't smoking. An insignia on the breast of his shirt read "MASA: Excellence In Flight."

"Sure," she said. He nodded and extended the tape measure, positioning it various ways and writing down the results. When he was through he stepped back and surveyed the debris, tapping the tape measure on the clipboard in a complicated rhythm, but he seemed to come to a decision about it and wrote nothing down.

"You live here, I take it."

"My husband and I, yes." She looked back at the couch. Paul had left.

"They told me you saw the wreckage."

"Yeah."

He looked back over his shoulder and narrowed his eyes, as if this could let him see through the trees. "Well," he said. He shoved the clipboard under his arm and stuck out his hand, up and into the hole. "I'm Chase. Montana Aviation Safety Authority. My partner and I are the crash investigators. For the state, I mean. The fed guys are always late."

"Anita Beveridge," she said, shaking the hand, then realized what she was wearing and backed up a step. If Chase noticed or cared, he didn't let on.

"No kidding? I Need a Beverage. I knew a guy named James Brown."

"I see."

"Yeah, well." He turned again to face the trees, and spoke to her over his shoulder. "They won't let us back there yet. Fire. Slurry bombers are coming in to drop retardant. That should about do it." He kicked a piece of splintered wood and it helicoptered over the grass. "Anybody out there? Any survivors?"

"No, nobody."

"Mmm," Chase said. He took the clipboard from under his arm and tapped on it with the tape measure. "They go down in trees, things get pretty ugly, that's for sure."

She went into the bedroom to lie down. She had the scattered feeling she always got when events conspired to mess things up, and nothing exhausted and frustrated her more than a mess she was incapable of fixing.

This was something she couldn't make Paul understand. To her, chaos was self-perpetuating, both in the real world and in her head; her life, for better or worse, was her struggle to defeat it. And usually she relished the task. Nothing thrilled her like a desk covered with paper clips and staples and little pieces of paper with things scribbled on them, or a long list of onerous tasks laid out in order of importance. These things were an invitation to battle, and she always won.

But today she felt like the underlying structure of her life had crumbled and was, even to her, beyond repair. She had decided that morning to give in to Paul for now—she was young, after all, and didn't strictly *need* a baby yet—but her short-term solution had failed. The second he opened the box, she knew it. It was as if she had cleared the clutter from her desk to find that the desk itself had vanished under its weight. And now, despite her best efforts, the desire was back on her.

It was that boy. He was the victim of circumstances that should never have been, and when she saw him and realized how far gone he was, she tasted for the first time the sheer folly of hope. Her moment alone with him was a series of first-priority demands that would, and did, pass into eternity unsatisfied. Of course his uncle would never pick him up, of course they would never go fishing—and that these plans were left hanging had thrown off the balance of the world forever.

She wanted babies, and she wanted to give them whatever they wanted. That was the bottom line. But Paul was still her best hope, and Paul wasn't budging, with his deep obstinance disguised as wishy-washiness and his cringing fear masquerading as sensitivity. She thought they were lucky to have fallen in love, that they should be kneeling on the ground thanking God that there was love enough for both of them, most of the time. But sweet Paul, who had lacked it all his life, thought that love was always there, around them like a pervading gas, and could be snatched out of the air and made to work. Love was radio waves to him.

But he was wrong. Love was finite. Love had its limits, and theirs was close.

She woke to voices in the kitchen. The bedside clock said 7:41 p.m., still early. She got up, unsticking her knee from the sheets, and dressed: T-shirt, shorts pulled on gently, over the wound. She balled the ruined nightdress and tossed it onto the floor, then limped out.

Chase and his partner sat at their kitchen table, asking Paul questions, and Paul answered animatedly, his hands describing shapes in the air. A group of men leaned against the counter, each with a glass of water. All heads turned when she walked in.

"Are you the wife?" one of the men said.

"I'm Anita Beveridge."

Another took a notepad from the pocket of his jeans. "Can I ask you some questions?"

More reporters. "You already talked to Paul?"

The reporters looked at one another. "Uh . . ." said the man with the notebook.

"I don't want to talk," she said.

"Anita," said Chase's partner. "We need to know a few things."

"I don't think we've met." At the counter, conversation sputtered and restored. She sat down on the remaining chair.

"Anita," Chase said, "this is Alan. Alan, Anita."

Alan wore a beard too, but his was bushy and black. His hand was sweating when she took it. "Now," he said, "please describe the crash, the way you saw it."

"Hasn't Paul done this?"

"Now, Mr. Beveridge tells us he saw a bright flash before the plane changed direction and began to fall. Did you see the flash?"

"No, I didn't."

He turned to Paul. "*She* didn't see a flash, Paul."

"I wasn't looking," Anita said.

"I just want to get these stories straight, Anita."

She stood up. "What difference does it make, really? Nobody's going to

be any less dead." She pushed her chair in. "Everyone," she said. "All of you."
The reporters fell silent. "Please get out of my house. All of you, please. Goodbye."

The reporters exchanged glances, then put their glasses on the counter
and filed out, trying to look as if they wanted to. When they were gone, she
turned back to Alan. "You too, please. Go, go."

"Mrs. Beveridge," he said with put-on patience, "This is a matter of—"

"Please. Go now."

"Come on," Chase said to him, touching his arm.

For a moment, nobody moved. Then Alan got up, and Chase after him. "I
think we have enough," Chase said. "Thank you both."

"Sure," Paul said.

"The fed folks will be coming from Seattle tonight," Chase said, his eyes
on Anita. "They're going to ask you a lot of the same questions."

"I don't doubt it."

She followed them onto the porch and watched as they climbed into a
green truck. They sat in the cab for a moment, talking. Several times Alan
looked up and scowled in her direction. Finally they started the truck and
drove away.

Paul came out behind her and touched her shoulder, then they stood there
and watched: the smoke, billowing out of the forest, firefighters running in
and out, planes swooping overhead and disappearing behind the treeline, then
rising up out of the fire like embers. As they watched, a dump truck appeared,
rumbling up their drive, with a giant white dumpster on its bed. It squeezed
between two police cars near the edge of the trees, and stopped. Two men got
out and stood behind it, guiding the driver, and it lowered the dumpster onto
the ground on long steel arms. Then the men detached it and signaled to the
driver. It was the cleanest dumpster Anita had ever seen.

After the federal people came from Seattle and left again, after the television crew showed up and flooded their house with blinding white
lights, they lay awake in bed. Paul had pulled the shade down, but the flashing lights still seeped in at the edges, and the room glistened around them
like a pot of boiling water. Paul's hand found her thigh and it patted her in a
gentle, monotonous rhythm.

"He said something, didn't he."

"Who?" Anita said, though she knew who.

"The kid in the woods. He said something to you." He rolled over to face her and propped his head up with his hand. "I know you. You're keeping it secret."

"He said hello."

"'Hello'?" He slumped onto his back. "Why are you hiding this from me?"

"I'm not hiding. It's over, okay, Paul? It's behind us." Liar, she thought.

"But—" he said, then stopped. She heard his mouth open again, then close wetly.

"I'm exhausted. Can we go to sleep?"

"Yeah, okay."

"Good night," she said, and kissed his cheek. His skin was warm and his hair smelled like smoke.

"Good night."

But even now, she didn't sleep. Paul was right. If this were a year ago—even a week ago, even yesterday—she would turn over and apologize for it, and tell him what had happened. But now she didn't want to. This thrilled and terrified her; she felt like she had swallowed a dangerous drug that had not yet taken effect. When it became clear to her that there would be no sleep, she concentrated on slowing down her waking self until she was indistinguishable from a sleeping person: she breathed through her nose and felt the plane strike the earth, over and over; she slowed her heartbeat, replaying the boy's death, dissecting every moment, trying to get it all right, each pine needle and turn of eye, and sap and blood and smoke.

She barely noticed when Paul got up, moving stealthily to keep from waking her, and squeezed out the door. But once he was gone, she became almost giddy with her subterfuge, and she giggled in the half-dark, filled with herself and her secrets.

And then, like that, it was gone—her concentration broken—and all that was left was fatigue and sorrow. I'll tell him, she thought, but it was too late—she was already asleep and never noticed when he came back.

It rained in the morning. The sound was so strange to her that she thought she was back in college in Tuscaloosa; that she was about to be late for a morning class and for once, only once, didn't care; that she would make herself a breakfast of Cream of Wheat and listen to the radio, the way she did on Saturdays. Then she remembered everything, and held the blankets to her chin until her equilibrium returned to her.

Quarter after six. She slid out of bed, trying not to wake Paul, and went to the kitchen. Through the window, she saw that floodlamps had been put up to guide the paramedics, and a bright path of light twisted into the darkness, interrupted by the trunks of trees. As she watched, two men in white carried a stretcher slowly along the path. They emerged from the woods and into the rain, angling toward the open doors of a waiting ambulance. On the stretcher lay a form under a white sheet, and the sheet fluttered in the wind. The men came to the ambulance and the stretcher disappeared into shadow.

"Ma'am?"

She yelped and whirled around, catching her cut knee on the handle of a drawer. Fresh blood rose to meet the pain. A man sat at the table, the paramedic from the woods. He stood up.

"I'm sorry. I didn't want to scare you like that."

"What are you doing in here?" she whispered.

"I'm real sorry." He turned to the window, then back to her. "I just needed out of all that for a minute. Didn't think anybody'd be awake in here."

"Jesus," she said, still shaking. Her knee throbbed.

"You cut yourself."

She looked down. Blood drooled down the knee, where the boy's blood had been the day before. Was his blood inside her now?

"I did."

"I ought to patch that for you," he said. "Make myself useful."

She nodded. "Okay."

He grinned. "I'll be right back."

She could feel her pulse in the wound, pushing blood out in thick little gasps. She thought about those suicides who slit their wrists in a tub of hot water. She could see the appeal of that.

He returned with a first aid kit and knelt on the floor at her feet. He pulled out a cloth and wiped away the blood, then dabbed iodine on the cut with a cotton swab. It stung, and she twitched. "Easy," he said, to himself or to her she didn't know. He smeared on something clear and cold and covered the knee with a neat patch of gauze and some tape. As he worked, he steadied her leg with a warm, dry hand on her calf, and she closed her eyes and inhaled the clean smell of antiseptics.

"Good as new," he said, standing.

"Thank you."

"No trouble, no trouble." He looked out the window again and sighed. "Back to the grind," he said. "Worst thing I ever seen." He turned to go.

"Do you need anything? Cup of coffee?"

This stopped him a moment, but finally he said, "No, that's okay. We'll send somebody to town for takeout."

When he was gone, she leaned against the counter, admiring the bandage. It felt good there, like a new pair of socks. In a little while, she went to the bedroom, quietly dressed, and left.

She took the car out to Valley Road, where a police car was parked. Inside, a cop was eating a sandwich. She rolled down her window.

"I live here," she said. "Are you here to keep people out?"

"Yeah."

"Remember me. I'm coming back."

The cop raised his hand to her.

She drove five minutes past some ranches and an ugly new housing development, and under the train tracks and highway. Very few cars were out at this hour, especially today, a Saturday. Downtown she parked near a coffee shop she went to during the week. No other customers were inside. She ordered a coffee and bought a newspaper.

NO SURVIVORS
MARSHALL VALLEY PLANE CRASH KILLS 58
31 Marshall Residents Believed Dead

Her heart sank when she saw it, though there had been little doubt. Nobody had lived. There was an aerial photo: the plane had come down in two pieces, the tail section and the rest of it. An inset picture showed the blackened engine. She skimmed the article and found little she didn't know. The police chief was saying that the list of victims would not be released until their families had been notified. "Nobody wants to find that out from the paper," he told the reporter.

She wondered how the boy's uncle had found out. Probably he was at the airport. She tried to imagine what he would be like, extrapolating from the boy's freckles, his hair. Nothing came to her. She wished she could meet him, could tell him that the boy was thinking about him when he died. Larry, the uncle's name was Larry.

She finished her coffee and walked around in the rain. She had loved doing this as a little girl—not just the feeling of being out in the rain when everyone else was inside, but knowing that there was a warm bath and dry clothes waiting for her, and the familiar comfort of her room.

Her parents were the kind of people to whom a rainstorm posed no more limitations than a sunny day, to whom the day was no more appropriate for doing anything than the middle of the night. They had been hippies when she was born, and to some extent still were; they could rarely see past the next couple of days, let alone years. "If we thought ahead," her mother once told her, "we probably wouldn't have had you." They never planned for her education, and Anita had to work her way through college, taking night classes at school and working days at the bank. It was there that she first got access to her parents' finances: they had no savings, and their checking account (riddled with bounced checks and service charges) rarely had more than a couple of hundred dollars in it. Her dad worked at an ice cream factory and her mother made jewelry.

So it was no thanks to them that she became a neat freak. That came from her second-grade friend Vanessa, the smartest girl in the class, whose mild British accent made her the butt of class jokes among those who envied her grades. Anita liked her, though. She took her licks with dignity and wore her hair in a French braid. She and Anita ate lunch together and made up elaborate stories based on their classmates' worst qualities.

Anita thought that Vanessa must be rich, as she assumed all British people were. But when she was finally invited to the house, she was surprised: it was modest, and her parents self-effacing and frumpy. They weren't rich; only *clean.* Where were the trays full of cigarette butts, the teetering stacks of books on the floor? The kitchen linoleum was unscuffed and unstained, and the trash sealed away in an upright plastic lidded box, instead of a leaky paper grocery sack. During dinner, Vanessa and her parents ate with unhurried dignity and washed their dishes as soon as they were through; afterward Vanessa's mother mended clothes and her father, a newspaper reporter, read a stack of daily papers from all over Alabama.

When Vanessa suggested playing a game, she led Anita upstairs to her bedroom, where she slid a board game out from under the bed and removed the pieces from the box one by one. When they finished playing they replaced everything, put the game away and selected a new thing to do.

Anita was enthralled. Vanessa's house calmed her, and when she went home she could barely breathe amid the dust and clutter. Her behavior at home began to change, and her mother grew puzzled. "You're cleaning your room," she said. "Why are you doing that?" Anita started washing dishes after dinner and cleaning up her parents' messes, and began a secret resentment of them that lasted until she moved out of the house.

She supposed she married Paul partly because he was a mess to clean up. But it was more complicated than that: he was a kind and affectionate man when he thought to be, and he had a delicacy about him—thin fingers and neck, and a sort of windswept gawkiness—that provided her a nearly bottomless attraction. Most significantly—and now she regretted having been so taken in by this—he was utterly loyal. He would never leave her. Such a promise was irresistible to her at twenty-one, her heart as lonely and open as an empty house; now it wasn't enough. She would no longer fool herself that Paul was going to turn into somebody else.

She left the coffee shop by seven-thirty, but stood for several minutes just outside the door, under the wide green awning, and watched clouds move across the mountains. From a distance, the world looked carefully orchestrated: the hills' simple rock carpeted with trees, the weather traveling, changing, as if with a specific destination. She remembered, as a child, noticing this apparent purpose up close too: the pattern of cells seen through a microscope, or the fastidious sameness of a flower's petals.

She walked a few blocks down Weir Avenue to the florist's shop. It was closed, but through the door, hazy with condensation, she saw its proprietor leaning over a desk, sipping a cup of something. She knocked, and the woman looked up, alarmed. Anita waved. The woman held up her wrist and tapped her watch. Anita made a pleading face. Finally the woman came to the door and opened it a crack. Moist, perfumed air breathed out. She was middle-aged, plump, a look of private self-satisfaction fixed on her face. "We're not open yet," she said.

"I know. I was just wondering . . . I don't want to come in, but maybe I could get some flowers." She dug bills out of her pocket and held them up. "Maybe some daffodils?"

The woman frowned, turned her head back to her desk and steaming cup. "Well . . ." She disappeared for a moment into the back of the shop. Anita kept the door open with her foot, breathing in the warm air. She felt water on her back and shivered.

"Two dollars?" the woman said when she returned. In her hand was a wrapped bundle of half-open daffodils, more than Anita had ever bought at once.

"For all those?"

"Okay, three."

Anita handed over the money and took the flowers. As she left, she saw the woman settling back into her chair, and felt a twinge of jealousy tickle the back of her throat.

By the time she returned to her car she was soaked and cold, but focused. The things she needed to do fell into place in her mind like ice cubes in a tray: she needed to drive home; she needed to take a hot shower. Dealing with Paul was far down on the list, pressing but distant. She got into the car, set the flowers on the passenger seat, turned the heat on full blast and watched the windows fog up around her.

Driving through town, she grew impatient at lights; pedestrians blocked her right turns and she pounded the wheel in frustration. An old woman tapped at her window while she waited at Weir and Cedar; Anita knew her. She was crazy. She had a gigantic account at the bank, and a safety deposit box so stuffed it could barely be closed. "Can I trouble you for a ride?" she hollered over the traffic noise. Anita had given her rides before, but when the light changed she raced through the intersection as if chased, leaving her with a vague sensation of wrongdoing.

When she got home, the cop guarding their drive was gone, as were most of the cars in the yard. They had left behind a muddy landscape of deep ruts. Only the ambulance and dumpster were left now, and the drab green Buick of the federal investigators.

Inside, all was quiet. Muddy footprints crisscrossed the kitchen floor. She checked in on Paul. He was still sleeping. What was it that she felt for him? She stood watching, trying to figure it out. Tenderness, she felt tenderness, she decided, and stopped there, for now.

She turned on the faucets for her bath, then stepped into the kitchen, where she stuck the daffodils into a glass of water. She set the glass in the middle of the table. It was by far the brightest thing in the room, but the flowers, still not completely open, struck her as pitiful and vulnerable.

Through the window, she saw a few straggling paramedics, looking limp and haggard as they walked back and forth in the yard. As she watched, a man approached the dumpster carrying a wet plastic bag, darkened by its contents. When he got there, he tossed the bag in.

5

Bernardo made his plane reservation, put the ticket on his credit card. Probably he would never pay for it. His hands were shaking. He copied down his departure time with difficulty, and in the dim light from the street the numbers came out lopsided and barely legible: 6:44 a.m. for his flight from Reggio to Rome, and then a few transfers to Seattle, and another to Montana. He hung up and looked at his watch: ten o'clock. He had all night to wait.

Even here, in his own kitchen, he felt exposed. He went to the painting studio, locked the door behind him, pulled down the window shade and turned on the light. He left the window open a crack, the better to hear anyone who might come looking for him. Paula had already been to the door twice, and the phone had rung several times. He hadn't answered.

There was a time when he could find comfort in this sort of solitude, when he could enter into a state of blissful concentration. Now there was only loneliness and fear. He went to the armchair, sat down, took the ashtray off the arm and set it on the floor. On second thought he dumped it out on the carpet—no point in keeping things tidy now—and lit a fresh cigarette. He crossed his legs and took on the demeanor of a relaxing man. He looked at the paintings.

He was a bad painter, the paintings were testament to that. In his lowest hours he had often tortured himself with his shortcomings: his technical ineptitude only heightened the shallowness of his subject, which was always the same. The sea. He was a seascape painter. This was not an unusual thing to do in Reggio di Calabria, as it was a coastal town, right on the strait, and seascape painters were a dime a dozen. They painted in the morning and sold the paintings to tourists in the afternoon. But Bernardo's paintings had never left the studio.

The one he liked best—the only one he liked at all, in fact—he had never finished. Like the others, it had no title. It leaned crookedly against the far wall, opposite his chair, just where he'd left it years before when he stopped working on it. He supposed he was afraid of finishing, of wrecking what little was good about it. It depicted a trio of turn-of-the-century Calabrian swordfishermen, floating in one of the old-style wooden boats, the kind with the upright cross standing in the center like an altarpiece. A lookout man, the *guardiano,* stood on the crossbeam, one arm wrapped around the pole, one pointing to the water somewhere beyond the painting's right-hand edge. Below him stood the *allanzatore,* his spear balanced on his shoulder, peering where the lookout was pointing. A third man stood with his hand on the pole for support, staring off into the distance, where another boat, a larger one, trawled deeper water.

Bernardo liked the desperation of the scene. The lookout's arm and fingers curled around the cross for dear life, and his legs, bent at the knees, seemed about to give way. The spearman's stance was defiant and dignified, even as his face betrayed his frustration. But the predicament of the third man, the oarsman, was Bernardo's favorite part. The ship he was watching spelled doom for his small boat. It was the future of swordfishing: the long steel hull, the gleaming spears that never missed. In the painting, it was only the oarsman who seemed to know this.

This oarsman was—or was supposed to be—Bernardo's grandfather, dead fifty years now. Ultimately, the oarsman was a failure. He didn't look enough like the old man, Bernardo thought. In moments of expansive optimism, he tried to convince himself that the mental image he had of his grandfather was idealized beyond recognition, that he would never be satisfied with any attempt he made to paint it, because painting it was impossible. But really, he knew better. What he had tried, and failed, to convey was not doom but hope. The oarsman knew what the big ships meant, but he didn't care. It wouldn't stop him. That persistence (perhaps foolishness), to Bernardo, was the essence of his grandfather. It just wasn't evident in the painting.

Nonno had come to Calabria from south of Messina, where he grew up, after he lost his family in the volcanic eruption of 1904. He was still a teenager at the time, but managed to establish himself in Reggio as a sword-fisherman, which he did until an earthquake hit a few years later. The strait was washed with tidal-size waves, and his crew lost their boat. The *albergo* he lived in was miraculously untouched, and he paid for his luck by helping to rebuild the town. The people he met doing so later helped him to open his market, the one Bernardo would someday take over.

Nonno never let Bernardo or his father forget this story; its theme of steadfastness in the face of disaster was intended as a guiding principle for generations of the family to live by. But so persistent was the old man that the story seemed, above all, like a curse. Bernardo felt like he'd spent his entire life anticipating a catastrophe.

Of course there were other problems with the painting. The spearman's legs didn't seem to be part of his body, for one. They looked like a marble pedestal on which his arms and head had been precariously set. And the boat itself, which should have been listing dangerously to starboard, appeared only to be a little larger on one side. But the main thing was the undeniable and corrupting absence of hope, which Bernardo could not dispel, neither in this painting nor anywhere else.

Bernardo pointed his cigarette at the painting. Sorry, Nonno, he thought, I'm going to let you down again.

Nonno's market was called Alimentari Patti. Bernardo's father, a quiet, beaten man Bernardo never really felt he knew, worked there. Later, Bernardo did too, and for a few years after the war, all three generations ran the market side by side. Those were lean times—the old man developed a desperate paranoia about Communists, and he chased dozens of regular customers away with his caustic and unpredictable rants. Bernardo was often sent by his father to seek these people out and pacify them so they would come back. Nonno died in 1948, and for a while the shop prospered. And then

Bernardo's father died of a heart attack, sitting in his chair during the night, and Bernardo was left to run the business and care for his mother, Mona, who had taken ill and couldn't, or wouldn't, get out of bed. He was twenty years old.

For a while he wanted only to leave, perhaps go to Rome, where he could go to school and get a job. But that would mean leaving his mother or bringing her with him, and she was unlikely to agree either way. And then he started making money. The tourist trade was picking up in Reggio, and the market had a good location, just off the Corso Garibaldi. Foreign faces began to appear, and he added sandwiches, light meals, sidewalk tables. Before he knew it, running the market was his life, and in comparison to staying at home with his mother, a fairly appealing way of passing the time.

He fell in love one summer. There was an American movie at the cinema, *Double Indemnity.* Maria was sitting alone two rows in front of him. He watched her watch the movie. Afterward, they talked about it, about themselves and each other, until late into the night. They saw one another every day for months, and finally married in the same church his parents had. Mona left the house and her bed in order to go to the wedding, the last time she ever would.

Bernardo was quickly in over his head. Maria proved demanding and bored at home, conscious of prevailing fashions and desperate to stay in style, to offset, she said, the indignity of working in the market. When money ran low she blamed him, complained he smelled of onions and meat and foreigners, and that his business wasn't classy enough to draw the kind of customers that would make them rich.

So he borrowed money to renovate: he bought new tables, an awning; he rebuilt the facade and had a new sign made. His idea was to hire new employees to handle an expanded stock, a waiter and a butcher. He would manage books in the mornings and run the restaurant end of things in the afternoon. He would design a new menu. The plan worked: the money came from family friends who remembered Nonno and wished his grandson well, and though Bernardo hated to involve these outsiders in his business, he had paid them off within a year and established the market as a place worth going to. Maria had gotten pregnant, and things were looking up.

They named the baby Antonio, after the grandfather it would never meet. He was a quiet, brooding child, much like the elder Antonio. Many years later, when Maria was dead and Antonio, not yet twenty, had fled to Montana with an American girl named Lila, Bernardo would remember that time as the best he had had, better even than the winter afternoons he'd spent sitting in folding chairs in the back of the market with his father and Nonno, listening to stories about the disasters and the war. He and Maria worked side by side preparing a room for the baby, and even their hours in the market together were happy. Their heads were clear and they were full of energy. Those were good days.

When he woke up he could see the first flickers of daylight glowing around the shade. He jumped up. What time was it? Five o'clock, according to the clock in the kitchen. The phone hadn't rung once during the night. He checked his wallet, still half-asleep. There was enough money for a cab, and he called for one.

Waiting, he realized this was it, he would never see the house again or the things in it. He walked through once more: past the bedroom where he first made love, quietly, to his wife; to the room, an unused guest room, where his mother had taken her time dying. He stood a moment in the hall, looking at photos of Antonio, as a baby peeking out from between the bars of his crib; in his filthy soccer uniform, holding a ball. His high school portrait. There was one of him sitting on a fountain, the last Bernardo had taken before he left for the States. That day they had walked around like tourists, eating gelato, taking in the sights. It wasn't much fun. Bernardo kept trying to talk him out of leaving, out of jumping into marriage, and Antonio told him to stop talking about it, but Bernardo couldn't help himself. So his son said nothing to him for most of the day, and that's how they parted, without a proper goodbye, without saying what they felt about one another.

And maybe this was a good thing. Bernardo wasn't sure he wanted to know what his son thought about him. Probably that he was weak, that whatever he touched was ruined. Now they exchanged infrequent letters, and it was clear to Bernardo his son was happy, finally, in America. He wondered how happy he would be to see his father in person.

He switched off the light in the studio and looked out the window. His cab was there, waiting. He walked out, leaving the door unlocked behind him, and an envelope on the counter with Paula's name on it. She had wanted to move into his house, and now, at last, she could. Inside there was the house key, and a note that read: *It's yours if you want it. I'm sorry. Bernardo.*

On the way to the airport, the cab passed the fountain where he'd taken Antonio's picture, past the rows of shops and churches and restaurants he'd known his entire life, that he'd been inside a hundred times each. It seemed inconceivable that he was leaving them, that he could have an existence separate from them. He felt his heart pulling from his chest, stuck as it was to this place.

No: this was foolish. He had given up such thoughts with his mistakes.

They passed, too slowly, the smoldering row of buildings where the market used to stand. He looked in spite of himself, keeping his face pulled back into the darkness of the cab. The wooden sign hung black and warped from the bent wrought-iron holder he'd installed years before. The two wide front windows and the glass pane on the door were shattered, and from them, detectable even through the closed cab window, issued the smell of meat and cheese cooked and consumed by the fire. He knew that half a mile from here the brand-new restaurant he had borrowed money to build stood unfinished and empty. It would stay like that until someone had the wherewithal to complete the job or tear it down. The land it stood on wasn't his, and with his major asset gone, the wood, the brick, the nails, everything, belonged to his creditors.

He had been uninsured for years. This kind of recklessness would have been unthinkable to Nonno, with his carefully cultivated circles of personal and business connections, his maniacal aversion to risk. But for Bernardo, every element of his life entrusted to someone else was a piece of himself lost forever to the world. He thought the new restaurant would let him take those pieces back—by creating his own success, being his own man—but it did just the opposite. Contracts, loans, permits, each spread him a little thinner, until he was wishing he could just have the market back and forget the new place completely. Then the market burned down.

He wasn't there when it started. A couple of part-time cooks, just kids, were grilling themselves sandwiches after hours and got into a fight. They took it outside. By the time it was settled, there was no inside left to go back to. Most of the market was gone by the time Bernardo arrived. He stood on the opposite sidewalk, listening to the fire roar through the building, as the potter's vessels in the shop next door exploded one by one and traffic jammed to a halt at the ends of the block.

There was no one to blame but himself—he knew the business had been getting away from him. He barely knew the kids he'd hired. In the end, after more than forty years as a small businessman, he could no longer deny he wasn't cut out for business. Watching the market burn, he felt a strange calm settle over him. It wasn't just his capital going up in smoke, but the entire lie he'd been living, the life he'd gotten himself into by mistake and had never been able to see his way out of. It was a mess of connections and obligations, finally gone.

Already he knew he wouldn't return. They would come after him sooner or later, but he didn't have any intention of being there for them to find. It was an act of cowardice, pure and simple. But never, he guessed, had cowardice felt so invigorating, so purifying and true.

So why, at the airport, couldn't he stop shaking? He found a bank of pay telephones, then dug in his pocket for his son's phone number. He didn't know if it still worked. Antonio might have moved. He knew only three things about Antonio's life in America: his phone number, his wife's and daughter's names, and that he owned and managed a carpet store. Carpet! Who could have imagined? Bernardo didn't even like carpet in a house. He dug a phone card from his wallet, dialed for an international operator, who put the call through. He tried to breathe himself calm while the telephone clicked and stuttered. It was difficult to keep in mind that nobody would find him, that nobody knew where he was.

The phone started ringing, once, twice, six times. He was about to hang up when a little girl answered, so clear he could swear she was right beside him. "Hello?"

"Hello, your father is home?" The English was clumsy and misshapen on his tongue.

"He's at work."

"Ah . . . your mother?"

"Please can I say who's calling?"

"Say I am . . . I am your father's father."

There was a long pause on the other end. "Really? This is my grandpa?"
"Yes."
"Are you coming to see us?"
"Ah, yes, very soon."
"Are you in *Italy*?"
"Yes, I am in Italy. Are you . . . Is that Angela?"
"Yes."
"Maybe I talk to your mother?"
"Why?"
"Well, ah, I talk to her, and . . ."
"I mean why are you *coming*?"
"To see you."

That seemed to do the trick. He heard the sound of a phone being set down. How old was she now? He didn't think he'd touched a child in thirty years.

"Hello?" came a voice.
"Lila!"
"Bernardo, is that you?"
"This is me."
"My God, Bernardo. We were thinking we'd never hear from you again." She sounded, beyond all reason, *relieved*. And so comfortable with his name, as if they'd only just parted. Her voice was as he remembered it from so long ago, perhaps more weary.

"I am in *aeroporto,* in Reggio," he said. "Tomorrow I come to America."
"Marshall? You're coming here?"
"Today Rome and Seattle, tomorrow Marshall."

She grunted, the sound of the words trying to form themselves. "But how . . . Why are you coming? I mean, we're thrilled, Antonio will be thrilled to have you, but why so sudden?"

"I have a little trouble."
"Trouble?"
"I have no money. I . . . It's no good here."

She sighed, and it was a little while before she spoke. "We could have helped you, you know. If you'd asked."

"No, no, I only want, ah, a vacation. You know?"
"Sure. I understand. You're coming tomorrow?"
"Yes." He gave her the time, the flight number. "That is your time, not Italy?"

"No, that's our time."

And then there was a long, empty space, which he knew she was filling with second thoughts. Why not? Of course they wanted to see him, but on their terms only, in a way that wouldn't disrupt the fine and quiet life they'd made for themselves. It wouldn't take long for them to start asking when he would go back to Italy, when he would straighten everything out and get on with it. He wondered if there were other places he could go. Mexico, maybe. It would always be warm. He'd heard you could live like a king for next to nothing.

"I go soon," he said.

"I guess we'll see you tomorrow then."

"You tell Antonio."

"Of course, Bernardo." She took a deep breath. "And please don't worry. We'll help you with whatever you need, okay?"

"Okay. Tell Angela goodbye from Nonno."

"I will."

"Okay."

He almost changed his mind. He sat in a plastic chair in the terminal, a discarded newspaper crunching underneath him, and almost decided to stay in Italy. It wouldn't be so hard, would it? To leave the terminal, perhaps try to get a refund for his ticket; to climb into a cab and have it bring him back to the house, where it was still too early for anyone to have discovered him gone, where he could settle back into the old problems and their familiar contours. Who could expect, after all, a truly simple life? Paula would forgive him, and he would make back the money he owed, maybe even be able to retire. None of it seemed so bad.

He went back to the phones. It would be easy enough to call her, wouldn't it? She would be sleeping now, or perhaps even awake already, worried about what might have happened to him. He held the receiver at his ear, doing nothing. The terminal was getting crowded now, as the plane was preparing to take off. A slick-haired, middle-aged businessman in a tailored suit moved up behind Bernardo, too close, and looked at his watch. He wanted the phone.

Bernardo dialed. It rang once, twice, five times, before she answered.

"Pronto?"

Paula's voice was full of sleep, and before the word had finished leaving her mouth, he knew he could say nothing, could never admit to this awful mistake. She had probably not given him another thought.

"Pronto!" Awake now. And then a sigh, and: "Bernardo?"

He reached out and cut off the connection, then took a deep breath. He could tell from the sound of his name, she didn't want to hear from him.

"Grandpa," somebody was saying. He turned. It was the businessman. "Are you going to use that? Or are you going to stand there playing with it?"

"I . . . I'm going to use it."

The man had a cigarette lit and was tapping ash onto the floor. "Well?"

Bernardo dialed again, this time automatically. The number of the market. He'd given it to so many people, had called it countless times from home or from out of town, to see how business was going in his absence. Always fine. Of course there was only a taped message now. He listened to it play through several times. *This number has been disconnected.* It was like listening to the eulogy at his own funeral. There was no going home. The only friends he had left were the ones he'd borrowed money from. A cloud of smoke filled the air around his face.

"Hey! Grandpa! Move along!"

Bernardo hung up the phone but left his hand on the receiver. He turned to the man. "Give me a cigarette," he said.

The man frowned. "Why should I give you a cigarette? Get off the phone!"

"If you don't give me a cigarette, I'll stand here until you go away. Give me a cigarette and you can use the phone."

There were two other telephones. A young woman cried bitterly into one, saying, "Yes, but . . ." over and over. A short man had the other. He listened intently, nodding and saying nothing. The businessman glared at both of them but neither noticed. Bernardo said, "You're a businessman, right? That's my deal. One cigarette for one telephone."

The man's eyes brimmed over with rage. "Motherfucker," he said, and handed Bernardo a cigarette. They were imported, Spanish. The smoke smelled harsh and sweet.

"A light, please." Bernardo kept his hand on the phone.

The businessman thrust out a silver lighter and flicked it to life before Bernardo's face. Bernardo put the cigarette into his mouth and drew the flame to it. He inhaled and exhaled before releasing the receiver. "Here," he said to the businessman, who was already crowding toward the telephone, "you can have this too." And he handed him the spent phone card and took a seat near the terminal gate.

For the first time since the fire, he felt ready to leave.

He had flown to the south of France or to Palermo, but it had been some time now and he had forgotten what it was like. Flying was not like the train, and especially not like a car. The land did not scroll by just outside the window; familiar landmarks did not rise up on the horizon ahead and vanish behind. Flying was a kind of stasis, a nothingness a person simply existed in. There was no control, above all no sense of travel.

And for this Bernardo was grateful. He could pretend, in the air, that he was not himself, wasn't anybody at all. Beside him slept a thick-faced man in a suit, his snoring low and steady like an enormous cat's, his head lolling toward Bernardo's shoulder, whereupon Bernardo would push it away. How could a man sleep on a forty-five-minute flight? Finally the head came to rest on Bernardo and he left it there.

He changed his last lire to dollars in Rome, got onto a larger plane, quieter but no more numbing than the last. He was waiting for the blow that would knock the feeling back into him, but it didn't come: he looked out every few minutes onto the gray expanse of ocean and saw the bleak, featureless landscape of his heart. The farther he flew from Calabria, the less a person he became, or so he thought. It was as if, while trying to touch up a painting, he had inadvertently washed out the entire thing, so thoroughly that he had forgotten what he'd been trying to paint in the first place.

In Seattle he bought lunch—tacos—panicking all the while over the unfamiliar money. The clerk took about half of it. Before he could protest, Bernardo found the tacos in his hands, in a paper bag, and other people moving to take his place in the line. Everyone seemed wild and ugly here. He found his terminal, sat down and ate. The tacos were salty beyond belief, and he ate them with blinding speed.

He bought a copy of *Time,* and watched other travelers while pretending to read it: the text was full of unfamiliar people and weird idioms, and he couldn't muster the presence of mind to decode it. The people around him looked bored. A mother held a sleeping baby, hitching it up reflexively on her chest at intervals; an old man talked to a young woman by the windows. A middle-aged couple dressed in garish jogging outfits held clothes bags and did not speak to one another. A boy sat alone, wearing stereo headphones.

When the time came, they filed into the plane, a small jet with seats grouped in twos. His was in the last row, against a carpeted wall, and wouldn't recline. He buckled his seat belt and read the ads in *Time*.

A young woman sat down next to him. He recognized her from the waiting area; she had been talking to the old man. She smiled at him and said "Hi."

"*Giorno,*" he said, forgetting. "Hello."

"Great seats," she joked. She struggled with the recline control and quickly gave up. Bernardo watched the operation with sympathy.

"Well," he said, "it is only small fly."

She raised her eyebrows. They had a shocking expressive sweep to them. "That's true. One point for us."

He nodded. "Ah-hah."

Her eyes were fixed on his face, and he turned away for a second, coughing. "Are you from . . . overseas?" she said.

"Italy."

"Wow. Always wanted to go. Visiting family?"

"My son."

"Well, hey. That's terrific." She turned to look out the window on the opposite side of the plane, where the ground was moving slowly past. In the front of the cabin, flight attendants demonstrated the safety equipment. The young woman cracked her knuckles, then extended a thin, smooth hand to him. "Megan," she said.

He shook it. "Bernardo."

"So where'd you learn English?"

He shrugged. "Everybody know a little."

"Well," she said, pointing to his magazine, "I'll let you read. I just thought we ought to do introductions." He nodded, unsure of how to tell her that he preferred this to the magazine, but before he could work out the words she had settled back into her seat and closed her eyes.

The flight was bumpy, but the view spectacular: there were no clouds, and below them the ground spread out, vast and blank. The occasional town came into view, but mostly it was mountains and plains, a river or two. He didn't know long he'd been looking when he noticed her face over his shoulder. He started.

"Sorry, don't mean to bug you." Both of them sat back. "Is this your first trip to Marshall?"

"Yes."

"Oh, you'll love it."

"Yes?"

"I go to college there," she said, leaning over him again, "and I absolutely love it. It's a funky town. It's going to be hard to leave."

"So you stay?" he said.

She shook her head. "Gotta move on. Things to do, et cetera. Got a boyfriend there."

"He will go too?" Bernardo asked, and it filled him with envy, the thought of a traveling companion. But of course he had one, if he'd wanted her.

"Yeah," she said. She pointed down at the earth. "Now keep your eyes on this. We're going to rise up over those mountains and land in that valley. That's the Marshall Valley."

He watched as the mountains grew closer and rose to meet them. Then the ground dropped away to reveal a wide plain dotted with farms and houses, then factories and a city, gray and bright in the sun. There was an electronic ping, and the seat belt signs went on. Bernardo hadn't taken his off since they left the ground.

"Doesn't it look nice?"

"The mountains have no houses."

"They're not allowed."

He looked at her. "No?"

"Yep. People like the hillsides bare."

He watched in silence as the plane banked and the entire sweep of the valley was exposed. She said, "How long has it been since you've seen him?"

"Seen him?"

"Your son?" she said.

"Ah." He shrugged. "Maybe twenty year."

He pushed the little tray into the back of the seat in front of him and slid the latch home. The plane had evened out, and drifted over trees interrupted here and there by open ground, and he could see it all clearly now: each individual tree, every animal. He could tell the horses from the cows.

Then there was a deafening roar somewhere in front of him that decayed into a loud and steady ringing, and everything outside jumped. People's voices rose. He felt hands on his arm. The window was like an old movie—dark, light, dark, light—and in the cabin objects moved across the floor like loose animals. Masks, oxygen masks, dangled comically before them like gag spiders. He reached out with his free arm for one, but couldn't catch it, and a jolt sent his hand back to the armrests. He felt the American girl's head on his shoulder, but if she spoke he couldn't hear her. Everything around was noise now, his head filled with it, as if it were coming from inside him. His stomach floated free in his gut like a buoy. And then a terrible knocking, a gush of summer air, and he shook in his seat until he thought he might come apart.

At some point he didn't feel the American girl at his side anymore. And then nothing seemed near him at all, nothing he could see or touch or otherwise sense. He was in a completely new place where no one had ever been before, or could go to, and for the moment this filled him with sweet relief.

Trees in front of him. A steady tone in his left ear, silence in the right. He shook his head and nearly fainted away with the pain of doing it. He looked gingerly down at himself and saw that he was still belted into his seat, still holding tight to the armrests. Just beyond his feet, a tongue of torn carpet, hanging out over a drop the height of a man, and dark soil below. He stuck his toe out over the edge. There was no one in the seat next to him. Where was the girl? Where was everything, the rest of the airplane, everything?

There it was, far off to the left, one wing laid flat along the ground and the rest of it scattered about. Trees felled, broken; an intact chunk of the cabin black and burning, a cigar butt on the forest floor.

It was very quiet. He waited.

I must be dead.

He released the seat belt and stood up. Got dizzy, sat on the sheared-off edge and vomited over the side. Every muscle felt torn from its moorings. He turned his hands over against the weird backdrop of the forest: not a scratch on him.

I must be dead.

The air smelled rank all around him. He turned and looked back at what he'd left: the tail of the plane, completely, impossibly whole, nestled up between two giant conifers. If he looked up he could see the path the rest of the plane had taken through the trees: it fell, taking their tops off clean, until finally they beat it down.

Nearer the wreckage now, he stopped and found himself surrounded by *things:* a six-pack of canned soda, spread-eagled on the ground ahead; a shining something that resolved itself into a pair of glasses; a length of shiny fabric, half blackened, with smoke rising off it. These objects were like clues in a mystery, the solution to which was both obvious and obscure. He could feel the answer rising up, dark and horrible, but his mind was unwilling to let him see it, the way a movie murderer pulls the cowl over his head before he turns to face the camera. And like that, the desire to see the killer's face left him, and then the desire to take another step. He could feel the numbness tamping itself into his fingers and toes, asserting itself along the length of his bones, and it made him so weary he sat down hard on the forest floor and lay back in the dirt. He was aware only of something tremendous having happened, something baffling and awful, and an urgency that seemed distant, far removed from his own predicament, whatever that might be.

"I must be dead," he said aloud now, and it shocked him to hear the hope in his voice.

part *two*

6

Monday morning, Paul woke sweating in the dark, unable to pry apart his jaws. He lay still a long time, willing the muscles in his face to relax, remembering the dream. Its predominant element was his teeth: he was clenching them together and couldn't stop, and the pressure on his molars grew until, with a sickening crunch, they shattered. Oddly there was no pain, only the salty, warm rush of blood and the weird scrape of tooth fragments against one another. He began to panic. He jumped into the car and soon found himself lost among labyrinthine streets in search of a dentist's office he couldn't find.

Awake in bed, he got his mouth open and probed it with a finger. The teeth were all intact. He looked at the clock. It was ten after six. Anita slept beside him. For a second he thought about waking her, but decided against it. All weekend, as the investigators and reporters came and went, he and Anita had gently pulled away from each other and settled into a mutual politeness in which unprovoked speech seemed rude and physical contact brazen. He worked his jaw, massaging the muscles, then slunk out from under the covers.

In the shower, the dream anxiety retreated, and at the breakfast table the space it left began to fill with the real anxiety of his first day on the job. Already, his having been hired seemed like an embarrassing and potentially disastrous mistake, and he wondered if somehow he had been taken for someone else.

He had responded to the ad on a whim, in person, a week ago. The office lay just off the strip beyond downtown, sandwiched between a popcorn and candy shop and a discount shoe store in a shrub-and-white-gravel "professional village." Paul walked in through the swinging glass door and was struck immediately by the overpowering smell of popcorn butter.

"I'm looking for Emil Ponty," he told the man at the front desk.

"That's me," the man said, looking up from a typewriter. He was short and thick with a wide, froggish face and ugly plastic-rimmed eyeglasses. Paul took a quick look around the office and saw, half-hidden by a carpeted partition, a teenage girl with purple hair talking on the telephone.

"I'm Paul Beveridge," he said. "I saw your ad." He held up a scrap of newsprint in the air between them.

Ponty rolled his chair over to a filing cabinet and pulled out several sheets of paper. "Okay," he said. "Have a seat."

"No way!" the girl in the back suddenly screamed. "No *way*!"

"My daughter," Ponty said. "On lunch from the high school. We're going out for a bite."

"I can come back . . ."

"Nah, it's no problem. If she's done on the phone before I'm done with you, you can come along. Now you want the assistant job, right?"

"Yes." He rummaged in his bag until he found his résumé.

Ponty looked it over for approximately five seconds. "Real nice-looking paper, Paul Beveridge," he said. "You went to Alabama, did you?"

"Yes, sir."

"Roll Tide!"

"Oh, yeah."

He tossed the résumé onto the desk and leaned back in his chair. "So the job's like this, Paul. You don't work full-time, exactly, but it's twelve bucks an hour, which in this town, I'm sure you'll agree, is a king's ransom. Job isn't for everybody. A lot of sitting and waiting for people, a lot of walking around town smoking cigarettes, a lot of time in the car. You got a car?"

"Sure."

"Okay, good. No drugs or drinking on the job, I hate that shit. You're not

Bogart, okay? Do you mind looking in people's windows? Taking snoop pictures?"

"No, sir."

In the back, the daughter screamed again. Paul jumped. "Oh God, Kate! He's such a little weasel!"

Ponty swiveled in the chair. "Hey, pipe down! I got a meeting here!"

"Sorry."

"Okay," he said, spinning back around. "This oughta be your only job. Sometimes you might have a week straight with nothing to do, sometimes you'll do forty-eight hours in a row, no breaks. You have to be around when I need you, is that all right?"

"That's fine."

Ponty looked at him for some time, until Paul began to think something was wanted of him. He began to fidget.

"Well?" Ponty said. "You want the job?"

"Do I want it?"

"Do you want it."

"Well, yes."

"Okay then." He handed Paul the papers he'd taken from the file cabinet. "Fill these out and bring 'em back to me."

Paul stared at the papers. "You mean you're hiring me?"

"Yeah, you're hired."

He picked up the papers and looked at them: I-9, W-4, employee information sheet. Ponty sat in his chair, hands behind his head.

"Can I ask why?" Paul said.

Ponty shrugged. "You look like you can blend in. You didn't come swaggering in here wearing a trench coat. That's what the last guy did. A trench coat? In August? This is not the kind of guy I want sitting in a tree for fourteen hours, you know what I'm saying?"

"Sure," Paul said. Fourteen hours in a tree?

The girl hung up the telephone, jumped out of her chair and threw her arms around Ponty's neck. Ponty patted her arm. "I'm hungry," she said.

"Yeah, okay." He turned to Paul. "Hungry?"

They walked to a hamburger place on the strip and sat in a booth, Ponty and his daughter on one side, Paul on the other. The daughter's name was Alyssa, and she was preternaturally beautiful, a fact she seemed dimly aware of and slightly embarrassed about. She kept her head down much of the time, looking up only occasionally to see, Paul thought, if he was watching her. Which, in fact, he mostly was. After they ordered, it occurred to Paul that he didn't have any money, and he told Ponty.

Ponty waved his hand in the air. "Ah, it's on me. Celebrating my new assistant."

"Did you have one before?" Paul asked him.

He nodded. "Yeah, for a while. But he was a pervert."

"A pervert?"

"Got off on looking in windows. He started turning in these reports . . . He'd tell me everything I wanted to know, but he also told me about what was going on behind every other window on the block. Then he finally quit. He took off with this woman he was supposed to be spying on. He actually called me from Portland to tell me this. He watched her and watched her and finally just went up and knocked on the door, and the next day, adios."

"I see."

"Maybe I shouldn't get the burger after all," Alyssa said to her menu. "I don't want to get fat."

"Fat!" Ponty yelled. "You're fourteen! You're a bean pole!"

"Fat runs in the family," she said.

"Your mother's a rail. I dunno who you could be talking about."

Alyssa giggled.

When their burgers came, Alyssa fell upon hers. She was the first to finish. Afterward she picked at the french fries, taking several bites to eat each one. When they were all done, Ponty stood up to pay the bill. His belly curled over the edge of the table and knocked over the pepper shaker, though he didn't seem to notice.

Outside, Ponty hugged Alyssa. "Gonna come by after school?"

"Going to Mom's."

"How're you getting there?"

"I got a *ride,*" she said. Paul noticed that the purple hair was all growing out of one side of her head. The other side was shaved clean, and the purple hair swept over it, like the bald man's trick. Now that they were outside, she kept touching it.

"Who from?" Ponty demanded.

"Dalene."

"Christ," he said. "That girl and her truck. Okay. You tell your mom to get you to school tomorrow, then."

"She *knows*." She backed away in a little skip and waved to Paul. "Bye, Paul."

"See you," Paul said. He watched her as she walked off toward the high school.

"She's a terror," Ponty said.

"Yeah," Paul said back, automatically.

Ponty looked at him. "Don't get any ideas."

He was still sitting at the kitchen table at seven-thirty, the milk drying up in the bowl in front of him, looking out the window at the trees. Anita came out of the bedroom and shuffled past him. She began to make coffee. When she finally sat down across from him, he felt suddenly like they had been on a long trip, had driven without rest from city to city, and had only arrived here the night before. He felt like last night was only the first step in catching up on lost sleep, and that they were here together, subtly changed, on a brief break from that sleep.

"Nice sweater," she said.

Paul looked down. The house had been chilly when he got out of the shower, and he had found the birthday sweater in the dark and put it on. "Oh, yeah," he said, and he reached for the buttons.

"No, leave it," she said. "It looks good on you."

"You think?"

"Yeah."

"Look," he said. "Can we just forget all that? The stuff on Friday? I was just under some stress, you know. This job starting . . ."

"Uh-huh."

"And now, with the plane, it all seems so . . ."

"I know."

They sat in silence for a few seconds. Anita sipped her coffee. "I just don't want to think about it right now, is that okay? I just want to go to work like usual, and not think about it." She waited. He didn't know what to say, so he just nodded. She pointed to the empty bowl. "What did you have there?"

"Raisin Bran."

"Hmm." She got up and poured herself a bowl, carried it gingerly to the table. Paul watched. She would drink about a dozen spoonfuls of milk before she ate any cereal. And when she finished the cereal, she would spoon up the extra milk. His heart swelled until he thought it would burst. How could I have been so rotten to her? he thought. How could I have let her down?

When she was ready, they drove through town in silence. He dropped her off at the bank, and from force of habit they kissed. It surprised them both.

He drove across town and parked in front of the popcorn shop. Inside, someone was pouring popcorn from a metal tray into a large plastic bin, one of half a dozen lined up under the counter. He looked up and smiled at Paul, and Paul waved.

There didn't appear to be anyone inside Ponty's office. He walked in and stood at the front of the room, tapping his fingers on the desk.

"Mr. Ponty?"

From the back, he heard water running, then a door opened and Ponty stepped out, wedging the tail of his shirt into his pants.

"Hi," Paul said. Ponty nearly hit the ceiling.

"Jesus Christ."

"Sorry."

Ponty looked at his watch. "What are you, early?"

"It's my first day."

"Well, okay, eager beaver." He looked Paul up and down. "What's this getup?"

Paul spread his arms. "What?" He was wearing a T-shirt tucked into a pair of chinos, and his hair was tied back in a ponytail.

"Here." He reached for Paul's shirt and pulled it out of his pants. "Slouch," he said. Paul slouched. "Now take the hair out of the ponytail. Mess it up a little. You don't want to look like a fourth-grade teacher." Ponty sat down, and so did Paul.

"What have you got for me?"

"Okay. You gotta go watch this guy Wozack. He's got a little shop out on the Cherry Street exit, next to the laundromat. It's a joke shop. You know where I'm talking about?"

"Sure. Montana Gag."

"Right. Go watch him all day. The place opens at ten, closes at five. Keep an eye on him, then follow him when he leaves. Write down where he goes. Do it for three days. Got that?"

"Got it."

He opened a desk drawer. "Here. I'm gonna give you a camera. If he looks like he's doing anything other than running a joke shop, shoot him. And please be careful."

"The guy's dangerous?" Paul said.

"No, the camera. I've only got the one."

"Right."

"The whole point is to disappear. There's a Kwik Stop right across the street there. You might want to sit and have a couple cups of coffee, or read the paper or something, watch him through the window. Or maybe find some weeds to sit in." Ponty handed him a notebook and two ballpoint pens, and a typed sheet that listed Wozack's particulars: his truck, his address, a physical description. "I'll be here all day pushing pencils. Gimme a ring if things go haywire, okay?"

"Got it."

Paul knew the spot well. He had occasionally done laundry at the laundromat, when the place he usually went to was closed, and he had eaten at an ice cream parlor in the same building. It was all part of a little cinder-block mini-mall. He parked a couple of blocks away, behind some houses, pleased with himself for thinking to do so.

From the café in the Kwik Stop, he could see clearly through the window of Montana Gag. It was only nine-thirty, and everything inside was still dark, so he helped himself to a cup of coffee, a doughnut, and a newspaper and sat at a table near the window. He opened the notebook, uncapped the pen, and wrote: *9:32. Shop empty.* Then he turned to the paper.

The crash was still front-page news. "31 Marshall Residents Dead in Air Crash," read a headline. "Five Still Unidentified, Three Unaccounted For." The byline was preceded by a little graphic of a plane, with the words "Flight 114" printed above it. He scanned the list of Marshall residents, not expecting to find any familiar names, but one was Pamela Kinyon, the woman whose purse he found. He remembered the film he'd taken and got a chill. They'd found someone, a body, and those pictures were hers. Next to the article was a photograph of their yard; in it two paramedics loaded a sheet-covered body into the ambulance. Paul wondered idly if it was her, and automatically leaned close, as though this would help him.

When he next looked up, a pickup was pulling into the lot in front of

Montana Gag. Paul fumbled for the camera, almost knocking it off the table, before he realized there was no need yet. He watched Greg Wozack—average height, thin hair, worn jeans and cowboy boots—step out, fuss with his keys, and open the door to the shop. He locked it behind him and disappeared into the darkness.

Ten minutes later, the lights came on. Wozack walked out from behind a shelf, did something at the counter, and opened and closed the register drawer. He went to the door and flipped the Closed sign to Open. Paul leaned over the notebook and wrote it down, referring to Wozack as "subject": *10:02. Subject opened magazine, read.*

For an hour, nobody came to the store. Wozack flipped the pages of the magazine. At eleven, he picked up the telephone and spoke a few words into it. Finally, at 11:15, an old gray Cadillac pulled up, and a short, chubby man wearing a baseball cap got out. Wozack met him at the door, and after a minute the man walked around to the back of the building.

Paul stood up, excited. He hurried to the other end of the store, where shelves of boxed doughnuts partially blocked a window. Peeking between them, he could see a gravel lot, and the back door of the shop. The short man stood near it, his hands in his pockets.

Suddenly Paul remembered the camera. He ran back to his table and grabbed it. When he got back to the window, the short man was walking to his car, shoving a folded paper bag into the pocket of his shorts. "Shit," Paul said, "shit." He groped at the lens cap, but the Caddy was already gone. He smiled at the counter clerk as he returned to his table, but she was engrossed in a tiny black-and-white television and didn't look up. He sat down, defeated and irritated with himself, and smoothed out the paper.

Not much else happened. A few people went in and bought things—fake handcuffs, a rubber chicken—which they carried out in plastic bags. Paul dutifully wrote it all down. He bought lunch from a nearby Chinese place and read most of a magazine he didn't bother to buy. At five, Wozack turned over the sign on the door, disappeared into the back for a few minutes, then came out.

Paul grabbed his things, then sprinted out the door and down an alley to his car. As he pulled out, he saw Wozack's truck pass on Cherry Street. He signaled and maneuvered himself into traffic behind it.

Wozack was a terrible driver. He switched lanes indiscriminately, without signaling, and entered intersections at the worst possible moment, cutting other drivers off. Paul followed him with difficulty through the West Side, a hastily built community of one-story houses, and into Bear Lodge, a shabby residential area behind a bend in the river. Paul lost the truck on the grid of streets, fearful of giving himself away, but caught up with it again on Brainerd Avenue, which to his alarm ended a few blocks ahead. He pulled to the curb and slumped in his seat.

Wozack parked in a driveway on the street's last block, got out of his truck and entered the house. Paul started his car and drove one block south to Beadle, where he peered between houses at the one Wozack had gone into. The number above the door was 2011. He was about to write this down when he thought to check the fact sheet Ponty had given him, and he found that 2011 Brainerd was on it. Wozack had simply gone home.

That night, after they'd eaten dinner, he sat with Anita on the couch, reading. She had that day's paper and was spending a long time looking at the plane crash article. Above them, the plastic bags he'd taped to the hole flapped in a breeze from outside. She sighed finally and put the paper down, but didn't say anything.

"What?" Paul said. He had been trying to read a book, but was thinking mostly about his day, what Ponty would say about his missing the photo.

Anita shook her head. "Nothing, I guess."

"You guess?"

"You've been quiet."

"Because you've been." Was this strictly true? He wasn't sure anymore. Their silence had become, it seemed, a matter of mutual consent, and he'd forgotten who had begun it.

She nodded slowly. "I feel so distant," she said, looking at something across the room. "I feel like you're distant."

"I'm right here."

"You know what I mean."

They sat, not speaking or moving, for some time, and then she reached out and put her hand on his hand. She did this quickly, as if she were in danger of falling off the couch, and he had to restrain himself from recoiling: the gesture reminded him of the way his mother clutched his arm a few days before she finally died, desperate enough to hold on to this child she didn't even like, to keep herself from sliding into oblivion. Anita kept the hand there, and he felt the sweat squeezing from her palm and seeping into the dry cracks of his knuckles. She kept her head turned half away, toward the ruined corner of the room, and he knew this hand on his really had nothing to do with him, that she was losing her grip on something and he was nearest, the most convenient handhold. He reached out and pulled her to him, and she leaned back reluctantly into his arms.

"You're so tense," he said.

"Work," she told him.

"Do you want me to rub your back?"

"Would you?"

He did for a time, though her shoulders refused to yield and she made no sound. Finally she disengaged herself, turned, and, her face creased in concentration, kissed him. He kissed back.

"What is this?"

"I don't know, Paul."

They kissed some more, and he moved his hands across her back, over the familiar landscape of bones and muscles. She leaned her head into his neck. "Make love to me?"

"You want that?" he said.

"We need it."

"But you want it?"

"Yes," she said. "I want it."

And they did, but they moved with the tentativeness not of unfamiliarity but fear. When it was over, they held one another, each unwilling to be the one to let go, and neither moved until they grew cold.

Paul couldn't sleep and got up in the night for a beer. While he sat at the kitchen table drinking it, a car started up outside, and he went to the window.

It was a police car. The interior was illuminated, and the cop was talking on her radio. When she hung it up, the headlights came on and cleaved the clearing, and in the bright light Paul saw movement just beyond the first trees. It was a man, backing away. The man was a bit chubby, dressed in a white shirt, though his face was obscured by branches, and as Paul watched he turned around and ran off.

The cop stepped out of her car and into the glare of the headlights, and peered into the woods. But the man was gone. When she got back into the cruiser she sat there a moment, as if deciding whether or not to act on what she'd seen, then leaned over the wheel. The car pulled away, its red taillights disappearing around a bend in the drive.

He waited across the street from Montana Gag for most of Tuesday morning, but Wozack never showed up. Instead, there was a skinny kid wearing a T-shirt. His hair was cut short and uncombed, and he moved slowly. Sometimes he just collapsed on the counter and leaned there with his head down. At other times he disappeared into the back for as long as fifteen minutes. Paul scurried to the doughnut shelves a few times, but nothing was going on at the back door. Nobody showed up. At around twelve-thirty, the kid picked up the phone and dialed, but no one seemed to answer, and he didn't speak.

Finally, somebody did come: a young girl wearing a black beret and black stockings under her cutoffs. She had come in a pickup truck, a blue Ford, and there was another person, a boy it looked like, waiting for her behind the wheel. She walked in and spoke to the kid for a few seconds. He shook his head. She spoke again, and again he shook his head no. The girl shrugged and came out. For the first time, Paul saw her face, and he immediately recognized her: it was Ponty's daughter, Alyssa.

Alyssa jumped back into the cab of the truck, and talked for a moment with her friend. Then the truck pulled out of the lot and drove away.

The kid in the shop had vanished again. Paul sat with his pen poised above his notebook. Should he write it down or not? Was he obliged to tell Ponty his daughter had shown up? In the end he just gathered his things, and walked out.

At first he'd only thought to get a breath of air and clear his head. But by the time he reached the street, he knew he had every intention of going into Montana Gag and talking to the kid there. Why not? He only had one more day to go on this job, and if he kept his cool the kid wouldn't know he was spying. He crossed Cherry Street in what he hoped was a casual jog, walked across the mini-mall parking lot, and pushed open the door of Montana Gag.

The air in the shop was musty and dry, and the kid had disappeared. From somewhere came a low hum. Two bare bulbs lit the front of the store, but the shelves, cluttered with merchandise, stretched back into relative darkness. Paul heard some shuffling in the back.

"Hello?" he said.

"Oh," a voice came, barely audible. "Be right out."

Paul began to walk around, making a show of looking at the shelves. He heard footsteps, and behind him the kid's voice: "Can I help you with anything?" He sounded like he would rather have been anywhere than here.

Paul came to the front. "Oh, I was just wondering if Greg's around." He peered over the kid's shoulder, trying to get a look in the back, but there was nothing really to see there: a tiny refrigerator, seemingly the source of the hum he'd heard, some cardboard boxes, a calendar on the wall, covered with marks.

"Nope. Everybody wants him today."

"Yeah?" Paul said. "What for?"

"I dunno." The kid was staring out the window at the highway above. Paul followed his gaze and saw only the tops of trucks passing above the guardrail. "None of my business."

"Sure, sure," Paul said. "You know when he'll be back?"

"No. Not today."

"Oh, all right." The kid's eyes were ringed with shadows and his mouth was sour and slack. It was clear he wasn't simply bored, but stoned maybe, or sad.

"I guess I'll come tomorrow, then."

"Yeah."

He gave the kid a quick smile, then left. Walking back, he thought about whether the trip was a good idea and decided that though he hadn't learned anything, it had been worth the risk. When he got back to the Kwik Stop, he documented the trip in the notebook, filling the space he would have used to tell Ponty about his daughter.

He looked up to find the kid's face pressed up against the window of Montana Gag, staring directly at him across Cherry Street. Paul backed away from the window, but it was obviously too late. He'd been seen. The kid watched for another few seconds, then walked out the door of the shop and crossed the parking lot toward the Kwik Stop.

Paul panicked, and hid the notebook and pen and camera on the seat beside him just as the kid was pushing open the door. He and the cashier nodded at each other as if they were acquainted, and he came and stood over Paul.

"Hey," Paul said.

"Are you spying on me or something?"

"Spying?"

"I saw you this morning, reading the paper, and saw you looking up at the store and everything, but I thought you were just killing time. But then when you came in . . ."

"Oh, God."

"So you are spying," the kid said. He sat down across the table.

"Not on you."

"Not on me?"

"Wozack."

"My boss." He nodded, as if this made sense to him. "What, are you a friend of his? Or the police? Is he up to something?"

"I'm just a detective. An assistant detective, actually. I don't know why I'm spying, I just am." Paul shook his head. "It's my first week on the job. I can't believe this."

"I won't tell him or anything," the kid said. "I can't say I actually like him." He tapped his fingers on the table. "So what have you got on him?"

Paul shrugged. "I think he's selling pot or something." He thought of Alyssa Ponty and her friend.

He nodded. "Probably."

They both looked out the window at the empty shop. The kid's face was reflected in the glass, pale and overcast, like a cloud.

"I'm Paul Beveridge." He stuck out his hand.

The kid took it and shook. "Lars. Sorry I can't help you much. I barely see the guy."

"That's okay."

Paul had run out of things to say, but the kid still sat there, gazing blankly out the window. One of his hands stroked the other. This gesture was, to Paul, uncomfortably intimate, and he said, "Hey, are you all right?"

"What? Oh."

"I mean, I've been watching you. You seem . . . low."

"Yeah." He rubbed his face. "Yeah, I, uh, lost somebody."

"Like they died?"

"Yeah."

"I'm sorry."

"It was my girlfriend," he said. "She died in the plane crash. I just got back from the funeral this morning." He went back to rubbing his hand. "It's unreal. I just can't believe it. It's all happened so fast."

"I'm really sorry." He thought for a second of telling him about having seen the plane go down. But what was the point?

"Yeah, well. What's your name again?"

"Paul. Paul Beveridge."

"I don't mean to tell you all this. It's just . . ." And he trailed off into silence.

"Why are you working today? Why not take the day off?"

"And do what? Sit at home? That's the last thing I want. Though it's not like the job is particularly distracting."

"I guess not."

"Well," Lars said. He thumped the table with his hands. "I should go. Good luck with your surveillance."

"Oh, thanks. Sorry to have to spy on you."

"It's no problem."

"I hope things improve for you."

He shrugged. "They can't get any worse, I guess."

"I guess."

Lars stood up and left. While he waited to cross the street, a car pulled into the lot, and he jogged to the shop soon enough to hold the door open for his customer, a middle-aged lady wearing a sundress and hat. Inside, she gathered an armload of party toys and dumped them on the counter.

Later, when he left, Lars waved to Paul. Paul waved back, then watched Lars strap on a bicycle helmet, walk to the back of the store, and pedal away on a mountain bike. Lars wobbled off into the distance, and Paul wondered where he lived, and what he would do when he got there, if he had friends he could call.

Paul knew he could get up and leave now, but he didn't. The thought of home only worried him. Despite the night before, he felt no more able to reach Anita; whatever lay between them seemed no less tangled and impass-

able than before. This was the week that was to set things right, he remembered, the week that was going to put him on the right track: the one to responsibility and reconciliation. And he was trying, wasn't he? He was
supposed to be feeling things falling into place, right?

A few more minutes in the Kwik Stop: nothing. Finally he paid for his
last cup of coffee and headed for the car.

7

Lars's first thought when he got back to his place was that there was no food in it, and that he hadn't eaten for nearly twenty-four hours. He left the apartment again with relief, and with the ample justification of a necessary errand, one that any civilized person had to make. Groceries. This made great sense.

On the way to Safeway, he pedaled past a fraternity house. The brothers were standing around outside, stiff and bulky in their matching T-shirts, barbecuing steaks. For a moment he forgot his distaste for fraternities and their calculated squalor and found himself salivating uncontrollably. He thought this a good sign; it was the first time he'd felt any urgency since Friday. A car honked behind him, and he realized he was standing in the middle of the road. He moved aside and received the middle finger from the driver, a teenager with a tiny mustache.

He pedaled to the supermarket, feeling the hunger drifting like a virus through his blood, settling in his bones. He locked his bike to a pole and beelined for the electronic sliding doors. Then he noticed a banner, out of the corner of his eye:

ADT Bake Sale
to Benefit Christine Stull

It was set up at the near end of the parking lot, next to what seemed to be a trailer house. Beneath it stretched a long buffet table where a lot of blond-haired girls were sitting. The table was covered with neat piles of baked things: brownies stacked into pyramids, blueberry muffins wrapped in cellophane, glass jars stuffed with cookies. He recognized ADT as a campus sorority, perhaps one of the very ones he and Megan had taken such joy in mocking. These girls evoked in him a jumble of conflicting impulses—to approach, to run, to retreat into Safeway, to cry—and he realized he no longer knew what to say to girls or how to act around them. Panic slithered on the ground near his feet and began to climb up his legs by the hairs.

Someone at the table—the girl behind the cookies—motioned to him: Come on over here. He did.

"Saw you looking," the girl said. "How about a cookie? Good cause." The girl wore big sunglasses and—oddly, for the heat—a long-sleeved T-shirt. Her hair was held back with a giant yellow clip.

"Uh," Lars said. The cookies were huge. "Okay," he said, "okay." He fished a dollar out of his wallet.

She handed him a cookie wrapped in a small sheet of waxed paper. He closed his eyes and bit into it, and the chocolate dissolved on his tongue like a drug. He only looked again when he lost his balance and stumbled, and he found the girl leaning forward, offering him another cookie.

"You look like you need another."

"Oh," he said, patting his pockets. "No, I'm cash-poor."

"On me."

Lars took the cookie. "You sure? What about . . ." He looked up at the banner. "Christine Stull?"

"No problem. She doesn't mind."

The girl was grinning. "You?" he said.

She extended her hand, and Lars had to switch the cookie to his other hand to shake it. "Me," she said. "I baked these. I don't know if I've ever seen anybody eat a cookie like that. You can have as many as you want."

He felt himself redden. "Sorry."

"Oh, no! I'm flattered."

He took a bite of the new cookie. "So, how are you . . . benefiting?"

"Kidney transplant."

"Oh."

"Insurance'll only cover so much. The sisters here are helping out. They've been real pals."

"You're in the sorority too?"

"Yup."

"You're lucky to have such good friends."

She shrugged. "I suppose so."

"Well," he said. The second cookie was already gone. He crumpled the waxed paper and shoved it into his pocket. "I hope you're feeling . . . you know, better."

"You need another one?"

"Oh, no," he said. "Thanks. I'm going to go get groceries."

"Don't let me stop you."

Lars smiled at her. "Nice meeting you. Good luck."

"Thanks."

But however the cookies outside had improved his mood, he realized how hopeless the larger fight was, once he'd set foot in the store. First, it was the red and blue plastic hand baskets with their twin metal handles: he would always hold one handle, Megan the other. And the bread display, which stood just inside the door, to the right of the bakery; they'd always get the sourdough loaf and smother it with butter and garlic and cheese at home, sometimes making an entire meal out of garlic bread. The shelf upon shelf of brightly colored boxes: food packaged to attract children or processed into unappetizing shapes. They laughed over these, and the kind of people who bought them. They had been smug in love. His throat burned and he steadied himself against the rows of grocery carts, the metal supercooled in the air conditioning and electric on his hot skin.

Her brother Frank had called him Sunday with directions to their parents' house in Seattle, where he said they should meet to go to the funeral. "I'm sorry I won't have much time," he said, "but I want to see you."

"I want to bring a friend," Lars said.

"Of course, sure."

"Listen," Lars said. "I have her car."

"She had a car?"

"A small one. I guess we'll drive it out there."

"All right." He sounded distracted, unwilling to think about these things, but Lars had wanted them settled and out of the way.

"Do you want me to bring her stuff?"

"No, no. We'll worry about that later. Just . . . just bring the keys to her apartment. Do you have those?"

"I have a set."

"Okay then."

He and Toth would have to leave around four in the morning to make it; Seattle was eight or nine hours, barring any problems with the car. He called Toth that night to tell him to get some sleep. Toth was in the tub with the portable phone, crying. Lars could hear his voice echoing off the tiles and water.

"I've been in here all day, man," he said. "I'm completely fucking wrinkled." He sniffed deeply.

"Don't drop the phone," Lars said. He gave Toth the details. "Bring a few bucks for gas."

"How are you doing, man?"

Lars had not been doing well. "Didn't sleep much. Megan's dad said 'Fuck you' to me on the phone."

"I'm doing terrible," Toth said.

"At least you're clean." And miraculously, they both laughed.

That night long shadows from the neighbors' trees crept across his sheets. He ate half a bowl of cereal in bed, and massaged his mind to sleep by tracing the road to Seattle, every landmark and stretch of highway he could remember. He woke to his alarm at three-fifteen and found he had kicked his half-filled cereal bowl over in the night, and Hodge sat placidly on the floor beside it, licking the puddle. Lars got up and tossed a towel onto it. He dressed—khaki pants, white shirt, blue blazer was the best he could do—and stuffed what clothing of hers he could find into a plastic bag.

He got some cash at the drive-up bank and went to her apartment. She had lived in a tiny carpeted studio downtown and owned nearly nothing. He let himself in with his key. The place was a mild but particular mess; there were no books or papers on the floor but both were stacked precariously on her desk, and though all her clothes were in the closet, they were stuffed there haphazardly. He tossed the plastic bag onto her futon, which was spread sheetless on the floor. He went to the bathroom and pissed, then rubbed his hands under the tap. In the medicine cabinet he found a tube of toothpaste and a barrette. He put the barrette in his pocket. As he did all this, the dull pain in his throat was constant and debilitating; it felt like someone had lodged a gigantic rubber ball there, around which he could breathe only the barest essentials of air. When he left the apartment he did so forever.

Toth was waiting on the porch when he pulled up. To Lars's surprise, he was wearing a black funeral suit, and under the streetlight, his hair tied into a tasteful ponytail, he looked nerdily elegant. Lars commented on the suit when Toth got in. Toth didn't look up. He seemed paler than usual and his eyes were red. "Yeah," he said. "I got it at the Goodwill. This is the first time I've worn it." He pushed his fingers up under his glasses and rubbed his eyes. Lars pulled into the street.

"It's funny," Toth said, finally looking at him, "I feel like we're going fishing or something. I mean, it feels like some kind of fun trip thing. Getting up early and all that. Except I feel like jumping in the river."

"It just feels lousy to me," Lars said.

They drove in silence for an hour and a half, into Idaho and across the panhandle. Occasionally Lars heard Toth crying but didn't say anything. What could he say? When they crossed over into Washington he suggested some music.

Toth nodded and opened the glove compartment. He pushed the tapes around for a minute, then shoved one into the cassette deck. It warbled out of the speakers, a song Megan had liked. Toth left it for a minute, then said "Fuck" very quietly and popped it back out. He tossed it into the back of the car, where it clattered against the rear window. From then on they listened to AM radio, farm reports and news, and the sun came up behind them.

They stopped in Spokane for coffee and a box of Fig Newtons, which they ate sporadically on the road. At one point Lars said, "A bag of these costs three twenty-nine."

"So?"

"These boxes are half the size, and they only cost one twenty-nine."

"Doesn't make sense," Toth said.

"People are dumb."

It was the only thing they said all the way across Washington. Toth slept for the rest of the trip, and Lars stared out at the bleak hilliness of the state, wishing it would never end, would just go on and on being empty and boring. He wouldn't have minded if he had to drive this road forever, listening to

the news. Not at all. When they came close to the city, Lars took the folded
envelope with the directions on it from his pants pocket. He exited the highway and tooled through town, stymied briefly by a series of one-way streets,
and ended up in a shady neighborhood, where giant stone houses loomed behind cast-iron fences and rows of shrubbery. The house that matched the address on his envelope seemed to have nothing to do with Megan at all. It was
huge, like the others; its fence was the tallest in the neighborhood, and the
front walkway led through a ten-foot wrought-iron arch over which ivy grew.
The house spoke, Lars thought, of concealment, of embarrassment, and seeing
it reminded him just how little he knew about Megan's family. She had rarely
mentioned them. It was a bright day without direct sun; the light was dif-
fused through a layer of gray cloud. Lars found the driveway and pulled in,
and the change of speed seemed to jar Toth awake.

"We're here, buddy," Lars said. He parked behind a blue Datsun station
wagon and a green BMW.

"What?"

"We're here."

Toth sat up straight, blinking. He had a red seat-belt mark across his face,
and as he took in the yard his eyes clouded over. "Oh," he said quietly. "I fell
asleep and forgot everything."

"Sorry."

They stepped out and stretched, then walked to the door. It was giant and
wooden with a huge iron knocker that Lars was certain never got used. He
rang the bell.

When the door opened, and he saw Megan's brother for the first time,
something heavy and cold came unbalanced inside him, and he had to steady
himself against the doorframe. His face was hers, round and open, several
years older. His hair stuck up on his head and he stood at about six feet.

"Are you Lars?" he asked them.

"I am," Lars said.

He offered his hand to shake, and Lars took it. "I'm Frank."

"This is Toth. He was a good friend."

"I'm glad you could make it," Frank told Toth, and Toth nodded wearily.

Frank looked tired—his limbs hung off his body like broken tree
branches after a storm—and Lars could hear voices behind him, in the house,
a man grumbling and a woman yelling at him. Nobody said anything for a
few moments, and the yelling continued. Frank slumped, holding himself up

with the doorknob. "Maybe we ought to sit out here," he said. "Just for a little while."

The only thing Lars could remember Megan saying about Frank was that he spent a lot of time in the sandbox in the Hellenbecks' backyard when he was a kid. He would build things—houses and their yards—and decorate them with bits of styrofoam cups and rocks and sticks. Now he walked between Lars and Toth, shutting the big door behind him, and sat down on the porch step. He was wearing black pants and a white shirt. Lars and Toth sat down on either side.

Frank pulled a single cigarette from his pocket and lit it with a yellow lighter. He turned to Lars and said, "She loved you, you know."

"I loved her too," he said. He had a picture in his head of Megan, sweating in her shorts and T-shirt and cap in the summer sun, laying sod next to Frank, telling him that she loved her boyfriend back in Montana. Did Frank even work outdoors? Or did he just go around assigning grunt work from his office? It didn't matter. Lars rubbed his eyes.

"She told me about you, too," Frank told Toth. "She loved you guys. I'm glad you could come out here. It was kind of short notice." He was silent for a second, then turned bright red, embarrassed at saying something so stupid.

"Was it a good summer?" Lars said.

"It was a great summer."

Behind them the door swung open and smacked against the wall. Lars felt the house tremble. Somebody stormed past them, off to the right, and he looked up to see a thick-bodied man in gray slacks stomping through a bed of flowers. He heard the jingling of keys. Frank stood up. "Dad!" he called out. He stood, tossing his unfinished cigarette onto the walk. "Dad!"

"Shit," Toth whispered. He wiped the sleeve of his jacket across his face.

Frank caught up to Mr. Hellenbeck in the driveway. Lars couldn't make out the words, but Frank's voice was edged with exasperation, as if this was the sort of thing that happened frequently. His father twirled the keys on his finger but didn't speak. Lars had never seen a man who looked so physically dense. He could easily have been made of lead, his features painted on. After a minute, Frank's hands fell to his sides, and the two men stood unmoving for some time. Then Mr. Hellenbeck turned and disappeared behind the corner of the house. Frank stayed put. Lars heard a garage door rolling up creakily, then a car engine and the squeal of tires. Another BMW, this one red, shot into view, careening down the driveway. It angled into the road, leaving deep gouges in the grass, and fishtailed loudly in the street.

Frank came back to the porch. "Sorry," he said.

Lars and Toth said nothing.

"He'll be at the funeral," Frank said. He leaned forward and picked his cigarette off the sidewalk. "I don't think he'd go off and miss that." He took a long drag and stubbed the cigarette out, then swiveled his head, looking for a trash can. When he found none he wiped off the ashes and stuck the butt in his pocket. Then he got up. "I should see if Mom's all right. Why don't you come in for now?"

Lars and Toth sat opposite each other in powder-blue wing-back armchairs. The room they sat in was spacious and lavishly—perhaps professionally—decorated; long opaque drapes hung over long windows and the floor was covered with Oriental rugs. Frank had gone down the hall.

"Come on, Ma," they heard him say. "You have to get yourself together."

"That man!" she cried, her voice dissolving in tears.

"You have to get dressed, Ma."

Toth leaned forward. "This is weird," he whispered. "Where are all the relatives?"

"I don't know." Lars was looking at a portrait above the fireplace of a man with white hair, wearing an ascot. Something in the forehead reminded him of Megan, though that could have been his imagination. He could not picture her even standing in this house, let alone growing up in it.

"Is this the dress you're going to wear?" he heard Frank say.

"I can't do it!"

"C'mon, Ma. This is for Megan."

"Don't you say that to me! Don't you say that to me!"

Somewhere, a door opened and shut. Footsteps, some fussing in what sounded like a kitchen. Then the footsteps again.

"Take these, Ma."

"Get those things away from me."

"You have to face these people, Ma, okay? Just this afternoon, and then it'll be over and nobody'll bother you anymore."

A long pause, then: "Give them to me."

"Okay," Frank said. "That's good. Now get yourself dressed, all right?"

"Get away from me."

"Okay," he said. "Okay, I'm going."

Frank walked wearily into the room, his hands in his pockets. "Maybe we ought to go back outside," he said.

The blue wagon turned out to be Frank's. He helped his mother into the passenger seat. She was puffy and rumpled in a black dress, like a poisonous mushroom. Her pupils were very, very small. Lars and Toth took Megan's car, and Lars's heart sank as he slid back into the seat. He hadn't wanted to drive it ever again.

Frank's car led them to a small Presbyterian church a few miles away. They followed Frank and Mrs. Hellenbeck up a narrow sidewalk that had some odd glittery substance embedded in it. Lars found this curiously inappropriate and felt himself actually getting angry about it, hoping a priest or somebody would walk by so that he could complain. Ahead, Frank held the door open for Mrs. Hellenbeck, who staggered through it as if pulled in by ropes.

There were only thirty or so people in the church, though a hundred and fifty could easily have fit. Lars scanned the crowd anxiously, seeing if there was anyone he knew. Every face was empty and unfamiliar. Then he looked toward the altar and saw the casket. What was in it? How had they found her? His first impulse, sudden and palpable as a knife at the throat, was to turn and run, and this is what he did, pushing Toth out of the way and plunging back into the gray light, back into the awful, flower-sweet air that surrounded the church like a fog. He dodged a middle-aged couple on the sidewalk and sat down hard in the grass, his palms against his forehead.

"Lars." It was Toth, standing in his light, reaching out to touch him. "Lars?" Were they kidding about all this, the casket, the flowers? Surely they had to be kidding.

"I can't go in there," he said. "Are you insane?"

"Come on, man, you have to."

"Who are those people? I don't know any of those people."

"Don't worry about them." Toth knelt before him. Lars let him pull his hands away from his face. "It's just you and me and Megan, man. This last time, all right?"

No, he thought, this isn't the last time. The last time was at the airport, dropping her off for her trip to Seattle. His last kiss had been on her neck, just under her left ear, her hair smelling of shampoo and her T-shirt of detergent. As she walked away he saw that the back of the shirt was half-tucked into her shorts, like she'd pulled the shorts on in a hurry, not noticing how they looked. And the last time he'd heard her? On the telephone, *I'll see you Friday,* she'd said, and he said, *Okay.* What else had they talked about? Had they joked about a summer without sex, without conversation that didn't entail a ring of sticky sweat around the ear? Had they given their I-love-yous? He would have thought this would all come back to him unadulterated by the flaws of memory, but it didn't. He barely recalled a thing. He lay back in the grass. It had been cut, and the scent of chlorophyll was sharp in his nostrils, and the dirt musty and fertilized beneath it.

"Come on, buddy," Toth was saying.

Forget it, he thought, forget it.

"Come on. If you don't want to do it for her, man, do it for me."

So he did. He got to his knees, wiped the grass off his pants. He stood up and went in.

He paid little attention during the funeral. At the ends of the pews were stacked thick stapled booklets full of hymns, and he flipped through one of these, hoping nobody would begin singing. Nobody did. There were some prayers, and a few people spoke. At one point he looked up and saw Mr. Hellenbeck standing in the doorway, panting, his face shiny with perspiration. He had come late and was staring at Lars. Lars stared back. It was Hellenbeck who turned away first, then sat down alone in front, his wide gray coat heaving as he breathed.

What if? Lars thought.

What if he had driven to Seattle to pick her up, as they both wanted but couldn't fit into their schedules?

What if he'd asked her to marry him?

They walked to the cemetery for the graveside service, mercifully un-eventful and brief. They lowered the box. When it was over, he and Toth stood in the grass outside the church. Nobody approached them. It then occurred to Lars for the first time that they couldn't drive back if they were planning to leave Megan's car in Seattle. They had made no other plans. He told Toth this.

"Oh, Jesus."

Lars pulled out his wallet. He had four dollars. And something else, hard and sharp, in his pocket. He curled his hand around it: the barrette he'd taken back in Marshall. "How much have you got?"

Toth emptied his pockets. "Seven and change. I got plastic, though." Twenty feet beyond him, in the church parking lot, an old woman was talk-ing to Mr. Hellenbeck. He was looking over her shoulder, at the cemetery.

"Where's Frank?"

Frank was in the parking lot with his mother, walking her in small, crooked circles. She seemed to want to leave, and for whatever reason, Frank kept pulling her away from their car. Finally she seemed to give in, and he led her over to a small group of middle-aged women, who surrounded her, touch-ing her on the shoulders and back. Lars's hand was sweating around the bar-rette, and he took it out of his pocket. Without looking at it, he dropped it into a nearby bush. It was a relief to be free of it. He waited until Frank was looking their way, and raised his hand to him.

Frank came over. "That wasn't so bad," he said, his face indicating exactly the opposite. "Are you guys okay?"

"We're not sure how to get back," Lars said. "We came here in her car."

"I'm thinking bus," Toth said.

Frank nodded with a stricken, sugary gaze. "Right."

"Can we walk there?" Lars said.

"No." He squeezed his eyes shut and opened them again. "No. Look, why not just take the car to the station? You can leave the keys under the mat." He gave them directions. "If you get lost you can ask."

"I really appreciate it."

He shrugged. "Yeah, well. I'd ask you to stay, but there isn't going to be much in the way of a wake. A lot of drinking and moaning." Something seemed to come to him then and he snapped his head up. "I'm glad we met," he said. "Both of you guys." They shook hands. "I'll probably never see you again."

"I guess not," Lars said.

"We would have, maybe. Maybe on holidays."

Lars winced, and he watched tears appear in Frank's eyes. Then they were gone, wiped away with a pass of his hand. "You're a good kid, Lars," he said. "So was she. She was a really good kid."

"Yeah." He wanted to look into the bush—could he still see the barrette? could he pick it up again?—but he held himself back.

"I gotta think about that more, when I get time."

"So," Lars said. "I'll be seeing you."

He looked hard at Lars, then at Toth. "Okay, then," he said, and walked away.

On the bus, Lars could feel the pain pulling away from him, as if it were a series of small, hot beads on a long string, and one end of the string was attached to Megan's car back at the bus station, and the rest coiled inside him. With every mile, more of the pain unspooled and stung as it left him, and then was gone. He slept for most of the trip, an entire night's worth in an afternoon and evening, and they pulled into the Marshall station in the middle of the night. He understood that the worst was not over, but the keenest part was. What remained would be duller and blunter, and he would have to stuff the burned-out hollows that sharp pain left with something new and different, something that didn't quite fit. When they stepped off the bus and into the cool night air, Toth said, "We'll have to walk."

"I know."

"How are you doing?" he said.

"Better, some."

Toth stared out over the trees and houses to the North Side Bridge rising bright in the distance. "Me too," he said. "Still bad, though." He turned back to Lars. "Can we talk about her sometimes? Would that be too weird for you?"

Lars shook his head. "No, I figure we'll have to do that."

"It's good we were together for it."

"I guess so."

And then they hugged clumsily and went off in opposite directions toward home, afraid to say anything more and suffer from scrutiny in one another's light. Lars kept his head up as he walked, so that he could catch the moment when the streetlights started winking out.

He gathered his groceries in a sort of fog, breaking the rules he and Megan had always so carefully followed together: never shop hungry, never shop without a list. Anything that looked good, he put into his cart. The shopping was dull, each item offering a modest lump of heartbreak as he re-membered eating it with her. His hunger, held at bay by the two cookies, was dull. Everything with Megan, on the other hand, had crackled, her energy so great that it buzzed like a force field around her; the best of times had been like touching a nine-volt battery to the tongue: a little uncomfortable, very exciting. But all Lars wanted now was this: the comfort of predictable hurt, eating and sleeping and breathing. Time passed, and when he got to the cashier he had four sacks' worth of groceries, far more than he could carry. He paid, then loaded two onto his bike, leaving the others behind with the cashier for the second trip. But when he returned from home the cashier was gone, his groceries with her.

"Excuse me," Lars asked the new cashier from behind the plastic bag rack. A considerable line had formed.

"What," the cashier said. He was a corpulent man with tinted glasses. He didn't turn his head, but continued to swipe items over the UPC reader.

"I left my groceries here? With the lady who was here before you?"

The man stopped and spun on him. "What?"

"Two sacks of groceries. I left them right here." He pointed at the bag-ging area, now cluttered with a lot of health food—vegetables, vitamins. He felt himself sweating from the bike rides.

The man scowled behind his glasses and grabbed a nearby PA phone. His voice boomed throughout the store. "Assistance at seven. Assistance at seven."

Lars noticed that the girl whose groceries were being rung was staring at him. She had a funny quality about the eyes, kind of tired and sick.

"Two-cookie guy," she said.

It was the sorority sister from the bake sale. "Hey."

"What was your name again?"

"Lars Cowgill." Somebody was trying to get past him in the exit aisle, an old woman, and she sighed loudly several times. Lars pressed himself up against the bag rack.

"Koggle?"

"Cow gill." He spelled it.

"Right. Christine Stull, remember?"

"Some trouble?" a man said behind him. Lars turned and met a plastic nameplate: Frank Banner, Floor Manager. The accompanying face towered above Lars by eighteen inches at least, and sat on a neck as thick as a pile of sandbags.

"Uh . . . I . . ."

"Two sacks of groceries? Got 'em in back."

"Oh. Good. I mean, thanks."

"Step aside there, son," Banner said. "Make way for Claude. He doesn't wanna be cramped."

The checker's lips thinned. "Ten forty," he said to Christine.

Banner brought the bags, and as Lars stood outside, fastening them to his basket with a pair of bungee cords, Christine came through the sliding doors and set her sack at his feet.

"You got out of there in a hurry," she said.

"Oh! Sorry."

"Oh, hey, I just gave you a couple of free cookies. No reason to chat."

"One free cookie," he reminded her.

"Okay, geez." She smiled. "You look like you haven't eaten in a week."

He looked down at his bicycle, teetering under the weight of the sacks. "This is only half of it."

"Well," she said.

"Well."

"Nice meeting you, Lars."

"Good luck with the, you know. The kidneys."

She rolled her eyes. "Yup."

That night he was sautéing vegetables when the phone rang. He carried his wooden spoon with him into the living room and picked it up.

"Lars Cowgill," said a female voice. "Here you are, right in the phone book." In the background, he could hear a low mechanical whooshing.

"Hello?"

"It's Christine."

"Oh, hi."

"Don't sound too excited."

"Sorry," he said. He picked up the phone and brought it into the kitchen, and the trailing cord reminded him of his call from the airline days before. He took a deep breath. "I just wasn't expecting anybody to call tonight."

"Ah."

"So what's up?"

"Dialysis," she said. "I have to do this every couple of days. They hook me up to this machine and all my blood goes through it."

He reached over the burners and turned the heat down. "Does that hurt?"

"I get tired. The day after, I'm okay, but then I start feeling shitty again fast."

"Where are you?" he said. "The hospital?"

"That's why our trailer's at Safeway. It's near the hospital. Gotta be close by if they find a kidney and all."

"You're *living* there?"

"Yeah. They let me call people while this thing's going. It gets boring."

There was a long silence, during which he moved his vegetables around in the butter and oil.

"So what's up with you?" she said.

"Cooking dinner."

"I mean in general. What's your story?" He heard her shifting, and she grunted and let out a long breath. "You sound like a sad fella."

"Not generally," he said.

"But specifically . . ."

He slid the pan off the burner and scraped the vegetables onto a plate, then rummaged in a drawer for a fork.

"Okay, don't answer."

"Specifically, my girlfriend's dead." How many times would he have to tell people? He decided that was it, that nobody else should know.

Another pause. "Oh . . ."

"So I'm sad." It didn't feel so bad to say this. It almost felt good. "I'm sad," he said again.

"Maybe I'm not the person to be talking to."

"I don't mind." When she didn't say anything, he said, "Do you mind?"

"No."

"I'm going to eat while we're talking." He crunched into a piece of broccoli. It tasted great. "Oh, God," he said.

"What?"

"This broccoli. It's really good."

"Ugh. Don't talk to me about food. I feel like blowing hash."

"Sorry."

They talked until he was finished eating, and when he hung up, Lars felt
like he had never slept before, like an infinite chorus of rock bands had been
keeping him awake since the dawn of time. Still, he didn't sleep for a long
time. "Just you and me," he said to the cat when he walked by. "Goodnight,
darling," he said to the blocks of street light that arced across the ceiling.
"Goodnight."

8

Sunday morning, the phone rang. When she dragged herself from bed to answer, Trixie saw that it was nearly ten-thirty and was stunned to find herself still aching and lethargic, things she usually shook off by nine. She picked it up and leaned heavily against the counter. "Hello?"

"Mother, it's Katerina."

The words were so foreign that it took her a moment to understand they were being addressed to her.

"Mother?"

"Yes, it's me."

"How are you, Mother?"

Trixie cleared her throat. That voice, still sharp as a spanking—she hadn't spoken to her daughter since Kat's son was born, seven years before.

"I'm feeling just fine. Older, still getting around."

A low tone escaped Kat, as if this was more than she had wanted to hear. She said, "I'm calling with bad news, Mother."

"I think I know it already."

"Father?"

"His plane."

There was a long silence, after which Kat said, "You know he's dead?" Her voice was incredulous and, Trixie thought, slightly disappointed, as if she had been looking forward to delivering the news.

"I know."

"Mother," she said, "what was he doing flying to Marshall? We didn't know anything about it."

"He was coming to see me."

"To see *you*."

"Yes."

After a long silence Trixie said, "Does Edward know yet?"

"He couldn't be reached."

"Oh. And Rachel and David—are they taking it badly?"

"They're children," Kat said. "They don't understand."

"I suppose not."

"Mother, why was he going to see you?"

"I can't say I know. He just wrote me a letter saying he was coming, and I wrote back telling him he should go ahead, if he wanted." She felt so tired, so helpless: this was not, she had imagined all these years, the way it would be at the end, nothing resolved, no impulses satisfied. She wasn't sure what the proper reaction was, not just for appearances' sake but for herself: how to mourn the man who left her when she was young? The man who was on his way to see her old self?

"I see."

"He was a good man, mostly," she said idly, almost to herself.

Then Kat said, "I really don't see how you could know that, Mother." The self-satisfaction of the statement, the insensitivity and arrogance, was so bald that it was Trixie's turn to be speechless now. It was not a comment that asked a reply.

When Kat spoke again it was more hesitantly. "There will be a funeral Wednesday," she said. "In Seattle. Janice is making the arrangements."

"Janice?"

"Caitlin's daughter."

"Caitlin, his second wife."

"Yes."

She reached for a pen from the cup on the counter. "Why don't you give me directions?"

"Well, Mother," Kat said, very quietly, "I was thinking it might not be appropriate for you to go."

"I beg your pardon?"

"I needn't repeat it for you. You heard what I said." Her voice had gone uneven, it seemed, and Trixie realized with a start that her daughter was crying.

"I suppose I did," Trixie said. "And why not?"

"Frankly, Mother, a funeral's for the living. I've searched my heart for the strength to forgive you, I've begged God for it . . ." She was sobbing freely now, all control gone from her voice. "But this service is for my father, for Janice's father. It is not . . . it is not for your husband."

"My God, Kat, you're a grown woman," she found herself saying. "This is—"

"I'm sorry, Mother. I won't take it back. You're not encouraged to come."

Years from now, Trixie knew, Kat would remember the funeral, would remember that her awful mother hadn't even bothered to come. She would recall her own strength in the matter, bearing up despite such a blatant and sinful affront. She would not remember this telephone call, that was certain.

"If that's the way it has to be," Trixie said.

"I'm afraid so."

"Well then," she said. "I'm sorry about the death of your father."

Kat answered in a whisper. "Thank you," she said, and after that they had nothing more to say.

Sundays were book group days. Trixie usually drove into town at eleven-thirty, parked at the public library, then sat quietly and went over the book for that day while she waited for the other ladies to arrive. There were four of them, besides Trixie: Diane Keeler, a divorcée ten years Trixie's junior and probably her best friend; Bette Spraycar; Margaret Cheatham; and Iona Sandburg. She'd known Bette for ages, but Trixie still didn't know her very well; none of them seemed to, though they had been meeting on Sundays for nearly four years. Bette was a barrel-shaped woman in her sixties and disliked anything out of the ordinary. When it was her turn to pick a book, she rarely suggested anything written after the turn of the century, and that suited

Trixie fine. Margaret Cheatham seemed to exist only in reference to her husband, who waited outside in his truck while they talked. She always found a reason to leave early and suggested only romance novels with exhaustingly repetitive plots; Trixie and Diane had often talked about writing one of their own, they knew the rules so well by now. And Iona Sandburg was old, older than Trixie, well into her eighties. For the past two years they'd skipped her turn to choose, as she had begun to forget her obligations and often didn't get around to reading that week's book at all. But some weeks were better than others, and Trixie guessed she had once been a wry, energetic young woman, gone confused and aimless in widowhood.

This week's book was one of Margaret's, and Trixie had stopped reading it about halfway through. She had promised herself she'd finish it yesterday, but after the crash, after talking to Kat, the ex–stable boy and his rippling muscles didn't seem worth paying much mind. At eleven-thirty, she was sitting in the library, riffling the pages and trying to find something to say later, when Diane came in and took her place at the table.

"You're early," Trixie told her. They met in a glassed-in room next to the history section, and it overlooked the parking lot through tall, thin windows flanked by bare brick.

"I was going to do what you're doing," Diane said. "But I don't think I'm going to bother." She reached across the table and touched Trixie's hand. "How are you getting on?"

"Fine, fine."

Diane nodded. "We ought to get together this week to shoot the bull," she said. "When was the last time we did that?"

"Months."

"That long?"

"That long."

Diane looked healthier than ever. When Trixie met her five years ago, she was still married. After her divorce a year later—the end of forty-five years, the worst ones of her life, Diane was fond of saying—she quit smoking and drinking and got a membership at a gym. "I should have divorced him forty years ago," she told Trixie once. "Thank God I'm not old yet."

Now she watched Trixie, her eyebrows raised, waiting. This is one thing she was good at: getting Trixie to talk. "Well?" she said.

"Kat called this morning."

"*Kat* did!"

Trixie shook her head. "She was calling to tell me what I already knew. Then she asked me to stay away from the funeral."

Diane dismissed this with a wave of her hand. "Well, you should go anyway. Go ahead and crash it."

"Oh, there's no point." She let the book slap shut and tossed it onto the table. "She told me I didn't really know him. What garbage! She barely spoke to that man when they lived in the same house. She was only a child."

"People will go to the greatest lengths to convince themselves of what they want to believe."

"I suppose."

Diane took a breath. "You expected to see him again, didn't you."

"I suppose I did. It seemed inevitable. Even when he wrote, and I thought about keeping him away . . ." She remembered the panic she felt watching the mailman's truck raising dust on the road.

"You knew he'd come."

"Yes."

Diane grinned. "I spent most of my life waiting for Frank to turn into the sort of person I wanted to be married to."

Trixie smiled at her, and at that moment Margaret came in clutching her copy of *Castle Hearts.* Torn strips of paper stuck from the pages, each neatly written on in ink. "Hello! Hello!" she said. She sat down across the table, as far from Trixie as possible, leaned forward and whispered, "I'm so *sorry.*"

"Speak up, Margaret!" Diane barked.

"It's all right, Margaret," Trixie said.

"If you need *anything.*"

"You're very kind."

"I was just saying to Edro, if Trixie needs *anything* . . ."

"I'll be sure to let you know."

Margaret set her bag down on the table, and the book next to it. "Well! I hope you both enjoyed this one." She straightened the book, lining it up with the edge of the table, and patted its cover.

"Oh, yes," Trixie said.

The door opened and Bette walked in, leading Iona by the arm. "Here, Iona," she said. "Sit here." She pulled a chair out and Iona sat. "I passed her in the car. She was standing on the corner of Main and Weir. She looked awfully confused."

"I plumb forgot," Iona said.

"Are you all right, dear?" Margaret said, reaching out to touch her arm.

"Why, yes. I'm just fine." She looked into her handbag and frowned. "Oh . . ."

"What is it?" Bette asked her.

"I've forgotten my book. I'm forgetting just everything today."

"Oh, it's all right," Margaret told her, "you don't need it. You remember the gist, don't you?"

"I certainly do. I certainly do."

Bette sat down to Trixie's right, and squeezed her forearm. "I'm sorry to hear about Hamish. We saw him a few months ago, in the city, first time in years." She quieted to a whisper. "He had aged well, Trixie. A very handsome man. I'm sorry."

"Thank you."

"What happened?" Iona said. "What happened?"

"I told you before, dear," Bette said quietly. "Trixie's husband passed away."

"Oh!" Her hands flew to her mouth, tiny and strange. "Her husband!"

"It's all right, Iona," Trixie said. "We'd been apart for a long time."

Diane nodded. "Iona, they were divorced. Estranged, you know?"

"It was the plague, wasn't it," Iona said.

"No," Diane said. "He died in that plane crash."

"Plane crash," Iona repeated, her hands falling away from her face, her voice as flat and fragile as a sheet of glass. Trixie wondered briefly what it was like to forget yourself; if it was, at times, a relief not to have your past pacing hugely behind you like a restless giant, or if you never really forgot, if the past only turned shadowy and indistinct and mastered you with fear. But Margaret, obviously sensing that they were off to a poor start, began to talk about her book, and Trixie tried to listen.

The discussion went badly. Trixie tried to offer a few nice comments about the book, mentioning parts she didn't exactly like but thought rose above the general mess. Diane didn't say anything at all, and Bette began, apropos of nothing, to talk about Jane Austen. Margaret was beginning to become visibly upset, even glancing out the window at the parking lot, where Edro was waiting, when Trixie noticed that Iona had begun to cry.

"Iona?"

Her chin was trembling and her eyes had gone hazy and wet. She had taken off her glasses and they lay upside down on the table. Trixie remembered that Iona had been a dancer once—a showgirl in the once thriving theaters of Great Falls, back when it was the fastest-growing city in the state. That she had once possessed grace, had been a living part of something grand and exciting, moved Trixie, and she reached across Bette and took Iona's hand. "Iona, dear," she said, "it's all right."

"I miss my Eugene," she said simply, and with her free hand rummaged around in her bag.

"Let me," Bette said. She reached into Iona's bag and pulled out a little plastic travel pack of Kleenex. She broke the seal and handed several to Iona.

"Thank you," she said. Her voice was weak and mournful, like a distant train.

"I think it might be time to stop for the day," Diane said. Margaret's face darkened, but she said nothing, only closed her book.

"I don't know what's come over me," Iona said.

"Speak your mind, Iona," Diane said.

"Oh, I don't know. I don't think there's much point to that." But then, after a moment, she did go on: she told them about the theater Eugene had helped build with his own hands, the famous men who came out on the train from the East. She told them about the local gangsters, who loved Eugene, who came to the theater for free, whenever they wanted, and the years when the labor unions began to break, when Anaconda Mining picked up and left for greener pastures, and attendance began to fall as people's money ran out. And then there was Eugene's heart attack, the day they knocked down the giant smokestack, and how she came out of the hospital after they lost him to find the stack gone from the horizon. Her voice took on renewed life for those minutes, and the other ladies were silent as she spoke.

Trixie's heart was breaking for Iona. She knew what it was like to watch life go bad for someone you loved. She recalled life in Marshall with Hamish as a series of relentless external pressures that changed the shape of their family, laying bare their weaknesses like an earthquake lays bare new and ragged earth.

She remembered an evening during a long period of idleness for Hamish: it was late winter of a year when construction jobs had proven few and far between, and he had been reading and rereading the classifieds in the kitchen, circling ads with a pen and crossing them out again. After nearly an hour, he stopped reading abruptly, capped the pen and folded the paper neatly on the table. An expression of dark resolve came over his face and he pushed back his chair. Trixie had been reading a book across from him. She looked up.

"Where are you going?"

He didn't answer. His eyes passed over her; they were focused on something else entirely, something beyond this house, their lives. She was used to his sudden decisiveness, but this look, its object unclear, frightened her.

"Hamish?"

"Be back," he said, and he grabbed his coat from the hook by the door and vanished, his keys jingling.

Kat and Edward were in the next room playing Monopoly. When she could no longer hear the truck's engine, she went to the living room and watched them. Kat had all the money, and Edward looked stricken. He said, "Where's Daddy?"

"He'll be right back."

This answer seemed to pain him. He turned back to the game warily, as if taking his eyes off Trixie meant he might doom Hamish never to return.

"You're in my *hotel*," Kat said.

"I'm out of money."

"You can give me your railroad."

"No!"

"Either that or you lose."

In the end, Kat allowed him to borrow money from the bank, and they kept playing, Edward tentatively, flinching as he rolled the dice, Kat with naked and gleeful aggression, building additional hotels on already crowded properties and giving Edward breaks to prolong the game whenever it seemed he might quit.

Trixie heard Hamish come in, and Edward sat up, relieved. When she went to the kitchen to see where he had gone, she found him sitting at the table behind a bottle and an empty glass.

She met his eyes, coldly. "We can't afford that."

"Priorities," he said, and unscrewed the cap.

"What on earth is that supposed to mean?"

"It means we bought it anyway."

She turned to the children. "Time for bed."

"No, it's not," Kat said without looking up. "It's only seven-thirty."

"It's time when I tell you it's time, Katerina."

"We're *playing*."

"Oh, let 'em play," came Hamish's voice.

"See?" Kat said. Edward's head swiveled between his mother and sister like a wind vane.

She turned back to Hamish, who offered his full glass to her. She shook her head no, and he drank it all in one swallow, tipping his head back like an old pro. He squeezed his eyes shut. Then he set the empty glass on the table and refilled it.

"That's three days of food, Hamish," she said. "Or a pair of boots for Edward. Or a hat."

"Nope," he said. "It's only this. No going back." He swirled the glass, and the booze licked the sides. "You could use some, Trixie."

The children were staring at her, Edward in astonishment, Kat with what looked like irritation, or impatience. As far as she remembered, this night was the real birth of Hamish's drinking, of Kat's ill will toward her. Could it have been that simple? Maybe not; maybe she'd assembled the memory from several sources. But the incident was so clear in her mind—the expressions on the children's faces, Hamish's words, the uneasy impression that latent threats had come to pass all at once, and would soon gather the strength to rise up and crush them.

The book group broke up early, and Trixie gave Iona Sandburg a ride. She helped Iona up the steps to her house and sat in the car a moment before pulling away, watching Iona move behind the curtains, checking that she was all right.

Driving home, Trixie thought that she was too old for everything to come back to her like this, that she didn't want to spend her declining years grappling with the past, and she began to consider what she could do to snap out of it: a trip perhaps, or a new hobby? But where would she go, and with whom? What could she find to do?

That night, while she was fixing her dinner, he came to her. She liked to make soup in the summer with the vegetables her neighbors brought her, and she always had some leftovers on hand, divided into serving-size plastic containers in the fridge. She took one of these and dumped it into a pot, then sliced some bread off a loaf and buttered it. While she was stirring, she heard the glass doors of the china cabinet open up with a rattle, heard some plates clinking together, and the sound of one being placed on the wooden tabletop. She stopped stirring. She heard a chair being pulled out, then pushed in again.

"Hamish?" she said, and turned.

He looked bleached, like a book left too long out in the bright sun, and adult: his body was mature but his face blurred. And he was handsome, the way he might be in an overexposed photograph. He didn't look up. Instead, he curled his left hand as if around a spoon or fork, and moved it across the plate and to his mouth, in a pantomime of eating. His face was absent with the repetitiveness of the task. The only sound in the room was the hiss of the burner, and without looking Trixie reached over the stove and turned off the gas.

"Hamish."

And now he did look up: not at Trixie but to his side, as though someone were there at the table's edge, eating with him. He tilted his head, listening, and her heart leaped to see it. She remembered him as a young man of twenty-five, listening to her questions about the cattle, the horses. How many times had she seen that gesture? As many times as there were things she didn't know. It was he, she remembered now, whose knowledge of ranch life made her want to become expert in everything, made her already sharp thirst for knowledge into an imperative, as necessary as food. His lips bent into a smile now, and he laughed silently, nodding.

Finally she said his name again, more loudly, and he looked up at where she stood. But he couldn't see her. He half rose, the chair scraping the floor behind him, and walked around the table. No air moved as he passed. He went to the far window, in the living room, and looked out. Then he returned to his chair and began to eat again.

He was like a sleepwalker, sure of himself in the motions and impulses of his dream, of which, in his presence, Trixie felt an invasive part. He dabbed his mouth with an invisible napkin, got up, and walked to the door, then stood in the doorway a moment, running his hand through his hair, another gesture of his as familiar as any of her own. And as she remembered, he stepped out into the dust and disappeared around the corner, toward the road. A breeze filled the house and threw shut one of the cupboard doors with a bang.

She went to the open door, but he was gone now, lost in the glare of the sunset. A car window gleamed at a bend in the road. She stepped back inside, shut the door behind her and closed the cupboard. She left his empty plate on the table. Her hands shook, but she turned on the gas under her dinner and watched the blue flame until the soup was hot enough to eat.

"*He came tonight,*" she told Diane on the telephone. "Hamish did." It was dark outside now, and she sat on her chair, watching the back of the door.

Diane took her time saying anything. "What do you mean by that, exactly?"

"I was making dinner, and he came into the house, and took a dish from the cupboard, and sat at the table and ate off it."

She heard something being set down on the other end—a drink, a book? "Are you all right? Do you need to go to the doctor's?"

"I'm fine. A little afraid."

"You saw Hamish."

"He didn't really eat. He just pantomimed eating."

"Forgive me, dear, but that sounds a bit funny."

"I know."

"Don't you think maybe you're seeing things?"

"I'm not," she said. "I feel fine. I'm not light-headed or confused, nothing's numb . . . It was strange, Diane—he could hear me saying things to him, but he didn't know what, or that it was me. It was like he was only half here."

Trixie heard her grunt. She was getting out of bed. "I'm coming over," she said.

"Oh no! You don't have to do that!" But suddenly she wanted Diane there; she wanted the house full of people.

"I'd feel better. Are you sure you're feeling all right?"

"Yes, fine."

"Hmm. I'm on my way."

"It's no rush."

"Well, it's not like I'm waking anyone up."

When they hung up, Trixie could sense, almost supernaturally, the emptiness of the house, just how much of the air lay fallow in the corners and around the ceiling, and she felt lonely there for the first time in years. It reminded her of her days alone in the old house, with Hamish at work and the children at school, and how quickly solitude turned to misery after he left them and Kat had moved out.

She could remember feeling this way once the year before Hamish left for good. It was a Saturday, the day after a night he had walked out drunk and not yet returned. She was sitting in the quiet of the living room, trying to ease herself down from panic, when she realized she hadn't heard the children for hours. She strained to hear them, but there was nothing. The silence began to grow ominous, and she went up to check on them. She found Kat's door wide open, her curtains drawn, and there in the darkness she and her brother knelt before her bed, their hands clasped before them in what struck Trixie as a grim parody of prayer.

"What are you doing?" she whispered.

Kat was sixteen then, and her face had begun to take on the firm lines of an adult's. When she looked up, it was filled with calm and righteous anger. Edward's face, still a boy's, was terrified beside her.

"We're praying to God," Kat said.

Trixie's first impulse was to march into the room and pry their hands apart. Instead, she stared at them, waiting for them to crack and run to her for comfort. But nothing happened. Edward buried his face in the blankets. Kat was glowing. Finally Trixie dragged herself away, and wept wearily when she heard Kat's door slam shut behind her. Now she wondered how she had let that happen, why the loss of Kat's trust only paralyzed her and stripped her of resolve. Her imagination had long provided a better end to that scene: she walks into the room, throws open the curtains, and confronts Kat. It isn't me, she explains, I'm not the one driving him away. You can trust me still. You can both trust me. And the three of them sit, cross-legged on the floor, and talk about what they'll do when Hamish gets home, when their problems have been solved and the family is back together again.

When Diane came, Trixie put on a pot of coffee and they sat together in the living room. Trixie recounted what had happened, and Diane nodded, her face resolvedly neutral. She glanced around the house as Trixie talked. When the coffee finished brewing, Trixie went to the cabinet for cups and saucers. They clinked together as she pulled them out, and when she set them on the counter she could see her own face reflected ash-white in a saucer's well. She trembled as she poured.

"Well," Diane was saying, "you look all right, anyway."

Trixie set her cup on the ottoman and handed Diane hers. "I told you."

"Yes." Diane pushed each shoe off with the opposite foot, then propped both feet up on the coffee table. She cracked her toes.

"You don't believe me," Trixie said.

"No, I do." She was staring off at the door, licking her lips.

"What, then?"

She turned to Trixie, as if just now noticing she was there. "I've never told anyone this," she said.

"What?"

"My miscarriage."

Trixie sipped the coffee. It was too hot, but her body came to life at the flavor. "When did you have it?"

"Before the kids were born."

"I think you may have told me about it, actually."

"No," Diane said, "not the circumstances. We were living on the second floor of an old woman's house—come to think of it, she was probably about the age I am now, but she acted *old*. She was awful, yelling up at us every time we walked across the floor or left a dish dirty for more than a few minutes, that sort of thing."

She smiled at this and drank from her coffee cup, then set it aside. "I was pregnant, about five months. One day I was sitting in this old rocking chair we had in our bedroom, trying to learn to knit, which was something I thought I was supposed to do. I was starting to feel like a fool, though. I couldn't do it. I don't have a logical mind, and all that counting . . . Anyway, I kept at it, making a mess of the yarn, and I started to feel sick. Finally I put the knitting down, but I kept feeling more and more nauseated, until it actually hurt—and I looked down and saw blood, a lot of it, and I knew the baby was lost."

"My God," Trixie said. Her own mother had miscarried the year after Schatze died. She remembered hiding under the bed in fear as her father rushed her to the hospital, and choking on the dust under there.

"I remember screaming, and the landlady coming up to yell at me. But when she saw me she ran to the doctor. She didn't have a phone, you see. I was terrified—I wasn't yet twenty and I thought I was going to die. I didn't, though.

"But the strange thing happened a few weeks later, when I was recovering. It was in the middle of the night, and I had had this dream—I can't remember it, but it was a nice one, the kind you're sorry to wake up from—but when I woke up, I was pregnant again. I mean, very pregnant, as much as I had been before."

"I don't understand," Trixie said.

"I mean I was pregnant." She shrugged. "My belly was big, and there was a baby in it, and it wanted to come out. It *kicked*. And years later, when I felt Eleanor kicking, I knew the kicking that night had been real, or had felt real. And there was this terrific, awful pressure. So I pushed."

"You pushed."

She nodded. "I just sort of knew what to do. Frank was asleep next to me and I prayed he wouldn't wake up. And after that, it was suddenly easy, not at all like Eleanor and Fred, it was easy and there was no pain. He just came out, like pulling a scarf out of a bottle. Zip! he was out."

"He?" Trixie said.

"This white baby. He just floated up out of the sheets. He was smiling in such an adult way . . . I'll tell you." She took her feet off the table and sat up straight. "He was like those medieval paintings of Christ, where He's a baby, but He's got those adult eyes, and hands and feet. You know the ones?"

"Yes."

"Like that. This white baby just kind of hovered there, and as I watched he covered up his mouth with his hand, like this"—she flattened her fingers together over her face—"and I was suddenly exhausted. It was like he had cast a spell. I felt like I had gone days without sleep. And as I was sinking, the baby just kind of . . . drifted away."

She stopped talking and sat back. Trixie was stunned. "That's it?"

"That's it. When I woke up I was fine. No blood, no nothing. We ate breakfast and Frank went to work."

"Don't you think you were dreaming?"

"No, it didn't feel that way." She touched her chin. "It's hard to explain. If it was a dream, it was a strange kind I haven't had since, where everything is very real. Oh, Trixie, it was so real. I thought I was going crazy. But after that, I could bear the loss. I was still sad, but I didn't want to kill myself. It was bearable. I felt like . . . I felt like he was safe, somehow."

"So you think . . ."

"It was a ghost? I don't know. The jury's still out on that one. My point is, it doesn't matter." She noticed her coffee with a start, as if she had forgotten, and took a sip.

"What do you mean?"

"I mean it helped me to get over what had happened. I'm saying maybe there's a parallel here. I'm also saying I believe you."

But the rest of that night, Monday, Tuesday, he didn't come again, and Trixie was left to consider what the encounter meant, left alone in a strangely empty house with her memories. For the first time she envied those who had God to turn to: these people knew what was to come if they had lived virtuous lives, had a collection of rules to turn to when things made no sense. She wondered if seeing Hamish meant that she was close to death herself; if, in fact, there was an afterlife and he was a messenger from it. A few weeks earlier, she had felt that her life, if not exactly what she'd expected, was at least settled. Now she didn't even have that.

9

She'd kept the list of names from Monday's paper and stuck the
article in her bottom left desk drawer. It felt like a betrayal. Neither had said
so, but when she and Paul made love that day it had seemed a partial reconciliation, and if she was serious about it, she would do her best to forget about
the boy. If he had triggered some need in her that Paul was unprepared to fulfill, then so be it; her marriage ought to come first.

This is what Anita told herself all afternoon Wednesday, when the teller
lines were overflowing and customers with all kinds of problems were spilling
into her office, demanding she solve them. This was not like Tuscaloosa,
where people were polite in banks. Now, a tiny, furious woman stared at her
with tired eyes behind large square eyeglasses.

"It says right here, five point five percent. You told me it'd go up that
much every day."

"You must have misunderstood," Anita told her. "You see, this is an an-
nual rate. It's compounded daily. That means it goes up gradually, see, not all
at once at the end of the year." She pointed to the print on the woman's CD
that explained this.

The woman stared at the paper for a moment, her mouth hanging open. Anita had seen this look before; it meant the customer was deciding not to believe what she'd just heard. She jabbed her finger at the print, looked up, and said, "My husband and me figured it. You owe us seven thousand, three hundred and ten dollars. That's what you told me."

"I'm afraid you're mistaken, Mrs. Leary. Do you know who you talked to when you came in to open your CD?"

"It was you!"

"It probably wasn't. I do loans, not CDs."

She looked down at the paper and back up again. "My husband just bought a brand-new car!"

"I understand your problem, but—"

She snatched the paper from the desk and stood up. "I'm sick of you people trying to rip us off! You're going to be hearing from Ted!"

"Please, Mrs. Leary . . ."

But she was already gone, stomping across the marble floor, her handbag swinging around her like a wind-whipped flag. People turned. She slammed through the door and out into the glare of the parking lot.

It was ten after four by the clock on her desk, twenty minutes until the lobby closed. The clock had been a gift from the electronics company that had installed their phone system; nobody else had wanted it. It was a five-inch Lucite cube, with the clock embedded in the middle. The cube was perfectly clear, and whenever Anita looked at it she thought of the Kreskin's Krystal she'd had as a kid—you'd swing a pendulum over the Krystal and it would tell your future. But all this clock told was the time. The clock itself was just a little plastic digital thing that she was sure would give out someday, but she was glad to have it there, blinking away, heavy and bright. There were tiny shafts that ran through the bottom of the cube to the clock, and it had come with a little metal spike you could stick in them to change the time.

When she looked up, she was surprised to find no one in the chair facing her. Except for the line to the tellers, and a young couple sitting in New Accounts, nobody was waiting. She organized her desktop, straightening the out box, brushing the dust off her desk calendar, setting the stapler and tape dispenser next to each other at an empty corner. She rearranged her dried flowers. Then finally, desperately, she opened her drawer and pulled out the newspaper article.

The paper had printed the ages of all the crash victims who had been identified, and the towns where they lived. She had recognized a lot of names, probably from the bank, and wondered if she'd notice, somewhere down the line, the absence of familiar faces. Three names were circled—all the boys between eight and thirteen who were from out of town. She copied the names onto her desk calendar, looked at the newspaper one last time, crumpled it up and threw it away.

She took out the phone book and looked up the boys' last names, then wrote down the numbers corresponding to those names in the phone book: three Huttons, five Butzes, four Rileys. Seven of these were men whose first name was definitely not Larry. There were two L's and three women.

Of course, it was very possible that the boy's last name wasn't the same as his uncle's. At least fifty percent. And there was a chance that even if it was, the uncle didn't have a listed number. She underlined L Riley, L Hutton, and the three women. Then, before she could change her mind, she dialed the first number. It rang four times, five, then an answering machine picked up. "You've reached Diane and Lloyd Riley," came a woman's voice. "Or rather, you haven't."

She hung up. It was four-thirty—most people were still at work. She crossed out L Riley and dialed L Hutton. It rang seven times. She was about to hang up when a man answered. "Hello?" He was soft-spoken, tired-sounding. He said it again: "Hello?"

She put on her business voice. "May I speak to Larry?"

"This is," he said.

"Larry Connell?"

"Oh," he said. "No, this is Larry Hutton."

"Hutton . . ." she said, feigning confusion. He sounded young.

"You must have the wrong number." And he hung up.

She set down the phone and leaned back in her chair. What were the chances that it wasn't him? It could always be another Larry entirely, somebody with a different last name, but she doubted it. It felt right.

She opened the phone book again and copied his address out of it: 2153 Keneally Drive. She knew where that was—down by the health food store, west of the Strip. There was a little neighborhood there that a lot of people didn't know about. She and Paul had found it driving around. Small houses with clean yards, and beyond it Laidlaw Creek, which ran down to the river from the southern foothills; the crummier end of the neighborhood was separated from the mall parking lot by a thin, trash-strewn line of trees. She could call him anytime now; she could get in the car and drive to his house if she wanted. It wouldn't take much to fulfill somebody's dying wish. *Tell him I'm here.* Not much at all.

That night she got a ride home and ate alone on the couch, a plate balanced on her leg. Behind her rattled the plastic garbage bags Paul had used to patch the hole, the clear plastic over the window. She watched the telephone, wondering if she should pick it up. The boy's name, according to the paper, was Sasha. She reimagined finding him, speaking his name. *Sasha,* she says, *it'll be all right. You know my name,* he says. And Anita touches his face, the side that still looks like a boy's face, and says, Shhhh.

It was just after eight when she heard the doorknob turn. She considered getting up to greet him. It was her duty, wasn't it, to get up and do that? But she didn't. She couldn't shake the irrational feeling that everything that had happened was somehow Paul's fault—the crash, Sasha's death, the chaos of the aftermath. She set her empty dish aside, crossed her arms, and waited, watching the kitchen through the doorway.

She heard footsteps, and Paul passed the doorway. He looked like he was carrying something bulky, like groceries, in his arms, and she was about to call out and thank him for shopping—immediately she felt like a heel for being angry at him—when it occurred to her that the man who'd come in was not Paul at all. He was too short and his hair was curly and darker than Paul's. And he was fat. That was a belly he was carrying. She surprised herself with how angry this made her. They were being robbed. Then she heard the refrigerator door suck open and the bottles rattle on the door.

He's *eating?* she thought. He broke in for something to *eat?* She heard the man grunt, and items move around on the shelves; then the door shut and she heard a plate being set on the table. There was a distinct crinkle of plastic wrap. She was wondering whether to announce herself or not—what if he had a gun?—when he stepped into the living room, a cold chicken drumstick in each hand and his lips slick with grease. He was around sixty and wore a pair of khaki pants and a white shirt, both filthy. He sucked in breath and Anita let out a yelp, and in the silence that followed, the man's eyes bulged and he dropped the chicken.

He was choking. He struck his ribs with his fist, and his face worked with the effort to find muscles that didn't exist deep inside his chest. I could let him die, she thought. It would be easy. But before she had even completed the thought, she leaped to her feet and grabbed him from behind. She made a fist with both hands just below his rib cage, and yanked. The man made a weak gagging sound. She yanked again. This time a chunk of chicken flew from his mouth and landed wetly on the floor. She let him go, and he staggered around, coughing. He doubled over in the corner and took two, three deep and ragged breaths, then collapsed onto the couch, his face gleaming and red and dripping with sweat.

"*Grazie,*" he said.

"What in hell are you doing in my house?" Anita yelled. The man looked at her another second, then turned away, wiping his face with his hand. She bent over and picked up her plate and the fallen drumsticks, then put them in the kitchen. She cleaned up the food he had choked on with a wad of paper towels. When she came back to the living room, he was still breathing heavily, and she stood in the middle of the room, her hands on her hips, watching him.

"Come on. What are you doing here?"

He shrugged and crossed his legs, then laid his hands down over his knee. It was an easy, elegant gesture, like draping a coat over the edge of a chair. He smiled weakly. "I am Bernardo," he said. He had some sort of accent.

"Oh, that explains everything," she said.

"I am hungry." He shrugged again.

"What are you doing out here? We're in the middle of nowhere." She looked out the window at the police tape, flapping in the breeze. "You came to look at the crash, didn't you?"

He nodded, uncrossed his legs and smoothed out his pants. It was a ridiculous gesture. They were covered with stains. She shook her head, then went to the kitchen and brought back a folding chair. She set it directly in front of him and sat down. "Where do you live? Do you live in town?"

"Ah . . . no," he said.

"Where do you come from?" She spoke each word distinctly.

"Italy."

"When?"

He paused, and his eyes glazed over for a moment. He was thinking his way around the question. "A couple months. I come for business, but it is no good." A lie. She noticed that he was wearing scuffed loafers and thin white socks that had been torn.

"So where have you been staying?"

He pointed behind him with his thumb. "In the woods. Like you say, I see the plane, and I stay up on the hill."

"And you've been eating what, bark?"

He shook his head and pointed toward the kitchen.

Anita turned, then looked back at him. "You've been eating *here?*"

"No car, I go in. But you are here anyway."

"Yeah, here I am." She sighed. "Look, I'll be honest with you. I can't give you much. This is a lousy time for my husband and me."

He nodded.

"And we don't have time for you, frankly." She stood up. "I can offer you a shower and something to eat. Then you're out of here, all right?"

He nodded, surprised. "Yes."

"You're awfully polite, for a thief."

"I only have . . . bad luck." He crossed his arms and leveled her a gaze that seemed almost a challenge. She didn't take it.

"The bathroom's in here, off the kitchen. And I can wash those clothes for you."

He had no answer to this, and she left the room to get his towel.

He undressed in the bathroom and handed out his clothes. As she carried them to the washer, she noticed that the shirt was made of silk. She also noticed that it didn't look like he'd been wearing it for months. Of course, he could have gotten it anywhere. His heavy steps echoed in the bathroom and she heard the water go on.

When Paul came home, Bernardo was still in the shower and Anita sat at the kitchen table with a magazine. He looked weary and disheveled and slumped into a seat across from her.

"Hi," she said.

"Hey. What a day."

"Do tell."

"Oh, you know. I watched this guy, and after that I followed him, and I got to see him buying pot from a hippie kid out of the back of his VW. I got pictures and everything. It's all very exciting."

"So what now?"

He shrugged. "I don't know what Ponty's going to do with the pictures. Give them to whoever hired us, I guess. He said I did a good job." Paul smiled, and for a moment she warmed to him again. It was good to see him taking pleasure in something, anything.

"I mean, what now for you?"

"Oh, nothing."

"So I can have the car back tomorrow."

"Sure." His face clouded suddenly and he blushed. "Oh, no. I do have something I have to do."

"What is it?"

He stood up and went to the sink, where he filled up a glass of water. "Oh, nothing. Just another little job I'm supposed to be doing."

She could tell he was lying. He leaned against the counter, drank and looked at the floor. Then he looked up again. "Hey, who's in the shower?"

"Another man."

He grinned a little, but uncomfortably, as if he were in on the joke. "Yeah," he said, "so it was a very interesting day. I sort of like the job, which—"

"Don't you have any reaction to that?"

"What?"

"There's another man in the shower."

He turned toward the bathroom door and squinted at it. "Well, you were kidding, right? You're flattening some pants or something?"

"I'm *what*?"

"You know, flattening stuff. With the steam. I've seen you do that." Then the water went off, and the sound of two footsteps—thud, thud—drifted into the kitchen.

"Hello?" Bernardo said. "Hello? You have my clothes?"

"There's a robe on the back of the door," Anita called out to him. "Put that on."

"That's my robe," Paul said, astonished. "Who's the guy?"

"This guy," she told him. "He just walked in and stole some food. I caught him. I told him he could take a shower."

Paul's eyes narrowed. He looked at the bathroom and back at her. He brushed his hair out of his face.

"You need a haircut," she said.

Bernardo's face appeared in the doorway. He looked at Paul first, then found Anita. "My clothes not finished?" His eyebrows were close-set and thick, and his wet hair lay flat on his head.

"No. Take the robe."

"A little small." He closed the door and she heard him fumbling behind it. Then he stepped out. The robe barely covered his belly, and he stood before them like a great plush toy, clearing his throat.

"Hello," Paul said.

"I am Bernardo." He made a little bow, and turned to Anita. "You don't tell me your name?"

"Anita."

"Anita," he said, as if it were the name of some delicious food he hadn't eaten in a long, long time. "Thank you very much." He cleared his throat again and raised his eyebrows at Anita. "You say I can eat?"

"Help yourself," she said. "You know where it is."

They set him up on the couch for the night with a couple of pillows and a blanket. Anita left their bedroom door open a crack in case he thought to walk off with anything. He had repeated his story for Paul—came to America a few months before for a business deal that fell through and had been hanging around Marshall ever since, looking for work, finding food where and when he could—and now she asked him what he thought the real story was.

"What," he whispered, "you think he's lying?"

"Of course he's lying. Somebody who doesn't have anything to eat doesn't just walk out here to look at a plane crash."

"Oh, I don't know . . ."

"You're too trusting," she said. "It doesn't make any sense."

"It's not a matter of trust." He turned over on his back, and in the moonlight folded his hands behind his head. "It's just that I've seen some weird stuff, is all."

"Oh, sure," she said.

He didn't speak for a moment, and she thought he might let it go. Then he said, "What's that supposed to mean?"

man was waiting outside and she held the door for him as he tottered in. The old man entered the roped-off teller line at the far end, and followed its labyrinthine path to the front. Two tellers were talking to each other and didn't notice him. Kathy called him over to her window and shot the tellers a look.

Anita picked up the phone and brought it to her ear. The dial tone was grating and unnerving, and she found herself searching her desk calendar for Larry Hutton's number. Then she found herself dialing it. After the first ring, she panicked, took the receiver away from her ear, and held it over the cradle. She heard the second ring tinnily, from two feet away. Then she brought the receiver back to her ear again. Someone picked up.

"Hello?"

I could still hang up, she thought. It isn't too late to hang up.

"Hello?"

"Is this Larry Hutton?"

"Yes."

"Mr. Hutton, this is Anita Beveridge. I'm calling from First Marshall Bank."

"Yes?"

"I'm calling . . . I'm calling about Sasha."

Immediately the line went quiet. "Mr. Hutton?"

"What do you want?" He was angry now. "I just got back from the kid's funeral."

"It's not . . . I'm very sorry. It's not bank business. It's me. This is a personal call."

"I don't think I'm interested in hearing what you have to say," he said.

"Wait, please, I . . . Mr. Hutton, I live on Valley Road, where the crash happened. I was with Sasha. When he died."

Again, nothing. She heard him breathing on the other end, and went on. "I was outside when the plane crashed. My husband and I saw it. We ran . . . I ran into the woods, and he was the first person I saw. He was alive. I . . . he talked to me."

"He was *alive*?"

"Yes, he—"

"Jesus Christ!" he said. "They said it was immediate! They told me everybody . . ."

"They didn't know. I didn't tell them. I'm really sorry." When he didn't respond, she added, "He told me about you. He said I should tell you he was here."

"Oh, God," he said quietly.

Her vision had begun to blur, and when she brought her hand to her face she found tears. She pulled some tissues from a drawer and pressed them to her eyes. "Look," she said, "I want to meet you. Let me buy you lunch."

"No, I don't think so."

"Really, it's on me."

"I think I just want to stay home. It's been a long week." And then, suddenly, he changed his mind. "No, no," he said, "I'll go. I'll go. I want . . . I ought to know more, I guess."

"There isn't much more."

"Whatever."

"Are you sure?"

"Yeah. This afternoon?"

They made plans to meet at the coffee shop on Weir, the one she'd gone to the morning after the crash. She told him what she looked like, and he wrote it down. When she put the phone down, she looked up to find Kathy, behind her teller window, staring at her.

He was late. She drank all of a cup of weak coffee and picked at her lip. If she had her choice, she thought, she would go back and undo their move to Montana entirely, stay at the bank in Tuscaloosa, save up for a house. Maybe there, where Paul at least knew his way around, he would have wanted a baby. Maybe it was the weather here, the land that cultivated his apprehension: unforgiving snow and dry air, every beauty an intimidation, every wild-flower brittle and covered with spines. She looked out at the mountains the river passed between: there they were, keeping an eye on everyone. No wonder people were suspicious.

She and Paul simply weren't taking here, like his garden. Every spring she told herself that the summer would make all the difference, that it would take off the chill she felt year-round, would ease the fatigue she got from hunkering down. But here it was, almost September, and she felt no different. Either they would have to tolerate the dank desiccation of this place another year, or they would have to go someplace else, home maybe. Paul would say it wasn't home anymore, but neither was this.

"Hello?"

He was standing before her, a serious-looking dark-haired man with rimless eyeglasses and a high forehead. He had a tan and a flannel shirt, which he wore fully buttoned and tucked into his pants, as if it were a dress shirt. "Are you Anita?"

"Mr. Hutton." She half stood and he waved her down. "Larry," he said and pulled out a chair.

When they had settled themselves, he said, "Well. I was expecting somebody older." He was probably about thirty-five, and he sat very, very still. She imagined she could see a little of Sasha in him, something in th sharpness of the nose, and the recollection made her look, automatically, a

"I want to thank you for coming," he said. "I was the phone. But he meant a lot to me, Sasha did." He r and spread it open on the table before him. "I want you t you can."

"Sure," she said. "There isn't much."

He nodded. "I understand." He ran his hand absently over the menu, as if it were in Braille. It was a thin, dignified hand, scarred, she guessed, from work. "He was my brother Arthur's kid. He and his wife . . . they've been having problems. They were going to try and work things out, you know, and I had told Sasha he could visit anytime. So he was going to come out here for a couple of weeks. They got him off school for it."

"I'm so sorry."

"Well," he said. "I was in Bellevue for the funeral." He shook his head. "I think they're done for, after this."

"Oh."

He managed a sad smile. "Why don't we get something to eat?"

They ordered sandwiches, and she found herself staring at him as he ate: he moved like a spy, bringing the food to his lips with strange precision and economy. He dabbed his lips after every bite with a purposeful manner that didn't seem, to her surprise, even slightly artificial. It embarrassed her to eat in his presence. When they finished, they sipped coffee and stole nervous glances at one another, until finally she took a deep breath and began talking. She stared at the tabletop as she told him, and her fingers clenched around a balled-up napkin, which she squeezed each time she thought she might cry.

When she was finished, she looked up and was shocked to find his face full of sympathy. He looked like he was about to reach out and gather her into his arms.

"I'm so sorry," he whispered.

"Oh, well . . ."

"No, please, it must have been awful. I . . . I can't thank you enough. For staying with him through it. Most people would have run."

"I don't think so."

"Well," he said, "it was a good thing, what you did." He wiped his face with a napkin. "It was the best you could do. I hope you understand that."

She nodded. Relief was spreading inside her. Of course! I did my best! This wasn't something Paul ever had bothered to tell her, had even bothered, she guessed, to notice. She'd done all she could.

When they parted it was as if they were old friends. Who hugged whom was unclear—she thought it was Larry who first leaned toward her, but something in her stance could have been asking him to. His body was slender, like Paul's, but there was substance to it, something surprising and alive when she pressed herself to it.

"We should get together again," he said.

"Sure."

"I'll call you at the bank."

Sure, sure, she was thinking, why not? Of course he must have seen her wedding ring, of course he wasn't getting any ideas. This is what she told herself on the way back to the office, when on the bridge the breeze from the canyon threatened to lift her into the air and set her adrift in the river: of course everything will be fine now, everything will be fine.

10

Every day that he woke on the rock outcropping, Bernardo sat bolt upright, terrified, unsure of what happened to him or where he was. It was as if this place was a nightmare he kept dropping into from the sleep of his real life, though what that real life consisted of, or where it had gone, was a mystery to him.

He had spent afternoons in the sun, looking down on the plane and the house and the tireless search-and-rescue operations, slowly working the soreness out of his body. For a couple of days he hadn't eaten anything but foraged sour berries, so crowded was the yard, so awful the pain in his muscles. But once the people began to clear away, he was able to sneak into the house and take what he wanted. It was easy. They never locked the door, and the refrigerator and cabinets were always full of things to eat. He brought them up here, to his hideout, and tried to find a pattern in the mess he'd made of things, a signpost that would tell him what to do next.

If the American movies he'd seen were any indication, it would be unwise to make himself known. He had lost his passport, and for all he knew, they still shot each other for no particular reason in the West. Surely the airline presumed him dead, and if he appeared, announcing he'd been in the crash, they'd probably interrogate him about what happened and then throw him in jail for a lunatic. He'd be found out, deported.

The obvious solution was to find Antonio. It wouldn't be hard. He had lost the phone number, but there was the town, off in the distance; all he had to do was go down to the road and walk along it, then look for his son in a telephone book. And though this increasingly seemed like a bad idea, though he recalled with greater and greater intensity that it wasn't coincidence that drove his son away from him, certainly that is what he had to do, sooner or later.

But right now he was a dead man, and this vantage point much like his imagined heaven: high, clear, uncomplicated. The problem was that he didn't belong here: he belonged down there, with the real dead, carried in pieces to a waiting ambulance. Until he was caught by the people in the house, he'd had plenty of time to consider this, to wonder what it meant. Now he could only do what he'd dismissed as foolishness years ago: pray.

Maria hadn't liked Bernardo's mother; for that matter, neither had he. She was an irreligious woman who wielded religion only when it was morally convenient. She had a deep klaxon of a voice, which she employed in issuing endless commands, and Maria steadfastly refused to help Bernardo obey them. Mona was the last thing he attended to before he left for the market, and the first when he returned. And now that he had a son, Bernardo found himself stopping home several times a day on errands for Maria: lotions and groceries and unfathomable baby things. Generally on these errands he would come in reeking of meat and sweat to find his frosty wife pacing in the kitchen, and the shrill cries of his mother echoing in the back of the house: *Bernardo, potete venire qui?*—sarcastic and loud.

Mona's room was hung with acres of home-woven lace curtains, pillowcases, linens and tapestries, all white. She lay in bed in the middle of it, skinny and pale, her sewing laid out around her like surgical instruments. The room was immaculate but had the dusty, sour smell of sedentary skin and hair and bone. "Bernardo," she would say to him, "that woman is trying to take over my house."

"She lives here, Mama. We need the room for the baby."

"It's my house! I should kick you out on the street!"

"Mama—"

"Get her out! Get her out!"

His mother wasn't even old—younger than Bernardo was now—but she had taken on, unaccountably, the obstinacy of the ancient and infirm. He could feel his bones go to rubber at the sound of her screams, and Maria had little sympathy for him and his inability to stand up to her. Looking back, he felt like he had spent every waking moment smoothing out the battles between the two women, and fallen to sleep every night exhausted, Maria's back to him across an expanse of empty sheet.

He had married too quickly, that was for sure, and he and Maria were proving incompatible. Talking to her, trying to get at the source of her dissatisfaction, he learned that she saw marriage as an escape from her own crowded family home and its dreary obligations. She thought that being married would make her free, like it did in the movies, but living in Mona's house she felt less free than she ever had.

"Let's live in an apartment," she said one night. "Just you and me and the baby." They were cleaning up the market after closing, Antonio asleep in the back room. This was when she could still enjoy helping him with the business, before she had come to realize their entire life might be played out here, in the service of strangers. "We need some time alone, Bernardo. Even when we're in bed, I can feel her there, listening."

"She needs me," he told her. Outside, the voices of young men echoed in the street, and a girl's voice answered from somewhere, distant and sweet. "I can't just leave."

"Go see her for an hour or two a day."

"I don't know."

"Hire a nurse! Do something!" She had been wiping the counter, calling across the room to him where he swept, and now she put the rag down and came to him. "Bernardo. Who's more important to you, me or her?"

"It isn't like that. It's not a matter of more or less important."

"Sure it is." She grabbed the broom from him. "I married *you*," she said. "Not her."

"*You* are, then. It's just that she's my mother."

Her eyes grew fiery, but then, suddenly, she gave up. She deflated like an old tire, hung her head, handed back the broom.

"I'll talk to her," he said as she walked back to the counter. "I'll tell her we want to move."

"She'll only get angry."

"Maybe not."

The next day he pulled a chair to the foot of his mother's bed, and asked her to let them move out. Mona had a stony, angular face, but before all the words had left his mouth her face went slack and soft as a rotting pumpkin and tears began to well in her eyes. "Okay," she said, groping for a handkerchief. "Fine, you go."

"Mama . . ."

"No, abandon your mother, I don't care. I can be alone. I've been alone before. Not while your father was alive, of course—your father would never have abandoned me, but you, you're something different entirely."

So they stayed. Bernardo would later see this as the moment when they gave up on their ambitions of independence and ease, when the old lady finally beat them. But now he only scrambled for an angle, a way to make this latest disappointment into a trifle.

He went to the kitchen, where Maria was waiting, and understood there was no reassurance, no platitude that could pacify her. Her face was a dull cipher, a grim mirror of his sleeping son's. Of course she had heard everything. And then, strangely enough, he saw only evidence of Maria in Antonio; his tiny fists seemed loaded with her defiance, his face weighted down with her defeat. Bernardo's own features were nowhere to be found.

He dozed on a rock for a while, and dreamed the plane had landed safely in the forest. It tumbled violently in the air, just like it had during the crash, but the passengers were perfectly calm. When they touched down, gently as a fallen leaf, the door opened into the trees, and outside stood crowds of happy people, greeting their loved ones, shaking hands and hugging and kissing. As the plane emptied, people walked off in different directions, disappearing into the woods. Soon they were all gone, and Bernardo found himself alone with the plane, a charred hulk already overgrown with weeds and grass.

He woke to the sound of his name, among markedly different shadows. It was afternoon. He sat up and looked around, but saw no one. Then he heard his name again, from far away. Below him, in the yard of the house, stood the blond-haired man. He was peering into the woods. He brought his hands to his mouth and put them down again, and a second later Bernardo heard his name a third time.

"Hello!" he called out from the rock. Paul leaned farther toward the trees, facing the wrong direction.

"Come out!" he called.

Bernardo considered a moment, then began to make his way down the hill. Dirt and stones got into his shoes, and he stopped several times to empty them. Once or twice he heard Paul call to him again, and when he got out of the woods Paul was still standing where he had been, in the middle of the yard, looking up at the hills.

"Hello!" Bernardo said.

"Hi." Paul walked across the yard to meet him. He seemed uncomfortable with the sunlight and walked shading his eyes. When they met he stuck out his hand.

"I didn't really get to talk to you," he said. "It's Paul, remember?"

"Ah. Well. Happy to meet you."

Paul nodded, and pointed over at the hole in the house. "Anita said you could fix that?"

"Oh, yes. The other, too." He gestured toward the shed.

He nodded again. "Well, you know, I've gotta talk her into it . . ."

"Yes?"

"I think you ought to do it. I mean, you need the work, right? And we're pretty busy. So . . ."

"I work slow. But a good job. In Italy, I fix my market."

"Oh!" Paul said. "So that was what you did. You had a market." He crossed his arms over his chest. "Is that what you came here to do?"

"Ah, yes."

"But it didn't work out."

"No."

Paul shook his head. "Yeah, I hear you."

He looked over Bernardo's shoulder into the trees and seemed to get lost there for a moment. Bernardo wondered what, if anything, to say now. He didn't imagine this would go over at all well with the wife.

"Well," he said. "We go look? At the house? Probably you need wood . . ."

"Oh, yeah. Sure."

They walked toward the house, skirting what looked like the remains of a large vegetable garden. A strip of gouged earth led to the airplane engine lying just beyond the treeline. Paul shook his head when he saw Bernardo looking at it. "You'd think they'd come and take that away," he said.

Bernardo had been thinking nothing of the sort. In Italy, the engine would probably stay there forever, disintegrating. When they reached the house, he could see that the damage wasn't as bad as it might have been; the window had shattered, but the frame wasn't crushed. The engine had sheared the corner off more cleanly than he would have thought possible. He shuddered to think of how fast it must have fallen to do this, how fast the plane too must have fallen. And the trough it made in the yard was deep enough to bury a body in. His stomach began to seize up. That he had survived seemed beyond comprehension.

"What do you think?" Paul asked.

"Well. You need new roof. Also the wall?"

"Hmm."

"And the window."

Paul frowned. He looked defeated. "Sounds expensive."

"Not so bad."

"No?"

"Well," Bernardo said. He looked around at the trees. "I do not know the cost of wood. But . . ."

"Maybe we can go to the lumberyard later and get the stuff we need."

"But your wife . . ."

He shrugged. "I gotta pick her up at work pretty soon. Depending on what kind of day she's having, maybe I can talk her into it. You never know."

"Work."

"Works at a bank." He grinned. "And I just started a new job myself. Private eye. Well, assistant to one."

"Like in the movies."

"Sort of," Paul said. "Not so exciting, I guess."

"So today you do this?"

Paul frowned. "Not exactly. Well, sort of, I guess."

For awhile, they talked about detective movies. *The Big Sleep, Chinatown.* Paul mentioned *Double Indemnity.* "Ah!" Bernardo told him. "This is my favorite."

Soon they sat at the kitchen table, making a list of what they'd need on a paper napkin. Bernardo found himself slightly put off by Paul's enthusiasm. There was something blind and unseemly about it, as if the enthusiasm wasn't for the thing at all but the fact that they had it to do. Did he think his wife would change her mind about letting this stranger into her life? Bernardo was certain she wouldn't, especially now that Paul had simply gone against her wishes and asked him to stay anyway. He could smell a bad marriage from a mile away.

Paul picked up his keys. "I'll get us a few things," he said, walking toward the door. "Why don't you go check out the shed? See what we can salvage."

"You have . . . tools?"

"Uh, yeah. They were in the shed."

"Ah."

When Paul had gone (leaving him in the house, to his surprise), Bernardo rummaged in the refrigerator and found some cheese, which he ate. He walked around the house, snooping. Their bedroom, for all its rustic simplicity, was strangely antiseptic, the walls devoid of photos or art, the bed covered by a plain gray quilted bedspread.

The bed. He sat down on the edge, testing, then lay back. It felt like months, though he'd been in his own bed in Italy only a week ago. This mattress was the way he liked them, just a bit resistant, as if to remind you of your own body. It was like Paula's—the sort of bed you wanted to be in with a lover, when awareness of the body was the point, and rest secondary.

For years he'd never visited that bed at night. He and Paula took their lunches at her apartment in the afternoons—a cup of coffee and a snack, and often love, when they wanted. There was no pressure; for both of them, obligations were elsewhere—for him, with his wife and mother and son; for her, with her art. It was only tenderness they relied on each other for, and in that each found the other generous and dependable.

Maria's illness had brought them together. By this time Bernardo had come to hate his wife in a familiar way. She complained she was like a slave to his business; he thought her expectations of him were too high, that she only felt she needed *things* because she hadn't accomplished anything herself. Divorce was out of the question. They still ate dinner at the same table, with Antonio, by now a brooding ten-year-old; they still slept in the same bed.

Then she began to grow thin. At first it stirred in him a new desire; it reminded him of the way she looked when they courted—slender and dark, with dim circles under her eyes. For some months they even made love again and spoke to each other when they didn't need to, for pleasure. And then one day she fainted in the market from pain and was diagnosed with an inoperable cancer—something they both secretly expected. She went to bed and grew worse. In her pain she needed more from him, and the competition between her and Mona intensified; each bossed the boy around and criticized Bernardo for his attention to the other. And their pain, he knew, was great, and this knowledge racked him with guilt when he thought about hating them, which was often. He hired someone new at the market to take Maria's place. This was Paula.

They fell into their romance easily. She was a painter, a realist, not at all bad, though she had the frumpy clothes and dull features of a housekeeper instead of the artist's Bohemian affect. Her body was round and farmy, and its solidness held a particular appeal for Bernardo, whose home was haunted by near-ghosts. He fed her, and she taught him how to draw and paint.

But later, after Mona and Maria had died and Antonio had left for America, things changed between them. Without any obstacles to something deeper, they began to drift together more often and under new circumstances, spending nights in each other's beds, dining out. Somehow, though, it felt forced. Much of the time they both wanted to be alone, and neither of them welcomed the change of pace that extra contact brought. Before long they had returned to their old habits, and that didn't feel right either; what was once necessity now seemed selfish. It took some time for them to adjust to this new revelation: that they were two adults who preferred distance.

And then, just recently, things changed again: Paula began to want more. Bernardo was wary. Her desire was to him a kind of flattery, and his immediate impulse was to give in to it. But something held him back: a strange portent of catastrophe, as if to give himself to her in any deeper way might mean the end of them both.

She finally proposed it a few months ago, while they lay awake in bed. She would sell her apartment and move into his house. "It's big and empty," she told him. "We could be near one another."

"We're already near," he said, hoping to defuse the situation. He hugged her to him.

"You know what I mean. Bernardo, we're *old*. Admit it, this is it for us."

He shrugged. "So why not keep it as it is?"

"Because I'm afraid we'll be lonely," she said after some thought. "That if we live apart like this for much longer, we won't know how to stop. I'm afraid of the day when it will be as easy for you to stay home without me as it will be to come be near me." She took a breath. "I'm afraid I'll get that way too."

"So then everything will be as it should. We'll do what we want."

She turned over and took his face in her hands. "Is that really what you want?"

"Not now, no. Of course not."

"Because if that's what you want—for our love to just wear away to nothing—then leave me now. I don't want to see us do that to each other."

"Paula!"

"No! Better to go out with a bang!"

"I don't want that," he said. "You know that. But what makes you think that will happen? Unless you think something's wrong now . . ."

"No, there's nothing *wrong*. It's just . . . we've been through a lot together, but we've never been obliged to do anything, not once . . ."

"And we've been happy."

"Yes, so far. But soon . . ." She shrugged.

"Soon what?"

"Soon we might not be able to get around so well. Or we'll get sick. I want us to trust each other to be around for that. I want you to know I'll be there for you."

"Ah," he said. "You mean *you* want to know *I* will. You mean you don't trust me."

She sighed. "I do trust you, as far as I've needed to. But as for the future . . ."

"Yes?"

"I want a promise," she said. "I need this from you, Bernardo. I want you to rise to the challenge." She sat up, the sheets tumbling off her like the unveiling of a monument. "I challenge you to invite me into your life."

He gave it a moment's consideration, though now—with the business in flux, and his hardest years, he hoped, behind him—now the idea made him terribly weary.

"I'll think about it," he said.

"You will."

"Yes, I will."

Of course all of that was meaningless now. For two months, he said nothing of that conversation, and their lives went on as usual, intersecting whenever it was convenient or desirable. And then, in the last few days, when the market burned, he panicked and didn't speak to her at all.

It was a mistake, all of it. There was a lot in his life he would like to have erased, a lot of bad decisions he'd like to have the chance to make again. But all he wanted now was not to have run away, to have instead run to her and made something of a life together. Of course it was too late to go back. He tried to imagine himself a year from now, two at the most, established in America doing . . . something. Would she give up her life and come live with him?

No. She owed him nothing, and he hadn't found the courage, when it counted, to give her his life—or his death, which now would come to him in a strange country, perhaps alone. At long last, he understood what a fool he was.

He gripped the sides of Paul and Anita's mattress as if it were a rowboat tossed by storm, and he let misery wash over him, bitter and worthless as the waves, and as cold.

Outside, he poked through the boards that used to be the tool-shed. It hadn't been terrifically strong to begin with—the walls were cheap plywood that had nearly rotted through in places, and the studs had simply been set in holes, no cement. He pushed aside a few planks and discovered a capsized workbench littered with loose tools. He found a hammer and a hand-saw, and a flattened cardboard box spilling nails.

There were also garden tools—a hoe and a shovel, the handle of each snapped off at the base, and a dirt rake. In a bent plastic bin were some hand tools, a tiny spade and a weeding hoe. The ruined patch at the edge of the yard had indeed been a garden, and he wondered why they dug it so far from the house, in the shade of trees. Probably simple ineptitude. He had a momentary flash of irritation—people shouldn't undertake things they knew nothing about. But who was he to criticize? He was hungry again and the sun was hot, and he decided to go back inside.

It was there, his head suddenly clear in the quiet and cool of the house, that it occurred to him for the first time that he was a bad man. Not just a fail-ure, or a rube, but a truly bad man, selfish and cruel, and rotten luck to any-one he touched. So terrible that he pushed away his son and his lover, that he drove his parents and wife to early graves. And hadn't he gotten an inkling of this on the hill, looking down on the ruins of the plane the way a murderer might stand for a moment over his victim, savoring the awful simplicity of killing, the finality of it?

He reeled, and caught himself against a kitchen chair. He was worse than a murderer, who, if nothing else, had the gun or the knife to believe in— Bernardo believed in nothing, trusted no one. He was useless and alone in the world.

He collapsed into the chair, lowered his head onto his folded arms and finally cried, the rough grain of the table blurring before him like the bars of a cell. For long minutes, there were only the tears and the incessant heave of his body, and slowly these things brought him back to earth. He felt the table under his fingers and the floor under his shoes, and his hunger, which always returned to him, no matter how miserable the circumstances. And soon enough he felt like himself again, a small, wrung-out version of himself that he could bear to inhabit, and he got up from the chair and breathed deep, thankful breaths.

That was when he thought to make them dinner. Anita was bound to be angry when she got home, and most people found it hard to maintain their anger when there was a plate of food in front of them. If he was going to get himself together, to make some sort of life, he would have to start here. Anita and Paul, for better or worse, were the only thing he had.

He looked through the kitchen cabinets. They had a lot of things in cans. He found dry pasta, tomatoes, a bottle of olive oil crusted stickily over with dust. Some flour in a plastic container, a few packets of yeast in the refrigerator. The ingredients began falling into place in his imagination, in their familiar way. If nothing else, he at least had a way with food. There were worse things to be good at.

When he heard the car pull up, he had a *focaccia* baking in the oven, flavored with sage he'd found growing outside, and a pot of what he considered passable tomato sauce, all things considered, bubbling on the stove. He felt, to his surprise, almost useful, a little less far from content.

Then the door swung open, and Anita said, "You!"

"Hello . . ."

"Get out of here! I told you to get out!" She tossed her briefcase onto the table, where it landed with a deafening clap, and pushed him away from the stove. "What are you doing!" she said. "You're *cooking*!"

He held up his hands. "Paul—he asks me . . ."

"Paul!" Her face was struggling; it twitched like a piece of frying bacon. "Paul?" She turned.

"I didn't ask her yet," he said ruefully as he came in. Bernardo could see the car through the door, spilling over with lumber.

"Ask me what?"

"I told him . . . I said I'd see if you'd reconsider . . ." He made a defeated gesture with his arm toward the corner of the house. "I'm so bad with fixing stuff. We could use the help."

"Oh, for Christ's sake."

"*Mi dispiace,*" Bernardo said. "I make you food . . ."

She turned on him, but her eyes fell to the oven. "The oven's on."

"I bake bread."

She shook her head. "I can't believe you left him in the house," she told the floor.

"You made food?" Paul said.

Bernardo looked at him, then at her. "Spaghetti. Tomato sauce. *Focaccia.*" He leaned toward the oven and opened the door. The smell of sage filled the air. "No problem."

"Mmm," Paul said.

"Paul." Anita was glaring at him now.

"What!"

"Outside," she said, shaking her head. She leveled a finger at Bernardo as she left. "Don't touch anything." He raised his hands to indicate he understood.

He watched them through the window. Paul had his hands shoved deep into his pockets and his head down. His hair cascaded over his shoulders, obscuring his face. Anita, her arms pistoning before her, seemed to be doing most of the talking. Bernardo's water had come to a boil, and he automatically dumped the pasta into it and began to stir.

When the door opened again, Anita walked through the kitchen without a word, and Paul followed her, plodding, into the bedroom.

"Pretty soon you eat," Bernardo informed him as he passed.

"Okay."

He remembered where he had seen the dishes and took out three matching ones, then found some silverware in a drawer. He listened to the grudging, negotiating mutter of the voices in the next room but could make nothing out. In another drawer he found a grimy pair of votive candles, and he lit these and set them on a small plate. He was filling glasses with water when Paul came out.

"Hey," Paul said, his eyes wide at the sight of the table. He solemnly took a seat. Anita appeared in the doorway and stood very still for a moment, staring at the candles as if she'd never seen them before.

Bernardo served the dinner. It smelled good after those days of foraging and stolen leftovers. Paul took the first bites, and Bernardo was pleased to see the sudden light it brought to his face; Anita said nothing, but ate anyway, her eyes locked on her plate.

They had nearly finished when she looked up and said, "Get the shed up as soon as you can. You can sleep there until you're finished with the rest."

This did not produce the effect he thought it would on Paul—a relieved, victorious grin. Instead, Paul hung his head again, as if he had just heard a papal decree. Bernardo found himself getting a little angry—*I need no favors!* he thought to announce, but of course he did need them, desperately—and managed a mumbled thanks.

"This is pretty good," she added, as an afterthought.

"Yeah," Paul said, and she glared at him. He went on, more quietly: "After dinner, we can get the wood out of the car."

"Good," Bernardo said. And this was what he wanted, wasn't it? To buy time, to keep himself in food and under a roof until he could figure out what to do next. But something had changed between Paul and his wife; suddenly they were careful, as if they'd only now noticed that something had come between them. Bernardo felt like he had tripped a silent alarm.

They finished eating in silence, and he gathered the dishes. Then, without a word, Paul beckoned him to the car, where he would get to work building himself a new home.

11

Three weeks later they had rebuilt the shed and were well into replacing the corner of the house. The new studs and joists stuck out palely like the bones of a half-carved turkey, and they had bought wood siding and salvaged the old insulation in anticipation of finishing the wall. The work had gone well, if slowly; Paul found himself increasingly busy working for Ponty. For several days he had posed as a college student to track down a kid who had vanished. He found the kid holed up, paranoid, in the bowels of the University dining hall, where he'd been stealing food and running heroin out the loading dock door at night. Paul was stunned at how easily he passed for a college student. None of the kid's confidants ever questioned his intentions; they only took a quick look at his long hair and longshoreman's cap, his baggy pants (which he'd gotten at a junk shop for a buck), and decided he was okay to talk to. It amazed him how guileless these students all were, and amazed him even further how much the paranoid kid reminded him of himself—the perpetually stoned Tuscaloosa version of himself, the one who partied through his father's death and burial without having heard a thing about it. He pitied the kid terribly, and with a little guilt, as if he had no right.

Another case was simple surveillance. He was supposed to watch a young woman from outside her apartment, and take unusually detailed notes. He had picked up the woman's photograph and some other particulars from a rich lady who lived on a ranch outside town. The rich lady had to be about eighty. Her face was heavily made up, and she wore a fringed rodeo shirt and spurs on her boots indoors. She smoked Marlboros through a plastic holder. Paul could gain little insight into why she wanted this younger woman followed, but he expected a lot of driving around, a lot of slipping into the darkest corners of bars, a lot of intrigue.

Instead, the young woman stayed home every night. Paul usually showed up around five, and watched her come home from work, cook some food, read the newspaper, and wash the dishes. She was about thirty, bespectacled, plump; she never had friends over and spent most of her nights looking at magazines and watching television. One night he was thrilled to see her come out and walk to her car; he followed her to a movie theater, where he sat three rows behind her. She watched the movie alone. It wasn't very good. Then she went home.

He learned to bring along things to read and eat, and a tiny flashlight. On his last night, he was munching on a bag of crackers when he heard a phone ring. He looked up at the window and saw the woman walk out of sight to get it; a moment later she reappeared at the window, the receiver cradled between her head and shoulder, and peered out into the dark. Paul ducked, but he was sure he'd been seen. When he heard a door slam, he fumbled in the glovebox and pulled out the owner's manual to the car, which he opened to a random page. The woman appeared at the car window.

"Hi," she said.

"I'm having some car trouble," Paul told her. "I think I've blown a fuse or something."

"I know who you are. Grandmother called to make sure you were out here."

"Grandmother?"

"The old lady with the boots?"

"Uh . . ."

"Do you want to come in for tea or something? I'm watching *It's a Mad Mad Mad Mad World*."

"I don't get it," Paul said. "You knew I was . . ."

"Not exactly. She does this sometimes. She's a little mad herself. Did you go up to the house?"

"Yeah."

"Did you notice there aren't any doors? When my brother and I were kids we had to stay there for a week every year, and there was no privacy at all. No door on the bathroom, and she has one of those showers with the sliding glass partitions. It freaked me out. Imagine being nine and your grandfather walking by to check you out while you were in the shower."

"Geez."

"It took years of therapy to undo the damage. Are you sure you don't want to come in?"

"I'm sure," he said.

She shrugged. "Suit yourself."

He stayed in the car until the woman had gone to bed. She waved to him before she turned out the light, and Paul waved back.

He kind of missed that assignment when it ended. It had given him a lot of free time to think. What he thought about mostly was Alyssa Ponty, whom he had been following around almost every day.

When he saw her at Montana Gag that Tuesday, he'd immediately been struck with strange and nauseating waves of empathy; these redoubled when she came back the following day, again with the boy in the truck. Wozack was in that day, and Alyssa and the boy walked away with a paper bag of pot. Paul had the camera ready behind the doughnut shelf, and he aimed it at her virulent shock of purple hair as it moved across the parking lot. At the last possible moment, before they climbed into the truck, he snapped three shots in rapid succession.

Wozack had a lot of customers that day, and Paul filled his roll of film. In the afternoon, when he waited at the mall photo shop for his prints to be finished, he tried to decide what to do about the Alyssa pictures. Was it his responsibility to turn them in with the rest, or would that represent some kind of betrayal? How could it be a betrayal when he didn't even know the girl? How was it his responsibility?—he was only Ponty's employee. He left the pictures on top of the stack until he was standing outside Ponty's door, then he shoved them into his pocket.

After that, he was obsessed. It was a familiar feeling; he'd never been very good at keeping secrets. In grade school, he alienated his friends by tattling their confidences to anyone willing to listen, which was everyone. Eventually nobody told him anything. He couldn't get hold of a piece of knowledge without acting on it. And if telling her father wasn't the way he was going to act on what he knew about Alyssa, he would find another way. That way was following her.

The day after he took those pictures—a day he was supposed to take off, to help Bernardo with the shed—he grew restless and took the car out to the high school. It was around two-thirty, about the time he expected the students to get out, and he parked half a block from the main entrance. He passed the time listening to some Celtic folk songs on the public radio station.

After about half an hour he heard a distant bell, and students began to empty out through the school's wide double doors. There were so many, and they came out so fast, that he quickly lost hope of identifying her. Then he noticed the battered blue pickup parked at the corner on the next block. If she was going to get a ride with the boy from yesterday, they would have to walk right past him. And sure enough, when the crowd of kids began to thin and the cars around him disappear in clouds of exhaust, he noticed them coming toward him across the school's wide yard, the boy with his arm around her and a red baseball cap hugging the dome of his head, she leaning precariously against him, her hair shoved up under her black beret, out of sight. Paul slid down in his seat and angled the rearview mirror to watch them approach: they seemed more at ease than he could ever recall being in high school. She was taking long, slow strides, and his steps seemed shortened to meet hers halfway, so that they walked together, bobbing like a pair of buoys on calm water. They passed within a few feet of Paul and didn't notice him; when they reached the truck they parted and got in their respective doors, only to meet again in the cab. They sat there a long time. Paul saw smoke curling out a half-open window. Then the truck started up with a rattle and pulled away.

He followed them to a suburban house in the South Hills, presumably the boy's parents', and watched them go inside. They were in there for a long time—Paul had no watch on, but it seemed like an hour and a half—before Alyssa came out alone, hitching her knapsack up on her shoulder. She walked around the truck and started off down the street, walking with a swagger that, in its blithe confidence and pleasure, Paul found heartbreaking.

When she was out of earshot, he got out of the car. He pushed the door nearly closed as quietly as he could, then leaned heavily against it until it latched; he began to follow her on foot, through the undulating grid of streets that had been carved into the side of the foothill. She walked ten, eleven, twelve blocks, turning frequently and cutting through the corners of yards, following no apparent set route, making it difficult for Paul to keep her in sight. Finally, when they had reached a slightly older, more run-down neigh-borhood (for this part of town, anyway, with its succession of in-ground pools and chattering sprinklers) than the one they'd left, Alyssa ran up the walk of a small ranch-style with yellow wood siding and walked in the door.

Paul stood on the corner of the previous block, blinking. There was a fa-miliar-looking car in the driveway, an old Jeep Cherokee with a dent in the passenger door. He remembered suddenly where he'd seen it: the parking lot of the strip mall where Ponty's office was. He'd followed her to his boss's house.

This went on for a while. He followed Alyssa to coffee shops and the movies; he sat behind her in the drive-up line at Burger King. Sometimes she was with her boyfriend and sometimes she wasn't; occasionally she hung out with a towheaded girl with impossibly white skin, and they leaned to-gether, giggling.

He wasn't sure how to treat this new behavior of his. He thought about her constantly, terrified whenever he was at home or doing real work that she was in some kind of trouble, had gotten herself into a situation that she would need to be rescued from. He began to have fantasies about just that: she and her friend, or boyfriend, get their hands on some beer (something, to his sur-prise, they didn't ever seem to do), they drive around and crash, and he resus-citates her on the hot pavement while lights flash around them. The boyfriend gets rough with her, she protests, Paul steps in. She finds herself in a tough part of town, and is threatened by thugs for her money; Paul shows up and chases them away. The fantasies always ended in a kind of haze, just at the height of Paul's heroism. Whatever happened next was always unclear. Did he drive her home, comfort her with fatherly pats on the back, bring her to Ponty ("I happened to be driving by," he says to his employer. "Lucky thing")? Or did it go in another direction—a kind embrace, the purple hair beneath his hands, his fingers on the smooth skin of her neck . . . ? It was this ending that made Paul nervous, and he always prevented himself from fully imagining it, the way he would occasionally entertain the horror, in his most miserable mo-ments, of some kind of awful self-mutilation, then pull back the reins on his imagination before something disgusting actually happened in it.

On one hand, the idea of romance with a teenager was highly unattractive to him. Pimples, gum, the characteristic combination of boldness and squeamishness. But the idea of romance with Alyssa was a different thing. He only watched her, he never talked to her, and at such distance he admired her for her independence and lack of gloominess. He was well aware of the difference between the Alyssa he daydreamed about and the one who probably existed, for real, in the halls of the high school. This knowledge did not, however, curb the frequency or intensity of his obsessions.

Meanwhile, he worked on the house with Bernardo. The old man knew his stuff, this was for sure, and Paul could see that he took great pleasure in it. He had been a big man when they met him, but since then he had lost weight and grown a black and gray beard that made him look ten years younger. They said little to each other that didn't have to do with the repairs. Bernardo talked about filling in the divots the plane engine had left and covering them with new sod; he gave Paul advice on bringing the garden back to life in the spring: planting it elsewhere in the yard, staggering the various vegetables in a different way, keeping bugs out at the times of day when they were most likely to appear.

It was the middle of September. Paul was on his way back from the lumberyard with siding and plywood when it began to rain. The drops were gigantic and left splashes the size of half dollars on the windshield, and before he had gone a quarter mile up Valley Road his visibility had fallen almost to zero. He found the side of the road and stopped there, letting warm air from the car heater widen the clear circles on the inside of the window. By now— after six—Anita was in the living room, relaxing after her day of work. Paul stared out into the rain and pictured her there, on the couch, dozing and waiting for him to come home.

He realized this was wishful thinking. She hadn't been herself these past few weeks. Or, rather, she had been herself—nervous to finish tasks begun, eager for whatever she was doing to end. But usually she felt that way only when she was tied up in something she didn't like. Now, evidence of that mood was cropping up all the time. She rushed through her dinners, went to bed soon after. She got up a little later than usual, forgoing her leisurely cup of coffee, and left for work early. She lingered only in the bathroom. Her baths could last for well over an hour, and sometimes Paul heard the faucet over the sink running for fifteen or twenty minutes at a time. He'd been thinking it was

Bernardo who bothered her, but lately Bernardo seemed to have sensed her mood too, and backed off as much as he could, only coming into the house to make them dinner, or to take something from the refrigerator for breakfast.

The rain slowed down. Paul pulled back into traffic, the lumber clunking in the back of the car, and drove slowly. The defogger was losing to the outside air, and he reached forward to wipe off the window: it was cool. Autumn, finally, was here.

He pulled up to the house and ran inside. The lights were off, the air still dry and flat from the morning's heat. Nobody was there. He looked at his watch: six-forty-five. He went back out to start unloading the car, slipped on the porch steps, and landed in the mud, banging his elbow on a rock.

It barely hurt, but he lay there, feeling it, trying to follow the last fluttering scrap of pain as it floated away from him. When it had all receded, he found his chest suddenly heaving and tears gathering hotly behind his eyes.

This took him by surprise, and it wasn't until his vision blurred and he felt the itch of humiliation in his face that he realized just how frustrated he had been lately—how much of the past few weeks had been spent deflecting Anita's brazen dismissiveness, how little affection she had offered him, how little he had risked offering her. In the mud, he felt doomed. He let himself sink farther, his head cradled by the accommodating muck, and breathed, his eyes closed, until it seemed that tears wouldn't come after all.

He stood up, and the frustration began to drain out of his body, and loneliness percolate up into it. This loneliness was great and hollow as an empty gymnasium, and he gulped air trying to fill it. He hadn't felt like this since his deathbed vigil, years before, with his mother, who rejected his every attempt at conversation as if they were offers to get up and play tennis. "Remember the time . . ." he might ask her, or, "Tell me about when Dad . . ." And she would slowly turn her head, her dry lips parting like the seal on an old jar whose forgotten contents had long since putrefied, and tell him with great effort to shut up. And he did, with relief, because he didn't want to know what might come out of her if she really started talking. She hated him, and he hated her, and he carried on his charade of compassion and gratitude until she was dead.

He wondered if he had ever loved Anita—if he had ever loved anything— with the unmitigated passion he hated his mother with during those weeks.

He rubbed the water off his face with a clean part of his hand, and found himself peering off into the forest, toward the wreckage. The rain had slowed, and the droplets shone in newly revealed sunlight over the trees. Nothing was visible from here, but the dark green was so strong, the new coolness of the air such a shock and invigoration, that he felt himself invited into it. He walked to the edge of the clearing, gave the sodden and rotting garden a wide berth, and stepped over the deep ruts the emergency vehicles had left.

Under the canopy of trees, the rain seemed to have stopped entirely, and the turpentine smell of pine needles was enough to make his eyes water. He hadn't come back here since the crash. The rescuers and investigators, now long finished, had left a clear path through the humus where they had carried their stretchers and clipboards, and he followed it to the creek, which from the rain had regained some life. He stepped in and over, and was shocked by the cold of the water. It rushed against his legs and lapped up to his thighs. When he stepped out he squinted into the distance and thought he could see a flash of metallic light. Then it was gone. He bent over and rubbed his legs, now nearly numb with cold, and began to jog along the new path slowly, looking at the ground around him for evidence of the crash.

Ahead now, the plane's pale outline was easy to see; it looked like a whale that had been beached here, the tail a great fin sticking out of its side, the torn fuselage its gaping mouth. Its flesh gleamed in the light, which had come almost to dominate the sky, shoving aside the storm like dust before a broom. Paul wondered briefly how they would get the thing out—surely it was too heavy to be lifted by helicopters.

The fuselage was surrounded by a strip of yellow police-line tape. He arrived at it panting—it was the farthest he'd run, perhaps, since he was a child—and was immediately surprised by the plane's size. It was not big. For a moment he thought he must have missed something. Such a flimsy thing—its metal skin bare inches away from the skin of its passengers—could never carry human cargo anywhere; it could only be knocked out of the air. And here, of course, it had been. He looked up and saw where the tops of trees had been shaved off as it fell; several trees had fallen completely, and leaned crazily against each other around the irregular clearing the crash had created.

He stepped over the police tape and stood before the wide maw of the fuselage. The backs of four seats sat before him, and the rows continued beyond them into the wet half-dark of the plane. A hole had been blown in the side, over where a wing, now doubled over and crushed beneath the wreck, had been. There was an accordion bend just beyond this, where the fuselage bunched up on one side and tore open on the other, and this bend allowed him only the slightest glimpse of the cockpit, with its glistening dials and switches. There was no rain at all now, and slivers of sun sliced through the trees to the ground; there was no sound save for the rushing of the creek in the distance behind him and the steady drip of water everywhere. The forest smell couldn't mask the sharp scent of metallic decay. The entire scene reminded him of a half-eaten meal, carnal and ruined.

He climbed into the hole and stood on the carpet between the rows of seats. It had not been cleaned up—there was still blood here. It stained the seats and carpet and ceiling, and the rain had brought it back to life, so that it drooled down the walls and windows as if the plane itself were bleeding. Muddy footprints tracked through the blood, where investigators had certainly been, where paramedics removed belted-in bodies. He walked forward suppressing nausea, around the strange and frightening bend, into the cockpit.

The control panel had been smashed and was brown with blood; the steering column had been snapped off and lay in a corner like a pair of antlers. A few shards of windshield remained. The entire thing was canted at an angle of about thirty degrees, so Paul had to grip the doorframe to keep from falling over.

Outside, chewing on a nut and staring at him through the windshield, was a brown squirrel. It was balanced on an upthrust fold of metal on the pushed-in nose cone and seemed undisturbed by his presence.

He thought, I will never fly again. How could anyone think it would work? Then he thought that there would be nowhere for him to fly, anyway.

He came out into the yard, which now, illuminated by full sun, sparkled like broken glass. He squished through the mud to the porch, took off his shoes and socks, and went inside.

Anita was at the table, sipping from a mug of something. She looked up at him and her face darkened. She managed a weak smile.

"When did you get home?" he said.

"Just now."

"I didn't hear a car."

She put the mug down and folded her hands. "Kathy dropped me off at the end of the drive. Her car can't handle the dirt road." Kathy was her coworker, who'd been giving her rides since Paul had started working. She'd never had problems with the dirt road before, though. Both of them knew this, and after a moment under his scrutiny, Anita hung her head. This gesture had the effect of sucking every last bit of energy from his body, and with great effort he removed his muddy shirt and tossed it onto the porch.

"What happened to your shirt?" she asked, trying to sound cheerful and failing.

"I fell in the mud."

She nodded, not bothering to ask where he'd been since she got home. She stared into her mug. Paul walked past her. "I'm going to take a bath," he said. "Just so you know where I'll be. In case there's anything you want to tell me."

He showered briefly, to get the mud out of his hair. It fell to the floor of the tub in thick dark chunks and dissolved in the water. Afterward he stepped out and drew a bath, then sat in it, and finally lay down, his nose and mouth just above the surface and the rest of his head underwater. He could not get warm.

He heard her come in. She said something he didn't catch, and then repeated it, a little louder. He cut her off. "Are you sleeping with somebody?" he said.

She said something else now. "What?" he said. "I can't hear you." Then he felt her hand in his hair, pulling him up. She brought her face down to his.

"Yes!" she said. "I am!"

"Thank you," he said, and sat up.

"I'm sorry."

"Ah! Sorry. Good!"

"Paul—"

"Yeah, yeah, yeah," he said. The feeling of exhaustion would not go away. He started to sink again but left his ears above water this time.

"I've been unhappy," she was saying. She sat on the toilet, her knees pressed together. Her voice bounced around the room, off the walls, off the surface of the water, which seemed to modulate it a half-tone too high. Or perhaps that was just the way she said it. "You promised me a family and it didn't come. And then, all this . . . ." Her arm swung out, toward the woods. "Everything just went to pieces, Paul."

"Not me!" he said. "I didn't go to pieces."

"We can't all be as steady as you, Paul."

"Oh, that's true. I suppose you'll tell your lover that. 'Paul was a *rock* through all this, poor brave guy.'"

"Paul—"

"So is it *serious*?"

"I don't know."

"So it just might be a casual thing, then? Just a little snack? Well that's certainly a relief."

She sat there for a moment, silent, and he closed his eyes and tried to will the heat of the water to penetrate him. He reached out with his foot and let the hot water tap run for a few seconds. When he shut it off he heard her moving, the sound of her clothes being taken off.

"Ah," he said. "The reconciliation."

She stepped into the tub at the spigot end and crouched there. He heard her splashing herself. "Jesus," she said. "This is hot." She tried to sit but his legs were in the way. "Move," she said.

"Fuck you!"

"Come on."

He moved, bringing his knees up to his chin and holding them there with his arms, trying with all his might not to touch her. When he opened his eyes, finally, she was staring at him, her eyes red, her hair sticking to her forehead with sweat. "Do you still want me?" she said.

He slammed his fists into the water. It splashed over the edge and spattered on the floor, and he felt his knuckles smash into the enamel, felt the skin on them break. "Of course I do! Of fucking course I do!" he screamed at her, and the sound against the tiles was incredibly loud, louder than he had ever heard himself or thought he could get. She flinched, and began, silently, to cry.

He felt his bowels loosen with the force of his anger and clenched himself inside, clenched every muscle in his body against it, to keep from screaming again. His hands were palms down in the water, curled like an ape's, and blood had begun to strip away from the knuckles in slow, widening strands, four to a hand. The blood dissolved like contrails, and he brought his hands to his face. Little flaps of skin pulled back and jumped with each heartbeat. His elbow throbbed.

"Oh Jesus, Paul," Anita said, and stepped dripping from the tub. He heard her rummage in the cabinet under the sink. Then she climbed back into the water, her breasts long and slender from the pull of gravity as she stood above him, her hands spilling with bandages and tape.

He understood that this was what he was in danger of losing—the privilege of seeing her body at its most raw and practical. The muscles in her thighs went taut as she sat, her shoulders bowed; this was unsexual and beautiful to him, and the loss was a great, awful vacuum in his chest, pulling at anything he seemed to have left inside him. "Keep still," she said. She patted his knuckles with tissues and swabbed iodine onto the wounds; she snipped up a gauze pad with a pair of cuticle scissors and taped the pieces to his fingers. The flat, medicinal odor of the gauze floated up to him. He closed his eyes.

"Done," she said.

"Thank you." He watched the skin move over her vertebrae as she got out of the tub to put the first aid things away. When she sat down again, they had nothing to say to one another, and she put her hands on his knees. He sat, unmoving, his bandaged hands elevated and tingling at his ears, and he felt a nagging sexual heat that angered and embarrassed him. But when she moved her hands down his legs, he let her, and when he came he was watching her face, placid and focused, where it lay on his knee.

He put clothes on, grabbed his jacket and keys from the dresser. "I'm going out," he told Anita when he passed her in the kitchen. She was sitting very still in a bathrobe at the table, her hands flat on the table.

"Okay."

He looked at her once more before he opened the door, and the look she met it with was only sad, nothing else. Any comment he might have made evaporated. He left.

Outside, it had begun to get dark. He walked to the car and stood by the door for a minute, watching the clouds turn color. Then he noticed, in the shadows at the edge of the yard, a dim angle of light coming from the reconstructed shed: Bernardo. For a little while, he had forgotten Bernardo was there; now his presence was a kind of relief. He didn't know where he'd planned to go, and the interior of the car looked drab and cold, so he walked through the mud to the shed and knocked on the door.

"Yes, hello?"

"Bernardo?" He pulled the door open and found Bernardo sitting on a stool at the workbench, drawing. By his side, a plate of votive candles burned.

"Close the door, please. The wind." He pointed at the flickering candles.

Paul did as he was told. He hadn't really looked in here since they'd finished rebuilding it, and Bernardo had made tremendous use of the small space he'd been given. The tools were stacked or hung on one side of the tiny room, and the rest was taken up by the workbench and a couple of blankets that lay opposite it. Paul had to push the blankets aside slightly to keep from standing on them.

"This is nice," he said, for lack of anything else. "I mean, you've fixed it up nice in here."

"Grazie." He looked at Paul's bandaged fingers, but said nothing.

"What are you drawing?"

Bernardo raised his eyebrows and leaned back, revealing a series of roughly drawn seascapes: men in boats, houses on hills in the distance. "What are they doing there?" Paul asked.

"They fish."

"For what?"

"Swordfish," he said. He looked up at Paul and smiled at him sadly. "My grandfather catches them, a long time ago."

Paul nodded. "I think Anita is going to leave me."

He didn't seem surprised. "Maybe not," he said.

"Were you married?"

"Yes."

"Not anymore?"

He turned back to his drawings. "No."

"Do you regret that?"

Bernardo waited some time before saying, "She is dead now."

But Paul had a lot of regrets, and they all came to him now, lodging in his head and chest like bullets: wasting himself and his dignity, thinking too hard about the wrong things, getting lucky with Anita and somehow blowing it. It wasn't so easy to pretend they weren't there. He reached for the door. "You might not want to go in there."

"Okay."

"You know," Paul said, "you don't seem like somebody who'd lose his shirt. You don't seem like a vagrant."

Bernardo turned again, this time scowling, and searched for the words. "No, no. Anybody fails, anybody."

"I guess you're right."

"Yes."

He walked out and shut the door behind him. He could hear Bernardo shifting inside on his stool, getting himself comfortable enough to draw. Paul didn't feel like he'd ever feel comfortable again. His hand, which hadn't hurt even when Anita was working on it, ached as if he'd broken every bone. And he was absurdly hungry. He walked to the car, still unsure of where he was going, only confident of the image of him behind the wheel, driving, somewhere.

12

Lars had been talking on the phone with his mother. She'd called frequently since the crash, and always, for his benefit, tried to sound cheerful, but it was clear that she was a little bit lonely and had been for some time. Lars's father died when he was five, and since then, though she usually seemed to be happy when Lars was at home, his mother hadn't had any lasting partner that he knew of. Stoughton, Wisconsin, was not a big town, and she was a homebody; she poured a lot of the energy she would have expended in a relationship into spontaneous and marginally useful household projects: graceless wooden furniture assembled with nails and glue, frequent rewallpapering. Lars saw these things whenever he went home to visit, and always felt a little sorry for her. Now he was wondering if maybe he ought to start a project himself.

His father's name was Ivar Cowgill. He had taught fourth-grade science at a public school in Madison. Lars could remember sitting at the kitchen table with him in the evening while he made marks in his grade book. The list of unfamiliar names upset him: who were all these other, older kids his dad knew and spent time with, who got to see a side of him that he, Lars, never could? Soon after, when his father was in the hospital with his cancer, Lars was consumed with jealousy at the neat rows of construction-paper get-well cards his students had made for him. He asked his mother, "Can't we *move* them?" He claimed the cards obstructed his father's view out the window. When his father told him that it was fine, that he should leave the cards there where he could see them, Lars went out into the hall and cried.

His death a few weeks later was a complete shock. Nobody had told Lars to expect this, and later he would learn that nobody had expected it. But at the time, he blamed the fourth grade. He vowed never to speak to a fourth grader and to skip the grade altogether when he got to it, though by the time he did he was twice as old and had only vague memories of his father.

Though his mother's eccentricities made a little more sense now, he was not comforted by the fact that, fifteen years later, she still had them. Their conversations, like the ones he had with Christine, were full of long silences that quickly stopped seeming odd; Lars often listened to his mother breathing in perfectly measured rhythms, like a weightlifter, while they thought of something to say. Usually they ended up talking about politics: Wisconsin's Republican governor, surrounded in the capitol building by the most liberal neighborhoods in the state; Montana's local militiamen and water rights and Canadian grain protests along the Hi-line. This last time, though, Lars's mother mentioned that she'd gone out. "I went bowling, by myself," she said. "In Madison. I wore tight jeans and drank a couple of whiskey sours."

"Jesus, Mom."

"And I got picked up!" she whispered.

"What!"

"Well, almost," she corrected. "I could have been, if I'd wanted. The opportunity was there." She spoke with a dreamy wistfulness, as if, in her imagination, the evening had turned out quite differently. It was unlike her, and it seemed to Lars that she was beginning, finally, to snap out of it. He wondered if she was doing it for his benefit, if he was expected to follow suit. He hoped not.

He had come to Safeway to get orange juice and noticed someone he recognized standing in front of him in line. It took a minute to place him: Paul, the detective. He looked bad, staring at his sandwich rolling down the conveyor as if it were the only life preserver on a sinking ship. Lars almost reached out and touched him, but changed his mind, afraid to frighten him.

The juice was for Christine, who was waiting for him in the trailer. They'd gotten to be fairly close, if touchy, friends in the past weeks, spending a lot of time on the phone and occasionally, when she felt up to it, hanging around together. Her mother didn't like her to go far; if a kidney suddenly became available for her, Christine would need to get to the hospital fast. So if they spent any time together it was usually in the trailer.

Megan's loss was changing him. Things reminded him of her frequently, approximately once every ten minutes—some music, somebody's sunglasses, a kind of food or a place in town—and at these times he felt himself going blank, his mind caught in a logic loop that he wouldn't come out of for several seconds. The result was a general spaciness he hadn't suffered before, and he was concerned that it might be permanent. It was akin to suddenly losing a sense: you switch on the stereo and remember that you can no longer hear. You have to learn how to live around the problem. And compounding this was the nagging feeling that it all might have been preventable.

The good thing about Christine was that she was used to this herself. She'd been through it—not being able to eat certain things, do certain things; not being able to leave the general vicinity of the hospital. She told him he'd get over it. He wasn't so sure.

Just now it was the juice he was holding. The cool condensation that had gathered on the carton, the gentle swell of its sides—this reminded him of running to the store in the mornings sometimes for juice or milk while Megan stayed behind in bed. It reminded him of breakfast together by the window, of weekends alone with her. His brain went haywire making the connections; synapses fired indiscriminately. He heard, dimly, the checker asking him to put down the juice, but it didn't occur to him to do so.

"Hey! Hey!" It was the guy who had been so brusque with him before, the chubby one. Claude. His glasses, thick lenses fitted into wire frames, looked a little like goggles.

"Sorry."

"Oh, just I gotta keep you moving."

Lars turned but saw nobody behind him except a woman at a nearby cigarette display, choosing a pack. Claude rang him up and Lars paid. When he stepped out onto the sidewalk, there was Paul, his mouth full of half a turkey sub, shredded iceberg lettuce sprinkled around him on the cement.

"Paul?"

Paul frowned. His eyes were red and deeply sunken, like the hidden wells of flowers. They glinted warily in their sockets. His hands were covered with clean white bandages.

"It's Lars. You spied on me, remember?"

"Mmm!" He nodded with what looked like false enthusiasm and swallowed his bite of sandwich. "Howyadoin?"

"A little better. You?"

"Eh," he said, wiggling a free hand. "Actually bad. Actually my wife is sleeping with somebody."

"Geez, sorry, man."

"I've been driving around, you know? In the car?" He blinked several times, rapidly. "It's like I just stepped into somebody else's life. Hello? Does this belong to you?"

"I wish it did."

Paul frowned, then turned a little red. "Oh, right. Oh, God, I'm really sorry."

"That's okay."

"No, really . . ."

"Look," Lars said. "Why don't you come along to my friend's? That's where I'm going."

"I don't know . . ." Paul said, but Lars could see his eyes starting to creep out from their pits.

"Come on." He started walking, and after a second, Paul followed, clutching his half-sandwich. They stopped at the trailer door.

"Your friend lives *here*?"

"Yeah." He knocked and opened. "Christine?"

"Juice!" She sprung into the doorway and her eyes narrowed. "Who's that?"

"Christine, Paul. Paul, Christine." The two shook hands gingerly, eyeing one another with suspicion. There was something creepily competitive about misery. People could sense it on each other, as if it were a smell or a way of walking. Since it had roosted on him Lars had seen it everywhere: in his apartment building, in line at the bank, on the sidewalk. If, for some reason, he had to talk to one of these people, their voices sounded different. They had an echo, as if the words had to travel a longer distance to reach their destination, and generally they did—the personal space expanded with misery. Misery buzzed around people like a repellent force-field. Paul and Christine crackled.

"How do you do?" she said, sarcastically.

"Oh, great."

And that kicked off their evening. The three stared at each other for a few seconds, then they all went inside to drink the orange juice.

Lars's relationship with Christine was, for all its downtrodden chumminess, a little uncomfortable. Part of the problem was that since Megan died women had taken on a tragic, painful cast to him. This was through no fault of theirs, he understood, but other women reminded him of her, and there was nothing he could do about it. He also knew this was a lousy reason to feel uncomfortable around somebody, so he pretended not to feel it. It was like trying to hide a pregnancy. They both knew, and there was little avoiding the mildly resentful silences that hung over them at times.

And Christine was a physical wreck a good portion of the time. Before her dialysis in particular, she complained of weakness and insomnia, dry skin, bleeding gums. She had problems digesting food and ran to the bathroom frequently. She gave off a foul odor: her breath was rotten, her body medicinal and rank. She became disoriented and irritable and took it out on him.

But they were respectful and open with one another. Her problems didn't embarrass her or disgust him, and he could speak his mind about Megan without irritating her. This understanding made them close, even as their indulgences kept them at arm's length, and they rotated around one another like a double star, throwing heat back and forth with little effect.

Toth, on the other hand, didn't get it. He'd heard Lars's side of several of their conversations and thought they sounded like an old married couple. He was convinced Lars was falling in love with her, a sick kind of love based on wallowing in unhappiness. A few days before, Toth had been complaining about this over pizza they'd ordered. They were in Toth's house, the rock band exerting themselves beneath them. "It just isn't right," he said, "you carrying on like this with her."

"I'm not 'carrying on.' We're just friends."

"You talk to her every night, man."

"So?"

"So you never talked to me every night," he said, staring at his hands, and Lars suddenly understood how jealous he was and had been. "We're friends, aren't we?"

"Toth . . ."

"Or maybe we're not. Maybe we just aren't the friends I thought we were." And with this he lowered his head to his hands and stayed hunched like that over his plate of pizza crusts. Lars was certain he was crying, but when he lifted his head his eyes were dry.

"You're my best friend," Lars said, almost meaning it. Without Megan he had no best friend.

"Ditto, man," Toth said, and it was obvious from his grimace that he felt the same way.

Now, though, he was beginning to wonder if Toth might be right: not that he was in love, but that he had become a little obsessed. The plasticky, close odor of the trailer triggered a rush of adrenaline that made his palms sweaty, and he was glad to have Paul here, even if he heightened the gloom. The trailer looked bigger on the inside than out, with bunk beds at the far end, and a television at the other, next to a stack of cardboard boxes whose contents weren't clear. The three of them sat in the middle, on swivel chairs bolted to the floor before a square table that folded down out of the wall. It was the dining area of a small kitchenette.

"So," Lars said. "How are you feeling?"

"Like dancing," she said.

"Really?"

"Hell, no!" She shifted in her seat. "I feel a little better than usual, though. I slept all afternoon."

Paul looked at one of them, then the other. "You're sick?"

"Oh, yeah."

"She's got bad kidneys," Lars told him. "She's waiting for a transplant. That's why she's near the hospital."

Paul's eyes widened. "Jesus. That must suck." At hearing himself say this, he reddened. "Sorry."

"No need," Christine said. "It sucks, for sure." She stared at the back of her hand. "So what's your beef, Paul? You look victimized. Been feeding the lions?"

Paul told her. She shrugged. "Sorry, buddy."

"Oh, you know, it's nothing . . ." he said, and his face began to melt.

"We should go out," Lars said quickly.

Christine raised her eyebrows. "'Out?'"

"Yeah, like out somewhere. I don't know. A movie?"

"Oooh. Exciting." She rolled her eyes.

Lars thought of his mother, bent over her scorecard, the ice melting into her whiskey sour. "Bowling," he said. "Let's go bowling."

Paul said, almost to himself, "I haven't bowled in years. I've never bowled in Montana."

"There you go."

Christine frowned. "Gimme a break, Cowgill. My mom would have my hide."

"She'll never know. She won't be back for a while, right?"

"She's at a *quilting* class, for Chrissake. Besides," she said, rolling up her sleeve, "how can I bowl with this?" A couple of tubes stuck out of her forearm, held fast to the skin with surgical tape. The flesh around where the tubes went in was bright red and crusted with something yellow. Lars had only seen this in passing, but now she held it out before them like a freakish creature she'd found. Paul started.

Lars said, "Uh . . . can you bowl with the other hand?"

She pulled the sleeve down, stood up, and swung her left arm in the air. She opened and closed the fingers. "Yeah, maybe. I don't know. I've never bowled. My brothers bowled, not me."

"You have brothers?" Lars asked her.

She looked at him as if this was not something she needed to tell anyone, as if people should just know. "I have four brothers."

"Oh."

"And their kidneys . . ." Paul said suddenly, as if nobody had thought of this yet.

"No," she said, looking out the small window at the street. "There's my dad, though, if anyone wants to try and find him." They were all quiet for a moment.

"So are we going?" Paul said. His fingers wiggled at the ends of his bandages.

She turned to him. "I guess we are."

The house lights at the bowling alley were off and the walls glowed with sparkling, outer-space decor: a bolt of lightning, a ringed planet, a UFO foreshortened to indicate speed. A spinning mirror ball glimmered above the twelfth lane, casting dots of light over the bowlers, and the alley's PA system blared an unintelligible rock song. Occasionally the sound of falling pins cut through the noise, and a scoring computer flashed a yellow X. People cheered almost unceasingly. Paul said something, but Lars couldn't hear what it was.

"What?"

"I said, is it always like this?" He seemed less impressed than dismayed.

"I've never seen it like this," Lars shouted. "Usually it's kind of less hip!"

Christine leaned into him, and he could smell her tired, stale odor before he could hear. "This crap is vibrating my guts! I feel like running to the can!"

They rented shoes from a short, curly-haired man with a handlebar mustache who seemed inexplicably irritated that they wanted to play. "You're gonna wait for a lane!" the man screamed ominously.

"What about that one?" Lars said. There was one empty lane near the far end of the alley.

The man stood on his toes, squinting. In the shifting fluorescence, his shirt glowed red. "Yeah, okay, twenty-three," he said, and punched a few keys on a computer. Then he turned and stalked off.

They picked house balls from the rows of racks. Lars found one for himself and a couple for Christine, who hefted them tentatively, as if they were porcelain vases. "We can use these? They don't belong to anybody?"

"They're the bowling alley's."

"This one's got a name on it." She brought the ball a few inches closer to her face. "It says 'Lanza.'"

"People sell them. They trade in their old ones at the pro shop. It's okay."

She stuck her fingers into the ball and frowned. "Gross. There's gunk in there." She took her fingers out and rubbed them together. "It's like using somebody else's toothbrush."

Lars was thinking: She's got tubes sticking out of her arm, and they run her blood through a machine, and she thinks a bowling ball is gross. He grinned and patted her shoulder.

"What?" she said.

"Nothing." She smiled back eventually, and they stood there with the light dragging across them, momentarily happy.

Lars was entering their initials into the scoring computer when Paul showed up at their lane with a gigantic pitcher of frothing beer. "I got three glasses," he said.

"I can't *drink*!" Christine yelled.

"Oh. Sorry."

"Pour me a glass," Lars said, picking up his ball. "I'm gonna start bowling."

He stepped up to the markers, fitting his feet to the third and fourth, as he always did. He remembered starting this habit, completely arbitrarily, in high school. It made him look like he knew what he was doing, and when, after every awful game he played, he told his friends he was having an off night, they believed him. Now doing it felt wonderful, like returning home after a long and not particularly satisfying vacation. The pins appeared and disappeared in the shifting light, and he hefted the ball in his hands.

He focused on the sweet spot between the first and third pins, where, if he curved the ball right, it would smack open the space and domino the other eight pins into each other, sending them crackling into the darkness at the back of the lane. The pins blinked in and out of view. He approached, raising his arm behind him like a catapult, then let it swing down, gathering momentum. He released the ball and it sped across the boards, then struck home with a hollow crash. The pins jumped. A strike. From behind him came cheering, and he turned to find Paul and Christine there, slumped in their chairs, Christine clapping and Paul stamping his feet. Not Megan.

Paul got drunk. Lars had maybe a glass and a half of beer, but the pitcher was drained before the second game was half over. He touched Paul on the arm when he got up to get another.

"Hey, I don't know if I want any more."

He gave an expansive wave of the hand. "Oh, sure you do."

"Well . . ."

Paul waited, breathing with a noticeable and labored rhythm, like a dog watching a passing car. Finally he said, "Ah, don't worry about it," and jogged off to the bar.

Christine was doing poorly but didn't seem to mind. Lars tried to coach her on her form. "You have to shake hands with the ball."

"Shake hands?"

"Like this," he said. He leaned forward, his right leg rising into the air behind him, and swept out his hand toward the lane. "Hello, ball!"

She mimicked his motions, switching the left for the right. "Hello ball," she said.

She was amazed at the ball return. "It comes *back* to you?" she said. "Automatically?" Lars was shocked that she'd never seen this, not even on television. She also didn't know about the pinsetter or the scoring computer or, she confessed when she had gotten more comfortable with her surroundings, the bar. She was surprised you were allowed to drink while you bowled. "Doesn't it seem dangerous?" she asked Lars. "With all these heavy objects?"

Lars shrugged. "I'm from Wisconsin," he told her. "Drinking and bowling are in my blood."

It had been Paul's turn for a long time, and still he hadn't returned. Lars turned and peered back at the bar. There was no line, and he didn't see Paul either.

"This is the most fun I've had since I came to Marshall," she said.

Lars was sitting next to her. "Oh, no problem." And without thinking, he set his hand on her knee.

He saw her, out of the corner of his eye, turn her head toward him, but he didn't look up. He was looking at his hand, resting there on her jeans. Slowly he picked it up and put it on his lap. A few seconds passed, and she lifted her leg and crossed it over the other.

"Lars?"

"Yeah."

"Thanks for taking me here. I would never have bothered to go anywhere."

He still could not look up. What had he been thinking? He slumped farther into his seat. "Sure."

They sat in silence a few minutes more, the sounds of the bowling alley swelling around them. Christine cracked her knuckles. "Where's Paul?"

"I should go look for him."

"Why don't you?" she said, and he got up and walked to the bar.

Paul was at the back of the room, next to the keno machines, at a pay telephone. He had the pitcher in one hand and the receiver in the other, and was blubbering desperately into the latter. When he looked up and saw Lars, he tried to wipe his face with the pitcher arm. Beer sloshed onto the carpet. "I gotta go," he said into the receiver. "Donworry. I gotta go. I gotta go." He hung up, then wiped his face a second time, again with the pitcher arm.

"Why don't you let me take that?" Lars said. "It's your turn."

"Uh-huh. Uh-huh. Okay." He handed over the pitcher. "I gotta . . ." he said. "I have to . . . I can't go—" And he burst into fresh tears. "You got a place I can stay tonight?"

"Oh, sure. No problem."

"You're a real pal."

"Come on. Let's go finish this game."

They finished off the game in palpably lower spirits. Lars didn't hit any of his spares and Christine threw a lot of gutterballs. Paul stood before the lane, reeling slightly, his ball dangling from his fingertips. He took a very long time to release it. Once or twice he simply replaced the ball and sat down without having thrown it. They didn't bother with a third game, and Paul insisted on paying for everyone. He leaned up against the counter and dropped his wallet. "Come on, hurry up," the attendant told him.

They had taken Paul's car. Lars took the keys from him and drove, while Paul slept in the backseat.

"I'm sorry, Lars," Christine said quietly, as they drove down Cedar Avenue. The river shimmered in the street light to the south, low and sluggish and unrippled.

"It's not your fault," he said. "I'm just so used to . . ."

"I don't care. It's . . . I like the idea that somebody would touch me like that. Just friendly."

"I'm sorry."

She was silent for a while. "I guess I am a little sad." She slumped against the window. "I'm a sad sack, Cowgill."

"No, you're not."

"I'm so *tired*," she said. "I want to wake up one morning and not be tired, you know what I mean?"

"I guess I do."

She sighed, and picked up his right hand with hers and put it on her knee. He left it there.

When they reached the Safeway, they could see Christine's mother moving behind the window. He pulled up in the car and she opened the door. "Thanks, Cowgill," she said. "That was the most fun I've had in ages."

"Me too," he said.

She looked out the windshield. "She's going to kill me."

Lars shrugged. "She'll get over it," he said.

She smiled at him. If this were different, he'd kiss her goodnight. But it wasn't. "Okay," she said suddenly, and stepped out of the car. The trailer door opened before she reached it, and her mother, a tiny, frizzy-haired woman, stood silhouetted by the kitchenette light. He could see the worry in her posture; her dress hung off her as if tossed onto a hook. Christine turned and waved one last time, and the door closed behind her.

Lars pulled onto Cedar and headed for home. He could smell Paul's breath even in the front seat, and he rolled down the window to let some fresh air in. Paul moaned. "Too bumpy," he said, referring, Lars supposed, to the road, but there was nothing to be done about that.

He slowed to drive over the tracks, and followed them with his eyes over the old train bridge. Trains no longer ran over it—the tracks dead-ended north of here at the wall of the dairy—but teenagers still dared each other to cross it, and at his apartment on the other side of the river, Lars could often hear them calling to each other in the dark. He remembered looking through a book of old photos in the library, and finding a picture of the old rail station, now a hunting club, that stood on the far side of the bridge. Trains angled in from Butte or Coeur d'Alene, clouds of coal smoke gushing out above them, and rail passengers idled in the haze over the platforms, their bags at their feet. He could make out the station's outline from here, and the red glow of the Coke machine in its bell tower. He could imagine the sounds of the passengers drifting across the river, broken up by the current. If the sounds were real, he thought, he'd leave tonight. He'd take the train to Whitefish, then east, over the mountains toward home. He would sleep as North Dakota and Minnesota flooded past.

He had only had his eyes off the road for a second. But when he turned back, there was a woman, a gray figure waving her arms in the glare of his headlights. He hit the brakes. The tires squealed and his seat belt locked across his chest. He felt something heavy strike his seat from behind.

"Paul! Are you okay?"

"Ohhh . . ." Paul was saying. "I'm going to puke . . ."

The woman had jumped off the road and was opening the passenger-side door. To Lars's surprise she got in. "Hoo-hoo!" she said. "Sorry if I gave you a fright." Her face was round and open and gently wrinkled; her lips were thin and long and she carried a bulging white handbag. She smiled.

"Uh . . . I guess I wasn't paying attention."

"No harm done!" she said, buckling her seat belt.

"Ohhhhh," Paul said.

Lars leaned back between the seats. "Are you going to be okay? Do you need to get out?"

"Uh . . . uh . . ." He had dragged himself back onto the seat, and now he blinked. "No."

"Good."

"Are you all right?" the woman asked Paul. She sounded vaguely disapproving. "You look *awful.*"

Paul raised his head, squinting, then moaned and fell back to the seat.

"Excuse me," Lars said suddenly. They had not yet begun to move. "Do you want a ride somewhere?"

"Oh, yes!" the woman said, laughing. She looked to be in her early sixties, as far as Lars could figure. "I certainly do!"

"Where to?"

She shrugged. "Oh, anywhere."

"I can take you wherever," he said. He restarted the car and put it in gear. "It's no problem."

"No matter."

Lars thought about that for a second. "Okay, then," he said, and turned onto Front Street. "How about Fourth?"

"Wonderful!"

Nobody said anything for a little while. Paul shifted in the back and sighed heavily. Lars turned onto the Cherry Street bridge. A grizzled-looking man carrying a bedroll was walking over in the opposite direction, and the old lady waved to him. He grinned suddenly and waved back.

"You know that guy?"

"Oh, yes." Out of the corner of his eye, Lars saw her staring at him. "You drive very well," she said. "I can barely feel you switching gears."

"Well, I'm not right now. I'm just in third."

"I have a driver's test next week," she said. "Wish me luck!"

"Good luck."

Suddenly she stuck out her hand. Lars took a glance at it, then shook it perfunctorily. "I'm Amelia Potter," she said.

"Lars Cowgill," he said to her, and she frowned. "What?"

"Have you been drinking? I don't accept rides with drunks."

"I had a couple beers." What was he feeling guilty for? "You probably smell my friend there."

Amelia's frown deepened, but she didn't ask to be let out. They went several blocks without speaking. Lars steered carefully, staying under the speed limit.

At his apartment, he pulled over and turned off the car. For a second he cupped Paul's keys in the palm of his hand, enjoying their heft, and wondered what the house was like that they would admit him to. "Well," he said. "I live here. Are you sure you don't want to go anywhere else?"

"Oh, yes. This is fine. Tell me," she said.

"What?"

"Can you make a left on red? That is, when it's onto a one-way street?" Her face was suddenly very serious.

"I think you can. Don't quote me on that."

She nodded. "Well, thank you. I've learned so much." She opened her handbag and pulled out what at first appeared to be a large candy bar. When she brought it into the light, he saw that it was in fact a box of number 2 pencils. He noticed that her white bag was filled with identical boxes. "Here you go. Use these well. Write down your innermost thoughts."

"Gosh," Lars told her. "Thanks."

And then she leaned across the space between them and touched Lars on the arm. Lars looked at her, his eyes wide. He could smell her, something like dead leaves drying in the sun. Then she pulled away and got out, leaning back in only to say, "I'll be comin' round the mountain, then."

"Goodnight." And she slammed shut the door and was gone.

"Anita?" Paul said.

Inside, Lars pulled some blankets from the closet and spread them on the floor. It was not much of a mattress, but Paul didn't seem to mind. In the same closet he found an extra pillow, Megan's, which he'd stuffed there weeks before. He held his breath as he pulled it out, and exhaled only after he had pushed it under Paul's head.

Hodge meowed and Lars fed him. Then he undressed and got into bed. He looked at Paul and noticed a shaft of street light falling over his eyes. They were wide open.

"What's the matter?"

"Spins," Paul said, his head absolutely still.

"You drank a lot. If you're going to do that, it shouldn't be beer. You'll get sick."

Paul seemed not to hear. "Excuse me," he said. He got up. Lars heard him vomiting behind the bathroom door. When he came back he looked better. "It's not so bad," he said to Lars. He lay back down and closed his eyes. "I'm sorry. You probably think I'm a loser."

"No."

"My wife, you know . . . and we have a houseguest. From Italy. It's all too confusing." He coughed.

"They're two different guys?"

"Huh?"

"The Italy guy and . . . you know . . ."

"Oh," Paul said. "Yeah." Then he was silent a long time. Lars thought he was asleep. Hodge slunk over to Paul and sniffed his nose, and Paul's face scrunched up. The cat seemed to decide he was all right and curled into a little ball on his ankles.

"I gotta tell you," Paul said. He shifted his ankles a little and the cat yawned.

"What?"

"This is weird, I know."

"Go on."

He sighed. "Well, that plane crash."

Lars stiffened. "What about it?"

"I *saw* it. It happened right by my house. I saw it go down." He paused. "It was the scariest thing I've ever seen in my life."

Lars considered his reply for a long time. "I don't think I want to hear any more."

"Okay."

"Can you understand that?"

"Uh-huh. But if you ever do," he said, "you can ask me."

"Maybe I will," Lars said. He turned over in bed to face the window, and looked out over the neighborhood houses, shrouded by trees. Backlit by the moon, they were blank, save for a dim light here and there in the windows. On the upturned milk crate next to his bed, he saw the box of pencils, and he snaked a hand out from under the sheet to pick them up. Potter, Potter Pencils. He wondered if there was a connection there. The plastic wrap came off with difficulty, and he took one out—the same kind he'd used in school, when he was a kid. Whatever happened to pencils? Why didn't adults use them? He thought to write this down, and even found a piece of paper to do it on, but the pencil wasn't sharpened. He was considering getting up to sharpen it when sleep took hold with uncommon strength, and he let it pull him away.

13

Hamish kept coming. It wasn't every night, but by now it was familiar enough to her that she could keep her heart from racing as he walked around the house. Usually he sat down to dinner, whether she was eating or not; sometimes he only paced from window to window. He always pushed the curtains aside with the same deliberate movement, the back of his hand sweeping them slowly up. He would stare out for long minutes, perfectly still, and then the curtains would sift through his fingers like a wooden fence swallowed by blown sand. And when they were closed he withdrew, apparently disappointed, and walked off, only to vanish again at the road.

One night, while he stood sadly at the window, Trixie got up and went outside. She watched him from the yard. He was faintly luminous, a paper lantern lit by a candle. After a few minutes, during which he didn't seem to see her, his eyes suddenly widened in surprise and he leaned forward, frowning. He pulled away and headed for the door; she saw him flash by in the kitchen window. But he never came out. When she went back inside, he was gone.

Saturday morning she woke up just before dawn from a strange and un-

settling dream, her body trembling and damp from what she recognized, after a moment's thought, as sexual warmth. This was the dream: she was treading water in a huge lake, the shores of which were too far away to see. She
didn't feel like she was in immediate danger of sinking, though it was obvious that sooner or later she would have to. She had the same seventy-three-
year-old body in the dream, with its same erosion and marks of age, but it
kept her afloat without strain.

Beneath her something huge and muscular was swimming, a creature she
sensed was deadly and capable of bringing her under. The water's surface
swelled around her with the creature's slow undulations. She woke up when
its skin—not scaly or slimy, but smooth, warm, like a Thanksgiving turkey—
slid across the pads of her feet. The contact sent waves of hot itch up her legs,
and the feeling persisted once she was awake. When she reached down to rub
her feet, she was surprised and frustrated to find that her stiff and sore old
limbs had been restored to her. She lay down again and noticed the slick
warmth between her legs; she touched herself there, pressing as she sometimes had, but the desire leached out of her and she fell back to sleep, her fingers drying on the air.

The dream left her with a drifting sense of urgency that followed her all
morning. After coffee and toast she decided to go to the University Library,
where she could bury herself in other things. Going out to the car, she noticed
that the air, which had been nosebleed-dry for the better part of a month, had
gone clammy. The temperature had dropped fifteen degrees overnight. The
change heralded the approach of uneasy breathing—the cold alone would be
tough on her lungs, as it was every year, plus there was the industrial sludge
and woodstove smoke the valley trapped in autumn and winter. She'd have to
stay inside more, soon, a fact that filled her with unusually deep dread. For
now, though, the air was damp and clear as a glass of water.

She wondered how Edward was doing in Glacier Park, where by now it
was certainly much colder. They might already have snow. She remembered
how much he hated fall when he was a teenager; he trudged off to school as if
to prison. The year before Kat left, he was thirteen and at his most brittle and
fearful. Meanwhile his sister had gotten more brutal. She dragged him about
the house by the arm, telling him where to sit, what to do. She listened dutifully when Trixie scolded, but her eyes were full of disdain, and Trixie sensed
that she was only paying attention to get a better sense of her enemy's flaws.
When Trixie brought home their meager groceries, Kat sneered at them, as if

Trixie held exclusive blame for the family's poverty. She endured Trixie's reprimands with unsettling patience before stealing away to her room. She studied the Bible passionately, masochistically, sometimes staying awake all night, and always returned from school over an hour late.

Edward, on the other hand, frequently didn't go to school, and the school secretary's tone of righteous disdain on the phone became all too familiar to her. On a September morning much like this one, she went to look for Edward down along the river, where she'd occasionally found him before. She looked in all his usual spots—crouched at the base of a bridge abutment; cracking rocks together in the tall grass—but he didn't turn up. She had decided to climb the bank to look for him in the street, when she heard a sound trickling from a corrugated drainage pipe. She came closer and recognized the sound as Edward's voice. He was talking, it sounded like to himself.

"Edward?"

She scrambled over the rocks at the water's edge and listened. "Edward!"

There was a thud in the pipe that cast a metallic echo onto the riverbank.

"Sweetheart, is that you?"

To look inside, she had to take a step into the shallow edge of a cataract. The water was cold, and her feet, protected only by tennis shoes, quickly went numb. It was dark in the pipe, and smelled gritty and flat with the collective runoff of the town's busiest streets. Above them, on the bridge, cars rumbled past.

"Edward, are you in there?" Now her eyes had gotten adjusted to the darkness, and she could see him, pressed into the pipe's curve with his arms wrapped around his knees. His toes poked into a muddy puddle. It occurred to her then that Edward was almost fourteen—fourteen!—no age to be crouched here by the river, mumbling. He was sitting just beyond arm's length.

"Please come out," she said. Her voice bounced off past him, and it took a few seconds for the echo to stop.

"No."

"It's dangerous in there. There might be rats."

He turned his face toward the darkness, then buried it in his knees.

"Please talk to me," she said. "I'm your mother."

"Why should I?"

"Because I care about you, Edward." She began to slip from the rock she was standing on, and moved to better footing. "I love you. I'm worried about you."

He sighed heavily and deeply, and for that moment he didn't sound like he was fourteen. He sounded like he was forty. "Kat says you lie."

She held the edges of the pipe tightly. "Edward, it's *me*. I don't know what Kat has been telling you, but I . . . we should talk about it." He said nothing. "What does she say I lie about? What?"

"Everything."

"Everything." She curled her toes in the shoes. It was hard to feel them. "Look, Edward, come out. I'll buy you something to eat. We can have lunch downtown. We can talk."

He looked up, his face filthy. "I won't have to go back to school?"

"Of course not. Not if you don't want."

He gave this a moment's thought, then began to crawl out. She offered him her hand. "I can *do* it," he said.

She moved away from the opening and stood shivering on the dry rocks. He came out a second later, gangly, glum, hugging himself against the cold.

"Come on," she said, taking his arm. "Where do you want to go?"

He shrugged. "Corner Deli?"

"Okay," she said, thinking about what she could not spend money on to make up for the extravagance of a restaurant. Powdered milk? Coffee. This week, no coffee. "Corner Deli it is."

In the restaurant, they sat at a small table near the window. She took her shoes off and rubbed her bare feet until the feeling came back to them. Edward was astonished that she would do this, and finally he slipped off his own shoes. They ordered hamburgers. Trixie hadn't had a hamburger in months. When the food came, a great pit seemed to open up inside her, and she ate with ravenous energy, nearly forgetting about Edward. She looked up and noticed that he was doing the same thing. They said nothing to one another until the hamburgers were gone. And then Edward, without prompting, said to her, "Kat goes to this religious place after school." He swirled a couple of french fries around in a puddle of ketchup.

"Religious place?"

"Some kind of church, except people live there. She gets all these prayer books and pamphlets and things. Sometimes she makes me read them, or she makes me listen to her read out of them." His voice was very small, and Trixie noticed that his hand, gripping the french fry, was shaking.

"I don't understand. A church where people live?"

He hung his head and she thought for a moment she had blown it. But then he said, "It's this *house* she goes to. These religious people live there. They call it a church but it isn't, really. I went there a couple of times."

"*You* did?"

"Yeah."

Her hands twitched and found each other. She moved them under the table. "So what did you think?"

He shrugged, his head still low. "I dunno. It was okay. They're into peace and love and all that, you know, God. But they're weird."

"Weird."

"They think the world's going to end. Also they're like . . . it's like they think everybody else is *wrong*. Like, the people who don't do their thing are all going to die when the world ends, but they're all going to live somehow. Marshall's supposed to be some sort of high ground, because of the mountains. Except most of the country's going to get flooded and everybody's going to get killed." He risked a glance to see how she was reacting. She must have looked okay, because he kept his head up. When he looked down at his hand he seemed surprised to find a french fry there. He ate it.

"So what do *you* think?"

"I believe in God, I guess." He sighed. "But not the other stuff. I think if there's a God He probably likes everybody." Now he braved a direct look at Trixie, and it froze her to her seat: he hadn't met her gaze for a long, long, time. The Edward she thought she knew was gone. "Kat does, though. She tells me you're going to die. Like she's trying to scare me." He shook his head. "It doesn't scare me. I mean, I'm not a little kid."

"Well, okay," she said.

"I think Kat's kind of crazy."

"Crazy?"

He nodded. "Yeah. I mean, she *hates* everybody. I think she's going to run away." As he said this a cloud seemed to lift from his face. His eyes gleamed. "She really scares me sometimes."

"I'm sorry," Trixie said. "If your father and I caused any . . ."

He shook his head. He didn't want, or need, to hear. "Is he coming back, or what?"

This startled her. Of course she had no hope of Hamish returning. She had assumed the children felt the same. "I don't think so."

"That's okay," he said. "It's better this way." He seemed to doubt this a little.

"It's not now," she said. "But we can make it better."

"Kat thinks he's coming back. Or she says so. I think she's going to go look for him if he doesn't."

"I have no idea where he is," Trixie admitted.

"Seattle. Or someplace near there."

"What!"

"Kat found out." He didn't offer any explanation and, for the time being, Trixie didn't ask for it. Seattle. She wondered what Hamish, who'd been so choked here in a small town, would do in a city.

"I wish I was older," Edward said after a while. "I wish I was in college."

"That's why you ought to be in school," she couldn't help saying.

"Yeah, yeah."

She drove slowly down her road, dodging potholes, then accelerated to the speed limit when she got to the new section of pavement. The windshield was fogging up on the inside and the heat was not yet hot. She tugged the sleeve of her coat over her hand to wipe away the condensation, revealing the hillsides on the way into town, dotted with new developments ugly in their uniformity. When she got to Cedar she turned right and headed east, toward the University. She had just passed the bowling alley and was looking south, to where the sun sparkled on the river, when she noticed a hand resting on the dash to her right. It moved back and forth, tracing a rectangular swath in the dust. Her heart lurched and she took her foot off the gas. The car rolled to a stop on the shoulder, and soon the only sounds were the noises of Cedar Avenue seeping through the closed windows and the shallow rhythm of her own breathing.

And then, the most gentle of brushings: that hand on the dash, moving again through the dust. Its edges were eerily, impossibly clear, the hairs upon it false, uniform; its skin was dark and unblemished, as if airbrushed there in heaven by a ceaseless and benevolent sun.

A scent in the car, like the sea: salt, a hint of fish. Rich decay that reminded her of swooping gulls.

Before she could gather herself, could consider the consequences, she turned, and there he was, dressed crisply in a light denim shirt, jeans, boots. As he moved, his clothes did not rustle against themselves; his chest neither rose nor fell. He turned to her. No hat, his face mature but youthful still, his hair combed neatly back across his head, exposing his wide forehead. It was and was not Hamish's face, precise in the shape of its features yet curiously emotionless. He seemed an apparition by committee, an average of her memories of him. He was fifty, thirty. He looked at her and did not look at her.

"Hamish?" Her voice sounded steadier and stronger than it felt, yet there was something curiously flat about it, as if this ghost absorbed all sound around it. Her skin felt dry.

His eyes narrowed and he looked blankly at her. He blinked.

"Hamish."

And now, instead of answering, he looked out the front window, frowning, and then craned his neck to see out the back, toward where the hills rose from the valley floor. She could see the outline of the passenger headrest dimly through his neck. After a moment he turned back to her, expressionless, and turned again to look out the back, like a dog who wanted out, but with military dignity.

She turned the car around and went back the way she had come, taking the first turn south, toward the foothills. In the minutes it took to get there, she stole glances at him, sure he would vanish if she didn't. They drove past condominiums so new the windows still bore their labels, and ranches, raced a freight train running along the road until the tracks gave way to a stream that thinned as they climbed. Hamish stared straight ahead, and finally leaned forward, taking in the mountains in the distance. He faintly flickered.

Soon the road yielded to dirt, and she turned around in a private drive that ran up over a ridge, out of sight. The car idled, and she sat there, looking over Marshall. Hamish looked too, until finally he turned to her, his eyes empty. He looked out again.

"I don't understand," she said.

He closed his eyes and lifted his hand to his face. He rubbed it there slowly, and took it away. Then he opened his eyes again and, smiling now, turned back to her.

She looked out at the town—so built up now, almost a city—to try to find what he had seen, and when she looked back he was gone.

———

She sat in the car on the hill, unmoving, for a few minutes. The sun had come out, and she rolled down the window to let in some fresh air. It was cold and clean, and swept away the ocean smell that Hamish had brought. When her head had cleared and she could think, she put the car in gear and started the trip back to town.

In the distance, to the west, smoke pushed from the twin stacks of the pulp mill and swept off toward the airport, curving hazily across the sky. The sight made her feel purged somehow, and the confusion of burdens she had been bearing lifted; for a moment her destination was unimportant. She felt like a little girl again—still thrilled and gratified by the ineffable rewards of experience. She remembered the smokestack that once stood over Great Falls, and how, before she was told it was an eyesore, she fantasized climbing it and looking out over the city for a view untainted by what she knew about the people in it, the way a new arrival might see it. The memory was strangely clear, the way images from books could imprint themselves perfectly onto the imagination. She was kneeling on a bench, leaning against the wooden slats of its back. It was late summer, and she was worried that her new stockings would tear on a splinter from the wood. The smokestack poured smoke. And Schatze, her sister—she was there too, next to her on the bench. Schatze wore a new hat, with wildflowers tucked under the band.

Then it all came back to her—it was the train station. They were there with their parents to meet Gran, Trixie's mother's mother, who lived in New York City and was coming to visit them. It was Schatze's voice that pulled her from the stack. "The train is here!" she shouted, and indeed when Trixie turned, there it was, its own smokestack visible above the trees just beyond the bend. They waited as close to the tracks as they were allowed.

Gran was the skinniest woman Trixie had ever seen. Her face was pale with makeup and shaded by a black hat, and her shoes were perfect, black and gleaming like little pieces of night sky. They looked like they would fall apart the second they hit the ground. But when she stepped onto the platform bricks, she and the shoes were steady as stones. Trixie's mother called to her— "Mama!"—and her voice was filled with hope and anxiety, feelings her mother rarely betrayed. Trixie was flooded with a sudden sense of her grandmother's power. When she hugged the girls it was perfunctory but fierce. Trixie thought it was like hugging a length of baling wire.

That night, Schatze, always the boldest, pestered her with questions, which Gran deflected as if they were flies. She only stopped asking when Gran lifted her up by the armpits and moved her across the room. "You may ask your questions from there," Gran said, but Schatze had been scorned. She retreated to the sofa, where she and Trixie played checkers and eaves-dropped.

Gran carried an air of constant disappointment. She pursed her lips at everything. When Trixie's mother put dinner on the table, Gran smiled and nodded her thanks, but closed her eyes while she ate, as if great concentration was necessary to endure the meal. She entered the guest bedroom with a re-signed sigh. Trixie's father did his best with Gran, cracking silly jokes, asking deferential questions about life in New York. She answered these with some-thing approaching animation, and for days her stories entertained them when nothing else did. But she refused to engage her daughter or her family in any other way—she played no games with Trixie and Schatze, and detested the musical that was showing at the Grand Opera.

Gran's train left early in the morning, and she was gone before the girls were awake. At breakfast, Trixie asked her mother if Gran had gone back to New York City.

"She doesn't live there, Trixie," her mother told her. "She lives in Buffalo, New York." *Buffalo,* she said with a self-satisfied pop of air through her lips.

In retrospect, Trixie could see how bitter and lonely Gran had been—she lived by herself, her husband long dead, in a sad, cold city. At the time, Trixie was disappointed by the revelation that she didn't live in New York—Gran seemed less real after that—but now, considering, she gave her grandmother a little more credit. She had a consistent way of dealing with her disappoint-ments, even if it was simply becoming more disappointed. Because now it was she who was disappointed, haunted, without family.

She found herself heading for the University after all, aware that some-thing had changed after this last visit from Hamish, but unsure what it was or how she should react. To lose herself in a book—such a reliable refuge from her memory reading had always been—seemed a nearly irresistible pull. She found the library parking lot, one of dozens connected by a baffling snarl of one-way paths, and pulled into a metered space. Inside, the building's auto-mated hush wrapped its arms clumsily around her; computers beeped behind the circulation desk, and the air conditioners—fooled by the sudden change in the weather—hummed in the walls. She paused on the stairs, blinded by the harsh light pouring onto the landing from the windows, and decided to head for the basement this time around, perhaps to look, as she had been fond of doing in years past, at maps.

Instead, her interest was piqued by a stooped old man shuffling through a glass door she hadn't noticed before, to the right of the stairs. His stunning white hair and beard reminded her of Colonel Sanders, gone to seed. The door closed behind him and she read: "Montana Room. Made possible by a grant from Mr. and Mrs. J. Doty."

She pushed the door open and walked in. There were about ten rows of stacks jammed into the tiny room, and the old man sat behind a compact metal desk. He looked up and smiled as the door shut behind her. He wore a name tag: "MSCM Library System: Nelson."

"If I can be of assistance . . ." he said, his eyebrow cocked as if he were kidding.

"That's all right," she said. Her voice cracked.

She hurried around the corner of a random stack, her heart racing. The smell of old paper folded over her, and she leaned against the cool metal of the shelves, breathing steadily. It was a good feeling, to lean here, so immediate and palpable that she could almost convince herself she had imagined the entire morning, from her dream to her encounter with Hamish on the hill. When she opened her eyes, she saw before her row upon row of old books: *Along the Lewis & Clark Trail. The Indians. Chief Joseph. Along the Blackfoot.* Montana history books. She reached out for *The Indians* and opened it to the title page. It read:

The Indians.
The SAVAGES' customs and traditions,
sought and recorded by DR. J. ALLEN WRIGHT,
anthropologist and scholar.

The publisher's date was 1904, and on the facing page, separated by a leaf of onionskin, was an overexposed photograph of Dr. Wright himself, his hand stuck into his shirt like Napoleon. He wore a pince-nez and muttonchops.

The following page was a photograph of a group of Indians, lined up as if for execution, in front of a massive tipi and a scrawny stand of cottonwoods. None of the Indians was smiling. The caption read, "Seventeen members of the SIOUX tribe posed after capture, eighteen hundred ninety." This photo was not covered by a piece of onionskin.

She looked closer at the group. They appeared ill: all were thin and several slouched under the weight of their possessions, which they carried in small pouches that hung from their clothing. A few of the women carried infants, none of whom seemed to be crying. Everyone looked at the camera with the same unflinching expressionlessness.

Except, she noticed now, for one child. It held something in its hand, and its head was tipped back in laughter. Its tiny mouth was open, its eyes dancing. What it held was hard to make out. Something light-colored—a piece of bone? Cloth? It didn't matter. This child's happiness was a private, incongruous happiness. She wondered if her own grandchildren were happy, if she would ever know whether they were happy, then suddenly she recalled one of the last images she had of Schatze before she took ill. She was in their room, dancing silently, the folds of her skirt suspended between her fingers while Trixie stood in the doorway, watching her spin and spin. When Trixie said, quietly, You dance pretty, Schatze stopped, shocked, and fell to the bed with her dizziness. But the expression on her face before she knew that Trixie was watching, before she knew she would be ill with a disease from which she would never recover, was a child's secret pleasure, was the smile on the face of this doomed Indian child.

"Are you finding what you're looking for?" She turned at the voice, guiltily shutting the book. It was Nelson, the white-haired man.

"Oh, certainly."

"Of course. It's just that few of our visitors know the extent of this collection." His speech was full of unnecessary pauses: "extent . . . of this . . . collection." It left her looking at him for an uncomfortably long time as he spoke.

"I see."

"Are you from . . . Montana?" he asked her.

"I grew up in Great Falls."

"And you were born . . . ?"

"In 1923."

"Ah, 1923! I would have had you born . . . much later."

"I should be flattered, I suppose?"

"Ah, no. I should be . . . chastised. For my inaccuracy."

"Yes, well, thank you," Trixie said. "But right now . . ."

"Of course," he said, and disappeared suddenly. She replaced the Indian book and considered leaving, but before she could make up her mind Nelson reappeared. "I think . . . you'll find this interesting," he said, and handed her an oversized volume, bound in red.

When he vanished again, she opened it. It was called *Great Falls: Yesterday and Today.* She opened to a random page and immediately recognized a photograph of the deaf and blind school, built when she was a girl, a few years after Schatze died. The building was brick and stood on a corner—one of the streets was Second Avenue, she knew it. A line of men stretched around that corner, wearing overalls and caps, and holding tools—shovels, trowels, pointed bricklayers' hammers.

Why, she could remember them building it. She remembered leaning on a crude wooden railing, peering into the dug-out foundation. Why, though? And then it hit her: her father. Her father had helped lay pipe. She walked past after school and waved to her father, laboring in the dampness of the foundation.

She thought for a moment he might be in this photograph, and brought it closer to her face. But he wasn't—these were just the bricklayers. She flipped to the index and scanned the names of businesses, philanthropists, and unions, and found what she was looking for: the United Association of Journeyman Plumbers, Gas Fitters, Steam Fitters and Steam Fitters' Helpers. She turned back to the book and found their photo—a group portrait on a row of bleachers—and there he was, in the second row, third from right. Heinz Hoffman. Her father.

"*I need some information,*" she told Nelson, who was bent over his desk. "This book you gave me—my father is in here."

"That does not surprise me one bit."

"Do you have anything in your . . . archives about these men?" She showed him the photo and he nodded.

"I just might," he said. She followed him through a metal door at the back of the room and into another room of equal size, every inch, save for a small buffet-style table at the front, jammed with old paper. The room seemed to suck every last bit of moisture from her. Her hair stood on end. Nelson disappeared into a row of shelves, reappeared a moment later empty-handed, then entered another row and came back with a thick, raggedly bound book. "Please sit," he told her. She did, and he gave her the book and left.

It was a collection of union minutes for the year 1930. Almost every union in Great Falls was in it. She pored over it for several minutes—there was no table of contents—before she found her father's union, and she read its minutes carefully in the secretary's shaky hand, searching for references to him. She found several: Mr. Hoffman nominated Mr. Bland to chair the committee on rate reductions. Mr. Cavendish queried Mr. Hoffman on the subject of temperature-related expansion and contraction of copper pipe. And then, finally, she found this:

> Mr. Hoffman was absent tonight, owing to the untimely death of his eldest daughter, Katerina Ute. Mr. Bland moved to organise a sign-up for all those willing to take on Mr. Hoffman's clients for a time. All present agreed to lend their services.

I *remember* this, Trixie thought. I actually remember it—Mr. Bland must have been Uncle Roger, Roger Bland, her father's friend. She remembered him coming to the house that evening, speaking to her father in a low voice. She remembered her father slumped in his chair, one arm hanging over the armrest like a scarecrow's.

For months, it seemed that nobody in their house spoke to one another. They were all recalling Schatze's terrible pain, her ceaseless coughing. Her parents listlessly played chess, or sat unmoving with books open on their laps. Trixie stayed in her room for hours during the day, hiding beneath the sheets, speaking out loud to Schatze the way she often did when she was afraid in the night. Every morning for months she woke and looked over at the other bed, then remembered, and the day ahead, which once would have lain before her like an empty basket waiting to be filled, grew roots and rotted away before her eyes.

And one morning Trixie awoke and the day was open to her again, and she imagined herself again doing the things she had done apart from Schatze: reading, swinging, listening to records with her mother and singing along, something her sister had never liked. She stood up easily, without, for the first time, Schatze's absence crushing her back to the bed. She breathed the air and it didn't sting. Before she went down to breakfast she lay her head and arms on Schatze's bed and apologized. She sang her sister a song. Then she walked out into her new life, went down to breakfast and told her father it was time to take her sister's bed away. Later that day, he did.

She closed the Great Falls book, and wondered what she didn't know about her parents' lives. She wondered what they did all that time she was struggling to make a life with Hamish, how they passed the days together when she had gone to Marshall to assemble her various failures.

They had died within months of each other; each was all the other had.

These were things she would never know. In the parking lot of the library, she was stunned to find that evening had come, the sun glared so in the west that she could barely see to pull out of her space. She had overstayed her parking meter, though nobody had given her a ticket.

If only they had talked to me, she thought driving home.

If only I had asked.

14

Anita spent Saturday afternoon with Larry Hutton, but much of the time she was thinking about Paul. She supposed it was a fitting way to pass the day. She'd spent much of the past weeks with Paul thinking about Larry.

She lay alone in Larry's bed, in the little house by the creek. The house looked exactly like she thought it would: a yellow one-story in the shade of some trees, set back from the road by a wide, patchy yard and a dilapidated white wooden fence. A perfect place to conduct an affair, if such a place existed.

He was in the shower. She'd been invited there, but had declined. The sounds of water were everywhere around her—his shower running in the next room, the creek murmuring outside, a lawn sprinkler. Larry had stepped out of bed after they made love and opened the window a crack—anticipating her need to breathe fresh air before it had even crossed her mind. That he was an unremittingly thoughtful lover took her by surprise every time they met, which by now was often.

She should have been relaxed here. Their affair was out in the open now, and that was what she'd wanted, wasn't it? If she'd wanted to keep it a secret, she told herself, it wouldn't have been difficult; she had an eternity of lunches to spend in Larry's arms. But she played her hand in plain view and confessed quickly. It wasn't even that hard.

So why was she still in bed, and not in the shower with her lover? Why did she find herself wishing she was here without Larry, that this house was hers, this good life of austerity and independence her own?

She felt around under the sheets for her underpants, and found them wadded into the crack between the mattress and blankets. She wriggled into them, picked her T-shirt off the floor and pulled it on. It was cold now. She went to the window and closed it, then sat cross-legged on the bed, gathering her hair at the back. In the drawer of the bedside table she found a rubber band, and tied up her hair. Also in the drawer were other things: a single ear-ring, a barrette, a bangle.

Of course he'd had other lovers. There wasn't any reason to get bent out of shape about it.

She stared out the window. There was his truck, the one he'd picked her up in when she called him this morning. She didn't have her own car because Paul still hadn't come home.

Paul had called her, drunk, the night before, from somewhere loud. Who was he with? What was he doing? Don't worry, he told her. He wouldn't drive. Lars could drive him. Who was Lars? He didn't say. By the end of the phone call he was crying, apologizing for nothing in particular, until he convinced her he was worthy of her scorn and she got angry. She intended to stay up all night waiting for him, and for half of it she did, feeding the fire of her anger with shovelsful of past offenses. Then she fell asleep face down on the kitchen table and woke up with sore shoulders and the beginnings of real loneliness uncoiling inside her. She made coffee, showered. Then, finally, she called Larry and told him to come get her. He didn't ask any questions—only picked her up, bought her breakfast (their first time in public together since they became lovers, which she cruised through with indignant effortlessness), brought her home and took her to bed.

And here she was. The rubber band and clothes cleared her head. She felt slightly more contained, wished for a bra. Had she worn one this morning? She didn't think so. Another first. The shower turned off, and she listened to

Larry push the curtain aside, pictured his body. He dried himself from the feet up. She thought of Bernardo, and his unfamiliar noises in their shower, and realized she had left the house locked before the old man had come in to eat. Tough. Let Paul come back and feed him. The weather had turned and their house still wasn't fixed.

She had to stifle the impulse to bolt for the door and go running half-naked into the street, in flight from this orderly home that wasn't hers, this easy, understanding man who wasn't her husband, a head full of junk she couldn't rid herself of. The bathroom door opened.

"Were you making that sound?" He was standing across the room from her, his towel wrapped carefully around his waist. His eyebrows rode high over his eyes, almost—but not quite—mocking.

"What sound?"

"A whine. Like water running through old pipes."

Her hand drifted involuntarily to her throat, which to her surprise was tense and sore. "I don't know. Maybe."

He nodded, letting it go for a moment. He walked to the dresser, picked up his comb and ran it exactly twice through his hair, set it back down. He plucked a nail clipper from a small ceramic cup and went back to the bathroom. The door was open, and Anita counted the staccato clips—thirty, three per finger. He came back without the towel, opened the top drawer of his dresser, pulled out a pair of light-blue boxer shorts and slid them on. Then, without a moment's hesitation, he came to the bed and sat facing her, cross-legged, so their knees nearly touched across the space.

"What is it?" he said.

"What's what?" He said nothing in response and stared into her eyes until she had to hang her head. "It's nothing. I don't know."

He took her hands in his, and she let him. He squeezed them. Then he put one down and ran the back of his hand over her cheek. She wanted to sink into the sensation, let herself become no more than the warmth of a hand on her face. But that quickly it was over.

"We're taking this too fast," he said.

"Oh, no," she said suddenly. She looked out the window. Now there was a cat curled on the hood of the truck, a ratty-looking brown long-hair with black ears. "It's not that."

"Anita."

"What?"

"Look at me, please."

She did. His face was searching, electric with complete concentration. How does he do that? she thought. How can he focus like this?

"It's all right with me if you want to slow down. I didn't expect you to call this weekend, you know. I expected to have to wait until Monday."

"You barely know me," she said, surprising herself. "I'm married. Why are you bothering? I'm so much trouble." She took his other hand back. "I just want to know."

He shook his head. "That's not the problem."

"It isn't?"

"No. You told him, didn't you? About us."

Was it that easy, she wondered, to read my mind? When she brought her face up to his she saw that it was truly pained, that this was important to him, that no matter what he was saying right now, he wanted her to stay here with him. This was a surprise.

"Yeah, I did."

He sighed and let her hands go to rub his face. "You want to go back to him, don't you?"

"No!"

"But you're thinking about it."

"No, I . . ." What was the real answer to this one? For a moment she lost all sense of herself, all context—if she wasn't Paul's wife, then who was she?— and with that loss came a terror deeper than any love she had felt for Paul, any she imagined she might feel for Larry. She felt the bed, the house, dropping away underneath her. She fell back to the pillow and squeezed her eyes shut.

"I'm sorry," he said after a while. "I should have known better."

"What do you mean?" she asked him through her hands. His voice had that quality of disappointment her mother had expressed when Anita announced her decision to start a career in banking.

"This is it for us," he said, so resigned, so quickly. She began to panic.

"Wait." She sat up, holding out her hands for balance. "Please just wait." When she opened her eyes she found he hadn't budged. He sat sourly before her like a monk, his legs crossed and his hands on his knees. "I don't not want you. I'm just worried about my husband, okay? It's not like him to—"

"Okay," he said, impatient.

"Do you understand? I don't—"

"All *right.*" He uncurled himself and went to his dresser. He opened drawers, taking things out, keeping his back to her.

She got up and put on her jeans and jacket. When she reached into her pocket for her car keys she remembered she hadn't driven. She stood a minute by the bedroom door while Larry fussed at the dresser. Then she said, "I need a ride home."

"I know."

"Larry . . ."

"You don't have to say anything else." He turned to her, eyes wet, and she started at the sight of him, rigid with dejection. "I get it."

"I don't know if you do. I just need—"

"Please," he said. "I know."

The cat looked up sleepily when they came out, and fled when Larry opened the car door. He was a careful driver. He steered with unwavering control, his fingers wrapped tightly around the wheel. He drove the speed limit. When they turned onto Valley Road, Anita began to feel heavy, and by the time they reached the drive she could hardly muster the energy to step out of the truck. He didn't make the left turn onto their road, only signaled right and pulled to the shoulder to drop her off. He had done this before: he didn't want to see their house.

The truck came to a stop. He pulled himself toward the wheel until his forehead touched it, and he extended his fingers. The joints made gentle cracks, like ice cubes dropped into water.

"Tell me, please," he said, "that this isn't doomed."

"It's not."

"I'm very serious about you," he said quietly.

"Oh . . ."

"No, no, don't say anything. Jesus Christ."

She reached across the cab to touch him but stopped short. He was right. She would have said something, anything, because it was called for, not because she wanted to. Being in love, she'd long believed, was a condition of being able to say it. Now she feared the opposite was true—that the word, spoken, could shake loose the emotion. She didn't dare speak.

"Okay, go," he said finally.

"I'll call." But she sat there, moving her fingers in a small circle on the seat.

His hand came down on hers and stilled it. "Go," he said. She went. She looked back only once from their drive, when she heard his tires crunching the gravel. He was leaning over the wheel, his dark face long and miserable and determinedly fixed on the road.

She heard a chain saw before she had walked half the way to the house, and she fantasized briefly that Paul had come back, charged with anger, to chop it into a thousand pieces. But the closer she came, the clearer the sound was: not just one chain saw, but a chorus of them. Up around the bend, the house came into view, intact, and beyond it she was stunned to find a swath shaved into the forest, already a hundred yards deep. There were gigantic trucks equipped with winches, some kind of crane, a flatbed with tall supports on the sides, onto which denuded trees were already being loaded. Men worked: half a dozen in the woods, cutting down trees, others gathering armloads of branches and feeding them into a buzzing chipper, which greedily consumed them and spit them out as kindling. Somehow the entire operation had materialized since this morning.

One man, wearing a white hard hat, surveyed the scene, his jaw frantically working a mouthful of chew. Anita walked up to him. "Excuse me."

He whirled. "Yeah!"

"What's going on here?"

"Building a road," he said. His face was plump and red as a football, and his eyes bugged out slightly, lending him an oddly theatrical expression of surprise. He frowned. "You shouldn't be here, lady."

"I live here." She pointed to the house.

He turned his head to take in the house, and stared blankly at it, seeming not to understand the connection. "Uh-huh."

"What road?" she said.

"Gotta get that plane out of there." He tilted his head toward her. "You see the crash?"

"I was here when it happened, yes."

"Uh-huh." It wasn't clear what he made of this admission. After a moment, he seemed to become uncomfortable with her presence and walked off toward the chipper.

Walking to the house, she noticed her car wasn't in the yard. Inside, she found that Paul had come and gone. There were dirty dishes in the sink, two of them, and a wet towel bunched on the bathroom floor. The door had been left unlocked. She walked outside again, to the shed, and tried the door. To her surprise, it was locked; she didn't even know there was a lock on it—sure enough, a shiny circle of brass with a keyhole in the center. The sight of it filled her with rage, and she pulled harder, kicked the door. It gave a little. She pulled again, and the handle came free in her hand. She held the handle tightly, crushing it in her fingers, and finally hurled it, with a scream, at the treeline.

All evening, she sat and waited. When it grew dark, she got up from the couch and searched the house for a note he might have left. There was none.

She lay awake in bed that night, wondering if Larry was doing the same. Probably not. It seemed that he could sleep through anything, eat through anything, regardless of the grumblings of his heart. He never failed at the logistics of living: his truck would never be broken down for more than a couple of days; his clothes never appeared on a bed or chair on the way to their hangers in the closet. He made schedules.

He was, in short, what she aspired to, but all too infrequently achieved. This was her greatest fear about him: that if she gave herself to him, he might make her into that perfect version of herself. And then what?

It was obvious why she had fallen in love with Paul. She saw in him a blank slate that she could quickly fill with the details of her choosing; she could teach him to be more like her. Now this seemed like the most infantile kind of folly, and cruel to boot. Paul was not a blank slate. He was Paul and always had been.

And the baby she had so wished for, the baby for which her marriage was falling apart? Another mirror.

When she was a girl, she often fantasized that she'd been adopted, or that her parents had taken her from a household of refinement and order. For the better part of her eighth year, she was convinced of it. She secretly dug through her mother's papers looking for her birth certificate, and when she didn't find it, held up its apparent absence as proof of her rightful lineage. Once, agitated by some childish disappointment she could no longer recall, she baldly accused her mother of stealing her and demanded she be returned to her real parents, her real house. Her mother seemed mildly alarmed by all this, but made no response. The next day, she brought Anita to the bank, opened the safety deposit box, and showed her the birth certificate—Anita

Jane Sloboda, seven pounds, nine ounces. Her footprint was on it, a smudged blob of black ink next to the state seal of Alabama.

She wouldn't speak to her mother for a week, thinking herself a victim of the worst sort of betrayal. But part of her knew that she could only blame herself for it. It was this part she most hated, the same part that had reawoken now.

In the morning, she woke to cold, and the already certain knowledge that he hadn't come back yet. She pulled the sheet tight over her body. There wasn't a blanket, and she had to pee, but the discomforts focused her and she reached deep into the muck of her heart to see if she could find out what she wanted, right now.

Not Paul. The thought of him here beside her—his warmth less comforting than unsettling, like the warmth of a bus station bench once a stranger has left it—made her legs ache with apprehension. She rubbed them. Were he here, he might have done it himself, his palms sweaty with self-loathing and guilt. The ache remained.

And not Larry, whose love, if that's what it was, seemed treacherous: there was a hardness to him that didn't want to forgive her for not being at her best at all times. More disturbing was that he thought he already knew what her best was. Even more disturbing was the possibility he was right.

And ultimately, she didn't want to be alone here either, which unfortunately for the time being was her only option. It was as if the walls were polished steel—everything in the house reflected back to her those qualities that had engineered her failures. What she wanted was really two things: to be elsewhere, and to be somebody else. Or at least a version of herself that had made better decisions, that had thought more clearly. She got out of bed shivering, put on the heat, and made her way to the bathroom in the half-dark.

After her shower, she stood in the kitchen in her sweater and jeans, waiting for inspiration to strike. None came. She noticed that the bulk of the cold was coming from the living room, where the wall was, at this point, nothing more than a piece of plywood nailed onto two-by-fours. Balled-up scraps of insulation were piled on the floor by the sofa. But, of course, it didn't matter. The house already felt like it wasn't hers. She remembered her last few weeks in Tuscaloosa, how much she hated those things she had long loved—the constant humidity, like the friendly embrace of a large, affectionate, slow child; history's weight over everything; the calm self-knowledge of people whose ancestors had been conquered on their own soil. She had longed for the mountains and towering, oblivious detachment of Montana. Now she missed the South, hated this house, and longed for nothing that she could actually have. It was time to jettison desire and begin treading the more familiar road of obligation. She opened the phone book and looked up Emil Ponty.

"Hello?" A young girl answered. A lover? A daughter.

"Is Mr. Ponty there?"

"He's in bed."

"This is Anita Beveridge. My husband works for your dad."

"Oh, yeah," the girl said, as if she knew Paul. "Sure."

"I'm wondering if he's . . ." But why explain it to the girl? She felt her voice going businesslike, the loan officer demanding a delinquent payment. "It's important I speak to your father."

She saw through it. "Right." And the clatter of a dropped phone.

Outside, a movement caught her eye. The trucks had arrived to cut down more trees. On a Sunday, even. She heard a chain saw start up, and a man walked into her view in the distance, holding the saw before him like a weapon. He laid it into a tree and the blade sunk in as if it were butter.

"Yeah?"

"Mr. Ponty? This is Anita Beveridge. I hope I didn't wake you."

"Just reading the funnies." His voice was nimble and slightly high-pitched, a gruff child's.

"I'm calling about Paul. Have you seen him?"

"Nope. Not since last week, anyway. When'd you lose him?"

"He called from somewhere Friday night, and he's been gone since."

"Ever do this before?"

"Oh, no. He's a homebody." She pressed the receiver closer to her ear, remembering Friday night, the bathwater she sat in pink with his blood. She thought that their separation would be something more than a sorting out of emotional goods. They were made of the same stuff. She wore molecules that used to be his. It would be like pouring the gin and the tonic back into their respective bottles.

"Mrs. Beveridge? Are you there?"

"Sorry."

"Have you checked the places he goes to? Bars, maybe? Friends in town?"

"He doesn't have any friends."

Ponty paused before saying, "Did you have some sort of disagreement?" And he added, "Maybe?," as if the question was somehow out of line.

"Um . . . yes, actually." As she watched, a tree fell in the forest. At the edge of their yard, a backhoe was unearthing stumps. One came up with great resistance, clods of dirt falling from the broken-off root ends.

"I have some experience with this, Mrs. Beveridge," Ponty was telling her. "Could be he's laying low."

"Experience. You mean your wife left you?"

"Uh. I meant in my work. My detective work." He waited a beat, during which she grew hot with embarrassment. "But as a matter of fact, yes."

"So she came back," Anita said, relieved.

He cleared his throat. "Oh. Actually, no."

"I see."

"If I see him . . ." he said finally. He sounded tired.

"Sure. Thanks. I'm sorry to get you out of bed."

"No problem. Hey—"

"Yes?"

"Tell him to call me when you find him? I have some work I need done."

When they hung up, she put on a pot of boiling water and sat down at the kitchen table. She stayed there most of the day, doing crossword puzzles and flipping blankly through catalogs. In the evening, she called Kathy, the head teller, and asked her for a ride to work.

"You two need another car," Kathy said.

That night she didn't sleep, only lay in the middle of the bed, alternately tugged by the wish that he would come home and they could get it over with, and a wrenching dread of the same thing. She fantasized a plan of action: herself, her car, her things, and a cashier's check for her life savings, all on their way to someplace better and new, maybe somewhere in the Southwest like Tucson or Albuquerque. She could already taste the dust, sharp as glass on her tongue, and feel the hot dry air plucking at her skin.

In the morning, Kathy came for her and they drove to work. Anita tried to act cheerful. But when a car approached close behind them with its lights on, she saw herself reflected in the windshield, her eyes sunken and wary like a rabid animal's. She hadn't eaten breakfast. Larry would have been disappointed and even slightly disgusted by that.

"Okay," Kathy said suddenly. "What is it?"

They were at the end of Valley Road now, on their way toward town. "Nothing."

"When was the last time you spilled your guts to somebody, Anita?"

The question took her by surprise. "Uh . . . not lately."

"So."

She shifted around in her seat and felt a draft on her thigh. *My God,* she thought, *I forgot my underwear.* But she felt around and found it was only a hole in her stockings. "I don't know what to say," she said. "I think Paul and I are breaking up."

"I'm sorry," Kathy said. She meant it. The unexpected sincerity choked Anita up, and she had to pause a second to keep from crying. Kathy was wearing a frilly blue western blouse and a black skirt. She had big hair. Anita had never really trusted her, always thought she was a bit ungenuine, a little tasteless. "How long have you been together?"

"Four years."

She nodded, like a doctor gathering information for her diagnosis. "What happened?"

"We want different things," she said. "It was my mistake." After a moment, she added, "I thought I could make him want what I did."

"You were young."

They were pulling into the bank parking lot. "I guess I was. Am."

All that morning, she pushed things distractedly around her desk. She approved several car loans automatically, with only vague attention to the credit reports. She passed her desk clock from hand to hand like a hot biscuit, as if doing so would jar the numbers loose and speed the time. At lunch, she passed up the leftovers in the doughnut box and walked across the street to the used-book store, where she thought she might be able to distract herself.

It was mostly a kitsch store. They carried a lot of Western Americana, gag books, ancient how-tos on the art of the love letter or postwar dinner party etiquette whose only value now was their age. It was uncomfortably warm, and she immediately began to perspire. At the back of the store she spied a wooden stool. She went to it and lowered herself onto it.

It was a very short stool. To sit comfortably she had to cross her legs in an awkward way, so that she took on a near-Indian-style stance. Her calves brushed the carpet. It reminded her of a visit she took to a first-grade classroom. The class was learning about money, and the teacher, whose home equity loan Anita had handled, had asked her to come in and explain how a bank worked. While Anita talked to the kids, she sat in one of their tiny chairs. At the time, the visit struck her as a preview of a world she would soon be a part of—a world of exuberance tempered by order, of regular schedules and parent-teacher conferences. This stool only made her feel like an oaf in a country of pixies.

There was a row of old books at eye level, which she wearily scanned. They were children's treasuries of fiction and poetry, all of them oversized and crusty with dried binding glue. She opened one called *Great Moral Tales,* and found a story about a sick boy who gives his toys away to poor kids. In one scene, he tries to demonstrate a bicycle to a little girl, but he is too weak to stand and topples like a rusted fence. Anita read it through to the bitter end: the boy's tragic death, surrounded by his admiring little friends.

In spite of herself, Anita began to cry. She slapped the book shut and shoved it back onto the shelf, and as she pulled her hand away a splinter found the webbing between her thumb and forefinger and drove in deep. She grabbed the hand with her other and squeezed her eyes shut. Now the sobs came up and out of her in great and ragged waves. God, she was sick of crying, of having to cry. She leaned heavily against the books.

"Miss?"

The voice took her by surprise. She righted herself, overcompensated, and groped for the floor to keep from falling. She groaned and pulled herself up straight. Then she looked at where the voice had come from.

It was a clerk, a woman in her thirties, bent over before her with a book closed on her finger. She had a large, blurry face that stayed blurry even after Anita wiped her eyes, its wide, rounded features blending into each other like clouds. "Are you all right?" she said. "Can I help you with anything? I don't mean to pry but it is very unusual, you coming in here like this and crying, and I don't know should I talk to you or call the cops."

Anita sniffed. "Have you got a tissue?"

The clerk produced a wad of toilet paper from her shirt pocket. "It's clean," she said. Anita noticed her thick, freckled wrists.

"Thank you." She blew her nose, tucked the tissue away into the pocket of her skirt. Her hand was throbbing. She held it up to the light, fingers spread, and saw the splinter: a tiny point of wood showed above the skin; the rest lay beneath, a shadow.

"What's that? You hurt?"

"A splinter."

The clerk knelt, taking Anita's hand and turning it over. Her fingers were thick and clammy, like sausages. "People think you're green if you cry over a splinter but I happen to know it hurts like damn."

"It wasn't that." Anita gently pulled the hand away. On the floor at her feet, lying open, was the clerk's book. It was called *The UFO Cover-Ups.*

"Well then what was it? You read something disagreed with you?"

Anita brought the hand back to her face, then grabbed the splinter with her fingernails and pulled it slowly out. She could feel her skin snapping back to fill the space it left, and only a dull ache, more like an itch, remained. There was no blood.

"You got it."

"Yep." And for that brief moment, she felt purged, as if the chemical that had been causing her confusion had left her body with the splinter. She dropped it on the floor and worked her fingers, each one individually.

The clerk's name was Callie ("Short for Corvallis, the town"). She led Anita to the counter and gave her a glass of cold, bitter, unsweetened iced tea, then asked where she worked.

"I have to confess I'm a bit suspicious of those who deal in currency," she said when Anita told her. "My brother Dick had a time of it down outside Hamilton with the feds over taxes, even though he does not participate in American Society at large. They sent out the black choppers? To monitor his activities?"

"Black choppers?"

"Government sends them around to check you out. If you live in town, you never see them."

"Actually I live—"

"So they saw him target-shooting out back of his place, he's got a lot of guns, you know, and they came in for a look. So he points his rifle up at 'em, just fooling, I mean what would you do?, and they're off like a shot. Week later they're at his door, all over him about back taxes. You can see the cause and effect here. I mean, I can see paying out here in town to ensure the crazies don't come into my house and kill me dead, but Dixon . . ."

)

"Dixon?"

"Dick, my brother. Named after the town. So you see my dilemma."

"Dilemma."

"With your job over at the bank." She swirled her iced tea and the cubes clinked against the glass.

"Sure," Anita said. "Sure I do. Actually I have to be getting back."

"Oh, right. Well, good talking to you."

"You bet."

Outside the sun had come out, dim and cold. The street, the buildings, the cars all had taken on an impossibly solid, yet detached quality, like giant objects stacked at the edges of a room. For the first time in a long time, Anita felt like Marshall was accessible to her if she wanted it, if only she would try harder.

"I'm staying," she said out loud. A passing bicyclist turned. She looked both ways, waited for a space in traffic, and stepped out into the street.

15

Paul came to the shed on Saturday looking frantic and demanded Bernardo come with him.

"Where?"

"Just out. You know, away. We'll go away for the weekend."

Bernardo had been drawing all morning, in a vain attempt to dispel the last traces of the previous night: he had lain awake for hours, trying to imagine his meeting with Antonio, each scenario ending with his son's astonishment giving way to fury. "Liar!" shouted the Antonio of his imagination. And the little girl cried in her mother's arms, fearful of the strange man who'd come to ruin them. Sleep proved no better. His subconscious got hold of his fantasies and corrupted them, and Bernardo found himself dragging his son's family onto crashing planes or responding to their disgust for him by committing acts of repulsive violence. And as he did so he whispered that he was a gentle man, a weak man; that he couldn't possibly be doing what he was doing: but there he was, watching his own hands exacting the terrible work. He woke gasping, starving, calmed himself by breathing steadily and tracing the walls of his shack with his eyes. Then he sat down at the workbench and drew.

He tried to draw Montana, but he couldn't get the knack of it. There was some kind of trick, he thought, to capturing the distinctive lack of softness the landscape seemed to have, even when it was obscured by clouds or smoke. But he couldn't tease the lines from his pencils. Paul, entering, snapped his concentration like a power line in the wind.

"Away?" Bernardo responded.

"I was thinking maybe of Glacier Park. You ever been there?"

"No."

"Oh, right. I guess you haven't. It's beautiful. Mountains, valleys, you know."

"Ah." It was not an altogether unappealing idea. "We eat too?"

"Oh, sure, you bet."

"I have a shower first."

"Whatever."

He nodded, and pushed his drawings into a pile on the workbench. "Okay, then. We go."

"Hey," Paul said suddenly. "You're drawing Montana."

"I do it bad."

"Let me see." He leaned in and lifted up the corners of a few drawings. "Did you do any with the house in them?"

The house. Bernardo remembered giving it a try once, the week before. He bent over and pulled it from some papers he had stowed on the floor. The house, looking very small at the foot of the mountains, done on a piece of lined paper torn from a spiral notebook. In retrospect, it wasn't too bad. He handed the drawing to Paul.

Paul's face arranged itself into a rueful smile. "This is really nice."

"The paper is no good."

But Paul didn't seem to mind. "Oh, no, this is great."

"You take."

His eyes widened. "You're serious."

"Of course."

He shook his head in disbelief. "Wow. Thanks a lot."

They set out in the car, clean and fed, around noon. Bernardo watched Paul as he drove. Obviously he had something to say, but for the moment kept it to himself. Bernardo had never met anyone so guileless, so transparent.

Bernardo knew that Anita had been having an affair. She had made no effort to keep it from him, and if he wasn't mistaken, even wanted him to know.

She made cryptic, mumbled phone calls when he was in the house and Paul wasn't, and several times walked to the end of the drive for her ride—the woman who picked her up usually came to the house and knocked. She came home late. Bernardo knew this game: she wanted Paul to find out but didn't want to tell him, and Paul wanted to avoid finding out what he must certainly have suspected was true. And by now, he figured, it must all be out in the open.

Bernardo would have none of it. He said nothing to either. His sympathies, however, were with Paul. Whatever faults she found in him, Paul was obviously loyal; it would not occur to him to be anything else.

But as they pulled onto the freeway, and the valley slid away behind them like a bad dream, Bernardo realized how tired he was of being the barrier they hid from each other behind. It was too much like his own family life, with its multiple stresses and unsteady allegiances, for comfort. The shed, the house, suddenly seemed suffocating to him, and he knew it wouldn't be long before he'd leave on his own accord.

They drove for hours, through mountains Paul told him were called the Mission Range. They rose up out of the ground at the edge of a flat valley, like a city built in a desert, and Bernardo found himself thinking that if he were a priest, sent to the New World to spread Christianity, this would be the place to do it. The mountains looked merciless, gigantic, treeless; it would take only the slightest change in perception to see them as the work of a powerful God, to fall to one's knees and worship them as such.

It was nearly evening when they reached the park. A lot of cars were leaving, their belongings bundled into trunks and onto roofs. Paul paid at a little log guardhouse and drove along a winding road that skirted a gigantic lake. Peering into the trees, Bernardo could see little clusters of dome-shaped tents, nestled between picnic tables and large American cars.

"What are these people doing?" he asked.

Paul stole a glance into the trees. "What people?"

"Back there."

"They're camping."

"Next to the cars?"

Paul shrugged. "Sure. People don't go camping in Italy?"

"Not so much."

"Well, here it's a big thing," Paul said. "It's the great American vacation. People like to go out and rough it."

"'Rough it?'"

"You know, go to the wilderness. Live a little while without the conveniences of home."

"Hmm." It didn't seem much different from Paul's house back in Marshall. Smaller maybe.

Soon they had passed the lake, and began to ascend. The road they were on was flanked by a low stone wall that would probably do very little to prevent a speeding car from sailing off a cliff, but Paul seemed unperturbed by this. Bernardo couldn't drive. All the streets in Reggio were too narrow, and they were full of holes. Besides, everything he needed was in town, or he could get to it by train. He could see that here, driving was a necessary thing. They hadn't passed a single bus all the way up the valley, and only freight trains seemed to run on the rails.

The higher they drove, the sparser the trees became, and the easier it was to see into the deep gorge they had left. He saw the road below, a ribbon covered with sparkling dots, and a creek that fed the lake. He had to admit, it was breathtaking.

"This is . . . magnificent," he told Paul.

"We're at around five thousand feet," he said.

"I think I am never so high."

Paul raised his eyebrows, but didn't take his eyes from the road. Ahead of them, a white van appeared to be full of nuns. "They have plenty of mountains in Italy, right?"

"In Italy, I am sea person. I never go walk on mountains."

They arrived finally at a visitor center, a building that seemed to combine architectural elements of both a log cabin and a filling station. Bernardo got out of the car and was surprised to find how much colder it was here. He hugged himself against it and stood on the log that marked their parking space, looking out at the not-so-distant mountain peaks. He saw a goat walking around about twenty feet from him, and he noticed that a nearby pine tree was not much larger than the goat.

Inside, while Paul went to pee, Bernardo read the placards that explained the wildlife of the alpine environment; the trees didn't grow much above a man's height and the flowers were as fragile as if they were made of sugar. The van full of nuns had arrived, and the women chattered to each other with what Bernardo thought was unusual animation, for nuns.

He wondered if Antonio came here, if this was his family's spot for vacations, and in spite of himself looked around the visitors center for him. Of course he wasn't there. When Paul was slow in returning, Bernardo went back outside, to take in the air, and spotted the nuns on the opposite side of the lot filing onto a path marked "Scenic Overlook." He turned back to the visitor center and back to the nuns, disappearing now around a bend.

Why not? He hurried between the cars and caught up. The nuns weaved past a patch of the fragile-looking flowers, through the shadow of a rock overhang, and gathered at a low stone wall, where they read from mounted metal signs. He sidled past them and leaned hard against the wall with both hands, to find there was nothing but empty air separating him from the gorge, thousands of feet below.

It had been different in the car, shielded by the window glass and the confident puttering of the engine. Now, he was met by the awful sound of exactly nothing—the sound of falling. Something cold and powerful gripped him by the neck and seemed to pull him down into it. He gasped and thought he saw, to his left, the nuns turn their heads. Here came the ground, rising to swallow him up; there was nothing in his hands but a mile of air, shaping itself like clay against his palms.

He jumped back, falling, and for a moment was lost in space before a patch of gravel found him. There were the nuns, gathering around him— You've fallen, you had quite a scare, are you all right?—and a man with a video camera. Children. They helped him up, and he thanked them, but he could not walk fast enough to get himself away from the ledge. How could they stand there, looking off into the great oblivion? Because that kind of distance could do nothing but crush a man, crack his bones like sticks, flatten a man's heart like it was so much mud. He could not stop shaking.

He was shaking still when he reached Paul, who leaned against the car door scanning the crowd for him. "There you are!" Paul said, but Bernardo could only nod his head and pull open the passenger door and collapse into the seat. Paul waited for an explanation but Bernardo couldn't give him one. He wanted to leave the park, get to the lowest point they could find and stay there forever. In the end, Paul asked him nothing, and now they both had something on their minds.

They drove back down as the sun was beginning to set, and before it was dark Paul had rented a couple of sleeping bags and a tent at a little log store at the edge of the park. This was the off-season, he explained, and they easily found an empty spot in a sparsely occupied campsite. Paul assembled the tent in the headlights' glare, and from the other provisions Paul had gotten, Bernardo found some wood and started a fire. For the moment, it felt good to be doing something unplanned.

They cooked food over the fire. Though it was stuff he wouldn't ordinarily have touched in a hundred years, he found it delicious: franks and beans, cooked in their own can ("Another American tradition," Paul told him), canned molasses bread with raisins. The smoke stung his eyes, and his knees and face baked in the dry heat.

In the tent, they lay side by side, uncomfortable with the hard ground and each other's nearness. Paul's silence was broken occasionally by loud sighs and lengthy fussings in the sleeping bag, but he didn't open his mouth. Neither did Bernardo. Somewhere nearby, some teenagers were laughing. Someone had a guitar and was playing it badly.

"So," he finally said to Paul. Paul stopped his shifting.

"So, what?"

"What you going to say?"

"Oh," Paul said. "Oh, nothing. I didn't say anything." For a few minutes he was perfectly still, then he sucked in a breath and let it out. "She's leaving me, that's the thing. She's been having this affair."

"Hmm . . ." Bernardo said. He said nothing else for several minutes, then: "This man—she wants to go be with him?"

"Yes," Paul said. "I don't know. Maybe."

He didn't reply.

"I don't know. But she's leaving." Paul turned over, and when he spoke again, his voice sounded far away. The tent smelled musty, as if it hadn't been properly dried out by the last people who used it.

"You said your wife . . . died."

"Yes."

Paul said nothing for awhile, perhaps out of respect. Or perhaps he was thinking about his own wife, about her death and how that would feel. "Any kids?" he finally asked. "Grandkids?"

The teenagers outside seemed to have gone to sleep, and there was silence now, asserting itself blankly over the ground like a fog. A car passed somewhere. Bernardo could feel the mountains looming hugely over them in the dark.

Then: "I have a son. And a granddaughter."

"Are you close?" Paul asked, accepting this without question.

"No," Bernardo said.

They left the park the next morning and drove to a nearby town called Whitefish. There, they went to a movie in a dilapidated theater that looked like an abandoned frontier building. It was an action movie called *Double Duty*. Afterward they went to a restaurant that was decorated with lacquered fish and stuffed animal heads. A row of gambling machines lined a wall at the back. They sat in a booth.

"I'm just getting a burger," Paul said.

"I never eat one."

"You never had a hamburger?"

Bernardo shook his head. Paul slapped the table, and the ice in their water glasses clinked. "No *way*!" he said. When the waitress came, he ordered two.

While they waited, Bernardo thought about the movie. He hadn't seen an American movie for some time, and a lot seemed to have changed. Its plot relied primarily on extraordinary coincidence—attack helicopters, for instance, arriving just in time to save the hero—and everybody spoke in short sentences, the words clipped like shot rattling in a pan. In fact, there was barely any dialogue at all. He'd had trouble keeping up with everything.

"The movie," he said to Paul. "It is hard to understand."

"What do you mean?"

He thought a moment. "They shoot the guns, and they talk like a gun." He made a gun shape with his hand and emptied a couple of rounds at Paul. "They don't talk like you."

"Well, you know, I'm from the South. Alabama. We talk different from your average movie."

"The South?"

"The southern United States. Like, the Civil War?" He raised his arms and made his own gun gesture, this time a rifle. "Mostly, the only time you see a southerner in a movie is if he's backwards. A hick." He made a stupid face.

"Ah."

Their burgers came. Bernardo stared for a moment at his. Its arrangement on the plate seemed an elaborate charade: around the burger itself lay a tasteful array of trimmings—lettuce, tomato, onion, a pile of fried potatoes—but underneath the bun, the beef was bright red, soaking the bottom piece of bread with its juices like a wound seeping through its dressing. Cheese melted over it and drooled down the sides. It was so unspectacular—so human—that he laughed out loud.

"What?" Paul said. He was trying to add ketchup to the mix. Bernardo noticed that all around the restaurant, people had bottles of ketchup on their tables.

"The tomato, the lettuce. It is like . . . you shake hands, then you fuck."

Paul looked down at his own plate, trying to see his hamburger from this new perspective. "Well," he said. "You're supposed to put them on. See?" He demonstrated, gently assembling a tower of meat and vegetables and topping it with the bun. Then he stared at Bernardo, waiting for some sign of understanding. Bernardo didn't know how to respond. He had never felt so foreign. "Aha," he said, and that seemed to be enough, but it pained him to feel so unwelcome and strange.

That night they stayed in a motel just outside town. The curtains in their room didn't close right, and a glowing sign at a gas station across the street bathed the room in lurid orange light. The burger hadn't agreed with Bernardo, and still didn't, but he could see the appeal. It was an impulse, eating it, and damn the consequences.

Maybe this was what it meant to be American. Everything and everyone struck him as *young*—the movie, badly acted, poorly written, was a puerile and impossible fantasy; these buildings, all hurriedly constructed, were like the makeshift toys of a precocious child. Nobody intended things to still be relevant years from now. For better or worse, these people did what they wanted and it made them happy.

And maybe, Bernardo thought, there was something to be learned from that. The incident at the visitor center was long over, but still he felt like he was falling. He said, "Paul, I tell you something," but Paul didn't answer him, only shifted in his bed.

He went on. "I am in the plane. When it crash. This is how I come to Montana."

Paul's breathing came to him, fast and steady, from across the room.

"I tell you lie before. Everybody dead. I have no passport, the people come and look for me, I don't know what I do. I come here to see my son Antonio.

But he thinks I am dead. Everybody dead." A car passed by outside, and its headlights swept the room. "I have no money, nothing, is why I am in the woods. I don't know where I go now."

Neither spoke. Minutes passed, and Paul turned toward Bernardo, his face finding the stripe of orange light. His eyes flashed, and they watched each other.

"I want to go home. But I lose everything, *capisci?*"

Paul nodded. After a while he closed his eyes. Bernardo watched him for some time before he too fell asleep.

The next morning Bernardo woke before Paul and put on a borrowed shirt and his old pants. He opened the window to let in the cool air, and turned the heater on. Paul stirred, awoke with a frown, and got in the shower. He put on the same clothes.

Without discussion, they began to head back toward Marshall. This time they drove down the lake's western shore. It was late Monday morning and there were few cars. Bernardo was surprised that so much of the lakeside property was undeveloped; they passed several towns marked by signs but few buildings. One was called Big Arm. He was thinking about this strange name when Paul said, "I won't tell anybody, if you don't want me to."

Until now, he wasn't even sure Paul had heard or understood. "Please. No."

Paul nodded. "Will you find your son?"

"Maybe. It not so good between us."

"You can stay as long as you want."

Bernardo considered this. Maybe it wouldn't be so bad. But no, he should leave. He would be no help to Paul. "No, I go soon. You very good to me."

After they had passed Big Arm's tiny cluster of houses, Bernardo saw, by the water at the end of a steep dirt road, a flat yellow building and its dock. And floating at the end of the pier was a small wooden boat with a crude-looking cross sticking up in the middle of it.

"Madonna mia!" he said. "Stop! Stop the car!"

Paul slammed on the brakes, and the car slid into the oncoming lane. Bernardo looked behind them and saw two black tire marks curving across the pavement. "What!" Paul was saying. "What! What!"

"There," Bernardo said. "On the water." He raised his eyebrows in apology. "Sorry. No . . . emergency."

Paul shook his head, less angry than disappointed, as if some dangerous and thrilling adventure had been averted, and turned the car around. He drove slowly back the hundred yards to the dirt road.

"Here," Bernardo said. "Here."

The dirt road slanted through tall grass into a clearing, where the house and pier stood. There was also a pickup truck, the same faded yellow as the house, and a gray dog that didn't bother to stand up as they approached. Near the dog was a small boy, sitting on an old tire around which weeds had grown. The boat bobbed on the water, smaller than the *ontre* Bernardo had known, but true in shape, if a little rough. Something white clung to the cross, a tied handkerchief perhaps, or a plastic bag.

"What is it you saw?" Paul scowled. "I think this is somebody's house."

"That boat." He pointed. "It is like the boat of my grandfather."

Paul squinted at it, then his face brightened. "Oh! You drew that!"

"Yes, yes." The little boy had stood up, but hadn't come toward the car. Paul parked it in a bare patch of dirt and they stepped out. The sun was pleasantly warm, and the smell of fish filled the air, possibly from the mud on the lakeside, which looked dark and viscous with rot. Bernardo walked up to the boy. "Hello," he said. "Tell me please about this boat."

"That one there?" The boy had been doing something with a stick, peeling the bark off it in long strips, and he dropped it on the ground. He was about eight.

"In the water. This is your boat?"

He shrugged. "It's my dad's."

"He is here?"

The boy shook his head. "Nope. You can go look at it if you want. Don't get in it though." He looked down at the stick, as if he was considering picking it up. Instead he kicked it. "Why, do you want to buy it?"

"Ah, no. Only look."

The boy looked disappointed. "Well, you could hang around until my dad gets back." He looked up the road, but nobody was there. "I helped build it."

"Yes?"

The boy nodded, then ran back around the side of the house. The dog, suddenly interested, got up and followed.

The pier was sturdy and new, and smelled strongly of pitch and pine sap. The boards didn't creak as Bernardo walked across them. Paul followed. The boat was about three and a half meters long; the cross, two meters tall, was rough and crooked. A fetid-looking puddle sloshed in the bottom, covered by what appeared to be pale circles of mold. It looked like the builder had never really seen a swordfishing boat, had perhaps heard one described over the telephone. He looked up and saw that what he thought was a white rag on the cross was actually a little statue of Christ, impaled there with nails far too large for the purpose. The nails had begun to rust, and orange stains dripped from their heads and onto the arms and feet of the statue. Christ was dwarfed by the oversized cross, as if He had been crucified by giants.

He looked again into the bottom of the boat and saw that the patches of mold were actually floating votive candles, surrounded by paddies of melted wax. The wax was dotted with pieces of sediment: bits of leaves and weeds, dead bugs, spiderwebs, as if they hadn't been burned for some time.

"It's some kind of shrine," Paul said.

"We built it when my mom died," the boy said. He had come up silently behind them. Bernardo jumped.

"I am sorry," Bernardo said, but the boy didn't seem to get the meaning.

"We went fishing on it some. But not much. Then Dad put on the candles and the Jesus." The peeled stick had materialized again in the boy's hand, and now he tossed it into the water, where it floated. "So who are you guys?"

"I am Bernardo." He shook the boy's hand.

"Paul."

"Caleb," the boy said, sounding strangely adult. Then something caught his eye behind them, and suddenly he was a child again: "Dad!" he shouted, and ran along the pier, his feet ringing hollowly underneath.

The man coming down the hill was whisper-thin and dark, and he carried a small, stained paper bag. He wore aviator-style glasses and his hair was tied into a long ponytail; his stride was long and had a horsy bowleggedness, though there was no horse around. He looked up at Paul and Bernardo and raised his hand in greeting. Then he went into the house, Caleb following, and came back out without the paper bag.

Bernardo and Paul walked into the yard to meet him. "Hey," he said. "You want to come in for a cold drink? I got some lemonade."

The four sat in the kitchen of the house, which was surprisingly spacious and cool. Their lemonade cups sat on cork coasters on an old wooden card table. The table had been refinished, its old stains sanded and varnished over.

The man's name was Arthur Luca, and he had lived in the house for ten years. He and his wife had built it. The land it stood on was her birthright— her family had been Flathead Indians and had lived on the reservation their entire lives. She had died of breast cancer.

"All the women in her family died of it too," he told them. His voice, Bernardo thought, had a strangely resonant quality, as if it were being reflected to them across water. It was a wonderful voice. If he lived in Italy, Arthur could talk on the radio. "And Caleb and me got the house. Most of her uncles and cousins thought that was only right, but sometimes a cousin'll come down here and give me a hard time about it. If they're drunk they threaten me. They never do anything, though. They wouldn't, since I was married to Ada." He drained his glass and got up. He went to the counter and picked up a green plastic pitcher. "Want some more? I got a lot of lemons. Most people drink it in the summer, but I like it when fall's starting. Tastes best with some smoke in the air."

They accepted. Bernardo said, "These men, why they are angry?"

"I didn't grow up here." He sat down. "I'm a Blackfeet. Some people think it's not fair, I get to live in this place. But I got Caleb and he's got the right, because of his mother."

"I'm going to live here my whole life," Caleb said.

"You should go to school," Arthur said. "Then you come back and wait on me when I'm old."

"I'm not waiting on *anybody*."

But Bernardo was still thinking about the boat. "This boat you have outside."

"Saw you looking."

"You build it with Caleb?"

Arthur nodded.

"My grandfather," Bernardo said, slowly, to get it right. "In Italy, he catches swordfish with a boat like this, for many years. It is called *ontra*. This is why we look. I think I never see this boat in Montana."

"Sure," Arthur said. He leaned forward, his hands flat on the table. "My grandfather was Italian. He lived in Great Falls and rode rail, stoking steam engines. He met my grandmother in Browning, and they lived there. He made a boat like that one, except if I remember right, it was bigger. He and my grandmother rowed it around on Mission Lake with my father, and they caught these gigantic brown trout in the spring with spears." He shook his head. "Everybody thought they were nuts, trying to catch trout with spears. But he did it. He was something else."

"So he fish in Italy!"

"Beats me. He didn't ever talk about it. He didn't talk much Italian either. He just wanted to be an American and live in Montana." He sat back, crossing his arms. "But I guess he probably did. He was dead before I was ten."

Bernardo wondered if this man's grandfather could have known his own grandfather, if they might have worked together on a swordfishing crew in the Strait of Messina. He considered the name, Luca, but it reminded him of nothing. He had known no Luca in Reggio.

The boy got up to get another glass of lemonade, and Bernardo watched Arthur watch him. His face was full of love for the boy, and Bernardo could read his mind: What if Caleb tripped on a loose floorboard and fell, what if he banged his head on the edge of the counter? What if he cut himself slicing a lemon? He remembered watching Antonio as a boy, remembered grinding his teeth together at night with fatherly concern.

Paul spoke up. "Caleb said you used to fish in this boat." He tilted his head toward the pier.

"Tried it a little. Best spots around here are on the bank, anyway. Or near it." He smiled. "We never tried fishing with spears, though."

Everyone laughed, but the obvious question—what he used it for now— nobody was going to ask. There was a brief silence, then Arthur leaned back in his chair. "I'm not kicking you out or anything, but I promised Caleb we'd go do a little fishing today. I got the day off."

"What do you do for a living?" Paul asked, a little intrusively, Bernardo thought. But Arthur didn't seem to mind.

"Gift shop in Polson. We carry a lot of Indian art. I know a lot of people on both reservations, and a few on the Spokane and down on the Crow, so I spend the day on the phone, talking to artists."

"That sounds great."

"It's not bad, yeah."

But it was obvious he wanted to be out on the lake with his son. Bernardo pushed his chair back. "Thank you."

"Oh, sure." Everyone shook hands. As they left, Bernardo took another look at the boat, and thought that there could be no better life than to live simply, alone with one's son, to give one's memories form and pull them in only when needed. He wondered if someday Arthur and Caleb might light their candles and cut the rope, let their shrine drift out into the lake to burn. He hoped they would.

On the ride home, Paul explained how the Indian reservations came into being, how the Indians were pushed into this corner of America from every direction and given the most meager of land to live on. Bernardo had seen a lot of American Westerns; the cowboys always fought the Indians but the Indians never truly lost the way they seemed to in real life. In the movies they were always a faceless and omnipresent threat, as inevitable and mindless as bad weather or disease. That so many Americans lived now among the people they had conquered was a surprise. It revealed to Bernardo an unexpected dark side to Montana, as if its people had only let the Indians live to remind themselves of their crime's great weight. He was not surprised to learn of the animosity between the races, and was grateful for the kindness of Arthur Luca and his son.

After this conversation, they didn't speak for a while. The Mission Mountains crawled past them like giant storm clouds brooding on the horizon. Bernardo recognized the pass that would bring them back into the Marshall Valley, and when he turned to Paul to remark on this, he found his chin trembling, his eyes wide and stricken.

"Paul?"

"All the time we were there, I was trying to change my mind," he said quietly. A truck stacked high with logs rumbled past them, and Paul seemed lost in the noise, like a dead leaf wheeling in high wind. "About a family. I tried to see it, you know, having a son, doing stuff with him. But I just couldn't." He shook his head. "And I got to thinking, what does that say about my life? I mean, what am I going to do with myself? I always used to think, no, I don't know what I want, and I kind of accepted it, and there it was."

He paused. So they had been thinking more or less the same thing. Bernardo didn't know if he ought to respond. "And now?"

Paul's face began to crumple. "And now Anita's leaving me! It's just me now! And if I'm nothing . . ."

"Not *nothing*."

"If I'm nothing, then what's the point of going on? How can I go on without her?" He smacked the wheel with his hand. "She leaves, she takes all I know of myself with her, you know? Now all I have is a lot of bad memories and a house I can sit in and think about them!" The car began drifting into the other lane. Bernardo reached for the wheel.

"We stop, eh? Take your foot off, okay?"

Paul slowed the car and brought it to the side of the road. He pulled the emergency brake and turned the key. When the engine stopped, he leaned over the wheel and stayed there, unmoving, for some minutes.

"You have a new start," Bernardo told him. "Me too. We start together."

"I don't want a new start."

He was at a loss. Paul's long hair draped over his hands like a creeping mold.

"You hair is too long."

"What?" He looked up.

"You need cut. Have it off. Then thinking is not so hard."

He leaned over and looked in the rearview mirror. "You think?"

Bernardo nodded yes.

Paul brought his hands to his head and, sniffing, pulled the hair back. He stared at himself a long time. "Weird," he said. And after a moment he started the car, and pulled back onto the road.

part *three*

16

Paul and Bernardo sat in the darkness of the car, staring at the wide ribbon of treeless ground that had materialized in the forest. It stretched from their yard all the way to the rise before the bank, illuminated by the last of sunlight as it receded along the horizon.

"When did this happen?" Paul said, though the answer was obvious. He felt like he had been away for weeks, instead of days. As they watched, several deer stepped out of the trees to graze in the new clearing.

"They take away the plane," Bernardo said.

"Oh, yeah."

Something moved at the edge of his vision, and he turned to find a figure in the illuminated window—Anita, looking out into the yard to see who was there. His heart dropped a notch in his chest. "I suppose I should go in now."

"Yes."

He turned. "Thanks for coming."

"I go again sometime."

"Do you think you'll stay in Montana? Or are you going back to Italy?"

Bernardo shook his head. "I cannot go back to Italy."

Paul pulled the keys from the ignition and dropped them into his jacket pocket. "You really can stay here for a while, if you want. Things are going to be a little strange, but . . ."

"No, no." He was waving his hand in the air. "I leave. Maybe I come back to visit."

"Oh, yeah. Definitely." Beside him, Bernardo had stiffened, as if steeling himself for the difficulties ahead, but now his eyes softened.

"Paul," he said. "You go in. You take me to town tomorrow."

"It's her car."

"We, ah, no problem. Tomorrow . . ."

He nodded, as much to himself as to Bernardo, and opened the door. Bernardo opened his, and they stepped out together and stood in the fading light.

"Go."

Paul went. Anita was already gone from the front window as he climbed the stairs. A board creaked underfoot—something he should fix—and he pushed open the door.

She was sitting at the kitchen table, waiting, her hands folded before her as if in penance. "I was so worried," she said.

"We went to Glacier."

"Jesus, Paul." She shook her head. Her eyes gleamed. "I didn't know what you'd done. I thought . . ."

"What?"

She didn't answer. Her hands untangled and she held them up, showing him they were empty.

Paul slumped against the door. It felt better to have the wood at his back, supporting him, and he pressed harder, until he felt the grain of the boards impressing itself on his skin. He said, barely loud enough for her to hear, "But you're leaving."

"Yes," she said.

"To be with him."

She wiped her eyes with her palms, like a child. "No, no. To be on my own. For now."

"Oh," he said. "On your *own*."

"Paul—" she said, and stopped herself.

"What."

"Never mind."

For a moment, he felt himself beginning to lose strength, his bones betraying him and going soft. But he pressed himself harder against the door, letting it bear him until the feeling passed. "I'll need the car for a few days," he said. "Then you can take it."

"You can have the house," she said into the table. "I won't fight you for it."

"Gee, thanks."

"I guess you want me out."

"I guess I do."

She nodded. "I'm sorry, Paul. I do love you. I just can't always be the one taking care. Maybe that's my great fault, I don't know."

Anger rose from the depths of him and burned on his lips, that she would absolve herself and claim blame in the same breath. But he let it drain away. "I'm not cut out for fatherhood," he said. "Maybe the family line ought to die with me."

"Oh, Paul," she said, so quietly that he barely heard.

"Can you leave tonight?"

"I'll call for a ride," she said after a minute.

"Not him, please."

"No. Kathy, from work. She said I could stay with her."

"You'll stay in Marshall?" he said.

She nodded.

He went out to the porch to let her call. He could hear her from there through the half-open window, speaking in short sentences, answering questions yes or no and offering little information. The phone clattered back onto the cradle, and there was silence: he pictured her standing, her hand still warming the receiver. Then her quick steps to the back of the house to pack.

He got up and walked across the yard, to where the still-fresh caterpillar tracks of a backhoe marked the entrance to the new road. The sun was down now, and the moon cast his long shadow over the gnarled remains of dug-up stumps and ragged tire ruts. In the dim distance hunkered the backhoe's yellow bulk, its bucket arm curled like a sleeping insect's; behind it lay a truck crane, with its boom folded over its back. He followed their tracks down toward the creek, trying to remember the pattern of trees as they had

stood, but he found that for all their familiarity he could not remember what
they looked like: in his mind it was only a forest now, one patch no more or
less worthy of his attention than any other. He closed his eyes, thinking of
Anita's face. He wondered how long it would take for it too to recede in his
memory, until it was only a face like any other. He wondered if it would shock
him someday to bump into her in town, if for that accidental second he would
recall everything about her, then forget again when she was out of sight.

The creek was swollen and muddy. This was where the workmen had
stopped, too tired perhaps to begin building the makeshift bridge they'd need
in order to cross. Several stumps remained, clinging to the ground that once
fed them, the trees they supported lying shorn nearby. Paul sat on one, listening to the creek's rushing, trying to coax its flow to enter him, to either make
this place as much a part of him as his wife had been—and still was—or wash
from him what little claim he had left. But it did nothing. It was only water,
and passed him by, fast and cold.

In time, he thought he heard a car engine, the slamming of doors, and
soon after someone approached him from behind. He didn't bother to open his
eyes.

"Hello." It was Bernardo, keeping his distance.

"Hi."

"It is a beautiful night," he said.

Paul tasted the air. It was sharp, thick, like a tonic. He said, "She's gone?"

"She says to tell you she come back in one week. She get a new place."

"All right."

The footsteps came toward him and stopped to his left. Paul turned and
opened his eyes. Bernardo had his hands in his pockets, his arms pressed
against his sides. "It is cold," he said. "Maybe we go back, eh?"

"I suppose," Paul said, but he didn't feel like moving. He rubbed his face
and the blood rushed to the surface, pricking him like a pine bough.

He felt a hand on his shoulder. "We go."

"Okay," he said, and he found himself happy to rise under Bernardo's firm
hand, to let himself be guided back by a benevolent stranger to his home.

In the morning Paul woke to find Bernardo cooking them breakfast. Omelets. He was wearing a T-shirt Paul had gotten at a rock-and-roll

show in Tuscaloosa and a pair of sweatpants. The churning of the washing machine was audible from the next room.

"Sorry. One more wash," Bernardo said.

"It's no problem."

"I find these in the dryer." He gestured toward the T-shirt and sweats.
Paul didn't remember washing them, and it occurred to him that Anita must
have, over the weekend, while she sat here in the house contemplating leaving him.

"You can keep those."

Bernardo looked down at himself, frowning. "I give them back."

Paul sat at the table, wondering what she would take with her. These
chairs? They had shiny red cushions stretched across metal frames. She'd
bought them at a junk shop in Omaha when they moved out here. The bed?
That was hers. The curtains, the kitchen supplies. It was of passing interest to
him that one of them laid silent claim to every object in the house, that, unlike a lot of couples he'd known or read about, neither ever forgot what was
whose. The couch was his, the records and stereo. None were much good if he
couldn't cook or sleep. He wondered what—or where—Bernardo would eat
tonight.

"Will you go to your son now? Anthony?" he said.

He didn't turn, but put down, for a moment, his spatula. "Antonio. Yes."

Paul pushed his hair from his face and looked around for a rubber band to
tie it back. He saw none. Across the room, the phone book lay grimy and dog-
eared on a small table (hers) under the phone (also hers). He went to it and
opened the yellow pages. No listings for barbers. He eventually found them
under "Hair." He picked up the phone and saw Bernardo staring at him, spatula in hand, from across the kitchen. "What?" he said.

Bernardo shook himself as if from sleep. "Nothing. You call."

He called the first few in the book until he found one sufficiently cheap:
six dollars. He hadn't gone to a barber since he was a kid. He called and made
an appointment—one hour from now—with a gruff-sounding middle-aged
man. By the time he hung up, Bernardo had put the omelets on the table.
They ate them in silence. Bernardo took his plate to the sink and washed it,
then took Paul's too. Paul let him. Then Bernardo sat down.

"So I go after an hour?"

"Sooner now. Half an hour."

"The house. We don't finish."

Paul shrugged. "I can do it myself."

Bernardo nodded. "Okay, good." He looked up and met Paul's eyes. If the line of sight between them, Paul thought, was a rope, it would be frayed and sagging. It would be hanging by a thread.

Bernardo went out to the shed to collect his belongings. He brought in a blanket and a pillow, candles, the pencils and paper Paul had given him, his drawings rolled up in a tube. He dumped these things, save for the drawings, on the table.

"You can keep all that."

Bernardo shook his head. "I don't need." He stared for a second at the pile, then looked up. "Are you ready?"

"Sure." Paul stood, his joints going off like firecrackers.

They drove to town, the sun weak and ineffective around them. Daytime struggled to assert itself across the valley. Paul's eyelids felt swollen and sticky, and he rubbed his eyes as they turned onto Cedar Avenue.

"I'm glad you showed up," he said to Bernardo. He knew it wasn't enough, but it was all he could think to tell him. "I hope your luck changes."

"I think so," Bernardo said. "Soon."

"I'll see you again?" He turned to Bernardo, then back to the road.

"When I . . ." Bernardo said, at a loss.

"When you're more established."

"Yes."

They came to Cherry Street, where downtown began. At the traffic light, Paul said, "You just want to be dropped off downtown?"

"This is good, yes."

"Are you sure there's nowhere in particular?"

"No, no. I find him okay, I think." He hung his head, turning the rolled-up drawings in his hands. "You don't tell people," he said. "About the plane."

"What plane?"

"The plane. That come—" And he noticed Paul's smile. "Okay, good."

"You know," Paul said, after a moment, "I don't know if I believe you. I hope that's not insulting to you or anything, but I saw it happen. I don't think a person could survive that."

Bernardo didn't reply.

"However you came here, it doesn't matter to me. You don't have to tell me the truth. I think one way or the other you'll make it here, and what came before that doesn't matter."

"It's good to me you say that."

"Well," Paul said, embarrassed. "Whatever."

Bernardo reached for the door handle. Street sounds rushed in. "Thank you," he said. "You help me very much." He looked down at the drawings in his hand, then placed them between the seats, a gift at the last minute.

Paul took his hand. "You helped me too." And then he let go, and averted his eyes until he heard the door close. He looked up and saw Bernardo crossing the street in a break in the traffic, and before long he had turned the corner and was gone.

Spruce Barbers seemed, in fact, to be only one barber, who operated in the daylight basement of a dilapidated house, in a residential neighborhood that abutted the railroad tracks. There were no other businesses for blocks around, and the dank little shop appeared to be some sort of zoning accident; either that or it had escaped the city's notice. The barber was short and bald and fussed over the gray head of a thin old man with a trembling jaw. There was one other barber's chair, but it was in the dark, apparently unused, half of the shop, and it leaned crazily, like a rickety carnival ride that had suddenly stopped.

Paul read the newspaper. In the back of the local section, there was an article about the crash; an AirAmerica spokesperson said the airline would begin to haul out the wreckage later in the week. The road that was being cut into the forest would be allowed to grow back over when the operation was finished. Paul's heart lightened at this news, as if the wreckage itself were the cause of his melancholy, the very weight that strained against his ribs in the night. He couldn't wait until it was gone.

The old man wobbled out, climbing the stairs with some effort. Paul thought he ought to go and help, but he didn't. He and the barber watched him until he had disappeared from view, then both sighed. Their eyes met.

"Been coming here for twenty-five years," the barber said. "Used to be mayor."

"Really?"

"Real mayor died in his sleep. Mr. Visser there was top man in the town council. He filled in." He shook his head. "Best couple weeks of his life. Used to talk about it all the time."

When Paul sat down, the barber walked slow circles around him, as if his head were a block of marble he was preparing to carve. "Shampoo?" he said soberly.

"Uh, no."

"Okay. How d'you want it cut?"

"Short."

The barber glared at Paul in the mirror. "You gotta give me a little more than that."

"Maybe leave a little on the sideburns. And the forehead."

His eyes narrowed. "Whatever you say."

He cut in silence for a while, spinning the chair with one hand, chopping with a skill that seemed indiscriminate. Heavy sections of hair fell away, and Paul heard them whisper against the barber's smock. For a long time, Paul was pointed toward the door, and when the barber turned him to face the mirror, he saw that his hair, while short, was messy and uneven. One ear was hidden and the other wasn't. The hair across his forehead was severely slanted, so that it covered one eyebrow completely and left the other bare. Then he noticed that the barber's head was gleaming with sweat and he was biting his lower lip.

"This'd be a lot easier if you gave me a particular cut to do. I'm no champ with this freestyle stuff."

"I don't know any hairstyles," Paul said. "I haven't gotten a haircut in eight years."

"I'm switching to clippers," the barber told him, after a moment's thought.

He plugged the clipper into the wall. It was a curved green thing with nasty-looking teeth on one end. When he switched it on, its buzz filled the room like an avalanche of metal filings. It set Paul's teeth on edge. The barber plunged it into what was left of Paul's hair and dragged it across his scalp. The feeling wasn't too bad. It filled Paul with a sort of nostalgia, as he recalled the buzz cuts of his boyhood. Meanwhile hair came away in graceful clumps and piled up on his chest and shoulders. The barber was sweating even more profusely now. "Okay, now," he whispered, apparently to himself. "Now we're getting somewhere."

It wasn't long before all of Paul's hair was gone, save for a smooth glaze of fuzz. The barber stood behind him, and they both stared at it in the mirror. For the first time in his adult life, Paul could see his own scalp: he had a prominent ridge that ran from just beyond the hairline to the back of his head. The clippers continued to buzz.

"Why don't you turn that thing off?" he said, and the noise stopped.

"Well, there you go."

Paul stared into the mirror. "You cut it all off."

"Looks good."

"I could have done that myself."

The barber didn't respond. He wiped the hair from Paul's neck with a soft brush, then whisked off the plastic apron with a flourish. "There you go!" he said again, cheerily. "That's six bucks."

"You're *charging* me?"

"Whaddya think?" The barber's hands were planted on his hips, his legs slightly spread, like a sumo wrestler's.

"But you screwed it up!"

"Six bucks!" the barber repeated.

Paul wanted only to leave now. "Forget it."

"Look, pal," the barber said, "you told me short and you got it. Cough up."

He ran his hand over his hair. Soft. He crossed his arms, uncrossed them, pulled out his wallet and paid.

In the car, he held his hands to his head and worked his jaw, feeling the muscles moving over his ear. They felt like new muscles, freshly grown. He pictured himself as one of his distant ancestors, crouching in the dust, gnawing on the leg of a fallen zebra.

There was no reason to go home. It was eleven-thirty, and he was driving aimlessly around downtown. He should call Ponty. Then he remembered first seeing Alyssa in Ponty's office, the phone pinched between her ear and shoulder; he thought of those thin shoulders and neck, seeing them through the rear window of her boyfriend's truck. How could Ponty sleep at night, knowing his daughter went to school every day, bobbed in a fast current of kids, with their drugs and weapons in their lockers? How could he sleep when she saw boys every minute of her day, leering at her from desks and in hallways, popping off the buttons of her dress in their dreams, reaching for her across a couch with the shades drawn?

He found himself pulling onto Weir, signaling into the lane that would bring him to the high school in time for lunch. Kids had already filled the streets around the school when he arrived, pushing one another, laughing in groups, passing things around. They leaned against trees and sat on cars. They crouched in hedges, smoking cigarettes. Paul drove by slowly, feeling like a fool but unable to tear himself away until he saw her, made sure she was all right.

He found a parking space adjacent to a practice field, where he had a clear view of the school, and slouched down to watch. No Alyssa. He could recognize her walk from a distance, even without the telltale purple hair: it looked like a shuffle but propelled her around with surprising speed, as if she were on skates; her head always down, navigating by some sort of teenage sonar. Even with the boyfriend she did this, a reflex he found profoundly moving. There was beauty in defense.

But she wasn't there. He was getting ready to leave when he noticed the boyfriend, his cap skewed ever so consciously an inch to the side, walking back toward the building with two others. Both boys. Their strides grew manlier the closer they came to the building.

Maybe she was sick today. Maybe she spent her lunch with other friends, or stayed inside to eat in the cafeteria. What did he know about how they worked things here? He started the car and (looking in the rearview, someone he at first didn't recognize: himself, without hair) pulled back into the street, drove two blocks to Weir and headed north, toward home. Home, where he had resigned himself to going. He could shingle the roof, or reinstall the insulation. Today could be the day he became a bachelor wilderness-survival type, living inside a healthy aura of self-sufficiency and masculine calm. He would keep to himself, own flannel shirts.

And then he saw her, sitting alone at an outdoor table in front of Taco Treat. Her hair wasn't purple anymore. She'd dyed it red over the weekend and had it combed down over the shaved sides in a sad approximation of normal hair. Her head was propped up by the V of her hands. She looked glum.

Impulsively, he turned onto Sixth and into the restaurant's narrow parking lot. He wedged the car between a pickup and a microbus and turned off the ignition.

Now what?

Through the side window and windshield of the microbus, he saw that she had a tray of food in front of her, but had made no move to eat it. He decided to go get some himself—it would be a chance meeting, him stopping here for lunch, her being here, except that he didn't much like Mexican food and the omelet he'd eaten that morning still sat in his stomach, undigested, like an unwanted guest who has fallen asleep. But he was here, he had parked. He went inside.

He watched her through the window while he waited for his food—just an iced tea and a single fish taco. She was wearing a gray hooded sweatshirt zipped up to her chin. Two knotted cinch ropes dangled from the hood, and she played with one of them as she poked her food.

When the taco came, it made him a little queasy. He pushed it to the far edge of his tray and carried the tray out to her table. Nobody else was sitting outside. It was too chilly. Cars raced past on Weir, and their smells drifted over them, faintly toxic.

Alyssa looked up.

"Hey!" Paul said. He put his tray down. "Mind if I join you?"

Her eyes widened. She didn't recognize him.

Paul touched his head and sat down. "It's Paul Beveridge."

Nothing.

"I work for your dad."

Now she leaned forward, squinting. The ropes from her sweatshirt trailed into her food, a wide, cold-looking plate of red beans and rice. After a moment, she opened her eyes and smiled.

"Oh, *you*! Hi!"

"Hi."

"What are you doing here?" she said. And then, soberly: "I think my dad's looking for you."

"Is he mad?"

"Not really. Well, maybe a little. I guess your wife called him, looking for you." She smiled again. "But here you are."

Your wife called? "I just stopped for lunch, and here you were."

"Uh-huh. Here I am." She rolled her eyes.

"So why aren't you in school?"

She snorted. "Oh, right. You're an *adult*." She hitched her shoulders once, let them sag. "I already learned everything," she said.

"Lucky you."

She rolled her eyes again, then shrank back a little. "Can I touch it?" she said.

"What?"

"Your hair."

"Oh! Right." He leaned forward, pushing his head across the table at her, until his nose hung just above his taco. His stomach groaned.

"Wow," she said. He felt her hand tickling across the tops of his hairs; each tingled at the root, starting a chain reaction that careened down his back, setting off every vertebra like a string of Christmas lights. Now she was using both hands, her fingers pressing into his scalp. He felt very warm. And then suddenly it was over, her hands gone. When he looked up they were out of sight, in her lap. "Cool," she said, and they both laughed.

"You haven't touched your lunch," he told her.

"I should have gotten *that,*" she said, pointing to his tray.

He looked down at the taco and back at her. "Here," he said, and pushed it toward her. "Take it. I'm not as hungry as I thought."

She was eating the taco in the passenger seat of his—Anita's—car, the paper basket held beneath her hand, catching drippings. They were heading south, toward the strip, toward her father's office, her house. "So you want to go home?" he said. "Or do you want to go to your dad's office?"

She shrugged. "I don't know."

"Well, think fast," he said. "The turn for the office is coming up." Ponty's street approached and passed. Paul watched as the office sped by. What would he think, if he knew where his daughter was? "Home it is, then," he said.

"How about we go somewhere else?" she said.

"Somewhere else."

"Yeah." She unzipped the sweatshirt to reveal a white T-shirt with the name of a local rock band on it. "I'm not, you know, *expected* anywhere," she said, her voice heavy with mock sophistication, and for a moment, Paul found himself imagining her in his arms, her ribs finding the grooves between his. And then the voice dissolved into giggles and the image disappeared, leaving him embarrassed and his mind soured with guilt.

But he didn't turn onto South Avenue, which would have brought them to her house, and he didn't turn onto Merriam Boulevard, which was their last chance to stay in Marshall. The light at Merriam was interminable, but neither of them said anything to the other, because to do so would mean admitting they were leaving town. Paul was so consumed with not speaking that he didn't notice when the light finally changed, and Alyssa bumped his arm with her shoulder. "Go, already."

Paul started. She sat up in her seat, alert. Horns blared. He rolled up the window, and they pulled away from the intersection.

And then they were on the highway, moving southwest toward the state line at sixty miles an hour, and neither had mentioned it. Paul pretended interest in the mountains and Alyssa, he could see, stared at the road with real excitement. Ten minutes later, when they'd crossed the Sapphire city line and Paul slowed down for the town's three lights, Alyssa leaned her crossed arms against the dash. "Up there," she said. "The second light."

He could hear the challenge in her voice as she said it, wielded uncertainly, like it was a weapon too large or complicated for her. He got the sudden urge to turn the car around and bring her home, but then there was the problem of the trip back, of what to say in the sullen silence after he backed down. And, of course, he wanted to know where she was taking him. He signaled right and turned onto a smoothly paved two-lane that snaked into the mountains and Idaho. For several minutes they said nothing to each other. And then, as if it were part of a conversation that had been interrupted, she said, "So he dumped me, and I didn't feel like seeing him."

"What?"

"This *guy,*" she said. "He *dumped* me. And I didn't want to see him, at school. So I left."

"Can't you get in trouble for that?"

She shrugged.

They passed a pasture at the base of a foothill, where some horses stood languidly eating grass. "How come?" Paul said.

"How come what?"

"Why'd he dump you?"

She shrugged again. "No reason, I don't know."

It was the sort of thing Paul would have said in high school; in college, even. But if adulthood had taught him anything, it was that there was always a reason. He thought about his mother, the way she used to react to such an answer: she would hold her gaze on him an extra beat, then capitulate to the lie with a tired nod and leave his bedroom without closing the door. And with his friends—none of whose names he could remember now—that kind of answer was de rigueur, so much so that none of them ever really knew one another beyond what drinks each liked, the way each held a cigarette.

He was wondering how he could express this to Alyssa, what he could say that wouldn't sound . . . *adult,* when she chuckled. It was a deep, strangely mature sound. She deadpanned: "Because I wouldn't."

"What?"

"He dumped me because I wouldn't."

"Wouldn't."

"Do it."

Paul's armpits began to itch. "Oh."

"Oh, geez," she said. "Does that make you uncomfortable?"

"Well . . ." He kept his eyes on the road, reluctant even to catch a glimpse of her reflection in the windshield.

"Because, you know, he just wasn't *the one.* I mean, everybody *does* it"—bolder now, enjoying his reaction—"but I don't think you ought to without a good reason."

"Well, good," he said, fatherly.

She fiddled with the seat, adjusting the angle until she was lying on her back, laughing. Then she straightened up a little, and stopped when she was a few degrees farther back than he was. She picked up the roll of drawings from between the seats but didn't unroll them, only looked through the tube out the windshield. Her voice came from behind him. "So what's your story? Where were you? Why'd your wife call our house?"

It irritated him that she knew this, and he groped for blame, landing briefly on Ponty and skimming over Anita until he settled, finally, on himself. "I went away for a few days."

"Why's that?"

He glared at her. She was leaning back, looking out at the mountaintops and clouds through the rolled drawings.

"She had an affair. She decided to leave me."

She said nothing for a while, then set the drawings back where she found them. "So I guess we're in the same boat."

"No," he said, as harshly as he could muster. "I'm married." And immediately he regretted it. Alyssa took a few minutes to absorb this, then curled her legs up under her and leaned against the door.

"Can I put this on?" she asked him quietly, pointing to the heat controls.

"Sure."

Soon they reached Sapphire Pass, where a sign told them that Lewis and Clark had camped only a few feet away. Those two seemed to have been everywhere. Paul parked at the visitors center to pee, and Alyssa stayed in the car. In the men's room he worried that this looked funny, like a man plunging into the wilderness with a girl half his age. Which is what it was. When he got back into the car, Alyssa said, as if she had read his mind, "How old are you, Paul?" She bobbled his name on her tongue like a ball tossed to her without warning.

"Thirty-two."

"Whoa," she said. "You're old enough to be my father."

He calculated. "I guess so."

"You have kids, you two?"

"No."

She nodded. "Good."

Paul paused before he pulled back onto the road. "Home?" he asked her.

"Not yet. A few more miles."

He obliged her, taking the steep decline in third gear, to save the brakes. When they had gone several miles, she pointed to a graveled lot on the right. "Here," she said, and he signaled and turned in.

They sat for a moment in silence. "Okay!" she said.

"Okay what?"

"You coming?"

"Where to?" he said. He wondered what a teenage girl could know about the Idaho woods, why she would bring him there. What would Ponty say if he could see them together, pulled over in Anita's car? She crossed her eyes.

"Don't be a dork, Paul."

Maybe this was what fatherhood was like: going along with things. He thought of all the times he'd begged his friends to go along with him—crashing parties, shoplifting, driving around—and how irritating that must have been. Then he pushed open his door and stepped onto the gravel.

A footpath led them through thick, close conifers. Alyssa ran ahead, suddenly childish and happy. The forest was much richer here than near his house, with a healthy dampness in the air and moss hanging from the branches of trees. He wondered briefly if, in the past three years, he had ever even been to Idaho.

No, he hadn't left Montana.

"Where are we going?"

"You'll see," she said. Something in her voice was excited and fearful at once, as if they'd come to hunt bears. "I can't believe you've never come here before."

They were quiet then, and the sounds of the woods mingled with their footfalls: birds and squirrels chattered, and off in the trees, Paul could see deer stepping carefully over logs. Somewhere, out of sight, there was a river running, and its noise grew louder and softer as they changed direction.

And then the path emptied out into a wide clearing that the river rushed through on its way elsewhere. Between the water and the ground beyond its banks, which lay bare except for thin moss and small boulders, were a series of still, clear pools, steam rising off them in thick, wind-twisted curtains. Hot springs. "Wow," he said, and Alyssa yelped with excitement and ran down to them, her hair tossing side to side like the flag on a child's bike.

He followed her. For a minute they stood and watched. Bubbles crept up from under rocks in the pools before them, the river running cold only a few feet beyond. The air was warm. Alyssa took off her sweatshirt, and then her shoes and socks: white tennis sneakers, white socks with gray pads.

"What are you doing?"

"Getting *in,*" she said, seemingly unable to believe the question.

And then, to his astonishment, she pulled her T-shirt up over her head and in almost the same motion pushed down her jeans, revealing a white cotton bra and a pair of underpants with carrots printed on them. The carrots were bright orange, and looked as out of place in this clearing as a tractor-trailer.

He gawked, at this woman's body exposed to the air, and was almost surprised when he looked to find her face still attached to it. Her eyes were wide, and she was breathing heavy and fast, through her mouth, from the run down the hill.

"What?" she said, but there was no concealing that she knew what effect this had had on him; her voice was full of it.

"You're not—" he said. "We can't—"

She turned from him, and brought her hands up behind her, to the hook of her bra, and unclasped it. She held the ends there, waiting, and said over her shoulder, "Either you're in, or no looking, pal."

Without thinking, he touched his head. He moved his hand to his face, and rubbed it, and said, "I'll meet you in the car." Then he turned and began the walk to the road.

In the trees, beyond where he thought he could see, he stopped and looked back. She was there, sitting in one of the pools, facing the river. Her shoulders were thin and bowed like an old woman's, as if she were no more substantial than a piece of paper, curled to conceal what was written on it. He thought of the photos he'd taken of her, and realized they were still in the glove compartment of Anita's car, where he'd left them the day he reported back to Ponty. Alyssa had been sitting inches from them for over an hour.

He jogged back down the path to the lot and took out the photos. He remembered them differently: Alyssa, he thought, was smaller in the frame and only distinguishable by her hair, and he recalled both her and her boyfriend hunched over slightly under the bright sun, shielding their eyes. But in fact Alyssa's face was clear, and the two of them walked easily, seemingly without worry. In one, Alyssa was punching his arm, and he was recoiling in mock offense.

Paul walked a hundred yards back up the mountain, to where the river met the road. He climbed down the rocky bank and crouched by the water, in the mild, cold breeze the current made, and he thumbed through the photos again. Now he had another picture in his head, this one of himself, walking slumped and alone off the school grounds long before the three-o'clock bell, on his way to meet his dealer so that he could get high in the car and drive out into Mississippi to visit the river. Rivers were different in the South, meandering and slow, and he often imagined he could lie down in one and wend through farms and homesteads and towns for days, wanting for nothing, swallowed by a larger whole that would let him forget who he was. He thought of himself washed out into the Delta, where he would simply vanish, quietly dissolved into the waters of the Gulf.

And if he did that now? He felt, for a split second, what it would be like to be broken on the rocks, and shuddered. Instead, he tore up the photos and scattered the pieces in the water. The river carried them away, and before they had gone a dozen feet they were indistinguishable from the play of light on the current.

He thought he had been spying on a young Paul Beveridge those days outside Alyssa's high school, but he could see he'd been wrong. She was at home here, and fearless, and needed nothing. The young Paul Beveridge was still him. What was he doing here? Why wasn't he in Marshall, doing his job? From now on, he decided, he would be an employed adult, and nothing more, and take it from there.

He stood up, his knees cracking. The river rounded the bend, laughing. He wiped the dirt off his hands, climbed the bank and walked back to the car to wait. The torn pictures, he imagined, were sweeping toward Alyssa Ponty, and heading for the ocean. They would reach her, pass her by, any second now.

17

Tuesday morning, when Lars showed up at Montana Gag, there were six police cars parked in the lot, their lights flashing, and as many cops walking around inside. He pretended to try the door of the Chinese place, which he knew was closed. Walking back to his car, he shook his head theatrically and thrust his hands into the pockets of his jeans. Sooner or later they would need to ask him questions, and Lars was content to let them track him down on their own time.

Out of a job.

When he got home, he padded around the apartment in his stocking feet, trying to decide if he should empty his savings, buy a car, and drive back to Wisconsin. It was probably a bad idea, though that had not always been an effective deterrent for him. Already he could see the confusion of emotions on his mother's face: joy at seeing him, coupled with the horror of realizing he would not be leaving. When he picked up the phone, he wasn't sure who he would call. It turned out to be Toth.

He answered, still asleep, on the first ring.

"Huh?"

"Toth, it's Lars." When he heard nothing from the other end, he added, "I'm sorry to wake you up."

"'Sokay."

In truth, this was something he needed to do, but had been putting off. Over the weekend he'd bumped into Toth and his roommate, Tim, at the Safeway. They were buying provisions for a camping trip that Lars had not been invited on. This simultaneously insulted him and filled him with pity; Toth didn't really like Tim, who was a hippie music teacher at the alternative elementary school and was always listening to tapes of himself playing guitar. At the store, a plastic bulk bag of peanuts dangling from his fist, Toth told Lars that he would have invited him "if I didn't think you'd be hanging around with your girlfriend all weekend." At this Tim snorted, and the expression of triumphant scorn on Toth's face faded away.

"What are you doing today?" Lars asked him now.

"Jesus," he said. "It still feels like yesterday."

"Maybe you ought to come over."

Toth paused, still breathing with the slowed rhythm of sleep. "Why's that?"

"To talk." And when he didn't answer; "I'll make you breakfast."

"French toast," Toth said.

"Okay, French toast."

"Okay. I'm on my way."

He arrived in half an hour, just as Lars was finishing the food, got plates and forks out for them and set them on the table.

"Thanks."

"No problem."

They ate, made small talk. Lars told him about the police cars and his feint to the Chinese place. Toth talked about his terrible weekend with Tim. "Man, the guy *eats,*" he said. "He ate peanuts and crackers all fucking night. I didn't sleep."

Afterward, they went outside to walk off the food, and ended up on a path down by the river, mostly obscured from view by trees and shrubs.

"I didn't know this trail was here," Toth told him.

"Not a lot of people know. Homeless guys." He broke off a branch that was sticking into the path. "I used to come down here with Megan sometimes." He didn't want to walk ahead, where there was a small curved bank of flat rocks around which the roots of cottonwood trees grew. The roots described the edges of an open circle of water, where eddies carved a deep pool.

He and Megan had tried to make love there, but found nowhere dry to lie down, and the rocks hurt them. They had finally given up. Lars remembered that Megan had lost a ring along here somewhere, and he automatically scanned the weeds for the glint of metal. But there was nothing.

"Here," he said, and pointed to a little clearing where a low, forgotten bench rotted at the water's edge. Once Toth had collected enough round stones to toss into the river, they sat there.

"I'm really sorry," Lars said.

Toth tossed the first rock, and the water shuddered beneath it. Then he shrugged it off.

Lars said, "I miss you, and I'm really sorry."

"So what's up with this Christine?" This very simple, nothing betrayed in the tone.

"She's a friend."

"Okay . . ."

"It's nothing romantic," Lars said. "She's too sick for that. And I'm not ready. You have to know that." He looked up at Toth, who was still staring at the spot where the rock fell. Suddenly he pushed the others off his lap, and they knocked against each other on the ground.

"I guess."

"I know it seems like a big deal to you." He touched Toth's shoulder, then withdrew. "It is, kind of. She needed . . . we both needed somebody who's not so much better off."

"I'm not good enough for that?"

"You remind me of her."

Toth turned to him. "You remind me of her too."

For a few minutes they watched the water pass. In midstream, just down-stream from a boulder that jutted from the water like an iceberg, a fish jumped. As if it were a signal to him, Toth said, "There's something you don't know, man."

"I don't know?"

"I don't think you know." He looked Lars in the eye. "No, you don't."

He felt a chill. "What."

Toth frowned suddenly, a reflex to precede tears, but the tears didn't come. "I was in love with her. With Megan." He kicked the pile of rocks and they scattered. "Nothing ever happened or anything, I just loved her. Like, ro-mantically."

Lars said, "No, I didn't know that."

"I don't know how it . . . yeah, I do. She treated me so *nice.* That's stupid. I mean, nobody bothered to get to know me like that. I could say whatever to her, and she'd know what I meant. That kind of thing." He shoved his thumb and forefinger up under his glasses and pressed them to the inside corners of his eyes. "And then, I pretty much knew you weren't going to break up, I mean, she wanted to marry you . . ."

"She did?" Another spike through his throat. He swallowed around it.

"Well, yeah." Toth looked at him strangely, apparently astonished that he hadn't known.

"Did she know?" Lars managed. "About you . . ."

"Uh-huh."

"Since when?"

"Since about eight months ago. We, the three of us, went to the Kwik Stop for beer, and I was in the front seat and she was in the back, and you ran in alone, and I just told her. I talked the whole time you were in there, and I just told her everything, how I felt and all, and I never looked back to see her reaction and she didn't say anything, and then you came out and we drove off. And you didn't notice a thing, I guess."

"I don't remember this at all."

"You wouldn't."

Toth took his glasses off, folded them up and dropped them into his pocket. It was an old man's gesture, and it made Lars deeply sad.

"I couldn't help it," Toth said. "I'm sorry."

"Don't apologize."

After that there was nothing more to say. They both seemed to realize this at once, and in time stood. On the way back to Lars's apartment, they talked about seeing a movie—a matinee somewhere.

But when they walked in, Lars's message machine was blinking. It was Christine's mother. They had found a kidney for her.

This is what had happened:

A group of teenagers, two boys and two girls, had spent the night camping illegally on a remote stretch of eastern Washington river. They got drunk, and were still drunk when they woke the next morning, when they drove their

Ford Bronco into the water. One of the girls in the front seat hadn't been wearing a seat belt and cracked her head on the windshield. She stayed conscious and climbed out, but her friends, ironically, all wearing seat belts, drowned. The survivor stumbled back along the dirt road they had taken the night before, until she encountered a group of picnickers, who drove her to the nearest town. As the picnickers' car pulled into the hospital parking lot, she suddenly screamed, "Oh my God!" and keeled over dead of a brain hemorrhage.

Of the three people within helicopter distance ahead of Christine in priority, none shared the dead girl's blood type. Christine did. The kidney was being removed from the girl's body when Christine's doctor called. She had been eating lunch, and when she hung up the phone she went to the bathroom, threw up half her sandwich, brushed her teeth and walked across the parking lot with her mother to the hospital.

Lars and Toth got all this information from Amanda Stull, who was sitting on a wheelchair that had been left in the hall outside Christine's hospital room. Christine was inside, undergoing tests in preparation for surgery; Amanda Stull was frantic. "I called all of Christine's brothers," she said. "Dennis and Leslie are coming, and Samuel . . ." And she switched off, as if the thought of these children, scattered as they were across America, almost out of reach, was too much for her to take.

She looked older here than she had in the trailer, where Lars had met her; her hair was an icy steel gray that seemed perfectly in place in the hospital, and it added to the already strong impression that she was emphatically and inconsolably nervous. Her eyes shone from the stone of her head like two glinting coins; her cheeks sagged under the weight of incipient jowls. Her hands were wrapped around the chair's push rims as if she might, at any moment, need to go careening down the hall in search of help.

Lars and Toth moved quietly away from her and waited near the elevators. "How long do you think it's going to be?" Toth asked him. They had been here twenty minutes, hoping to see her before surgery.

"Can't be much longer. How much can they do to her?"

Down the hall, there was a noise: Christine's door had opened and her mother was launching herself from the wheelchair. As they watched, she disappeared inside.

Lars tried to recall when he had last been in a hospital. The memory that returned most easily to him was of his father's illness, though there had been other visits since then. He remembered his grandfather's bypass surgery, which had been a failure; the operating doctor came out of surgery and told them that his arteries had been like wet paper towels. In high school, his soccer coach had broken his ankle when, running along the sideline after a play, he stepped in the water bucket and fell. And Megan's strep throat, which Student Health had refused to treat because of a filing error regarding her tuition bill. He brought her to the emergency room here, where they sat for two hours before anyone would see them. She lay across two waiting room seats, her head in his lap. Her forehead burned, and it radiated the scorched scent of a baked potato, and he brushed hairs from her face and read aloud to her from a copy of *Highlights for Children,* which neither of them had seen for years.

He wondered how these doctors and nurses, how anyone on the staff of the hospital, could stand to work in a place where everyone is angry or miserable, watching the lives of their loved ones drain away.

He thought: I took such good care of her. And in the end for nothing.

After a few minutes, a nurse came out to find them. She led them back to Christine's room and through the door, where her mother sat opposite them, mashing her daughter's hand in her own. Everything in the room was beige. Behind Amanda Stull hung a beige curtain. Lars could see the wheels and frame of another bed underneath it, and the feet of a man and woman, presumably doctors or nurses. Christine's head poked out from under her sheets, looking slightly waxen in the fluorescent light, but all in all she looked healthy and alert, more so anyway than she often was out of the hospital. Lars told her so.

"Well Jesus, it's pretty damned exciting, don't you think?" she said, her voice quieter, less sure than usual.

"I guess so."

She pointed at Toth, smiling. "Who's the kook?"

"I'm Toth," he said. "Lars's friend." He stuck out his hand and she took it.

"Christine. Lars told me about you." She looked down at herself, and gestured to her body underneath the white sheets. "Sorry I can't get up and show you around."

Toth looked flustered. "Oh, that's . . . I mean—"

"We came as soon as we could," Lars said. "They had us waiting outside . . ."

"They were sticking things in me." She made a dismissive wave with her free hand. "Business as usual. Did Mom tell you about the kids who drove their truck into the river?"

"Yeah."

She shook her head. "This kidney was cleaning out some kid's blood a few hours ago."

"Jesus," Toth whispered.

"Yeah," she said, and to Lars's utter astonishment, she began to cry. Her mother reached out, and with great and trembling gentleness ran her fingers over Christine's forehead. She whispered, "It's okay, baby," and Christine nodded.

"Christine," Lars said. "Do you want—"

"No, no, stay." She wiped her face with her free hand. "It's just, that poor girl had to watch them go down. I'm going to think about her every time I pee."

"Are you afraid?" Lars asked.

"Yeah."

"It's a perfect match, baby," her mother told her. "They said so. It couldn't be better."

"Yeah, I know."

The curtain behind Christine's mother parted, and two nurses, a man and a woman, stepped out. "Excuse us," the man said. Lars caught a glimpse, as the curtain fell closed, of a still figure under sheets. No sounds came from the other bed, only the low hum of some machinery—a monitor perhaps. They were all silent for a moment, suddenly aware of this presence they had forgotten, until Christine spoke again.

"You know," she said, "I've been totally confident about this transplant ever since all this started. Why shouldn't I be, right?" She swallowed hard, looked at her mother and back to Lars. "But now . . . they're gonna cut part of me out and put something else in? How can that work?" Her face tightened. "How can that be anything but the most ridiculous bullshit?"

Before they left the room, Christine asked him to make a couple of calls. "The Alpha chicks," she said. "Just call up the house, okay? It's in the phone book."

"Okay."

"I know you probably think they're stupid, but they're good to me."

"I don't think anybody's stupid."

"It's in the yellow pages. ADT, under 'Fraternities and Sororities.'" She paused. "As if sororities don't deserve their own listing."

"Got it."

"Come here," she said. Lars wasn't sure what she meant. He raised his eyebrows, questioning. "Here," she said, and waved him close.

When he leaned over, she touched the back of his neck and kissed him once, on the lips. He let it happen. Her lips, her fingers, were a little cold. It felt good.

"Go ahead," she said.

"Good luck."

"Don't tell me. Tell the surgeon."

He smiled at Amanda Stull, who managed a thin smile in return, and looked once more at Christine before he took hold of Toth's shoulder and walked with him out into the hall.

Lars called the sorority from the lobby. "I'm Lars Cowgill," he told the girl who answered. "Christine Stull's friend."

"Really?" she said. He heard her whispering something to someone else.

"She wanted me to call you. She got a kidney. They're putting it in now."

There was a pause. "Oh my *God*!" the girl said. Lars told them how long it would take—six hours—and about the accident that brought her the kidney.

"So do we come down there? Will they let us see her afterward?"

"I don't know," Lars said, and he wondered when he would next see her. Possibly never. Don't think that.

There was no use staying at the hospital. Lars looked at his watch: twelve-fifteen. It would be evening when she came out. Would she wake up before the day's end? He felt his blood scraping along the inside of his veins. It was as if he'd been poisoned.

In the lobby, they passed by a vending machine full of starchy junk food: pretzels, snack mix, potato chips. Lars was drawn to it. Just the thing to soak up the toxins. He pulled a dollar out of his wallet and fed it into the machine.

The machine spit it out, over and over again. He felt something electric and uncontrollable creeping into his limbs, and he stepped back, panting. The machine ejected his wrinkled dollar onto the floor.

"I have one," Toth said. He unfolded a crisp bill from his pocket and stepped toward the machine. "What do you want?"

His mouth was dry and sour. "Snack-'Ems."

"You got it." Toth fed his dollar in without incident and punched the appropriate buttons. A package cascaded down into the tray, and Toth pulled it out. He handed it to Lars, along with the crumpled bill.

"Thanks."

On the sidewalk, Lars ripped the bag open and ate. His body sucked the salt out of the food, and he shuddered as it coursed through him. They had biked here when they heard the message, and now they were faced with either returning home, where Lars emphatically did not want to be, or spending the afternoon hanging around downtown, sitting in cafés, waiting to come back to the hospital.

To the south, beyond the river, green clouds churned over the foothills. Somewhere within driving distance it would rain. It was the kind of sky that, in Wisconsin, would make people start thinking tornado. Lars remembered once, as a child, watching tornado clouds just before they gave birth to a funnel: he was in the parking lot of a shopping center in Madison with his mother when the sirens started (and before that, he now remembered, when he was even younger, he had thought those sirens were the tornadoes themselves, pulsing in the air like giant revving engines). He and his mother were standing, loaded down with bags, on opposite sides of the car. They looked up and saw, seemingly close enough to touch, two clouds passing one another at the same elevation. They clung briefly, the strands of each trailing off in the opposite direction as they parted. It was not something that was supposed to happen; Lars knew this without understanding why. It filled him with excitement and fear. And when he looked at his mother—he would not be afraid, he decided, if she wasn't—he saw her head tipped back and her mouth open, laughing, and she said, "Lars, if only your father could see."

Every kind of weather, for Lars, evoked a complicated layer cake of emotions, based on every thing he'd felt on similar days. Sunny, dry, and cold meant the embarrassed anticipation of opening presents at his fifth birthday party, the one his parents had thrown for him at the skating rink; it meant the impending sense of both defeat and relief in the last seconds of the final soccer game of his freshman season in high school; it meant the crystal diode radio he had made in sixth grade with Matt Acheson, and the wire-hanger antenna they had strung in a tree in his backyard. And this weather, today's weather, meant that afternoon with his mother, when they had gone Christmas shopping early, because it would be the first Christmas without Dad. And now the mingled pain of both loss and worry, each for a different woman, one who was gone from the world and the other struggling to stay in it.

He had eaten the Snack-'Ems down to the crumbs and hadn't offered Toth any. "Sorry," he said.

"You needed them."

He thought again of the amazement and terror of watching those clouds passing above him, and he wondered what the crash had been like for Paul and his wife, if they had actually seen it go down, or if they only heard and felt it. Did it take a few stunned seconds to understand what was happening, what had happened?

"What?" Toth said.

"What what?" Lars's jaws were tight, and he brought his hand to his cheek.

"You sighed."

He looked at his friend, who was still waiting for some explanation. "It's been on my mind awhile, I suppose."

"What?"

"The wreckage. I mean, it's right there, isn't it."

"Of the plane?" Toth rumpled his face as if from a bad smell.

"I got this idea I should go look at it. I decided not to, but now I don't know." His heart was racing, and in spite of himself he looked at his wrist. His watch wasn't there. He could see it lying next to the dish rack by the kitchen sink, the last place he'd taken it off.

"I do," Toth said. "Forget it."

Lars's hands were tingling, and he shook them to dispel the needles. "I think I have to go. There isn't much time."

"You don't have to do anything."

"I do." His hands were shaking on their own now. He felt like someone who is compelled to take five, six, seven showers each day, someone who has to fill in all the *e*'s and *o*'s in the newspaper. Suddenly the six hours that Christine would be in surgery seemed like a strange and urgent window of opportunity for him: it was as if doing this awful thing, which had for so long eluded his capability, would put something of Megan to rest. Lars was aware that this was not rational—even now, in the wake of the crash, he still found himself occasionally gripped by the impulse to call his father on the phone, something he had never done in his life—but he had finally lost much of his fear. The hospital breathed out its stale air behind him. This is where it would have ended up anyway, right? With one of them dying and the other doomed to watch it happen? Lars had never thought that Megan would want to marry him, and for this failure he got to live through her death early. Proposing might have kept her in Marshall for the summer; almost anything could have, and this was the fact that he had been avoiding, along with the fact of the wreckage, still out there, quietly rusting. He pictured a dripping glade, the scraps of plane scattered around it like the remains of a chicken. Not a battle-field, a cemetery. He turned to Toth.

"So are you coming or not?"

Toth squinted, as if against bright sunlight, though there was none. "I don't think so, Lars."

"Then I'll see you around, I guess."

He spun and headed for the Safeway, where they had locked their bikes. It was a sudden, impulsive exit, and blood pounded in his head from the sheer impoliteness of it. It occurred to him on the way that he didn't strictly know where the crash was, and he hoped he could make it that far and back before they closed Christine's body, the new and foreign kidney pulsing inside her.

He passed the bike rack and walked into the Safeway lobby, where the pay phones were. He looked up Paul in the book: 21540 Valley Road.

For a moment his conviction waned, and he slumped against the booth, feeling tired. He watched people walk in and out of Safeway, half-hoping somebody he knew would show up and he could bail out. There was a check-out clerk he often encountered, coming in for his shift, and a chubby man, burdened with bags, leaving with his red-haired teenage daughter, who Lars thought he knew. Then he remembered: Montana Gag. She and her boyfriend used to come in, looking for Greg. Briefly, Lars suffered under the weight of a despairing wish to be her: to buy groceries with her father, to eat dinner in front of the TV, to dip carelessly into the stash of weed stuffed into a hole in her box spring and drink in the smoke from her bed, the open window ad-mitting cool night. He watched the girl and her father get into a car and drive away. And then, there in the lobby with him, was Toth.

"Okay, I'm in," he said. A bicycle helmet dangled from one hand.

Lars pulled himself from the phone booth and looked his friend in the eye. "Good," he said.

The ride up the valley was long and windy, and darkened by the threat of rain. Cedar Avenue widened and followed the tracks, where freight cars clanked into each other like thunderheads, and cars and trucks raced past them, freed from the speed limits of town. Lars was exhausted before they even reached the exit to Valley Road, but seeing the green and white sign gave him new energy, and he rounded the corner at a smooth coast, a breeze at his back. It had taken them only half an hour so far. Once onto Valley, he and Toth were able to talk, as trees broke the wind and the traffic was light. But they didn't. Their mission retained some kind of sacredness, despite the bikes.

Soon, as the road evened out into a gradual climb, Lars was able to set his breath and motion into a smooth rhythm, and he let the scenery distract him. It had been a long time since he'd come up here; he and Megan went cross-country skiing one weekend in the woods. They passed the last convenience store and gas station, rode through wide meadows on which planned communities had been built along perfect curving paved streets. They came upon small ranches with sport utility vehicles in the driveways, and these petered out, leaving only trees and large log houses, set far back on the edges of hills. Soon there were posted signs—"SALMON NATIONAL WILDERNESS: NO HUNTING, BY ORDER OF MONTANA FISH & GAME"—and he heard Toth's voice, small behind him: "You think we're about there?"

Lars coasted to a stop, and listened as Toth did the same. Silence fell around them. "I suppose."

"They can't live *in* the wilderness, right?"

"I don't know." He scanned the horizon, then saw, up ahead, a gray metal mailbox, its flag hanging loose at its side. Across the two-lane from it was a dirt road, brown tracks fountaining out to the left and right.

"There?"

"Maybe." He straightened on the bike and started pedaling again, his muscles popping in protest.

The mailbox had the street number scrawled on it in black magic marker. There was no name. They crossed the road and stashed their bikes in the trees, out of sight from passing cars. The dirt road was heavily rutted and just wide enough for two cars to pass with great care. Water pooled in the tire tracks. They walked in silence, listening to the distant sounds of machinery.

"What is that?" Toth was asking.

"I don't know."

They rounded a corner and found themselves in a wide arc of churned-up grass, half-buried in drying mud. Off to the right, a piece of yellow plastic tape was tied to a tree and flapped in the breeze; nearby there was a dirt road, wider than the one they'd just been walking on, cut far back into the forest. It looked crudely new. From over a rise at the end of the road came a white pickup, driving slowly, and as it neared them Lars could see its tires bouncing over chunks of debris that lay in its way. Two men sat in it, both wearing caps. Lars was sure the men would stop and ask them to leave, but the driver simply raised two fingers in solemn greeting and nodded hello. Something rattled in the bed, beneath a large blue tarp.

Lars gazed out over the truck's path. "Down there," he said to nobody.

"Are you sure about this?"

He turned and looked at his friend, possibly for the first time since they left the hospital. Toth's eyes were weary and rimed with dried sweat, and his glasses sat far down on his nose, like a crotchety librarian's. Seeing Toth, his chest rising and falling, his lips slightly parted to let the air in, Lars had the distinct sensation of falling from a great height, and closed his eyes against hitting the ground. He felt dizzy, filled with the overabundance of life around him: the trees, the dirt, this panting, sweating Toth. "Yeah," he said. "Let's go."

They walked, side by side, down the road. Most of it was littered with pine needles and small rocks, and occasionally they passed a deep divot, where a tree must certainly have been. Here, the soil was exposed to the air and was darker than the ground that surrounded it; they avoided stepping into it, as if it were cursed. Another truck came over a rise and they moved out of its way.

And then they were standing at the bottom of the rise. Beyond it they could see the upper halves of trees, swaying gently. From behind them, there was sun. Toth went up it first, and stood at the top, perfectly still. Then he turned his head back to Lars, and in his face the wreck was reflected, as if in a shallow pool of water. A gulf opened up between them, Toth's expression, his thin body, unfamiliar to Lars now that he had seen. Toth extended his hand.

"Come on."

"All right," Lars said, and he climbed to the top of the rise.

The wreck was distant, but clear; gleaming metal attended to by yellow machines. People wearing blue baseball caps bent, examined things, wrote on papers flapping from clipboards. Things were lifted into pickups; a wheel loader scraped at the ground around a large piece of half-embedded airplane. Lars and Toth walked toward it slowly, letting the details accumulate gradually the closer they came. The entire scene was less like a wreck than an archaeological dig, every item from the teetering tail section to the sheared wing to the massive bent fuselage exhumed and examined with care, even reverence. There was something like elation in the air, the collective sense of chaos being brought back into line, and Lars felt himself moved by it, by the workers' absorption in the task. And Megan, he was surprised to notice, was nowhere to be found. He stopped walking.

"Lars?"

"No closer than this," he said. Because his sense—that this place was far from death, was more like a spot where Megan had waited for him, then given up, finally, and left—this sense, certainly, encompassed loneliness and loss, but not despair. Any closer and he might be set back again, sure to grieve without relief. But this sadness had some consolation to it, like reaching out and taking an offered prize. He did this, took what was offered and held it.

They stood a minute more, then turned back.

Though they had not been gone six hours—the sun was bright and high as they returned, and shadows still short on the ground— they returned to the hospital waiting room to find Amanda Stull pacing by the swinging doors to the operating rooms. Nearby an orderly sat behind a desk, watching over her. And in the chairs and couches arranged along the walls, big-haired girls in anxious poses. Sorority sisters.

"Mrs. Stull?"

She whirled upon Lars as if to grab him by the shirtfront, but when she recognized him she closed her eyes and inhaled deeply, gathering restraint. Lars felt himself flinch. "I'm sorry."

"I thought you might be the doctor."

"Any word?" Around them, the sorority sisters watched, their eyes wide.

"Somebody came out. It went okay. Or it's going. They're . . . closing." It seemed a great effort for her to say the word. "It's in there, anyway."

"Good." And for the moment, that was all that mattered: that a bad thing had been removed and a better thing put in its place.

Amanda Stull turned and peered through the door's porthole, and when Lars moved away he found that the girls had stood up behind him, six, seven of them, and were watching him and Toth, waiting for them to speak, to explain themselves in light of Christine's dramatic and anomalous life. Lars didn't have any explanation. He smiled, and nervously, a few of them did too. Then he held out his hands to them, and they took hold.

18

The man who answered the phone at Glacier Park Market was kind to her, but he failed to put her on hold, and she could hear him ringing up customers while she waited for Edward. "Going to have a few hot dogs tonight?" he asked someone. "No, ma'am, we're all out of those. . . . I'd just try singing. . . . No, ma'am, if you don't bother 'em, they won't bother you."

When Edward came to the phone, he sounded tired. "Hey, Mom."

"Did I wake you?" Trixie said.

"No."

"You sound tired."

He sighed. "I was in the back, trying to finagle some more bear whistles. Everybody's all riled up around here over the bear thing."

"Bear thing?"

"These people got mauled. They were sneaking up on some grizzlies in the backcountry, trying to take pictures. Now everybody's bought out the whistles." He sighed again. "It sounds like a Fourth of July parade out there."

"Well," she said. No use putting it off. "I have a little something to ask you."

This was a difficult thing for her to do. On his twenty-first birthday, just after he'd gotten his first job in the park, Edward had declared himself a family neutral zone. He would talk to or see anyone in the family (at that point Trixie, Kat, and her husband), and wouldn't talk about them to anyone else in the family. This included Hamish if he ever turned up. Edward moved into the mountains and was only accessible by telephone or long drive, and she noticed a subtle shift in his personality: he acquired a polite reserve, his letters became shorter and chattier. Trixie thought also that he might be homosexual, which, if so, he had never been candid about and probably never would be. Knowing his sister, this was the best tack if he wanted to remain on good terms with everyone.

In the end, the new Edward was a genius of restraint, a package that embodied all the quietness and delicacy of his childhood self and simultaneously jettisoned his fear. Trixie had tried to express her pride in him, in his self-control and even temper, but he resisted talking about it.

Still, she had a feeling he preferred her to his sister. Kat was likely to be suspicious of Edward, as he didn't share her faith, and the few times he mentioned her—which came very, very rarely—he seemed weary of bearing her scrutiny. So between mother and son there had evolved an unspoken trust, which is what made this phone call so difficult—she was going to ask him to lie to Kat.

"What is it?" he said, suddenly concerned. It was his misapprehension that she was frail, and he would soon need to move to Marshall to care for her. Though she supposed it was possible.

"I'm having a little get-together I want you to come to."

A pause. "Really?"

"A little thing. Just you, and . . ."

"Who?"

"My grandchildren," she said. "I'd like you to bring them along."

He snorted, a sudden and, she thought, contemptuous gesture entirely unlike him, and afterward fell into a silence broken only by the continuing sound of the cash register ringing, and the genial patter of the checker.

"Come on, Mom," he said finally. "I can't do that."

"Now don't say that so quickly," she said, and she could feel the opportunity vanishing, like so much precious water into the floor of a vast and lonely desert. "I'm getting old, and there are things I want known. You don't know about my parents, do you?"

"Grandma and Grandpa?"

"And my sister. Did you know I had a sister? Your sister was named after her. I'll bet those kids don't even know who their own mother was named after."

"I think I remember something about this, Mom, but really. I can't bring them to you. That's ridiculous." His voice had that sharp, particularly male, edge of finality she had grown to resent. Hearing it disappointed her.

"Do you intend to have a family, Edward? You're forty years old. Will you have children?"

Another silence, and this time the ambient sounds seemed to move away. When he spoke it was quiet and close, a deep and confidential voice. "No."

"I didn't think so. None of this will be passed on, Edward. I know this isn't so important to you—there is a lot you'd rather forget—but it is my life we are talking about. And my parents', and their parents'. It's our *family,* Edward." She paused, decided to play the only card she had. "And I'm getting to be so old, you know, I could forget it all. I want to pass it on before that happens."

"Is this about Dad?" he asked her. His voice took on that patronizing quality it had when he called after the funeral, as if she were the child now.

She sighed. "It is and it isn't."

"I can't violate Kat's trust," he said.

"Kat doesn't have to know."

"Oh, sure," he said. "I'll just whisk them away and have them back before she notices."

"You take them on a trip to the park. Just don't tell her about me."

"Think about this, Mom. They're kids. Do you think they're not going to tell their mother what they did on the trip? Do you think if I tell them it's a secret, they'll listen to me?" He chuckled, a low and sad laugh that made her heart ache. "You don't know these kids. They're tough customers. They don't trust anybody except their parents and God."

She hadn't known how well he knew them. Did he visit often? she wanted to know, but didn't ask. "I see," she said.

"You're asking me to undo Kat's hard work." He paused a moment. "You know, Mom, she's told them that you're dead."

"What!"

"That's why she didn't want you at the funeral."

"They think I'm dead?"

"They think you're dead. You've been dead since before they were born. That's the party line."

Trixie sat down now, on a kitchen chair, to catch herself from a sudden swoon: she felt for a moment that it was true, that she really was dead and had never existed in the first place. The ends of her fingers went cold and numb, and she loosened her hold on the receiver until the blood flowed back into them. How could Kat tell such a lie? Maybe part of her actually believed it. She could see how it might happen: the hatred beginning in isolation, a nacreous bead that floated, hard and inert, inside her; then something happening—their move to Marshall maybe, or Hamish leaving—to dislodge it and let it float free, and gather smaller hatreds like oil congealing on water. And soon it would be big enough to kill Trixie in her mind. To her daughter, she thought, it was better that she was dead. Trixie felt like she was groping at the last threads of her life, her past, things she wanted with a desperation she feared she did not have the strength to maintain.

"I am not dead," she said.

"No."

"Then you wouldn't need to tell them who I really was. I could just be an old lady you knew."

He let out a weary breath. "They would tell Kat, Mom."

"It would be the last thing on their minds. They're going to see mountains and bears and canyons, and that will be what they tell their mother." He said nothing. "When have I ever asked you for a favor, Edward?"

"I'll think about it," he said finally.

"Well, all right," she said, and hoped the excitement was not so obvious in her voice.

"I have to go."

"I love you, Edward."

"You too, Mom," he said, and hung up.

She pushed herself out of her chair and her muscles resisted, as if they might snap. She straightened slowly and hung the phone on the cradle. It had felt, as they talked, like Edward was here in the room with her, like one of the many talks they'd had in his sister's absence the last few years he lived at home; now she noticed that it had become dark outside, and the darkness in the corners of the house challenged the kitchen's single lamp, stranding her in an island of dull yellow light.

The effect depressed her immensely. In the half-dark, the room's objects

sat with an indifferent, immutable confidence, the way other people's possessions looked in their houses to a visitor waking in the night. Her hands trembled, not from nerves, she imagined, but to shake off the skin and muscle and
blood, easier then to settle in their grave. She felt like her body was launching
its first offensive against her mind, which it had decided had run its due
course.

Her thoughts startled her: so macabre! She remembered Hamish's
strangely smooth hands, the patterns they traced in the dust of her dashboard.

She walked around the house to get her blood flowing, and turned on
every lamp. It helped, a little. In the light her things looked less threatening.
Still, they distinguished themselves mostly by the shadows they harbored—a
smear of dark behind a chair, the black patch behind a photograph.

She took her jacket—a red windbreaker, worn at the cuffs—and slipped
it on. It felt a little big on her, the way Schatze's clothes had felt when they
were girls together, the way Hamish's had when they were married. Outside,
the air had taken on a rough texture, like burlap. She inhaled it and the burn
in her lungs felt like an infusion of new life. The moon was bright and nearly
full, and she could just make out the worn paths into the woods behind the
house. She had walked them enough to know them in the dark, especially
with the moon bright and the lights of the house still blazing.

She wondered what it would be like to meet them. How much of herself
would she see in them? The genetic line between herself and Kat, always clear
in her imagination, was in fact broken by a husband she had never seen (or
had, barely, in a photo Edward had shown her: he stood with Kat, at a great
distance, beneath a blossoming magnolia, a thick man with a round face and
the sun's glare in his glasses). She imagined the children fidgeting, their restraint learned, not innate, and polite. His hair cut short, hers long, with a
bow slightly ratty from travel. They would be wearing blue jeans bought especially for this trip, the only ones they had ever owned. They would have
white sneakers on their feet and would refuse offered food.

She hadn't really walked this path during the summer, and it had grown
halfway over. She didn't recall its having grown so quickly in previous years.
Perhaps the plants had saved up their growth during the drought, and exploded after the rain. Several times she thought she might have lost her way,
but the path reappeared before her in the moonlight. She came to a rise, which
she scaled with some difficulty, and looked down at her house from between

the trees. The lights cast squarish beams into the weeds in the yard and the split-rail fence that ran around it. From here, it all looked small and inert, pulsing out light that nobody would see or care about. How many people passed it on the road as they returned home in the evening, without noticing it? Her neighbors used to stop by to see her, but the ones who did so had moved, and those who replaced them never came.

It wasn't the company she missed, but the acknowledgment that she was there, living.

Hers, she thought now, was a life without consequence. It would vanish when spent, the way the house would one day be claimed by lupines and knapweed. She'd always had faith in the forces that combated entropy, but now it seemed like her life, everyone's lives, were only wounds in the fabric of the universe that would heal up in time, despite everyone's best efforts at preservation. The evidence was everywhere—the path, growing over faster than she could clear it; the stems of plants around her that would, if clipped, heal and grow double; the rain washing ruts from the mud and making new ones where it wished them to go.

And her family, eroded beyond recognition, leaving and marrying and dying as if they'd sprung fully grown from the dirt, without the intervention of her flesh.

She was cold, and the back of her hand stung and itched. She brought it to her lips and tasted blood; she must have been scratched parting the underbrush. It was time to go back inside. For a second, looking around her, she saw no path at all, and couldn't remember how she had gotten to this place. She took a step in a direction that felt right, but there was a bramble there that tugged the laces of her sneaker loose; in another direction was a fallen tree, rotted through and overgrown with moss. And then she remembered: she'd stepped over a thick root. The moon had grown dim behind a cloud, so she felt for it with her feet. There was nothing at first, and then it materialized beneath her. In the face of a rising and inexplicable panic, she leaped it, crashed through the groping branches of a thick bush, came down with her foot sideways on a rock and fell.

She landed on the path, the air knocked out of her. The impact was more a shock than a pain, her bones recoiling at the sudden pressure; she felt pine needles dig into her stockings and prick at her knees, and something hard drove itself into her chin. She rolled over instinctively, her hands finding her face in the dark, and she coughed until her breath returned to her, ragged and desperate. She tried moving her jaw: no problem. But her hands came away sticky. She found the wound with her finger, and it stung her terribly.

She got to her feet slowly, fearing a sprain or worse in her ankle, but it had held up. The hurt parts of her throbbed dimly, like electric coils, just beneath the surface of her skin. She felt dizzy and panicked, as if the woods themselves, or something in them, had done this to her; she stood perfectly still, taking deep, cool breaths, trying to calm her thudding heart. When she thought she had the strength, she hurried back down the path, taking it as slowly as her panic would let her, her hand clamped over her chin, stanching the blood. She burst out finally, letting go of a cry that seemed to come from somewhere else, so horribly and perilously weak was it, and she ran into the house, slamming the door behind her.

Inside, she rushed to the bathroom. Her cheeks were scratched, and blood welled thickly in the gash on her chin. Spots of it darkened on her jacket. She opened the medicine cabinet, her hands shaking, and fumbled with a tin of gauze and bandages. It clattered into the sink. She picked it up, set it on the toilet, and went to work cleaning her wounds, washing them with soap and water and swabbing them with iodine. Then she bandaged the cuts, and watched in the mirror as the gauze on her chin sprouted a red blotch that grew and then stopped. Now, finally, she calmed. She cleaned the blood off the sink and floor and went to her room.

In bed, the sensation of falling returned to her, and the room spun. She reached out and gripped a bar on the headboard for support. She wondered what Hamish saw when the plane went down, if he ever saw the ground he would die on or heard the other passengers. Or if it seemed he was alone, everything else just a blur around him, as he hurried to meet the forest floor.

The telephone woke her. She wondered who would call so early until she saw her bedside clock: noon. She hadn't slept this late in years. When she tried to lift her head, the pillow stuck to her face, and came away streaked with the dark brown of dried blood. Her face felt bloated and sore.

"Hello?" The room was still hazy, the light in the windows a bright affliction, as if the sun had risen in the yard.

"Mom."

"Edward!"

"You sound funny. Are you okay?" His voice was distant and tinny; a bad connection.

"I'm fine. I had a fall, and I'm sore."

"A fall! Is anything broken? Do you need—"

"Everything's fine. Just a few scratches."

"Okay," he said doubtfully. "I wanted to tell you that I called Kat. She liked the idea, believe it or not. Not the part about you, I mean, the trip. I'm taking them for the weekend, and I can put them up in one of the chalets, and then we can hike on some—"

"Wait a minute, you mean you're coming?" she said, her sluggish blood starting to flow.

"Well, maybe. I'm picking them up Friday morning." His voice was buoyant with excitement.

"So you're coming?"

"Well, I think."

"This is okay with Kat? She's letting you take them."

"They have some church thing this weekend," he said. "There was some kind of shake-up or something, a priest getting drunk, I don't know. It's like a retreat. They were going to leave the kids with some neighbors, but they don't really like the neighbors . . ."

"You'll bring them."

He sighed. "I will *try* to bring them, Mom. It's a little out of the way. I have to think of some reason to get them there."

"You'll bring them, please, Edward," she said. Her wounds stopped their dull throbbing and began to sting like fresh cuts. She touched her face. It had the mealy tautness of a tomato. "Tell me you will."

"I can't guarantee—"

"Edward!"

"Okay," he said. "Okay, I'll bring them. But I don't know the details. We'll have to make up something about who you are, I don't know. There's still time to think about it."

"I have to get ready," she said. "What can I do for them? We can go walking, and—"

"Look, don't make any big plans, okay? It's supposed to be no big deal, just some old lady."

"Right," she said, though she was loath to hear it.

"I'll get back to you on this. Let me think about my schedule here and I'll try to whip something up. Brainstorm, Mom, okay?"

"All right."

"I'm gonna go," he said. "I love you, Mom."

She had heard of her granddaughter's birth from Edward. Rachel, he told her, her name's Rachel. Trixie hadn't even known Kat was pregnant. Edward got hold of a picture of the baby and made her a photocopy of it. Even grainy and cracked from folding, Rachel's face bore the shadows of Hamish, and a little of Schatze. Somewhere she still had this photo, though she hadn't looked at it for years.

But after that, Edward sent no pictures. Maybe he had been optimistic that Rachel's birth would smooth out the rift in the family. If anything, it widened. Kat called only once, and that call had only been a curt declaration of her intentions, an almost defiant (and at that point entirely unnecessary) gesture. "Our spiritual adviser suggested I call," her daughter told her, and little else. And when David was born, nothing.

In the bathroom, Trixie was stunned at her reflection: last night's scratches had swollen like streambeds in a flood, and the wound on her chin reopened, turning the gauze and even the tape that held it a gruesome brown-pink. Gingerly, she tore off the bandage and replaced it with another, and the stain quickly stopped its spread.

That afternoon she ate lunch with Diane, at the same place she had eaten with Edward years before. It had a different name now, and the pressed-tin ceiling was gone. Now the water pipes and air shafts were left exposed high above them. Long cords hung from the rafters and ended in lamps that dangled directly over each table. It had been many years since the place changed hands, but this decor still seemed like an affront, a surface change that marked a larger movement in Marshall away from its humble beginnings. It reminded her that she wouldn't die in the place she had come to so full of hope for a new life, but in the urban landscape that had been built around it, which she would never fully know.

Even so, Marshall was more familiar to her than her own son was. Marshall had built itself out in the open: retail warehouses grew out of prairies, housing developments crept across fields like renegade weeds. But Edward grew up in private, like a greenhouse plant. He read books and listened to the radio, and if she had a tangible effect on him, it was only the fretful leniency that allowed him space to change in. And Kat, finally, seemed less her child than a piece of her broken off and lost, a piece she had lived so long without that it had stopped being hers.

When Diane arrived she gasped and touched Trixie's face. "I know," Trixie said. She explained the scratches and told Diane about the welling of panic that had sent her sprawling, the fear that something would find her in the dark.

"Well," Diane said, "you aren't getting any younger, now are you?" She raised her eyebrows. "Did your ghost come back?"

She was tempted to confess the episode in the car, but something in Diane's tone prevented it—an amused restraint, colored with the hope that the answer would be no, that the delusion, if that's what it was, had stopped. Instead, she told about her grandchildren, that they might be brought to her soon.

"You're kidding!"

"No, I'm not."

"So what will you say?" Diane said, happy to get off the subject she had brought up. Trixie shrugged.

"I don't know. You're the one who has a way with words. You tell me."

Diane shook her head. "Not a chance."

"I don't even know how to start thinking about it. I'm at quite a loss."

A waitress came and they ordered lunch. "You know," Diane said, "it might help you to write down your thoughts. Script it. When Frank and I were divorcing, I always took notes before we met. I kept them on note cards in my pocket. Never had to pull them out, but it helped knowing they were there."

"That's a thought."

"I say, give 'em something to think about someday. Make it a visit they'll remember."

"But won't tell anyone about," Trixie said, and thought for the first time of the risk that Edward was taking to try this. A cloud of doubt and guilt drifted through her and she took a deep breath.

They ate, talking about other, easier things, and paid their bill. As they parted, affection swelled in Trixie, the kind you get when leaving on a trip of indefinite duration, when you tell somebody you'll see them again someday. "You've been such a friend," she said, and almost wept at the sound of the words, thin and empty out on the sidewalk, against the noise of traffic. Diane took her hand. "Well, I'll keep on being one," she said, but Trixie could see

she was afraid to be moved, as if she saw, in her friend's confusion, her own future, and wanted desperately to believe it wouldn't be so bad.

Driving home, she noticed the handprints were still visible on her dashboard, not yet covered by new dust. She reached out during a red light and fitted her own, smaller hand into the wide fingers of his. The surface was cold,
and the cold seeped into her, stiffening the fingers. She worked them, wiping
the dust off onto her palm, and now there was another cleared space within
the first in the spidery shape of her hand.

Edward called that night; the trip was set, and he would
bring the children to her house on Sunday, sometime in the afternoon, as he
drove them home. "Your name is Mrs. Kurtz."

"Kurtz?"

"You're the mother of a friend of mine, okay?"

"What's the friend's name?"

A pause. "Oh, Jesus . . . uh, Mark."

"Mark Kurtz," she repeated, trying to fix the name. Her son.

She had three days to prepare whatever she was going to say. When she'd
hung up, she looked through her kitchen drawers for a package of note cards
she thought she had. She didn't find them. Eventually she uncovered a yellow
legal pad, its pages dusty and brittle with age, and pulled it out from under a
pile of pot holders and dishrags. She threw it onto her table, where it shone
dully under the kitchen lamp, and turned back to the drawers for something
suitable to write with. A pencil. It was unsharpened, clean and yellow and untouched by anyone but her. With a kitchen knife, she shaved it to a point, then
she sat down at the table, the legal pad before her, and set the pencil to it.

It was harder to start than she'd imagined: the memories that had sur-
faced were less parts of a narrative than evocative and fleeting images, and she
could no more commit them to paper than she could justly describe a painting or symphony. There were no words at her disposal other than the words
she recalled people saying. When she started, finally, it was at the beginning
of her family history as she knew it: *My parents,* she wrote, *came to Great Falls
from the state of New York.*

She was up late that night, setting her story in motion. She found that her
efforts to describe one incident stirred up memories of others, until, by the

time she usually went to sleep, her head was so spinning with stories that she could barely write them down fast enough. Her handwriting became nearly unintelligible, and she whittled her pencil into a little pile of graphite dust and wood shavings that steadily grew beside the paper.

She slept lightly, and in the morning emptied her shoebox of Hamish's things onto the bed. She sifted through them, holding each item for a moment in the hope that it would surrender something of the past. The box itself gave off a rich, musty odor that she recognized as an element of the old kitchen; this reminded her of the grave silence of family dinners in Hamish's presence, during his days of construction work, and how after his absence he was never mentioned, not once, by any of them during dinner.

Her memories of Schatze yielded a sense of their bedroom back in Great Falls, the yellow window shades with their dark stripes, and the single bowed floorboard at the foot of the closet that made a bench for Schatze's dolls. She remembered her parents' discussions, which she listened to from the top of the stairs when she couldn't sleep. They argued affectionately about how they thought the world was put together, sometimes for hours, and though Trixie didn't understand what they meant, she always was confident that the world was put together well, hearing it from their lips.

These three days of recollection were a kind of bliss for Trixie. She understood, writing, that it was a rare concentration, one she was not likely to see again. She had, for the first time in many years, a real sense of herself and what came before her. It was like talking to the dead, asking them those things she had always wanted to know. For the moment she let herself forget about what she would tell the children. Such was her state that she assumed she would come up with the perfect thing when the time came.

But then it did, and she had nothing. She was in the bathroom, trying to cover up the marks on her face, when Edward's knock came at the door. He came in before she had a chance to answer it. "Mrs. Kurtz!" he said, to her puzzlement: she had completely forgotten about the assumed name. She hadn't seen her son in a year. He had a thick beard now, the same color his father's hair had been before he left—dark, dark brown, with strands of gray bright throughout, like moonlight. She went to him and hugged him.

"Hello, Edward," she said, and she marveled again at how much he felt like Hamish, and how his smell, that smoky, cherry brandy smell, was so familiar to her, his childhood smell intensified with age.

And then she saw them over his shoulder, standing in the doorway, backlit and shadowed by the light outside, and remembered her role. "Mark," she said. "Does Mark look well?" Could Edward hear the apprehension in her voice? Could the children?

"He's excellent, Mrs. Kurtz."

"Oh, good." She had prepared nothing, in her worry over what to say. Did she have tea or coffee? Cookies for the children? "This must be your nephew and niece."

"Mrs. Kurtz," he said, "this is Rachel, and this is David."

The children stepped into the house and Rachel, like an adult, closed the door behind her. "Hi," David was saying, his eyes straying around the house.

"It's nice to meet you." There was nothing of her in David's face. But then, in response, he hung his head just slightly, his neck vanishing into his shoulders, and she recognized in the gesture her father, that strange manifestation of his politeness. She thought of the stack of yellow pages in her pocket, that this was something she would add to it.

"I'm Rachel," Rachel said, and Trixie was astonished—the little girl might have passed for Schatze. She stood perfectly still, wearing a simple dress and sneakers. How Trixie wanted to tell Edward! But she couldn't, not right now.

"It's nice to meet you, dear," she said, trembling.

"Mrs. Kurtz." It was Edward, at her side now, touching her shoulder. "Did you hurt yourself? Your face."

"I had a spill out on the path."

"You have a path?" David said. "We saw a mountain goat and elks."

"You did!"

He nodded. "And this huge bird."

"A raven," Edward said.

"Except real big, like this." And he held his arms out.

And then Rachel suddenly said, "How do you know Uncle Edward?" It was not quite an accusation, but Trixie feared, for a moment, that they had been found out.

"His friend Mark is my son," she said, quietly.

"Did we meet Mark?" Rachel asked Edward.

"No."

They were all quiet, and then Rachel, satisfied, went to the cupboard and peered through the glass doors.

Trixie broke the silence. "Well," she said. "Let me see what I have to eat." She went to the cabinets over the sink and found some ginger snaps and chocolate syrup. She got the milk from the refrigerator and mixed it up for the children, who had found their way, along with Edward, to the table. The three sat there silently as Trixie set out the cookies and milk. David thanked her and drank his milk immediately; Rachel smiled and took a single sip before pushing it subtly away. She was a serious girl, nothing at all like Schatze in manner. "David," she said.

"What?"

"Say your prayers."

Trixie and Edward exchanged looks as the children bent over the table, their hands folded before them as if they concealed some found treasure. The girl's voice had real authority. When they had finished, David set upon the cookies but Rachel did not.

"Edward tells me you live in Butte," Trixie said to them. "Do you like it there?"

"Yes, very much," Rachel said. David nodded.

"Do you get to go camping much?"

"Mommy doesn't like it," David said.

"Because she's so busy," his sister added, with a note of warning in her voice. Her eyes turned to Trixie and lingered there, sizing something up. Trixie turned away.

In the silence that followed, Edward talked about the trip: they had gone into the backcountry, where they slept two nights in a rustic cabin, cooked over a fire, and took long hikes. David interrupted several times to add his observations, but Rachel only sat and listened.

"It was real cold," David said. "I wore gloves to bed."

"Shoes too," Edward said.

"Rachel," Trixie said now, "how did you like the park?"

"It was glorious," she said soberly. "I'd like to go again."

"I'm sure you'll get the chance," Edward told her.

They went outside to take a walk. David ran back to the edge of the woods and Rachel walked quickly after him, leaving Trixie alone with Edward. She turned to him, keeping her distance in case the children were watching, and said, "Thank you."

"I wish we could be out in the open." He looked about to cry.

She nodded. "They remind me of you and Kat."

"Maybe," he said, smiling. "David's a little more thick-skinned than I was. And Rachel's cleverer than her mother."

"She is clever."

"Yes."

They grinned at each other. "You go alone with them," he said. "I'll stay back."

"All right. I love you, Edward. I feel like I haven't been mother enough."

"I haven't been son enough either, I guess, out in the woods." He sighed. "I'll come for Thanksgiving, if you'll be here."

"I will," she said, and took his hands.

Out back, David was calling to Rachel as he ran about: "Look at this! Look at this!" Rachel followed him at a distance, like a worried parent, and made no response.

On the path, David ran ahead, calling back to them about the things he saw. "Don't go too far!" Trixie yelled to him, and to Rachel she said, "This is where I fell the other day. I don't want him hurting himself."

"He gets excited," Rachel said, and then, without the slightest change in tone: "I know who you are."

Trixie did not stop walking. Rachel was a stride behind her, her light steps making almost no sound on the trail. If not for her words, it would have been easy to think she wasn't there at all.

"What do you mean?"

"Mom has pictures of you and her and Uncle Edward." She paused, waiting perhaps for a reaction. Trixie didn't give it to her. "She keeps them hidden, but I found them."

Ahead, David left the path and ran into the trees, toward the ruin of an old stone springhouse. The spring, Trixie knew, was dry. She stopped and turned on her granddaughter.

"You mustn't tell your mother. She doesn't want me to see you."

"She says you died."

"I know that."

"She says you drove Grandpa to drink."

Trixie knelt in the dirt. In the pocket of her jeans, the papers crackled. "Don't tell her. She would be very angry at your uncle."

Rachel seemed to consider this. She took a handful of her dress and bunched it in her fist. When she let go, the creases remained. "I won't tell," she said.

"All right," Trixie said. "I trust you."

Later she would wonder what sent her hand to her pocket for the sheaf of papers. By the time they were out, she had reconsidered, but there they were between her fingers, like an ill-spoken confession that couldn't be taken back.

"What's that?" Rachel set her hand on the papers but didn't take them.

"It's about our family."

Her eyes narrowed. "It's for me?"

Trixie pushed the papers toward her. "Yes."

Rachel took them, unfolded them, looked for a moment at the writing. "Okay," she said, and refolded them and slipped them into the pocket of her dress.

Trixie took her arm and held her fast. "You mustn't tell."

"I *said*," she said. "I thought you trusted me." Her eyes, gray and brave, her grandfather's eyes, met Trixie's and held them there. "You do, don't you?"

Trixie tightened her grip. "I do," she said, and let go.

19

Kathy wasn't home when she called, so Anita left a message that she was coming and called Larry. He was subdued in the truck, but apparently only with great effort; he tried to start several conversations that she didn't want to have.

She hadn't wanted to see him at all, not yet, not until she had her own place, which she had taken a week off to look for. Her bag was stuffed with essentials—clothes she needed for work, for putting together an apartment. There were some books, some things she had grabbed in a moment of bitterness: a few pairs of men's boxers she bought for herself that Paul had appropriated, stolen from his bureau along with a roll of film he must have dropped there by mistake. She'd savored the prospect of denying him the pictures, which probably were of her and Paul in happier times, but now she only felt mildly guilty about it, as if for a nasty prank pulled years ago on someone nobody liked.

Anita had never seen Kathy's building before, but it was more or less what she'd expected of Kathy: a big concrete block covered with gray wooden siding and surrounded by well-pruned shrubbery set in beds of white gravel. There were six apartments, each with a little balcony. Most of the balconies were jammed with recreational equipment—kayaks, waders, rafts, inner tubes—but one, on the second floor, overflowed with flowering plants and weathered-looking redwood porch furniture. Kathy's. The building filled Anita with despair. She knew that the sill of Kathy's single tiny window would be caked with a mixture of dust and kitchen grease, and that the carpet would smell like a new car.

"If you have any trouble," Larry said. He had turned off the car. She would have been more comfortable if he'd left it running. "You know. You can come stay with me."

"Okay," she said, suddenly weary. She rested her head on his shoulder. Not the sort of gesture she'd pictured herself indulging in on this trip, but now it made her feel a little better.

"Doesn't look like your kind of place."

"It isn't. She says she got it because of the balcony."

"I like the balcony, though. At least there isn't a dead elk hanging from it."

It made her laugh, and for a moment she felt relaxed and wondered why she was bothering to stay with Kathy at all when she had Larry's house, with its yard and creek. And then she remembered the awful fantasy she'd conjured for herself: never finding a place, and simply staying there indefinitely, neither of them mentioning it. And then, without an adequate space between one man and another, not having the time to figure out who she wanted to become, and gradually accepting her identity as a subset of his. And finally, an image: years from now, a lonely moment at the house, Larry away with friends fishing, and she tries to comfort herself with food and spills it onto the floor, and she's kneeling there cleaning it, and the grit on the floor is rubbing itself into her knees, and she just gives up. She lies down there and does absolutely nothing until he returns.

Forget that. A week with Kathy, tops, and then a decent studio apartment. Near downtown.

She untangled herself from his arms. "Well," she said, meaning everything she'd been thinking.

"Can I call you here?"

"Larry . . ."

"No, okay, I'm sorry."

"I'll call you, I promise."

"Anita." He was looking at her intently, as if she were a tricky mechanical problem.

"Yes?"

"I love you."

She stiffened. How could he? She watched his face fall as she said nothing, and he began immediately to apologize.

"No, wait," she said, but they both knew there was no way she could make him happy at this moment. She took his disappointed face in her hands and pulled him to her and kissed him, deeply but, she hoped, without the desperation she felt. She held him, and whispered, "Soon," and then she got out of the car.

She stood before the door, listening to a strange sound: a sort of dim, scraping thud accompanied by a high, dull metallic clinking. A pause, and then the sound again. Anita knocked, hitching her bag up on her shoulder.

"Be right there!" came Kathy's voice, and a flurry of clinking with her footsteps. Then the door swung open. "Hey! You made it!"

"Hi there."

"This is it," Kathy said. She took Anita's bag and ushered her into the apartment. "In, in, in."

Against the far wall stood a gigantic wooden object strung with wires. It looked like a complicated musical instrument, and was about ten feet long and half as high. It dominated the room. As Kathy walked off with the bag, her footsteps made the wires vibrate and clink against each other. Anita was stunned. She thought, Every step? Every step you take in this apartment makes that sound?

"I see you've noticed the loom," Kathy said from the hallway.

"Loom?"

"I made all these," she said, gesturing around the room, and now Anita noticed, for the first time, the walls: they were covered, every inch, with intricate tapestries, each in jagged patterns of subtly shifting colors. They looked a little like Navaho blankets, but with a disturbing touch of madness. She had to admit, she liked them.

"They're terrific."

"Thanks." Kathy was wearing a baggy wool sweater and stirrup pants. Anita thought they made her look chubbier than she already was, but she also looked comfortable, and this was her own house after all.

Kathy led her to the extra room, where she'd be sleeping. The loom tittered as they walked, and Anita tried to tread lightly to keep the noise down. Kathy didn't seem to notice. The extra room turned out to be a sewing room. A sewing machine sat on a drafting table, and swatches of fabric lay in little piles on the floor and spilled off shelves. There was a large wooden rack covered with spools of thread, and a pincushion in the shape of a frog, its face full of dismay.

"I did the frog," Kathy said.

"It's something else."

There was a certain cluttered charm to the apartment Anita hadn't expected. It had all the distasteful elements she'd imagined, but they didn't add up to anything; Kathy had transcended her environment. It put Anita on the defensive. Not since junior high, when she attended various powwows in her friends' bedrooms, had she seen a place so obviously designed for one person's comfort—the couch was draped precisely with an old blanket, its tassels frayed at the ends, the walls covered with framed magazine covers from the twenties and antique-shop oil paintings of Victorian-era scenes.

Anita set down her bag. "You can sleep on the couch," Kathy told her. "It's comfy. There's a towel for you on the chair, and some bath stuff. I've got tea on. Get yourself situated and come on out." She disappeared. Sure enough, there was an upholstered chair with a folded white towel on it, and on the towel was a bar of soap wrapped in paper, some bath beads, a little bottle of shampoo.

She sat on the couch. It gave beneath her with a whoosh, and lowered her slowly into a deep, soft pocket of cushion. She felt held. She reached for the chair and pulled the towel out from under the other toiletries. It was thick and fuzzy, with flowering vines embroidered into the hem; she noticed now a washcloth and hair towel (she hadn't seen one of those since junior high, either) of the same design. She laughed, and thought she heard Kathy stop puttering for a moment. To fill the silence, she called out, "Everything's so *nice!*"

"Well, good," Kathy called back.

She unpacked her things, trying to form neat piles on the floor around the couch. She folded up her bag and stowed it under the sewing machine. Then she went out to the kitchen and sat down across the table from Kathy. The table was covered, at an angle, by a lace tablecloth, and a blue porcelain teapot steamed in the center, next to a small lamp. Anita's cup was full, and a tiny pitcher of cream and a bowl of sugar cubes sat next to it.

"This is some place," she said.

Kathy sipped her tea. "You sure you don't think it's funny?"

"Funny?" But she felt herself reddening. "Oh—no, I was just . . . It's just a surprise. How nice it is."

Kathy nodded slowly. She seemed unsatisfied with this answer, and stuck her spoon into her tea for no obvious practical reason. She stirred it.

"Who was the guy?" she said.

Anita laughed. "Larry."

"You looked unhappy getting out of the car."

Unhappy? Anita looked up, trying to gauge Kathy's intent—if she had been offended or if she was simply probing for information. "I guess I'm just generally kind of unhappy."

"You're seeing him, though."

It was asked like a rival sister might ask it, a challenge.

"Yes."

Kathy smiled. "Is he Your Future?"

"I don't even know what I'm going to be eating for breakfast tomorrow, let alone who'll be my future."

"Porridge," Kathy said. "With almonds and dried apples."

Usually she had trouble sleeping in unfamiliar places, but on the couch in Kathy's sewing room, sleep found her quickly. It was as if the apartment had wrapped itself around her and was rocking her. She dreamed, for the first time, about the plane crash. It started out familiarly, more or less the way it really happened. She and Paul were in the yard, having a disagreement, though in the dream she couldn't quite tell what it was about. Paul mumbled, she mumbled back. It was hot. When the plane came, its engines mingled with their argument, until the three sounds were indistinguishable from one another. The plane's shadow appeared in the yard and grew steadily, like a storm cloud.

Then she noticed Larry standing miserably in the shadow, like a cartoon character beneath a falling anvil.

"It's Larry!" she said.

"Ah, don't worry about it," Paul said.

The shadow moved toward the forest, and Larry began to jog, then to run, to keep under it. "I'll catch it!" he called out to Anita. Then he was swallowed by the trees, and the plane's shadow ballooned ridiculously over everything, bringing the yard into an ominous half-dusk. In a blur of sickly gray, the plane plunged into the ground, sending a smokeless silo of apocalyptic fire into the air. The dusk spread itself out over the forest, as far as the eye could see, and the treetops were bathed in firelight. She was cold when she woke, and the bright outdoors looked queer and false.

"You look shell-shocked," Kathy told her at the breakfast table. There was the porridge, steaming in twin bowls before them, with brown sugar and cream poured over it. "Did you sleep badly? Is the couch okay?"

"Fine. It's fine. I had a bad dream."

Kathy raised her eyebrows. She looked perfectly rested, serene and un-wrinkled in her white nightgown. Her hair was frizzy from sleep and rose above her like a halo. She rustled the newspaper and took part of it out. "Here's section C," she said. "Classifieds."

"Oh. Right."

Anita tasted the porridge. It was very good, and she said so. Kathy thanked her and went back to her section of newspaper. This manner of Kathy's—a seemingly effortless nonchalance, even around a relative stranger—was incomprehensible to her, an inexplicable weirdness that made Kathy seem, at times, barely human. To Anita, the situation was basically wrong, an uncomfortable anomaly of which the best had to be made. To Kathy it seemed only like another fairly pleasant day, flavored with a few in-convenient quirks. Anita cleared her throat, though she had nothing to say. Kathy didn't look up.

She opened the paper to the apartment ads, spread it flat in front of her bowl, and began to read. At first the ads were impenetrable. Everything was in code. She felt out of her element, as if people who looked for apartments were people who were always looking for apartments and that she was an un-wanted visitor to their peculiar country. But slowly the listings began to sink in. They weren't what Anita wanted.

SUNNY 1-br daylight basement. No smokers. No pets. 1313 Hood Way. $450/mo. Call Petra, 276-9915.

SPACIOUS, CLEAN bsmt studio, cool in summer, garbage pd.
No pets, smokers. $375 + $300 dep, call Dave with references,
276-3818.

"Are they *kidding?*" she said.

"What?"

"These ads! Four fifty for a basement? In Marshall? That's insane!"

Kathy laughed. "That's how much it costs to live now."

She looked up. "What are you paying for this place?"

"Five fifty."

"That's half your salary!"

"It is," Kathy said. "Heat included, though. Except they keep it at a brisk
sixty-five all winter."

All the ads were like the first two, dismal and demanding. She borrowed
a pen and began to circle the ones that didn't seem too bad: downtown one-
bedroom, no pets, $470; "huge studio" near the University, heat paid, $400.
She'd never thought of rent as a major expense. She lived in a room of a large
house in college and paid ninety dollars for the privilege, and since then she
hadn't had to pay a thing. Thanks to Paul.

But she had money. She'd been saving since they came here, mostly in a
joint account that they would have to settle (she would give him half, probably, though she thought that if she wanted to she could keep more), but some
in her own account that Paul had never known about. She never had any real
plans for it, but it had long been a comfort to her, and now she would probably need it—for her rent and deposit, for some new furniture. For a divorce
lawyer. Would they need one? Would it be an amicable parting? She knew
nothing about this, and now didn't want to have to. This was not a new life
she was starting, but a backtracking upon the old one. There was no such
thing as a new one.

She took a breath and circled another apartment: spacious room in family
dwelling, private bath, $300, call Denise.

"How do you know my salary?"

Anita looked up. "What?"

Kathy wore an expression of amicable distrust. "You said my rent was half
my salary. How do you know my salary?"

Anita shrugged. "I just do. It's a teller's salary. I used to be a teller."

Kathy seemed to accept this and looked down at the paper, open to the comics. But it dawned on Anita why she really knew: she looked up people's accounts on the computer sometimes, just to see what they deposited each month. She felt caught in the act. Embarrassed, she folded back the classifieds and stood up.

"Beetle Bailey's getting beaten up again," Kathy said. "A shame."

"Can I use the phone?"

"Sure, go ahead."

Anita went to the telephone and started dialing.

Five possibilities today. She dropped off Kathy at the bank, then borrowed her car and filled it with gas. She bought a giant paper cup of coffee from the gas station.

Her first appointment was the downtown one-bedroom. It was in a large brick building, the landlady had told her, "right across from the detached facility." This turned out to be a lobbyless drive-up bank, the one all the tellers at her bank used to work at and hated, where a long row of idling cars was lined up for their transactions. It was the primary view from the apartment building, which, though brick, still managed to look like an abandoned warehouse. The windows were little arrow-slits and the door was made of steel and painted green.

The landlady was waiting for her on the stoop. "I've been waiting," she said.

"I'm on time," Anita told her, and the woman frowned. She had an aggressively combed head of puffy silver hair that stopped just above the shoulders. Anita watched it sway as she followed her through a dark hallway that smelled like cat urine.

"Current tenant's still here," the landlady told her, knocking on the door. Nobody answered, and they went in.

The floor was covered with clothes and dirty dishes, and the curtains were drawn. There was an overwhelming odor of a human body, and the smell of cigarette smoke. Anita remembered that smokers were not allowed, but the landlady seemed not to notice. She stood in the center of the room and pointed. "Bathroom, closet, bedroom, kitchenette, closet."

"I don't think it's for me," Anita told her.

"Garbage and water's paid. Not heat and lights."

"Really, I don't think I'm going to take it."

The landlady's hands fell to her hips. "Do you know what kind of schedule I have here? Do you understand that my time is valuable?"

"Well, I . . ."

"You can see yourself out, lady."

Anita drove to the place "near U." and found it was actually nice—wood floors, which she liked, and lace curtains that had been left by a previous tenant—but it was small and there was a fraternity next door. A window opened onto a window of the fraternity, and through it Anita could see a Ping-Pong table and a brightly glowing Coke machine. The guy from the rental agency was thin and had round glasses and a sunken chest. He adjusted his necktie incessantly. "Do those guys have a lot of parties?" she asked.

"No."

"Really?" Through the window, she could see a cluster of crushed beer cans lying under a bush.

"Not at night, anyway."

Outside, in the yard, Anita said, "Well, I'm a little concerned about noise. I know students can get pretty rowdy."

Beyond the fraternity house rose the clock tower of the University's Main Hall. "This isn't a real student-y neighborhood," he told her.

They were all like this. People lied baldly to her and snapped at her questions with gleeful rudeness. Roofs sagged, faucets wheezed moist air; walls were dark with spray-painted graffiti and carpets were torn into long, curling strips. One place she actually liked was above a veterinarian's house; the veterinarian confessed that there had been a suicide in the apartment weeks before, and responded to her horror with an extemporaneous lecture on euthanizing animals.

This went on for several days. In the evenings she cried and in the mornings she read the newspaper. By Thursday she was considering leaving town.

"I'm going to call Larry," she told Kathy.

"You shouldn't. Not until you have a place."

"I miss him."

"You miss the *idea* of him. You're really calling because you're desperate and you want him to talk you into moving into his place." She threw up her hands. "You're not bothering me. You can stay as long as you want, unless it's like a month."

But she broke down and did it. She called his house and got the answering machine, then hung up just after it beeped. After that she went to "her" room and tried to ignore the apartment's lushness, which at this point had come to seem aggressive and burdensome to her, like an impossibly heavy coat. She thought about him, about his smell, which she had thought was as familiar to her as her own face in the mirror, but which she had, to her surprise, completely forgotten. She could only remember Paul's. She had always liked the smell of Paul's sweat, which had a sweetness to it, even when it was the lazy sweat that came from not moving in the summer; she liked his hair, which smelled like toast and pine trees. She remembered loving him, and for the moment anyway was not sure she didn't still.

Now she got up and went to the phone again, intending, she tried to conceal from herself, to call her own number, Paul's number. Just to see how he was. She stopped in front of the phone and shoved her hands into her pockets. Kathy looked up from the table.

"What now?"

"Nothing."

She closed the book she was reading and came to stand between Anita and the phone. "Which one are you thinking of calling?"

"Neither. Both. I don't know."

And then it rang, startling them both. Kathy picked it up. "Just a minute," she said, and covered the mouthpiece with her palm.

"Who is it?"

"Larry. I think."

They stared at one another, and Anita stuck out her hand. Kathy put the phone into it. She held it for a second, then handed it back. Kathy lifted it to her lips and said, "I don't think she can talk right now." She nodded. "All right. I will." She hung up.

"You will what."

"'Tell her I miss her.'"

At that moment, there wasn't a person in the world she wanted to talk to or see. "Whatever," she said, and went to bed.

She lay there awake, thinking that she should have taken the veterinarian's apartment while she had the chance. She was beginning to feel the understanding of home slipping away from her—by leaving the place she'd been all her life, leaving the house she'd lived in for years afterward, she was losing her innocence by degrees. She wondered if someday she would forget how to live in one place, how to know its quirks so well that they ceased to be quirks, that they appeared as important to its existence as its streets or walls or people. Now, Marshall seemed static to her: people came and went, buildings were built and destroyed, but those things were simply the endless trade of interchangeable parts and had nothing to do with a place's identity. When you went there, you simply sunk into the changeless whole.

In the morning, she fussed over the newspaper and gulped the tea that Kathy had made her. Everything was an irritation: the tablecloth, the hot tea, even the paper itself, left neatly folded for her on the table when she stumped out of the sewing room. She found herself reading every ad twice, three times, and when she finally gave up and put the paper aside she found Kathy staring at her over the centerpiece, a spray of dried flowers stuck into a teapot.

"Do you like your job?" Kathy said.

"My job?" It felt like a picked-up strand of a conversation they'd left off some time before, one Anita didn't remember.

"Yes. You're the loan officer at the bank?" They both laughed at this, but Kathy stopped first. "So do you like it?" she asked.

"Sure, usually."

"Would you say most people are like you? They like their jobs?"

She shrugged. "I don't know. I guess they do."

Kathy leaned toward her. "Anita," she said, "people *hate* their jobs. I hate my job. You've been in the teller line, haven't you?"

"Of course."

"And you don't notice? The tellers hate each other. At First Marshall, all the tellers hate me and they hate being tellers." She noiselessly sipped her tea. "I might be exaggerating a little, but really—it's boring, thankless, bad on the feet."

This surprised Anita—she had enjoyed being a teller—but she didn't understand why Kathy was telling her this. It must have registered on her face, because Kathy said, "What I'm saying is, I have a life. Most people have lives that don't have anything to do with their jobs. You probably don't think your loan officer life is really separate from the rest of your life. It's all one big life, right?"

"Well, I don't know."

"I have this nice place, and this is where I live my real life. I like to make stuff, and if I have a lover he comes here and never to the bank. It's a good life, and I'm very happy with it."

She has lovers? Anita thought. But of course she must have. "Why are you telling me this?"

"Because you have a little contempt for me, and you shouldn't." She held a hand out. "Don't start denying it, it doesn't bother me. It's just that you can't go around thinking like that. You'll end up hating yourself for getting into a relationship that didn't work, and you won't be able to enjoy trying again." She paused, her eyes bright. "I want us to understand each other, if we're going to be friends."

In the silence afterward, Anita thought she heard, somewhere outside, a child screaming, and before the sound had died out, before she could replay it in memory, she was lifted and thrown back down by a tide of loneliness so strong that her chair groaned and she slumped in it like a dummy. "Oh!" she said quietly, and Kathy's hand, still extended toward her across the table, took her own and held it. "What have I gone and done?" she must have said, because Kathy told her, "You did the right thing." All she could do was believe this, so she did, digging her fingers into it like it was the last clod of dirt sticking to the cliff-edge that had fallen away beneath her.

"Are you all right?" Kathy finally asked her.

"I guess."

"Okay, then." Kathy pulled her hand away and folded it into the other, leaving Anita to grab hold of the chair's arms to keep from slipping farther. She felt like a child. "Time to pull yourself together."

And then, as if by decree, an apartment fell into her lap. The newspaper had turned up nothing, and she spent that morning driving around, looking for For Rent signs on doors and lawns. She found several, but the owners were never home; she peeked in through windows at dingy houses full of worthless crap, and decided that there were no apartments in Marshall she could live in, that she belonged in Paul's house, with Paul, no matter what he would and would not provide her, that she should move back in with her parents, that she should sleep on the street, quit her job, buy a rifle and a cabin in the woods and kill and eat things. Her joy at the passing of each minute was cruelly and endlessly obliterated by the arrival of the next.

Then, driving too fast down Ninth, she saw a black blur jump out at her from the left. She slammed on the brakes and squeezed her eyes shut, and when she opened them it was gone: under the wheels? Dead in the gutter? Was it a dog, a cat? The car had stalled. She took the keys out of the ignition and sat a moment, breathing, and her breath appeared dimly on the cool of the windshield. She opened the door and crouched at the side of the car, looking under the tires. Nothing there. The gutter, empty. There were several other cars, parked along the sidewalk, and looking under them turned up nothing. She got back in, restarted the car and pulled over.

To her left was a brick building, tall for Marshall—three stories—surrounded by shrubs. Directly in front stood a small cardboard sign attached to a thin wooden post, and next to it a wide yard, where a middle-aged man was cutting the grass with an old-fashioned push mower. It looked like strenuous work. He was putting all of his weight into it, and was working in a T-shirt. A blue ski parka lay in the already-cut lawn nearby.

She stepped out and walked across the lawn to the man. He was lean, slightly stooped, his face a rictus of exertion. He wore glasses that made his face a little foggy around the nose. When she approached he looked up.

"Hi," she said. "Have you got a dog? Or a cat, maybe? A black one?"

"I have a black dog."

"I think it ran out into the street. I might have hit it, but I didn't find it lying anywhere."

The man frowned, then picked up his jacket. "Otto?" he called out. "Otto?" They stood still in the grass, listening. "Otto?" Anita called.

"Let me," he said.

They walked around the building, peering into the shrubs. When the dog didn't appear, they crossed the street and walked around the neighbors' house. "Otto?" the man said, and a quiet whine came from behind a white picket fence dividing this house from the next.

Anita followed the man. They found Otto in a rough dugout between the yards, cowering in a little black ball.

"Hey, boy," he said. "You okay, boy?" The dog emerged, his tail swinging slowly in a tentative wag. He seemed to be walking fine. The man knelt in the dirt and scratched his head, and the wag turned full force on him. "Good boy."

"Is he okay?"

"He's fine," he said, seeming to add silently, *No thanks to you.*

"He just ran out." She noticed that the man's hair was the exact color and texture of the dog's.

The man lifted the dog into his arms. It whined in protest, and the three of them walked back across the street. Anita felt bad about the entire incident, and scratched the dog's head. His tail wagged, and thwacked against the man's jacket. No one spoke.

"Okay, well," she said, back in the yard. "I'm really sorry."

"No harm done."

They stared at each other for several seconds, and then Anita returned to the car. It was then that she looked back and noticed that the building was an apartment building, and the small sign she had seen earlier read "For Rent."

She got out again and looked more closely. A studio was available, three fifty a month, utilities included. She went back to the man, who was bent over the lawn mower, doing something to the blade. "Excuse me?"

"Yes?"

"Do you know anything about this apartment for rent?"

He nodded. "I'm the landlord."

"I want it. The apartment."

He looked over at Otto, who was snuffling in a patch of weeds at the edge of the yard. "You nearly killed my dog."

"It was an accident! Or it almost was."

He stood up and sighed. "You want to take a look, I guess?"

"Oh, yes," she said. "I want to see it, yes."

She moved in the next day. It was a lovely and reasonable place, if a little small; it had a lot of turn-of-the-century perks to it, like a built-in bookcase and a gas stove, a laundry chute and a dumbwaiter that didn't work but that you could look up into and see where it emptied into other apartments. Kathy took her out to get furniture and helped her set it up. She got a futon, the kind you could turn into a couch without anybody's help, and a soft chair. She got a dresser and a small dining table.

From Kathy's apartment, she called Paul and was relieved when the machine picked up. She left a message—her new address, where he could bring the car. She kept herself from tears until Kathy had dropped her off at the new place, and then lay on the floor, where it was hard and she could feel her bones and muscles grinding against one another.

And here, she tried laying bare those things about herself she had come to see as poisonous: her rage to make life safe for others, which had less to do with what they needed than what she needed to see about them; the plane crash, which no more belonged to her than the land it fell onto; the control she strove to exert over herself, which had leaked out into everything around her and corrupted it into the appearance of general and lasting imperfection. She lay on the hard floor struggling to make these ideas, which she knew to be true, take physical form inside her, a form that could be beaten down. But it was too difficult, and she wasn't moved. Instead, she drew the sobs out through force of will, inventing the first so that it charged her body for the second and the third, until they came of their own accord. They shook her, rattling those deadly parts of her, giving them rudimentary definition. For once, she could feel them living there, waiting for expulsion, and after a while she slept dreamlessly, the floorboards pressing their shape into the softness of her cheek.

Afterward, she sat on the porch, eating ice cream from the corner grocery two blocks away, and watched children playing in the park, under the street-lights. Later a van came, and the children all bundled in and were taken away.

The next morning she would take the film she'd found to the mall, and have it developed at the one-hour place. She would hold her breath opening the envelope, certain its contents would sting her, certain she would find herself adrift in sentiment for what surely would not be the last time. But the photos would be as opaque as the black canister they came from—blurry shots of a drunken party in an apartment she'd never seen before, filled with people she didn't know. A plump, red-haired woman posing in most of them, a beer bottle held close to her head, to make sure it got into the frame. She would wonder where Paul had gotten the film, if the pictures had been switched at the developer's. But by the time she thought of that, she would be out of the mall, and her relief such that she would toss the pictures into a trash can without a thought for her ten dollars, or whoever else would never get to see them.

She shouldn't have slept with Larry. Now, when she saw him again, she would be picking up the threads of something already in progress, and it would be difficult and complicated and not fully her own. It would not be a new love.

But then again, new love wore off. She wondered exactly how long that took: weeks? seconds? Or maybe love could just miss the opening act entirely and never be new. They had histories, after all; their lives were messy.

And that was something she knew she would have to get used to. Clutter. It might even be fun, like falling asleep in a leaf-strewn yard with the rake lying unused beside you. She would call him, and he would come to her new place, and they would be nervous together, the way strangers are when they've met before, have maybe talked about mutual friends, but have never had an actual conversation.

20

Bernardo looked for a pay telephone, but for some reason there weren't any. A haze of gravel dust hung over the streets—they had just, it appeared, been resurfaced—and though it didn't seem to bother anyone else, it made Bernardo cough, and he had to squint to keep it from his eyes.

He walked along Weir, which seemed to be the main street through downtown, and peered down all the cross streets. He saw no phones. Soon he came to a road he recognized, Cedar, the one that Paul had come into town on. He'd walked in a circle. On the corner, somebody was tottering around in some sort of inflatable costume. A gray box? When he came closer he could see that it was a telephone, a gigantic cellular telephone.

He'd seen these around Reggio. He hated them. At first only the businessmen and drug lords had them. Then they started turning up among teenagers, who talked loudly with the windows open at stoplights. Why would you want a phone with you all the time? Now apparently they were in Montana, USA. The costume was elaborate and silly, with every button painted onto the keypad and a thick rubber antenna wobbling on top. It was coming toward him now, its arms wiggling at its sides.

"Hello! Hello!" The phone stepped into his path.

"Hello." He looked closer, to see where the eyeholes were, but he didn't see them. "Do you know where is a telephone?"

"Ha-ha!" the phone said, in a young man's voice. "I'm a phone."

"No, no. A phone you pay." He pantomimed feeding coins through a slot.

"No need for that, if you've got a Cellular One cell phone."

Bernardo shook his head and continued walking. The phone yelled: "Hey, wait! Here!" He turned to see it running toward him, holding out a tiny folding phone. "Use this."

"No, I . . ."

"Please." It handed the tiny phone to him. "Go ahead and make your call. Notice how clear it is! That's because we have cells all over Montana and the West, guaranteeing crystal-clear . . . Actually, is it a local call?"

"What?"

"Actually, maybe I shouldn't . . . Here, let me dial." He snatched the telephone back. "What's the number?"

"No—I need a book!"

"You said phone, not phone book." The phone's hands found where its hips would be, if it had them.

"Goodbye."

"Don't mock me!" the phone called after him. "It's honest work, man!"

He found a bank of phones on a corner in front of a small grocery store. They were covered with graffiti, and the cords that had once held phone books dangled emptily. He walked another block down Weir, but now he could see that it dead-ended in the weeds next to the train tracks. There weren't any other booths.

He stopped walking. This was his new home, this dry and unfriendly place. This was where he would be without a house or job. There were no cars on this stretch of the street, and the sun shone down blankly out of a grim sky like muffled music from a neighbor's party, as if it only shone upon this place incidentally, as if it were doing its real shining elsewhere. Bernardo took a deep breath, and his body rejected it, coughing it back out in a series of painful spasms. He felt forsaken by God, if there was one.

He turned and saw himself in the window of a nearby storefront. It was strange to see his own body in its entirety: he used to look pudgy and sallow. Now, beyond all likelihood, he was lean, almost rugged. Behind his reflection, he noticed a painting in the window, propped on an easel, of a cowboy kissing a cowgirl near a campfire, backed by a blazing red sunset. There were some lumpy horses tied to a nearby tree. It was a bad painting. Deeper in the relative darkness of the shop, he could make out a man standing behind a counter, talking on the telephone.

He walked in. The place was an art gallery. On the floor before him was a large clay pot with Indian-style drawings on it: bison running around, people shooting arrows at them from horses. Nearby, also on the floor, stood a wrought-iron sculpture of a cowboy that rose six feet into the air; the iron bars formed the cock of his hip, his raised arm, the brim of his large hat.

"Oh, certainly," the man was saying to somebody. "Oh, most certainly."

Bernardo went and stood at the desk. The man didn't look up. A painting hung over the man's shoulder, this one an arrangement of paint splatters that vaguely resembled a cow. The colors were extremely bright, as if the cow were bathed in fluorescent light.

"No," the man said. "No. No. No, he's not." A long pause. "I'm afraid not, no."

Bernardo cracked his knuckles.

"You're entitled to your opinion," the man said. He was short and wore a white silk shirt with a band collar, black pants. "You can think that if you want. I'm not going to stop you." He listened for a moment, then abruptly hung up.

Bernardo waited. The man didn't raise his head, but began instead to shuffle some papers. He picked one from a pile and read it.

"Hello?" Bernardo said.

"Yes." The man did not look up.

"I look for a telephone book."

"We don't have a public phone. Go over to the Kwik Stop."

"No, only the book. I look for address."

Finally the man looked up. His face betrayed a mild contempt, but mostly his features looked so bored and lethargic that they seemed in danger of sliding off his face. It was hard to take offense at such a face.

He reached under the counter and came up with a ragged-looking phone book covered with scribbled notes and numbers. He handed it to Bernardo, folded his arms over his chest and tilted his head.

"Thank you."

There were no Pattis in the household listings. His heart lurched. He lingered on the P's, staring at the space between Patsun and Paul.

"Are you finished?" The man hadn't moved.

"No."

"I'm very busy."

Bernardo looked up. "You go work, then. I don't take anything." The man did not seem satisfied with this. Bernardo, irritated, heard himself adding, "These things too bad to steal."

The man's face reddened and he stalked off.

Bernardo turned to the business listings: bowling, cabs, cafés. "Carpet." And there it was: a small display ad, a tiny icon of two men unrolling a carpet. "PATTI FLOOR AND WALL, 2110 SPEEDWAY." And beneath that, a list of services marked with bullets—"linoleum, wallpaper, tile, paint, Marshall's largest selection of fine carpets for home and office."

He looked around for the proprietor, but didn't see him. From somewhere in the back of the gallery came a quiet voice. He tore the page from the book, folded it three times and stuck it into the pocket of his pants.

On the way out, he stopped before a freestanding wooden totem that stretched from floor to ceiling: a series of grotesque human heads. The top head had wings sprouting out where ears should have been, and the bottom rested upon two bloated feet. Each face was carved in a cartoonish expression of disgust. Tongues stuck out, cheeks ballooned, nostrils flared. Was it supposed to be funny? The place bugged him, and he headed for the door.

But it was blocked by a couple of thick, short men in uniform. He thought for a second they were twins. Their hair was cut to the same length—barely any at all—and shone yellow in the sunlight; they both wore tiny blond mustaches. He noticed that one was fatter, the other older. The older one had a steely cast to his hair, and his bulk seemed to be mostly muscle.

"What's the problem here, sir?" the younger one said.

Bernardo held out his hands: empty.

"He's a nuisance in here," the proprietor said behind him. He had returned without a sound, apparently from calling the police. Now he came around the counter and stood directly behind Bernardo, as if some mistake might be made about who should be arrested. "He tried to steal my phone book. He's been touching the art."

"Maybe you should leave now, sir," the young cop said. He leaned slightly forward, resting his hand on his holster the way police did in American movies.

"I touch nothing. He gives me the book."

The cop raised his eyebrows in the direction of the proprietor.

"He is a danger to these valuable works. He has no right to be here. He is trespassing."

"Why don't you just come outside, sir," the cop said now. Bernardo looked at the other cop, the silent one, whose arms were crossed over his chest. The face, the posture seemed to indicate that it was only a powerful act of will that kept him from swinging at someone, anyone.

"I have done nothing."

"Please, sir, step outside."

Bernardo turned around to face the proprietor, and was pleased to note that this upset him. "Why you do this?" he asked, but the proprietor turned his head away and sighed loudly.

The older cop's hands fell to his hips, where an array of objects hung: a radio, a gun, a pair of handcuffs.

Bernardo walked out. As he did he heard an electric beep somewhere in the gallery, and the sound set off a wave of rage. All he wanted was one simple thing from these people: what was the problem? He saw a beer bottle lying on the sidewalk and he rushed up and kicked it. It clinked across the street, spewing beer in all directions, and rolled to a stop against the tire of a car.

"Was that yours?" came a voice. "Was that yours?" It was the silent cop. In the dusty sunlight, the gunmetal of his mustache gleamed. It made him look like his insides were made of lead. He walked up and grabbed Bernardo's arm, and a bolt of pain coursed through it, thinning to a tingle at the fingers.

"No."

"Why'd you do that? You could hurt somebody, do you know that? You could damage property." This last seemed to have a mesmerizing effect on the man, and he pulled Bernardo closer. "You could damage property!"

"What! No, I . . ."

"You come off the train?"

"The train?"

The other cop approached them now, holding a small notebook and a pen. "Sir, do you have somewhere to go this evening?"

"Go?"

"Is there someone in town you're staying with?"

He looked down at himself: the torn shirt, the wrinkled pants and worn shoes. "I . . . my son."

The older one shook him. He was beginning to lose feeling in the arm. "Are you drunk?"

"Drunk!"

"You heard me!" The man's forehead had become slick. Behind him, the gallery owner stood in his window, calmly watching.

"Your son, sir?" It was the younger cop, moving closer.

"Yes . . . yes. I . . . He does not know I am here. I try to call him . . ."

"Maybe you should let us do that, sir." He set the pen to his notebook. "Your name?"

"I tell you when he leave my arm," Bernardo said.

"I'll let you go when I think you won't be kicking shit into the street." Veins pulsed in the older cop's face. Bernardo tried to yank his arm away, but the grip only tightened.

"No!"

The younger one closed the notebook and clicked shut his pen. "Maybe we'd better handle this at the station."

He rode in the backseat of the police car. There were no handles on the doors, a metal grate between him and the policemen. Nobody spoke.

Perhaps it was fitting that it would end this way—it wouldn't be the first time Bernardo had procrastinated until it was too late. He should have told the authorities right away that he survived the crash, and thrown himself on their mercy. Or asked Paul to help him—why didn't he ask Paul to help him? Instead, he was a crackpot plucked off the street. If he still thought it was worth learning lessons, Bernardo told himself, this would be a good one, that stupid pride only led to humiliation. He closed his eyes.

They drove three blocks down Weir before the older cop pulled the car into the parking lot of what appeared to be a deli. He opened the door, leaving the car running, and walked in. Bernardo watched through the front window as he wended his way through the shelves of snacks—bright plastic bags, bottles, colorful boxes—and brought something to the counter, where there was a line.

"You riding trains?" the younger one asked him.

"Trains? No."

The man nodded. "You're not from around here." The formality from outside the gallery was gone now.

"No."

"You mean that about your son?" He turned in his seat and faced Bernardo through the grate. "You have a son here?"

"He does not know I come to see him. A surprise."

The cop nodded, then looked back at his partner, still in line. "Why don't you go now? If you can keep out of trouble."

"Go?"

"Yeah. Get out and disappear?" He reached for the dashboard. Something clicked and the locks on the doors popped up.

"I don't understand."

"I'm letting you go. It's no big deal. The gallery guy, Dale. Calls every time a bum looks in the window." He shook his head. "A faggot if I ever saw one."

A *bum*? The cop was silent a moment while he looked in the deli window. "Officer Puhl doesn't really want to bring you in. He just wanted you out of Dale's hair, you know?" He opened his own door and stepped back to open Bernardo's. Even in those two steps Bernardo could see the swagger, a sort of proud, sexual manner that at once repulsed and fascinated him. The door opened and a plume of air pushed into the car. Compared to the air inside, it was fresh, a profound relief.

"Hurry it up. Puhl doesn't give a rat's ass if I do it, he just doesn't want to be around to see it."

Bernardo stepped out tentatively onto the pavement, still unsure that he was free. He looked back at the young policeman.

"Go ahead."

He went. He walked around the car, past the door of the deli. He looked in and saw Puhl looking back from the counter. His eyes followed Bernardo and Bernardo nodded once at him. Puhl turned away.

The police in Italy would never waste their time with something so insignificant, he thought. They wouldn't let themselves be used by a fool the way these men had. For some reason he was reminded of the cellular phone (which seemed to have vanished from its corner), and thought of it as part of a larger picture of waste that was drawing and erasing itself around him. He had exiled himself into a country of sad proxies.

He also understood that he could never disappear here. He felt like the pea under the mattress—his presence in Marshall so insignificant as to mean nothing to anyone, yet the cause, already, of more commotion than he would have thought possible. Reggio had been so popular with tourists for so long that he had forgotten: nothing sticks out like a foreigner in a small town.

And that's what he would always be here. But Marshall was all he had, and for whatever reason, it had just been given back to him. A second chance. He unfolded the torn-out phone book page and reread the address. Somewhere in this town was a part of him, something no one could know, could understand, the way he did. That was a start.

He found a bench in front of a coffee shop and sat there to rest. Teenagers walked in and out, the cuffs of their jeans dragging along the ground like mud flaps. How the girls would laugh in Reggio! He wondered if these kids had jobs, who would hire them if they did. Grocery stores? Movie theaters? Or maybe they all worked in coffee shops like this one, and visited each other all day long.

Of course he'd have to get a job himself. Could he start a restaurant? Work in one? A market was out of the question here—it had taken too many years to find all the things he sold at the old market. How would he find them in Montana? He wasn't about to go sniffing around the American West for Italian meats and cheeses. Everyone around him looked like frumpy Swedes.

He considered just how far he had gone carving out his little niche in Reggio. He had been comfortable, if not perfectly happy. He was never lonely. He spent most of each day doing exactly what he wanted. He thought of Paula: why had her company seemed like such a burden to him?

Nothing had ever seemed so burdensome as leaving his burdens forever.

He leaned his head back against the plate glass window of the coffee shop, exhausted and miserable. The air was getting cold. If Antonio and Lila didn't take him in, he would soon freeze in the night, like a stray dog.

And then somebody was sitting next to him. He'd heard a car parking in a nearby space and heard this person shuffle across the sidewalk to his bench, and felt the boards sag as the person sat down. He got the feeling he was expected to speak, but he didn't. He heard a little throat-clearing: it was a woman.

"Excuse me, you look like you need to be someplace else."

Not the comment he expected. He looked up. She had gray hair and a small round face. Something gleeful and strange twitched in her eyes.

"You give a ride?" he said.

She slapped her knees, excited. "I knew it! I was driving along—very slowly, I drive slowly for safety, though it seems I'm the only one in this town who does—and I saw you there and thought, that man needs to get some-where! That man needs to move!" The woman was dressed in a long black skirt and a red cardigan, and a white handbag hung over her arm.

"I go see my son."

"Well, that's a good thing to do. Amelia Potter. You know, Potter Pen-cils?"

He shook her hand. "No."

She looked at him with suspicion, then understanding. "Oh! You're not an American, are you?

"No."

"You're from . . . let me guess . . . France!"

"Italy."

"Well, I was close, wasn't I." She leaned toward him, as if to disclose a se-cret. "The one thing everyone in America has in common is that they've used a Potter. The name Potter is just about synonymous with pencil in these parts." She giggled. "And that's my family. Potter."

"Ah."

"And I've got a car now! Uncle Sam sent me his first check this month, and I thought, what better way to celebrate being an American than getting my own car? And I passed my driver's exam." She elbowed Bernardo, as if this was a little private joke between them.

He noticed that they were facing a car—a squat compact whose previous paint job showed through a fresh coat of red. He could make out a few words and symbols in black, a number of scratches and dents.

"This is your car?"

"Isn't it a beaut?"

"Beaut?"

"Beautiful! Isn't it beautiful!"

He nodded. "Very nice."

"I owe the people of Marshall more than a few rides!" she said, suddenly loud. "And now I'm paying them back for their kindness! So tell me where you want to go."

He didn't understand her, and he wasn't a person of Marshall, at least not yet, but he dug into his pocket for the phone book page he'd torn out. "Do you know Speedway?"

"I certainly do."

"I want to go . . ." He unfolded the page. "Two-one-one-oh. This carpet store. My son work there."

"Well, you must be proud."

He shrugged, nodded.

She was smiling at him conspiratorially. "Well? Hop in, hop in!"

Amelia fussed. She fastened her seat belt, then took it off and smoothed out her skirt and sweater, then put it back on. She tucked her handbag under the lip of the seat, patted it. She rolled down the window, adjusted the side mirror, rolled the window back up again, sighed heavily and rolled it back down and readjusted the mirror and rolled it back up. She adjusted the rearview mirror, said "Oops," adjusted it again, peered into it, touched her hair, nodded to herself, and readjusted the mirror.

"Buckle up! Buckle up!"

She had to go through her bag to find her keys, then restowed it under her seat and put the keys in the ignition. She started the car, then looked over her shoulder. "Ohh . . ." she said. "Tell me how close I'm getting, okay?"

Bernardo craned his neck. A large pickup had pulled in behind her, leaving about an arm's length for her to maneuver. He noticed that the back seat of the car had been pushed down, and the entire rear section was filled to a considerable depth with cardboard boxes full of pencils.

"Maybe a meter."

"Metrics!" Amelia shouted. She backed up carefully and skillfully, put on her turn signal, and pulled out into traffic. "Now, what is your name, sir?"

"Bernardo."

"Bernardo. Now, I'll bring you where you want to go, but since you're new in town there are a few things I want to show you." She turned to him and frowned. "You are new in town, then?"

"Yes."

She smiled. "Oh, good. Have you been to the courthouse? The Red Horse Wilderness? Have you been to see the river?"

"No."

She eased onto a side street. "Well! Then we have a few things to do. And we'll eat lunch at the Sandwich Barn, my favorite place. Do you like sandwiches, Bernardo?"

"In Italy, I make sandwiches many years."

"Wonderful!" She flashed him a brilliant crackpot grin, and made an unexpected left turn down a hidden street. At the bottom of it was a large brick building, and beyond the building flowed a river, wide and swift. He hadn't had any idea a river ran through town, let alone one this big. Then he remembered seeing it from the plane, twisting between mountains, how it seemed to flow out of its way to hook through Marshall. The sight instantly filled him with calm, and he realized how scared he was of what was to come, of meeting Antonio.

"Beautiful," he said, as she pulled into an empty space in a large, freshly paved lot.

"I'm so glad to hear you say that." She pointed. "This used to be a train station."

He'd meant the river. "But there is no tracks."

"Oh, no. The trains stopped running here years ago. There are still freight trains, but they're on the other side of the river." She pointed again, and he could see another brick building in the distance, its tower barely rising over a jumble of telephone wires. "They run from here through Butte and to Billings." She shook her head, but her eyes shone. "But the passenger trains are gone."

"In all the movies," Bernardo said, "there are many railroads."

"Everyone drives now."

Bernardo leaned into the windshield, to see the brick building's tower. High above, where a bell should have been, was a red glow that he could see came from a Coke machine. "What is this building now?"

"Hunting club. They let you go in and look around, but it isn't worth it. There's a lot of ugly carpet and the walls are covered with dead animals." She made a face. "Carpet! No offense to your son, but do you know what's under there? Marble! Imagine what it took to get marble to Marshall!"

They got out of the car and stood at the river's edge. In a section near the bank, where a small island diverted current away from them, the water was calm. Fish rose to the surface, leaving concentric circles in their wake.

She took him back downtown, to the courthouse, where Paul had dropped him off earlier. Amelia told him the building was designed by a man named Gibson, who also designed the Museum of the Arts, the post office, some buildings at the University. They drove past them all, and she pointed out the granite chevrons on the corners, the jagged corbels two bricks thick under the eaves, tall windows packed with tiny panes—the architect's trade-marks. They were sturdy-looking, functional buildings. Afterward they skirted town to the south, drove under the highway and rails, and watched as the city gave way to condominiums and half-built neighborhoods of identical houses, and these to small ranches, where horses walked around eating grass or trotting along lengths of fence. When the trees became dense, she turned onto a gravel road and into a small parking lot, where several cars were parked. They got out and walked on a well-worn trail for several min-utes, Amelia so full of energy that, even in her stockings and pumps, she put a considerable distance between them. They came to a ridge that looked out over a narrow canyon, along the bottom of which ran a creek. It reminded Bernardo of the ridge he had camped on after the crash, and the creek, white below him in the sunlight, gleamed like the plane's cracked and scattered bones.

"What way is that?" he said, pointing back over town, which was visible to them beyond the slope of the hill they'd climbed.

"North."

"That is called the . . ."

"That's the Salmon Wilderness, there. And that mountain is Elk Moun-tain, because it looks like an elk's back."

He was as far from the crash as he could be in this valley, and still see where it happened. "This is a beautiful place."

"It goes on and on." She was smiling, a smile utterly without guile. She looked youthful now, though he knew she must be his age.

He said, "Do you think . . . it is too late for a new life?" Not because he needed to know. He thought he did know. But he wanted her reaction, wanted to see something he said register on another person's face.

She turned to him, her eyes full of dismay at the question, full of delight at giving her answer. "Oh, of course not!"

"I am almost old," he said. "I am sixty-five. This is when people stop to work?"

"Oh, sooner, these days." She swept her hand through the air, as if lecturing the canyon. "People are so lazy, they have so much. People don't know loss. They think when something bad happens it's the end of the world." She touched his shoulder. "You know, I used to be so *confused,* Bernardo. They had me put away for it. But I'm your age, and I'm pretty much all right, and I just learned to drive."

"So you not confused now?"

"Well, sometimes. A lot of the time, I guess." She grinned. "But not right this minute."

Perhaps he had been living his life wrong all along, he thought walking back. Perhaps the disaster that dropped him here was not the point, and the point was his survival. It was possible there was no one who had ever beaten such odds. It was possible he was the luckiest man in the world. What to make of that?

They ate sandwiches at Amelia's favorite restaurant. Bernardo had an Italian hoagie. It wasn't too bad, considering, maybe a little mild. He was halfway through before he realized he had no money.

Amelia laughed when he told her. "When you get going on your new life, you buy me a sandwich."

They drove to an ugly part of town she called the Strip. All the buildings were low and dingy, and he saw no people walking. When they passed a side street, he noticed they were on Speedway.

"My son work here?"

"Oh, yes. A little further now."

"I don't like so much."

"Well," she said, "you can sure get what you're looking for. There's hardware, and books. And a boot shop." She pointed.

Bernardo said nothing.

"You seem nervous, Bernardo."

"Yes."

"But you're going to see your son."

He wiped his palms on his knees. "I don't see him a long time."

She signaled and turned into a parking lot. A long, flat building housed a row of stores. He thought she was stopping to buy something until he saw the sign, on the roof above a set of double glass doors. "Patti Floor and Wall."

Well. This was it, then.

"Is this going to be a surprise visit?" she said.

"Yes."

She pulled the car into an empty space, halfway across the lot from the store, then turned off the ignition. From the pile in back she produced a small box.

"You can write down your new life!" she said, as if the thought of his new life filled her with the same excitement her own might. His hands felt thick and damp. They throbbed. With one he accepted the pencils.

"This is the only thing that I have."

"Good thing it's pencils," she said, and when he didn't move, "Time to go."

"Yes, yes," he said, and made himself open the door. "Thank you. I never find without you."

They shook hands. "Friends!" she said in a near-shout. "You'll see me around, of course."

"Goodbye."

She hunched over and offered him a small wave, and he returned it. When he shut the door, she pulled out and steered carefully away toward the road. He stood and watched her pull into traffic, and followed the car until it was out of sight.

He walked across the parking lot. Inside was probably a young salesman, who would have to run and find his boss. And Bernardo would wait, smelling the new carpet, barely able to stand from the fear. But he pushed open the door and found a middle-aged couple near the door, their heads over a sample book, and at their side, holding it, a man their age, the top of his head black, whorled with gray hairs, and this man looked up, smiling. "Hello," he said, and looked back down.

"Antonio." The word a current across his tongue.

His son looked up again, tilted his head like a dog's, deciding whether to wag or run. The professional smile still stretching crookedly across his face, but the eyes clear and astonished.

"*Antonio, sono Papà.*" And now the couple looked up, and together, slapstick, turned their heads from Bernardo to his son.

Antonio crouched and set the sample book on the floor, his eyes never leaving Bernardo. He stood, took a step. "Papa . . ."

And tears, rising in him like a sweet wind. Why? Had he expected anything different?

"*Sono vivo,*" he said to his son, I'm alive. "*Sono vivo, sono vivo.*" He couldn't stop saying it, even as Antonio ran to him and took him into his arms, as if it was a surprise to him, as if he had never noticed it before. I'm alive.

For their help reading and editing portions of this manuscript, thanks to Kate Gadbow, David Gilbert and Julie Grau. James Welch checked my facts on the Blackfeet and Flathead Indian tribes. John McCormick of the National Transportation Safety Board in Seattle answered my questions about plane crash investigations.

For their attention to my work, I'd like to thank Lisa Bankoff, Amy S. Fisher, Allyson Goldin, Andrew Sean Greer, Cary Holliday, Mark Holthoff, Kristen Hunter-Lattany, Alicia Ieronemo, Bill Kittredge, Jill Marquis, Richard Nuñez, Chris Offutt, Mary Park, Jocelyn Siler and Ed Skoog.

I reserve my greatest thanks for my family and their kind advice and support, for Ann Patchett, and for my wife, Rhian Ellis.

J. Robert Lennon grew up in Phillipsburg, New Jersey. He studied creative writing at the University of Montana and now lives with his wife and son in Ithaca, New York. *The Light of Falling Stars* is the winner of the 1997 Barnes & Noble Discover Great New Writers Award.